THE KINDLY ONES

THE
KINDLY
ONES

CLIFF JAMES

LETHE PRESS

Copyright © 2021 by Cliff James

ISBN: 9781590216903

Cover Art by STAVEN ANDERSEN
Interior Design by INKSPIRAL DESIGN

Published by Lethe Press.

Para Alvaro, por aceptar el desafío.

CHAPTER ONE
EXODUS

THE ROAD WAS NOT SO much a road as a following. A slow following of incidents and auguries, divination rather than any conscious deliberation of where they should be going. It was Enoch, the eldest son, who determined which way they should take and when. They left at dawn when the weather was good, drove against the wind on back-roads and trackways until the sun began to slip beneath the empty horizon and it was time for evening prayers. There was always the risk that someone might hear the engines of their cars during the daytime, but they judged this to be less of a danger than driving by night.

'They can see where we are in the dark from the headlamps,' Luke explained to his little brother. 'In the daytime, it's tricky for them to know where we are just from the noise of the cars.'

Luke was simply repeating something that he had overheard his eldest brother, Enoch, say, but he still felt important saying it. He hoped he had remembered it correctly. Luke used a stick to draw a diagram in the dirt, a dot and a circle, though this did not make things any clearer to his younger brother, Abel, who nodded appreciatively at the drawing, pleased that Luke was sharing such a solemn piece of information with him, something so grown-up serious that it felt almost forbidden to the younger ones. Abel frowned to demonstrate that he comprehended the significance of the information and said nothing to show that his lips were sealed.

'Aye, and you shouldn't ask questions either,' continued Luke, scrubbing out his diagram in the dirt, perhaps ashamed that it held no real meaning. Best leave no trace of it at all.

Abel nodded again. He decided not to look at his brother but to stare thoughtfully at the ground as he had seen the adults do at night around the fire when one of them said something of significance. As the youngest of the six surviving children, Abel held a privileged position. He had turned fourteen some weeks ago, but Mother said that childhood was a precious state of innocence to be protected at all costs and treasured for as long as possible. Abel had been treated as the baby of the Mann family for so long that he was still considered an infant. Traditions like that were difficult to break. When Abel spoke, his father, his brothers, even the dogs, looked through him or over his head until his words dried up. When there were things that needed to be done, the chores were usually meted out to his older siblings. Keeping-an-eye-on-your-younger-brother was one such task, more often than not allocated to his sister, Ruth.

As the youngest, Abel was also reckoned to be less aware than the other children, deficient in reason and ability, useless. After evening prayers, the older ones were sent early to bed in the back of the pickup truck or on the caravan floor, whereas Abel, if he could not sleep, was allowed to stay up late as a spectator at the grown-ups' serious, firelit discussions, so long as he was quiet and remained mute and innocuous. It was here that he learned a great deal more than anyone would have suspected, let alone approved of.

Since they had left home, since even the concept of home had been extinguished on the Last Day, some things were changing beyond recognition whereas others had become fixed in a permanent state. Abel's babyhood was one such static fact. Another was Mother's expression, which had set into a condition of imperishable disapproval.

Among the things that had changed forever was the relationship between Abel and Luke. Once upon a time, the three-year age difference between them had meant little: they would chase, catch, pinch, push, scrape knees, bleed and tell-mum almost as peers. But this closeness had been neutered overnight, the night that the old world had been turned upside down to be replaced by a new Heaven and a new Earth. Luke was now a half-man with half-man responsibilities. Abel, on the other hand, was stranded in infancy.

The two boys, late-infant and early-man, sat side-by-side on a fallen pine tree and stared at the dirt where Luke had erased the diagram. They were unmistakably related and shared the same looks as their other siblings: dark eyebrows arched in perpetual shock or delight or it-wasn't-me innocence, brown eyes that flitted from one uncertainty to another and back again, and thick black hair that hung over their ears, eyes and into their collars. Luke had already grown a patchy beard, whereas a soft mist of adolescent whiskers barely began to shade Abel's chin and upper lip. Each wore a pair of tired blue jeans, patched at the knees with scraps of old cloth, and a red-white-blue checked shirt with mismatched buttons sewn on with odd-coloured threads. Clothes were passed down from their elders: from firstborn Enoch to Matthew and Mark, to Luke and finally to Abel. Ruth's position in the hierarchy of age was ambiguous, although Abel suspected that she had slipped out somewhere between Matthew and Mark. As the only daughter, Ruth belonged to a separate, ancillary, not-quite-defined category from that of the boys. For practical purposes, she also inherited her brothers' old jeans and faded shirts.

'No,' Abel said to Luke after some thinking time. 'No, I shouldn't ask you questions. And I won't.' He swept the dark fringe away from his eyes. It fell back at once.

'You can ask me stuff,' Luke said with a generous air. 'Of course you can ask me stuff. I meant you shouldn't ask them,' he nodded towards the road from where they could hear the voices of the others. 'It's not right. It's not fair on them. They don't know everything that's happening, or they might know things they don't want us to know because it's bad—like really-bad bad—so you shouldn't bother them. But you can ask me. I guess that's all right.'

'But what if, say, what if I ask something and it bothers you because it's bad?'

'Bad like what?'

'Bad like the burnt man,' said Abel. They looked at each other.

'What's the burnt man?' asked Luke.

Abel wondered if Luke pretended not to know about the burnt man or if he was hiding something really-bad bad. The pause lasted for such a long time that Abel guessed his brother did not know. Abel now understood how it felt to know bad things that maybe ought not to be shared.

3

'What's the burnt man?' Luke repeated impatiently.

Abel sighed and looked back at the ground. He used his own stick to draw a diagram in the dirt: a box-house with a chimney, a body without a head. 'When we stopped at that garage-house yesterday, and there were baked-beans and petrol in the shed. And I wasn't supposed to go in the garage-house so I waited outside with Mother, and we saw a man in a funny shirt standing by the tree but he had his back to us and Mother shouted and everyone came running, and our Enoch went up to the man—and Enoch had his axe, of course, because Enoch always has his axe—but the man didn't move, and Mother put me in the pickup, and I don't know what happened next, but I think I heard her say that he was a burnt man or something like a burnt man. And then we had to leave, but I don't know about the burnt man because, like you said, it's best not to ask questions.'

Luke looked at the drawing that his little brother had drawn on the ground and said nothing. They each brushed their fringes away from their eyes, an identical, familial gesture.

'I know the burnt man was dead, but I don't know why he was burnt,' Abel concluded. He thought that saying the words "burnt-man" again might prompt some answer.

'I don't know,' Luke shrugged. 'Like I said, you shouldn't ask questions.'

Someone called their names from the road. They jumped down from the fallen tree and Abel kicked the sense out of his own drawing.

Back on the road, Abel sat with Mother in the front of the pickup while Uncle Joe drove. In the back of the pickup, underneath the tarpaulin sheet, Luke sat with the dogs. The others travelled in the caravan-and-blue-car following along behind.

'You know what I think,' said Uncle Joe.

Abel did not know what Uncle Joe thought. He could not see much of his uncle's face behind the sunglasses and baseball cap pulled low over his brow. Abel looked at Mother to see if she knew what Uncle Joe thought. She stared at the road ahead but moved her face the merest fraction away from Joe to show that she both knew what was on his mind and disapproved of whatever it was.

No one spoke after that.

Abel watched the little gold crucifix dangling from Mother's neck. It danced with the movement of the truck, twinkling in the light and going dull when it turned away. The skin on his mother's neck looked different, he thought, more lined and looser. Her hair was the same, still glossy black with only a few flecks of silver here and there and long enough to hang halfway down her back, but her neck belonged to a much older woman. Abel wondered if the effort of preserving that fixed expression was finally taking its toll on the rest of her skin.

He turned his attention to the wedding ring on her finger. He wondered if it was the colour of the metal that people valued or something else, some essential quality he did not quite understand. Perhaps, after the Last Day, no one did value gold anymore. They certainly used to. Mother still wore her gold ring, so that must mean something.

Abel's attentiveness must have irritated Mother. She said nothing but rearranged her hands so that he could no longer see the ring. Then she lay her arm over his shoulder so the ring was well and truly out of sight. She shared the smallest portion of a smile with him, enough for him to notice, then she returned her gaze to the road ahead. Abel looked out of the side window at the passing trees, a slight wind stirring the branches and leaves, thought about the properties of air.

The forest went on for days and days, well into autumn. The leaves were inflamed, liver-spotted, rust-brown, cracking yellow and falling. The tree trunks were menacing, thick ribs of a pagan monster that had swallowed them and the whole world too, and in which they drove around in blind circles. Dark branches arched over the road, cut triangles of the grey sky, clippings of cloud and occasional blue. At night, nothing but black whale-belly emptiness overhead. When at last the forest thinned, the trees grew sparse and the fine geometries of sky turned into open expanses, Abel felt as though he had come up for air. They drove over potholed roads out of the forest and through flat fields, grass as high as the bonnet of the pickup truck, close-up watercolour-green fading into faraway-green and disappearing into distant mist, sometimes the bare shoulder of a hill on the edge-of-world horizon. There was so much sky that Abel thought they must now be driving in circles around the grey eye of a giant. Somewhere in the centre of it all must be the deep, black pit of an all-seeing pupil. Maybe that was the thing they were looking for. Maybe that was the thing that was looking for them.

Early evening at a quiet house, a roofless house in the middle of a field, chickens running around an overgrown garden. The heads of their two black dogs, happy to be out of the pickup truck at last, bounced up and down, up and down, breaking two tracks through the long grass. Enoch walked towards the house carrying his long-handled axe. Just ahead of him, Mark and Matthew cut a path through the grass with machetes. None of them spoke until they had reached the house, searched all the rooms to find them empty. Enoch whistled the all-clear, his head poking through the hole in the roof.

'Keep an eye on your younger brother,' Mother said to Ruth as she went to investigate the kitchen. Ruth glanced at the house, at the flat fields that went on forever, at Abel. Taking in everything and showing nothing, Ruth's face was as closed as her mother's.

'Can we do something? Can we explore the house?' Abel asked her.

Ruth shrugged. She sat on the step of the caravan and put on her trainers, tied the laces, buttoned up her cardigan. 'They're all in the house,' she replied flatly.

Abel nodded, appreciating that she did not want to go where the others were. Ruth pulled her hair back into a tight ponytail and stood up, fiddled with her sleeves. 'You want to play hide-and-seek?'

'You're too old for games like that.'

'So are you, but we played it last week.'

'I've got to keep an eye on you,' Ruth reminded him.

'But you're not keeping an eye on me, you're looking at the field.'

They both smiled. Abel thought for a moment, then said, 'You want to play this game where I keep an eye on you and you go wherever you like, say, in the field or wherever, and I follow to see where you've gone, and we can call this game the keeping-an-eye-on-each-other game?'

Ruth agreed, but said they should stay close to each other.

The sun had almost set, but there was still plenty of light. The broken clouds in the west were saturated orange and soft red, and the field glowed wedding-ring gold. Dust played over the grass, dust or insects or drifting seeds that the last of the sunlight had caught in the act of dispersal. Ruth made her own path through the long grass, which was too tall for her to see over, and she glanced playfully behind her to make sure Abel was following. When she came across something hidden in the grass, an old bunker made of breeze blocks and covered with a rusting sheet of corrugated iron, they both stopped to take a look.

'Was it for animals?' asked Abel.

'Or a bomb shelter?'

Ruth lifted the iron roof off to see inside. Straw, cigarette butts, broken cups and mildewed pillows, an empty green bottle that once held wine. It reeked of piss.

'It smells like animals,' said Abel.

Ruth snorted. 'It smells like boys.'

'I think it was a place for goats. I think goats lived here.'

Ruth used the corrugated-iron roof as a table and poured pretend tea from the empty wine bottle into the cups, handing first one and then another to Abel to pass on to their imaginary guests. They knew they were both too old for this game too, but neither of them minded. When all the cups had been pretend-filled, Ruth mimed the cutting of a cake on an invisible platter. The clouds shed their sunset complexion and the light began to fade.

'He says he would like some more, please,' said Abel.

'Who's he?'

'The burnt man.'

'Who's the burnt man?'

Abel shrugged but insisted on holding the burnt man's cup for Ruth to refill. She obliged and everyone, real and imaginary, was content. When they had finished their tea, Ruth said they should head back to the house. She could just about see the path they had broken through the grass, but they had walked for longer than she had realised and the house was quite some distance away. The falling darkness made everything seem distant.

Neither Ruth nor Abel could see over the tall seed-heads of grass. He kept his eyes down, following Ruth's white trainers kicking ahead against the current of fallen stalks, trusting his sister to find the way back through the field. It was taking a lot longer to go back than it did to come out.

'Shall we play the keeping-an-eye-on-each-other game again?' he asked, stumbling to keep up with his sister.

'Not now. Just stay with me,' she said, breathing faster, becoming afraid.

'What?' he shouted after Ruth, but she had gone, her footfalls fading in the canyon of grass, dispersing into a thousand seeds of direction.

Abel stopped running. He walked a few steps along the passage his sister had broken through the field, but the way was so dark and the wall of stems bent this way and that against his outstretched hands, closing him in. He listened to sounds, whispers of leaf and things that were not leaf but intentional and sensate, deliberate presences in the grass around him. The air was rich with flavour, with damp and humus, the old-meat smell of the earth. He made a small animal noise of fear, swallowed it whole, made another and looked up, startled, over the top of the grass and into the cold white face gazing down at him.

Abel must have seen the moon before. Even in the forest he must have seen the moon, or glimpsed portions of it through the branches, or at least heard the others talk about the moon like they talked of anything that existed in the abstract. The moon had been taken on trust as part of his universe, much like the sea or air or God—though he could never remember seeing any of those things either. But here she was, the immanent moon, an immediate being. If it had been an archangel hanging over the field with its gorgeous outstretched wings, Abel would have been no less enchanted. She was so close and attentive that he felt like she was looking at him for the very first time. And perhaps it was something of a mutual epiphany, he wondered. Perhaps this was the moon encountering Abel as much as the other way round. She must have seen herself reflected in his eyes, scarred and serene and tin-beaten white.

'What are you?' the moon asked curiously, not at all discourteous.

'I don't know,' Abel whispered, barely moving his lips and not thinking what he was saying. 'What are you?'

'I?' she said. 'Why, I am. I am with you.'

'Forever?' He smiled, though his eyes filled with tears of wonder.

'No, not forever. For now.'

'For now,' Abel repeated. Now was enough; now was everything. He did not know what else to say to her. He knew so many prayers, gave thanks and praise every morning and evening, and yet none of those mumblings would ever be fitting for this moment with the moon. If only he could speak with the tongues of angels. At last, something familiar and frequently recited came to mind. 'The Lord is with thee: blessed art thou among women.'

'Enough of that,' said the moon with a slight shake of her head.

'You want to play hide-and-seek?'

'Yes, let's play. You hide. I'll find you.'

When at last Abel's mother arrived running through the grass with a torch and a face harder than iron, she found him staring up at the sky and crying.

'Boy,' she said, 'Silly, silly boy.' She knelt down, swept the hair away from his eyes, examined his clothes for rips, tears, signs of injury. Finding nothing wrong, she slapped him.

'There, something to cry about.'

She took Abel's hand and walked him back towards the house. Ruth was sitting on the step of the caravan, anxiously scratching both of her wrists. She stood up and almost spoke, would have apologised for the thousandth time if given the chance.

'No,' said Mother coldly, passing but not looking at her daughter. 'No.'

Later that night, after evening prayers, after they had all shared a silent dinner and gone to bed early, Abel lay awake on his bed of cushions on the floor and thought about the moon. He knew that, if he climbed the stairs and stood on the landing, he could look through the open rafters of the broken house and see her immaculate face consoling the night. He would have to be quiet, would have to tiptoe between his brothers' sleeping bodies on the floor and pray that the stairs gave not the slightest tell-tale sound or else the dogs would go wild and Enoch would be there in a flash holding his axe. Abel wished that he were the one doing penance, that he had been told to sleep outside instead of Ruth, then he could talk with the moon all night without troubling anyone. He thought of Ruth out there all alone, not even allowed inside the caravan. She was always doing penance for something or other. He hoped that she was looking at the moon. Because she had lost Abel, Ruth's punishment was that no one would speak to her for days, weeks or for so long as Mother decided. Penance could last forever. Abel hoped that the moon was consoling Ruth now.

From behind the closed door of the other room, the room that his parents had taken for the night, Abel heard the sound of their voices. Quiet at first, his and hers, sometimes the sense of a mood broke through, sometimes whole fragments of sentence. Father was requesting, Mother refusing. His father asked again, whatever it was, his tone rising, pleading.

'No,' Mother told him firmly.

There was silence for a while, whole minutes of nothing, then Abel heard his father sobbing. The sound was eerie, came and went in such regular cycles that Abel wondered if his father had fallen asleep and was snoring. But, no, Father was crying. Abel felt ashamed for hearing what he knew was wrong for him to hear.

Abel closed his eyes and summoned the face of the moon. I am with you, she had said. I am with you for now. But that was then, and how long does a 'now' last? What about now in the dark? Was she with him in this moment, this particular now, too? He pictured himself walking up the stairs. He pictured her full face looking through the hole in the roof. He prayed that he could have wings like an archangel, like Gabriel or Michael, to fly through the firmament and briefly touch her cracked face. Would his fingertips burst into flames or would they turn to ice?

He heard a different sound from his parents' room, a new kind of breathing. No more words, only the sense of a mood, two moods, a mismatched rhythm of dissonant sighs. Abel turned his back to the door, felt his fingers tingle. Later, he dreamed of snow falling on sea.

IN THE MORNING, THE BREAKFAST prayer went on for longer than Abel could ever remember. There seemed to be so many things that Father was thankful for. Abel lifted his head and ever so slightly opened his eyes. He looked at Father, thin-cheeked and pale as usual, though showing no trace of last night's bout of tears. The sunrise blazed through the kitchen window, turned the rising tea-steam to gold, melted butter.

'We thank you, Lord, for teaching us obedience: wife to husband, younger to elder, sister to brother,' his father continued with the long list of gratitudes. 'Aye, and for the grace to overcome our own wayward natures. We thank you for blessing our family, for protecting us from the tricks and games of the Adversary, and for bringing our Abel back home to us safe and sound.'

Mother squeezed Abel's hand. The boy closed his eyes and lowered his face.

'And we thank you, Lord, for casting all them that you despise, the wicked, the god-haters and the unbelievers, to the bottomless pit on the Last

Day. For as you have promised: "I will give unto thee, and to thy seed after thee, the land wherein thou art a stranger, all the land of Canaan, for an everlasting possession; and I will be your God." In the name of the father, son, holy spirit.'

Amen.

They released hands, opened eyes, reached through the sunlit steam for plates, bowls, unleavened bread, fried tomatoes, baked beans. Mother ladled scrambled eggs onto Abel's plate, twitched him the faintest smile, a secret between them, and then served herself. They had not eaten eggs for many weeks. Father had forgotten to be thankful for those.

'There are chickens here,' said Uncle Joe.

'We know there are chickens here,' Father replied.

'And the petrol's getting low,' Joe added.

'And the petrol's getting low,' said Enoch, crudely imitating his uncle's voice.

The table went quiet but for the sound of chewing, cutlery, the knife in Enoch's hand tapping the edge of a plate. Outside, a rooster crowed, corroborating the presence of chickens.

After a careful pause, Uncle Joe continued, 'Greenhouse, garden, good land too, good soil. All in all, not a bad place to stay for a spell.'

Abel watched his eldest brother, watched what he would do next. Enoch would do something, Abel knew; Enoch never let anything go. Enoch chewed his bread slowly, deliberately, glared at the table. He stopped tapping his knife, seemed to be waiting for something to follow.

'Our Enoch says this place isn't right,' said Father. 'It's too flat, too wide open. The house can be seen for miles around. Enoch says this isn't the place that's been promised us.'

'This isn't the place,' Enoch confirmed.

Uncle Joe opened his mouth to speak, hesitated for a moment, and decided to bite on his bread instead.

'This isn't the place,' Enoch repeated, and that was an end to it.

When they had finished breakfast, Mother scraped the leftover scraps into a bowl that she handed to Abel, saying, 'Take this out to your sister. And remember, you're to say nothing to her, not a word. Your sister's doing her penance.'

'Give it me,' said Enoch. He took the bowl from Abel and turned to face Mother. He was about to go outside without her consent, would have gone, but her look told him not to try.

For the first time in his life, Abel noticed how fragile his mother looked. He had always imagined that she was impossibly tall, a pillar of light, a tower of white iron that reached to the heavens. But here in the kitchen, he could see that Enoch was so much more than her, bigger in muscle and shoulder and neck and knuckle. If Enoch knocked her aside, she would shatter against the wall like a china cup. But her will was unbending and she would not give ground to Enoch, her eldest, the firstborn, the son who was burdened with the inheritance of the Earth. Enoch's challenge lasted for barely a breath before Mother flicked her head towards the door.

'Aye, you take it,' she said to him. She seemed not to care but some boundary had been reached, some limit stretched. The next contest, whenever it came, would be a harder struggle.

Outside, Enoch kicked his way through the overgrown garden. He did not look up until he reached the step to the caravan where Ruth had sat all night, scratching herself to keep warm. As she stood up, Enoch threw her breakfast bowl over the field, scattering the contents in the grass, and pushed his sister hard against the ground. He would have done more to her, wanted to do more. If she had cried out or said something pathetic or looked up at him in pain or fear or accusation, he would surely have done more. But Ruth stayed facing the ground where she lay, though the palms of her hands throbbed where she had fallen against stones. She did not move until after Enoch had shuffled away, kicking his way through the grass. She did not need to look back at the house to know that all this had been observed, reckoned, sanctioned by Mother. Mother would have seen everything from the kitchen window.

When Enoch returned from the field, he said that the wind was blowing from the direction they had come, the road that they had taken from the forest.

'Then we'll head back the way we came,' said his father.

They loaded up the vehicles with useful things from the broken house. Luke found a fishing rod and big box of tackle. Uncle Joe put three of the chickens and the rooster in a wooden crate in the back of his pickup truck, which meant the excited dogs had to go in the caravan. Abel had found a wooden musical instrument, which he thought might be a pipe or a flute, in the cupboard under the stairs. None of this was stealing. Abel knew it was not stealing because that is what he had been told. Since the Last Day, all the things that had been left behind were theirs for the taking. It was their inheritance. Stealing was only stealing if they took from one another.

Abel planned to surprise Mother with the wooden pipe-flute thing once they had left the broken house and were back on the road. If he could show her that it was not taking up any space, she would probably let him keep it. He slipped the instrument down his sock, pulled his trouser leg down and sat in the front of the pickup. Looking out at the golden-green field, at the grass swaying in the breeze and the wide-open sky, he wondered who used to own the pipe-flute thing, whether they had played it in this field maybe looking up at the moon, and what wicked things they must have done to be sent to the bottomless pit. Then he thought about the other people who had been left behind after the Last Day, the ones that they hid from and who might see their headlights in the dark or the broken house from miles around. If all the god-haters had been sent to the bottomless pit, then who were those other people? If they were not wicked, why must he hide from them? And if the Last Day had happened, then what were these days they were living after the Last Day? It did not feel like a new Heaven and Earth. Abel brushed the fringe away from his eyes. There were so many questions he was not supposed to ask. He suspected that the answers must be really-bad or else not known.

Enoch was right. The wind was blowing from the direction they had come. Uncle Joe turned the truck around in the field and left a perfect arc in flattened grass. The caravan-and-blue-car followed in their wake.

'There it all goes,' said Uncle Joe. 'Greenhouse, garden, good soil, the lot of it.'

'That's enough,' said Mother.

'As long as we've the grace of obedience, wife to husband,' he added.

Mother did not reply.

They drove slowly down the potholed road. The wind turned fierce as they left the flat green grasslands and breathable skies behind and headed towards the tight forest. The wind brought clouds and an end to the autumn sunlight. Abel watched the rainclouds rise above the coming horizon, mountains of grey and purple that never seemed to change unless you glanced away and then looked back to find that they had all the time been advancing, tumbling over themselves to become something else: castles, turrets, battlements. He turned aside to the passing fields, watched the wind beat acres of grass into eddies of spiral, signatures of air. Ahead again, the towers of cloud had all tumbled down, their ruins reborn as a stampede of airy, angry dogs. Abel lost that light sensation of relief that the wide-open spaces had given him.

'You seen the sky look like that before?' asked Uncle Joe. He sounded uneasy.

'And I saw a new Heaven and a new Earth,' said Mother, reciting Revelation matter-of-factly, 'for the first Heaven and the first Earth were passed away.'

'Doesn't look good to me,' said Joe, taking off his sunglasses and scowling heavenwards.

By the time they reached the edge of the forest, autumn had transitioned into winter. Leaden clouds overran the sky and brought an end-of-world darkness to a world that had already ended. Though there was still no rain, the wind battered the windscreen of the pickup, rattled the caravan from side to side behind the blue car. They parked on the grass verge at the turn-off into the woods, waited for the storm to die down. The treeline provided some shelter from the wind but also an armoury of forest shrapnel for the storm to collect and spit in all directions, leaves to slap against windows, branches to fall, boughs to break.

Mother announced that they would all be sleeping in the caravan, except for Ruth who was still doing her penance. She would keep the chickens company in the back of the pickup.

'She'll be fine enough under the tarpaulin,' Mother added without looking at her daughter.

Enoch said he would keep watch all night in the cabin of the pickup. Mother said that, yes, he could, though everyone noticed that Enoch had not asked for permission.

'And you'll keep the dogs with you,' she said.

Enoch protested but Mother repeated herself, and that was that.

Instead of prayers after dinner, they recited Psalm Twenty-Three: 'Yea, though I walk through the valley of the shadow of death, I will fear no evil: for thou art with me; thy rod and thy staff they comfort me.' They said the psalm together just as they had done during that storm on the Last Day, though the memory of that night gave comfort to no one.

Later, Abel listened to the bodies breathing all around him, knew who was asleep and who was awake. He shared a blanket with Luke on the caravan floor, though Luke was already kicking his feet in a dream of running. Mark and Matthew shared their own blanket a few feet away, took it in turns to snore, an antiphonal chorus. Outside, leaf hands rapped against the sides of the caravan, wooden legs stumbled over grass and stone. The wind sang an uncanny song in the trees, a ghostly lament that wavered between two minor notes and never once stopped for breath. Abel thought of all the souls who had gone to the bottomless pit. If they could still cry out, if he could hear their torment, would they sound just like that wind? He wondered if the moon was singing for him behind the clouds. He reached under the blanket and touched the tip of his pipe-flute still hidden down his sock. Luke kicked him away.

THE STORM CONTINUED TO HOWL for weeks. Though there was never a drop of rain, the clouds twisted vascular overhead, heavily expectant, but tight and ungiving. Abel wondered what colour the rain would be when it eventually fell. Like oil or petrol probably, he thought: purple-black and bitter.

'Didn't I say we should have stopped at the broken house?' said Uncle Joe in the caravan when Enoch was not around to hear.

'And the Lord went before them by day in a pillar of a cloud to lead them,' Mother replied, 'and by night in a pillar of fire to give them light.'

She closed her eyes as though things were now settled. Father sat on the caravan floor and said nothing. He often sat at Mother's feet like that, like a devotee or a dog. Sometimes he would touch her foot and she would sigh and tell him to stop it and move her legs away.

'Pillars of cloud and pillars of fire,' said Uncle Joe. 'All we ever get is this wind taking us round and round in circles, going nowhere.'

'You doubting the word of the Lord, Joe?' Mother said sharply, a voice she reserved for the crushing of resistance. 'You dare to doubt the Lord, Joe? The Lord?'

'I'm saying nothing.' He looked out of the caravan window to make sure Enoch had not overheard. 'But a pillar of fire would be something.'

Mother prayed under her breath.

ENOCH SAID THE LORD WAS testing them. Enoch said the wind was a sign. Enoch said they must go back into the forest, take the road they had come down all those weeks before.

'Then it's back into the forest we'll go,' Father confirmed.

It was darker than ever inside the tunnel of trees, so they drove with the headlights on all the time. Above the creaking branches, the storm clouds bruised purple and black in the wind, maimed and heavy, but they never stopped rolling, threatening to split at any moment. Daytime was reduced to a few short hours of twilight, late dawn to an early dusk, punctuated with two small meals instead of three. Abel counted the nights without moon. He wondered if she was still up there somewhere or if she too had been swept away by the wind. Nothing was certain. Nothing could not be extinguished, not even the moon.

The pickup truck was the first vehicle to run out of petrol. The blue car had less than a quarter tank left, and the spare cans were all now empty. Enoch prophesied that the windstorm would be over by morning. He said they should camp where they were for the night. Tomorrow, the Lord would tell him what to do, where they should go.

'Course we're staying put,' Uncle Joe shouted through the open window of his truck. 'How the hell-fire can we go anywhere on empty? Got an answer for that, have you, lad? Eh, Enoch?'

Mother grew anxious and attempted to silence Uncle Joe, but he took off his cap and thumped the steering wheel, shouting all the while. Abel heard words he did not understand, though he knew they were bad, unforgivably bad. God may forgive him; Enoch would not.

Enoch held his axe in both hands. He kept his back to the vehicles and stared at the trees ahead of him, the heavy darkness between and beyond. Nothing seemed to concern him now but whatever absorbed his attention in the intimacy of the forest. The wind pulled at his long black hair, tugged at his jeans and his chequered shirt, but he stood solidly against the gale. Out of nowhere it seemed to come him, that sound that no one else could hear. He reached out an open hand as though accepting an offering of help from the empty air and stepped forward, one faltering step after another. Slowly, he climbed the embankment of nettles and twisted roots, and entered the forest.

As Enoch had predicted, the wind died down before dawn. The eastern clouds fragmented into strips of sunlit orange, broken strands of tinted white. Not a raindrop had fallen during the month-long storm. Enoch returned from his night-time wanderings with muddy boots, axe in hand and no explanation. Mother had waited for him to return all night, sitting in the front of the pickup with Abel asleep on her lap. Enoch sat down on the caravan step and stretched out his legs. Mother lit the camping stove, brewed him a mug of steaming sweet tea.

'You were right about the wind,' she said.

'Lord was right about the wind,' Enoch replied. He sipped his tea.

She nodded in agreement, felt for the little crucifix around her neck. 'Your uncle has something to say to you.' She nodded towards the back of the truck. Uncle Joe emerged from the tarpaulin flap, jumped to the ground with unlaced boots and an open shirt, coughed an apology of sorts.

'Been doing your penance, have you, Uncle Joe?' said Enoch.

Joe mumbled something under a cough, went to piss against a tree.

'I bet you have, Uncle,' Enoch added with an unkind smile.

They ate breakfast sitting on a blanket under the trees. Now that the wind had stopped howling, Abel could hear the sounds of the forest: wood pigeon, blackbird, crow. It was cold but he felt relieved to see blue sky through the branches overhead. It reminded him of the breathable, wide-open countryside they had left behind. He wondered if he would be able to see the moon tonight, if the moon was still there, if the storm had not sent her to the bottomless pit.

Warmed by the change in weather, Mother announced that Ruth had finished her penance and could eat with them once more. Ruth looked at no one, sat a little apart and did not touch the food on her plate. It still felt like a holiday.

Enoch said that they should leave the vehicles behind and continue on foot, just like the Israelites in the wilderness. Enoch said that he had seen signs in the night, found a trail of animal tracks through the trees, seen the way to go.

'Then we'll go on foot,' said Father. 'We'll take only what we need, carry what we can.'

The road was no longer a road, not even a path or an old track, but a following of Enoch through the trees and undergrowth until dark. Enoch stalked ahead, axe in hand, stopped and stared at the accidental patterns made by fallen branches. He walked ahead, stopped, moved on, said nothing. This and then this was the way to go.

CHAPTER TWO
REQUIEM

THERE WAS A MAN STANDING in her room. Fran knew it was a man because she could hear him breathing heavily, as though he had water in his lungs or his throat had been cut, or perhaps he had been running all his life to stand there at the end of her bed at that particular moment on that particular night. She knew that he could hurt her: that is what made her most afraid. Not of the things he would do, but of the things he could. Nothing was inconceivable. The possibilities were endless once the box had been opened. The man hesitated in a rapture of power, absolute and incontrovertible. Fran understood that whatever she did next would determine what he would do next, and all the things after that, and then that one final, terrible thing. Or perhaps she was wrong. Perhaps nothing she could do would change the order of things that he had predetermined. And was there enlightenment, she wondered, in the knowledge that everything he did was predetermined? Was there freedom in accepting the futility of her own actions?

Fran closed her eyes and whispered calmly, simply, so as not to provoke the man who stood at the end of her bed, 'She's behind you.'

But the room was as empty as it had always been. Fran did not need to open her eyes to know that now she was alone. She turned onto her side and listened to the voices downstairs, to the older woman, Rhea, reminiscing in the sitting room, to the endless say-so of the wind.

THE WIND WAS A SONG that never stopped singing, sometimes played kettle-drums with the bin-lids and jerry cans in the tool-shed outside, sometimes sang treble through the gaps in the tiles. It was a mischievous entity, the wind, both performer and performance, composer and opus, everywhere at once and yet nowhere to be held accountable. When the song did rest for a minute or more, the women downstairs thought that it might have finally passed away, though it had not ended at all, of course, but merely crescendoed to some unimaginable altitude where the air was thin, to fall back to earth with the weight of mountains, a fanfare of trumpets.

Rhea was not musical, but she did like to listen to music. When she had worked at the university before the troubles, she would go to the free rehearsals or almost-free concerts in the college auditorium all the time, occasionally attend chapel for choral evensong—for the music not the theology. She had once bought a wind-up gramophone player from an antique shop, a genuine tabletop phonograph with an oak cabinet and brass horn, on which she played her vinyls. In those days, she had taken pleasure in performing the quaint rituals of disc, turntable and needle, winding the handle to summon those crackling orchestras and long-dead composers who lived forever in works she loved but knew next to nothing about. It felt like sorcery, as if she were the medium at a musical séance, physically involved in the conjuring of voices, strings, woodwind and trumpet. Of course, she had also possessed, or thought she had possessed, a vast library of virtual music, but all that had been snuffed out in a flash when the servers were knocked out, the off-switch was hit and the lights went down. More than anything else, Rhea wished she still had that wind-up gramophone.

'Not more than *anything*, of course,' she said aloud, carrying her thoughts into the open. 'I don't quite mean that.'

Ky looked up from her book. 'Don't quite mean what?'

'Oh, nothing, I was just reminiscing about this funny old gramophone I used to own. Lamenting the loss of music, I suppose. I know it's silly but...' Rhea paused mid-thought. She tilted her head to consider the matter and then changed her mind. 'No, it's not silly, is it. I do miss listening to music, I really do. It's something I used to do every night when I got home from work. It took me out of myself, like a meditation. Stopped me brooding. And, once in a while, one of those old records, some piece or other, would really get to me, like here and here.' Rhea clenched her fist at her stomach and then at her heart. 'And we could all do with being taken out of ourselves a bit, couldn't we, dear. Especially now. So I do miss the music, I do.'

'And I miss it too,' said Ky. She closed her book, rested her elbow on the hardback cover, chin on knuckles, and smiled at Rhea through half-closed green eyes, as content as a cat. Ky liked it when the older woman emerged from deep thoughts and shared something random and personal, something she really cared about. Since circumstances had thrown them together— first on that train out of the city, and then at the relief camp, and after that on the boat to the mainland—Ky and Rhea had talked so much about patients and treatments and supplies and survival and so little about themselves that Ky had felt that they barely knew each other. But now they had found this remote house away from all the troubles, with the mountains on one side and the sea on the other, they could begin to relax and share precious fragments of their past lives, express more than mere outrage or urgency.

Rhea was in her late sixties, old enough to be Ky's mother or even, just conceivably, her grandmother. In fact, there was something fundamentally grandmotherly about Rhea, with her small blinking eyes, large spectacles and an expression that flickered between indulgence, mischief, all-purpose concern and occasional crankiness. Ky also knew that, if compelled, perhaps if cornered in an impossible situation, the older woman could still throw a mean punch. Back at the relief camp, Rhea had been stubborn enough to unload boxes of medical supplies from the delivery truck by herself while shouting at the bystanders, 'Stop playing with your balls and give me a bleeding hand, will you?' And because Rhea was cocky and confident and playful, and because times were extraordinary, the onlookers had laughed and done as they were told.

'I do worry about people sometimes,' Rhea had said to Ky at that time. 'You think those supplies would still be gathering dust in the truck if I hadn't shouted at those lazy arses?'

'I expect they would, but perhaps there are times when people want to be told what to do. They need it. Especially when the old certainties have all disappeared.'

'You mean people need a battle-axe like me to kick them up the backside once in a while?'

'I mean: cometh the hour, cometh the battle-axe.'

Now, drinking tea together beside the glowing fireplace while the wind wassailed calamities outside, Ky wondered how she could ever imagine Rhea kicking backsides and throwing punches. The older woman was even knitting while she harked on about gramophones.

'I bet you had an impressive library,' said Ky. 'Wall-to-wall vinyl in alphabetical order.'

'Oh no, hardly anything at all.' Rhea gazed absent-mindedly at the mantelpiece, at the wooden clock which had stopped forever at half-past twelve. 'I knew next to nothing about classical music—and it should be something classical on a gramophone, don't you think? I even asked the man at the shop what records I should buy for it. He said—and I'll never forget what he said because it was remarkably prescient as it turns out—he said, "If the world should end tomorrow and only these four pieces survive, then the soul of humanity will have been preserved". How about that for foresight? Such a pity he didn't have all four of those records, whatever they were, but I did take home two of them: the Saint Matthew Passion by Bach and the Requiem by Mozart. Maybe I haven't got the right ear, but I thought the Passion was quite dull in places. Actually, a lot dull. But I did like the Mozart. I suppose that was half of humanity's soul saved, wasn't it? Except, I don't even have those two anymore: Passion or Requiem. Such a pity.'

The wind rattled the fence posts outside the back door, skipped over the roof tiles and pushed a lungful of woodsmoke down the chimney. Rhea waved her knitting in the air to clear the smoke from their faces. This had been such a regular aggravation during the month-long storm that neither of them saw any point in complaining.

Ky rubbed her tired, smoke-bothered eyes and placed her book on the floor. She really should remember not to read in candlelight or firelight, she thought. If she should damage her eyes, if she should lose her sight, well then she would prefer not to live at all. She relied on her eyes to keep everyone safe, to watch over things.

'At least the wind is singing for us.'

'Because we don't sing for ourselves anymore,' Rhea said but regretted it immediately. 'Oh, I am maudlin tonight. I'm sorry, dear, it's not like me. It's just all this weather—'

'We have been having a lot of fucking weather recently.'

Rhea forced a laugh. 'An awful lot. And it's been such a relief to find this house, hasn't it? And, when you think about what happened to others, we've been very fortunate. But just when we thought we were safe here, there was all that bother with the man—oh, I don't like to think of it—because of what could have happened, what would have happened if I hadn't heard—and poor Francesca sleeping upstairs and waking to find that man—'

'You did what you had to, Rhea. I wish I'd been the one to do it. Really, I do.'

Ky knelt on the floor and put her arm around Rhea's shoulders, tried to hold her gaze but the older woman was too agitated to respond to such comfort. Rhea turned to the ceiling, the stopped clock, towards the back door in the kitchen that would not lock, to the ceiling again – above which was the bedroom where Fran slept. Rhea continued to utter pieces of sentences, broken images of what had happened, what could have happened and what she had done to end it. Ky knew that this was not a time to interrupt but to listen to Rhea's confession. It was unlike Rhea to be quite so emotional, but Ky knew this outburst had been brewing for days: it had to happen sometime. Far better that it all came out now when the two of them were alone.

When she had finished unburdening herself, Rhea stared at the fire with a face that had closed down. She had cast out her demons and bolted the door.

'It's done now. You did what I would have done. What I should have done,' Ky said as she stroked the older woman's hair.

They both listened to the wind's plainsong outside, the sound of logs crackling in the fireplace.

'What happened?' asked Fran, standing unexpectedly at the doorway to the sitting room.

Ky smiled as she always did when she saw Fran and then gave her a meaningful look, a frown and slight shake of the head. She and Fran often spoke to each other in these deep looks and heavy silences. She hoped that Fran would leave Rhea's confession where it lay. It did not need to be reopened so soon.

'I was sleeping,' Fran added quickly and pretended to stifle a yawn. She was wearing a long white shirt and pyjama bottoms, her feet were bare and her long, auburn hair was loose at her shoulders, so it was possible she might have been telling the truth.

'Oh, Francesca,' said Rhea, looking troubled again, 'I didn't wake you, did I?'

'No, it was the wind, the wind, always the wind.'

Fran sat down on the carpet in front of the fire, rested her chin on her knees and hugged her shins. Both she and Ky were in their late twenties, though Fran gave the impression of being the younger of the two. For one thing, Fran never seemed to be entirely present. Her eyes, a North-Sea blue, were wide and watchful and always found interest in some other distraction beyond immediate concerns, something in the corner of the window perhaps, a blackbird in a tree, the way a leaf moved. Her mouth was forever slightly open as though she were preparing something to say but could never quite find the appropriate words because, look, there was a moth trapped in the folds of the curtain.

Ky, on the other hand, was olive-skinned with almond-shaped eyes and a fiercely attentive expression. She gave full, feline attention to whatever matter was placed in front of her, whether it was a book, a refugee camp at the end of the world, or a friend confessing to murder. Her assessments were quick and her decisions utilitarian. She cut her own black hair functionally short, wore hard-wearing, military boots and a black boiler-suit, all of which had been looted from warehouses. She kept her essential items in an army rucksack beside her bed so that, if some new disaster should befall during the night, she would be prepared to evacuate in a moment. Among those items which Ky considered most indispensable was the heavy, hardback encyclopaedia she had been reading before Rhea had begun to reminisce about gramophones. It was this book that Fran now touched with her foot.

'What's the lesson tonight, Zachariadou,' asked Fran, using Ky's surname.

There was an uncomfortable silence. Ky and Rhea exchanged a glance, but Fran tapped the encyclopaedia with her big toe.

'You still on the B's? What you been reading? Butterflies, bee-keeping or Byzantium?'

Ky smiled. 'Oh, the book. I jumped ahead to the P's—to Plato. He keeps cropping up.'

'So tell me about Plato. I can't sleep. Tell me something new.'

Ky resisted but Rhea agreed with Fran and said it would be nice for them to hear something different, anything that was not the wind. Ky sighed, gave an outline of what little she could remember having read in the encyclopaedia—Athens, Socrates, *The Symposium*, *The Republic*—and said that most of Plato's books had been lost over time.

'I suspect all the rest have gone now too,' she concluded.

'As long as there's still bee-keeping,' said Fran, gazing into the fire.

'I'm not so sure about the bee-keeping, my love,' said Ky. Not for the first time, she stopped herself reaching for the mobile phone that had not been in her pocket for months. Instead, she took the encyclopaedia and flicked through the pages. 'The entries are too short. There's barely any detail at all. No instructions, nothing practical. Why? Are you thinking about keeping bees?'

Fran shrugged. "I wouldn't mind. I like bees. I miss honey.'

'What is justice?' Rhea said suddenly. She had been quiet for some time, trying to retrieve some half-forgotten idea. Now she had it, she had to share it. 'That's it, isn't it—the question he asks in *The Republic*. Plato. What is justice. It's been bugging me since I heard his name.'

'You've read it?' Ky asked in delight, as though Rhea had said she once met Plato.

'Oh no, dear. It was a lecture, I think. What is justice. If I remember rightly, someone tells Plato that people are only good because they are afraid of being punished. If you take away the threat of punishment—give them a magical ring of invisibility, say—then they will do whatever they want. In other words, is there any reason to be good or behave well if there are no consequences? I think that's the gist of the question, isn't it?'

Ky shrugged. 'No idea. Encyclopaedia's short on substance. How does Plato respond?'

'I imagine he would have disagreed, but I'm afraid I don't quite remember.'

'Guess we'll never know,' said Fran.

The three of them sat in silence for a time looking at the dying fire. The wind had taken this moment to settle down, reflecting upon its devastation and the things it was yet to break. Fran said she would go outside for more logs. She was just putting on her boots when there was a noise in the bedroom, a thump on the floorboards overhead.

'The boy,' said Rhea unduly distressed, perhaps remembering another disturbance upstairs on another night not that long ago.

'He's alright,' said Ky, touching her arm. 'Look, the back door's jammed. No-one can get in.'

Fran offered to check on the boy, but Rhea was already on her feet and up the stairs.

'We need to fix that back door,' said Ky. 'She won't feel safe until it locks. None of us will.'

'We need to give that boy a name,' said Fran. She raised her head at the sound of Rhea's voice upstairs. Rhea was talking to the boy, commiserating with him, reassuring him. Perhaps he had had another nightmare.

'Are you okay, my love?' asked Ky.

'Of course,' Fran replied vaguely, still listening to the voices overhead.

THE BOY HAD NOT SAID a word since they had found him standing alone on the roadside. That had been a month or so earlier, the same day that Rhea, Ky and Fran had arrived on the mainland. They had landed on a pebbly beach beside a small, deserted seaside town. The runner had dropped them on the shore and pointed towards a bus shelter on the promenade. He told them all, about forty passengers on a boat designed for ten, to wait inside the shelter until another runner showed up to take them to the next drop.

'How long will that be?' someone had shouted, but the runner was busy untying a rope and said nothing.

'Why is this place so empty?' Ky had asked him. 'Where is everyone?'

The runner spat over the side of his boat, started the loud engine again and cruised away.

'We're not staying here,' Ky said to Rhea as she heaved her rucksack onto her shoulders and tugged at the straps.

Rhea protested and said that they had spent all their money to reach a safe destination, but Ky shook her head. She waited until the other passengers had climbed up the shingle towards the promenade and were out of earshot.

'Do you trust me?' asked Ky. Rhea agreed, of course, that she did. 'Then we're not staying here. Something's wrong. Maybe this town is in quarantine or exposed, or maybe it's already been occupied and all the people have been rounded up.'

'Rounded up? What do you mean, my dear? Taken where, and by who?'

'Wherever people are taken at such times. Rhea, we have to leave now.'

'And them?' Rhea nodded towards the other passengers from the boat. They had all reached the bus shelter. Some were sitting on seats, stretching their wet legs, talking in relieved voices now they had reached the assumed safety of the mainland. One man, just one, was laughing. His voice sounded forced, too loud for the empty street. Ky shook her head.

'We'll attract attention if they all come with us,' she said. Without waiting for an answer, she started walking along the beach, away from the crowd in the bus shelter.

'You coming, Francesca, dear?' Rhea called to Fran, who had been staring at the wake of the disappearing boat on the waves.

Fran turned from the grey sea and picked up her rucksack. 'Coming,' she said and the two of them followed Ky along the beach.

At the bus shelter, the loud man stopped laughing. One by one, the other passengers fell silent as they watched the three women go their own way.

Ky led them down side roads and back lanes, past curtained houses, black windows that reflected the clouds, the empty streets and their quick passing. Only the sound of their footsteps and the whistling wheels of Rhea's suitcase broke the unsettling stillness. The sudden, occasional cry of a seagull caused them to flinch and quicken their pace towards the edge of town and the countryside. A dog barked forlornly in the distance, his yelp becoming wolf-like, wind-like.

An hour or so after leaving the seaside town, they spotted the boy standing as still as a tree at the roadside. He was staring at the mountains with his back towards them and was so perfectly motionless that they did not notice him until they had almost passed him. Rhea surmised that he must be about twelve years old, a short thirteen at a stretch. He was wearing an old school uniform—grey sweater, black trousers, muddy trainers—as though he had been waiting in all weathers for a school bus that would never arrive.

Rhea called out something silly to catch his attention, alert him to their presence. 'Have they blinked back at you yet, those mountains?' she said. 'If they have, you've won.'

The boy did not reply. Rhea left her suitcase on the road and peered into his dirty, sunburnt face, brushed the chestnut-coloured hair out of his face. Beneath long eyelashes, his blue eyes refused to look into hers. She asked for his name in English, then French. Ky tried Greek and basic Arabic, but the boy responded to nothing, just stared distractedly at the mountains.

'Perhaps we should leave him,' said Ky. She followed his gaze towards the distant peaks. 'Looks like he's waiting for someone.'

'We're not leaving him all alone like this,' Rhea said firmly. She spat on her sleeve and wiped the dried mud from his cheeks. 'See, there is a boy under all that muck after all. Handsome boy, too. You live somewhere near here, do you? You want to show me where you live? Maybe we can find you something to eat. What do we have here?'

She pulled out an old bar of chocolate from her coat, a rare delicacy she had been saving for a special occasion. She ripped the wrapper open with her teeth and held the bar to his mouth. At some point during its long months in Rhea's pocket, the chocolate had melted in heat. Now misshapen and white with age, the sight of it filled Ky and Fran with forgotten memories. They each looked away when the boy refused to take it.

'Come on, he's probably with someone,' said Ky. She did not like to be standing out in the open for so long. They were conspicuous on the road, surrounded by nothing but empty fields and grey skies, and she was keen to be back under cover. Though she would not verbalise it, some small, mean, conservative voice in her mind said they should simply abandon him.

'You want to stay with us?' Rhea asked the boy. 'You want to show us where you live?'

Ky pulled a face, scratched her hair and was about to object but Fran interrupted her.

'You speak Arabic?' she asked Ky.

'What? A little. Enough to get by. Why?'

'I didn't know you could, that's all. I don't think he speaks Arabic.'

Fran walked up to the boy and, without looking at him, took his hand. The two of them stood side by side staring at the same horizon for a while, holding hands and not speaking until Fran gently tugged him away from the road and into the field. The boy did not resist but let her lead him in the direction of the mountains. She swung their hands a little as they walked.

After a time, she slowed down and let him lead the way.

'Where the fuck are we going now?' Ky shouted, losing patience. She immediately regretted swearing at Rhea.

'We're going the fuck this way,' said Rhea crossly. She took her suitcase by the handle and pulled it into the field after Fran and the boy. Ky kicked the kerbside and reluctantly followed.

The boy led them through a field of whiskery grain, sown in some spring but never harvested, to a blackthorn hedge and a cattle path that bore the craters of old hoof-prints in dried mud. Over a wooden stile and onto a farm track, they arrived at last at the house. The boy let go of Fran's hand to unlatch the gate and, for the first time, looked up at her with the same frown he had used to scrutinise the faraway mountains. Fran nodded and entered the farmyard. Rhea and Ky were still some way behind, so the boy closed the gate behind him and led her into the house.

The lock on the back door had been broken; someone had smashed it open. Fran put her rucksack on a chair and looked for food in the kitchen cupboards, the unlit, stinking fridge.

'Well, this is something,' Rhea said when she arrived. She was breathing heavily from the effort of pulling her suitcase. 'Where's he got to, the young master of the house?'

'Upstairs,' Fran replied. She held up a tin of plum tomatoes. 'I think he's gone to bed.'

'What, all mucky and dirty like that?'

'No, I heard him running a bath. I believe he's house-trained.'

Ky took a reconnoitre of the grounds, the tool-sheds and empty barns with a knife in her hand. When she was satisfied there was no danger out there, she did the same inside, inspecting the windows and cupboards in every room. In the hallway, she lingered over a small bookshelf that contained almanacs, gardening books, some cheap thrillers and a hardback encyclopaedia.

'Seems abandoned, apart from the boy. But we have to do something about that back door,' Ky said when she returned to the kitchen. She lay the encyclopaedia on the table and her hunting knife beside it. 'What's the food situation?'

'Put that nasty thing away, dear,' Rhea said with a disapproving glance at Ky's knife.

Ky smiled and put the knife on a high shelf above the range cooker. 'Now only the big people can reach it,' she said.

'We shouldn't have to see that thing lying around,' Rhea added, shaking her head.

THE STORM ARRIVED A FEW days after they had found the house. Though it did not rain, the wind was ferocious, a thing of destruction that tore through the pine forest on the mountains and flattened the unharvested fields below, broke branches from the old oak and apple trees around the house, and ripped the roof off the barn, the door from the tool-shed. Heavy, gunmetal-grey clouds whirled overhead threatening to overwhelm them with a deluge of thick water but never spilling a drop. When the storm showed no signs of subsiding after the first week or so, they knew that this thing was different.

'Is it natural for a hurricane to hang around so long?' asked Rhea.

She was sitting at the kitchen table with Fran. They had found an old wooden chess set in one of the drawers and were playing a game by candlelight. The boy sat a little way off, watching the pieces move with the same puzzled expression he always wore.

'Ex-hurricane,' Fran said. 'You don't get hurricanes outside the tropics, only ex-hurricanes.'

'Where on Earth did you hear such a thing?'

'Ky's encyclopaedia. When hurricanes leave tropical waters, they become ex-hurricanes.'

Fran picked up a castle and held it hesitantly over the board. She had also read that hurricanes travel surprisingly slowly, about as fast as she could sprint. Still holding her castle in the air, she calculated the distance the storm would travel if it ran for ten days. It must have covered half the Atlantic or more, she thought, because it just kept flowing overhead without catching its breath. She pictured the whirling face of clouds over the curve of the Earth. From her imagined vantage point in the silent, upper atmosphere, the hurricane was an aesthetic curl of colours that made no sound and barely moved at all. Outwardly serene, it let loose hidden violence on the landscapes beneath. Straying in those unthinkable distances, Fran felt giddy. She dropped her castle on a vacant square.

'So,' she said, relieved to be back in the kitchen, 'this has to be an ex-hurricane. Check?'

'Nothing ex about this wind,' said Rhea, returning Fran's castle to its original position. 'Castles move up, down, left and right, not diagonally, dear. But is it natural to last this long?'

'Maybe it's the new natural,' replied Ky. She was standing beside the range, looking through a bundle of papers. She did not know what was natural, unnatural or ex-natural anymore. There was no one to tell her, no more TV or radio debates between experts and non-experts: all that had been done away with. Ky had made a conscious decision to no longer fret about things beyond her immediate control. If the wind howled against the windows and walls until the end of days, it was simply one more thing to accept.

'Look, here's a bill,' Ky said, changing the subject from the unknowable to something within her grasp. 'Tax bill, three years old, addressed to a Janet O'Byrne. Is that your mother?' She held the letter up like an item of evidence and smiled awkwardly at the boy. He cast a quick, uninterested glance at the document and then returned his frown of concentration to the chess board, giving nothing away.

'There's also a couple of school exercise books. This one belongs to a certain L. O'Byrne.' Ky held up the book, item number two. 'I bet that L. O'Byrne is sitting in this very kitchen right now learning how to play chess.'

'How not to play chess,' said Rhea, returning Fran's bishop to its original square. 'That one moves diagonally, like so. Try to concentrate, dear.'

'Why not ask him in Greek, Zachariadou,' said Fran, moving her queen, 'or Arabic?'

Ky pulled a vicious face, hunched her shoulders like a witch and swore dramatically, excessively in Greek. She winked at the boy who blushed and pursed his lips, trying not to smile.

Late one night during their third week in the house, a man had climbed through the window into Fran's bedroom. Rhea had heard the noise upstairs. She did what she did without thinking. Afterwards, she and Ky had carried his body outside. They did not have a torch and no candle would last a moment in that wind, so they stumbled around in the dark farmyard with the body. Ky went first with his legs, said they should put him in the tool-shed for the night. Rhea lifted him by his shoulders, said nothing. They must have forgotten to lock the shed securely because, when they looked out in the morning, the door had been taken by the wind. The man's leather boots lay at the entrance, his soles pointing towards the house.

'Oh, damn and fuck it. Would you look at that,' said Rhea.

'I'll take care of it,' said Ky. 'You go upstairs. Don't let them see anything.'

Ky went out with a shovel, did not return until late in the afternoon.

After a month, the windstorm finally moved on. It had not died, it had not disbanded nor run out of elemental voltage. It had simply decamped to some other place and left an uncanny, uncomfortable silence. Before Rhea opened her eyes, she knew that the storm had gone but that it was not over. A beast of that magnitude would never be over. It was looming somewhere else: a wolf at someone else's door. For now, at least, it was not lurking at theirs.

The fire in the range cooker had also died during the night. Rhea wiped her eyes, put her glasses on and stood up to get more firewood. She always slept in the kitchen chair now with Ky's hunting knife on the table beside her. Although the door with the broken lock was jammed shut with a chair, it could easily be forced open if someone was determined to break in. Now that the wind had gone, the silence would serve Rhea well at night. No one would break in unnoticed.

When Rhea turned around, she was startled to see she was not alone in the kitchen.

'Someone's up bright and early,' she said to the boy who was still in his pyjamas and looking out of the window. Rhea stood beside him and laid a hand gently on his shoulder. 'Shall we take a look outside, see what the storm has left us?'

The boy did not respond. He was staring at the battered old Ford Cortina that had driven onto the farm track in the night and parked outside the kitchen. Its headlights were broken as was one of the windows. The bodywork was so dented and scorched that Rhea wondered for a moment whether the storm had tossed the car into their garden as a parting gift. Then she noticed the dark outline of a man hunched over the steering wheel.

'Go and get Ky,' she said quietly, keeping her voice as calm as she could.

'No,' the boy replied.

'I see,' was all Rhea could think to say.

The boy looked up at her with the same deep-thinking frown he always wore, but now he was pouting in a hard-fought effort to keep his lips from trembling.

'The man that's out there, do you know him?' asked Rhea.

The boy nodded slowly and looked back towards the car.

'Is that your daddy?' she ventured. This time the boy did not respond.

'Is it your brother?' asked Fran who moved so quietly that neither of them had heard her enter the kitchen, though neither were surprised by her gentle arrival.

The boy shrugged an answer that could have been either a yes or a no.

'What do you think? Should we leave him out there or bring him inside?' asked Fran.

'Inside,' the boy said firmly. He looked up at Fran and this time his eyes were filled with tears, though he was still doing all in his power to control his lips.

'Then you have to go and wake up Ky so we can bring him inside,' she said.

The man in the car was unconscious and seriously wounded. He had several deep cuts on his cheek and forehead and his shirt was soaked with blood. It took all three women to haul him from the car and carry him upstairs. The boy led the way and opened one of the bedroom doors so they could lay him on the single bed. It was the room that Fran had been sleeping in.

'This is his room?' she asked, and the boy nodded. She looked around as though for the first time at the posters on the walls, heavy metal bands from decades earlier, a few science study books on the desk, an empty bottle of aftershave.

'Good,' she continued. 'Listen, Rhea and Ky need to look after him now. They know what to do, but they have to do it alone. Will you let them do that?'

The boy nodded again and cast one more glance at the man. They had already turned him on his side into the recovery position. The man was no more than a youth himself, younger than Ky and Fran, perhaps not yet in his twenties, though injury and infection made him look older. Ky stretched his neck to clear the airways. Rhea cut through his shirt with a large pair of scissors.

'Should I go and look for a pharmacy in that town by the sea?' asked Fran.

'Thank you, dear, but I doubt any shops will be open,' said Rhea.

'I mean, should I break in to one?'

'No one's going to that town,' said Ky resolutely. 'No one.'

'If you want to make yourselves useful, you can sterilise some sheets, shirts, towels, anything like that, in boiling water,' said Rhea.

'And bring my bag,' added Ky, shutting the door on them, 'and what's left of the whisky.'

The bedroom door remained closed for hours. Fran carried two mugs of tea upstairs mid-morning. She returned to find the boy sitting with his head in his hands at the kitchen table. She had set up a game of chess for them to play, but he would not take his move. Fran sat down opposite him and walked one of her knights over the empty squares and up to his king.

'Hey,' she said, or rather her knight said to his king. 'You know what's good for someone who's been injured? Fruit. Apples, for example. Apples, apples, more apples. If only there was somewhere we could get a load of apples.'

At first, the boy did not respond. Fran's knight shuffled over the chessboard, searching here and there, in every corner and over the edge of the board, but he always returned to the boy's king empty-handed, shaking his head. After a while, the boy took his turn.

'I know where there's apples,' said his king. He limped like an old man up to the knight. 'There's tonnes in the orchard.'

'Are there really?' the knight said, falling over in surprise. 'But wouldn't the storm have blown them all away?'

'I don't think so,' replied the king doubtfully. 'Maybe there's some left?'

'Maybe there are. Maybe we need to go on an apple-quest?'

The king agreed, so Fran and the boy went outside.

The passing of the storm was a momentous event, but one that had been overshadowed by the arrival of the wounded man. The wind that had torn relentlessly at their senses for weeks had departed so abruptly that the world was left mute, unnaturally quiet, bathed in a bright, unfamiliar December sunlight. Fran and the boy walked around the grounds noting the aftermath of the storm: gaps on the roof where tiles had been taken, wooden fences down, tree limbs scattered across the yard, the body of a colossal oak lying prostrate in the field. There were no apples left on the orchard trees, but the boy helped Fran salvage the least rotten fruit from the grass. These she stewed in a little water and sugar on the range cooker.

'You think your brother will like it more sugary?' she said, passing a spoonful for the boy to taste. He considered his mouthful for a moment and then nodded.

'Or perhaps salt. Sugar or salt?'

'Not salt,' he said, pulling a don't-be-silly face.

'You don't think so? What about some pepper?'

'Seriously not pepper.'

'Okay, more sugar it is for—what is your brother's name?'

'Michael.'

'Michael. Michael O'Byrne,' she said it like she had always known. 'And L. O'Byrne is…?'

'Lugh.' The boy licked the spoon once more and returned it to Fran.

'Do you know what I did with the sugar, Lugh? Can't see it anywhere.'

He did and went to retrieve it.

Rhea and Ky did not emerge from the bedroom until early afternoon. Fran assumed it was early afternoon, though the broken clock on the mantelpiece said it was still twelve-thirty. She boiled a saucepan of water for them to wash the blood or iodine from their faces and hands. After they had cleaned up, the four of them sat down at the kitchen table. Fran poured the remaining whisky into three small glasses and waited for someone to tell them what had happened upstairs.

Rhea was too tired and despondent to say much. Ky gave a brief, clinical report such as she might have once provided at the relief camp. The man had numerous injuries, she said, the most critical of which was a gunshot wound to his abdomen. Significant blood loss, trauma to the intestines, probable infection and indications he was haemorrhaging internally. He was alive but, without the right treatment, antibiotics and so on, his chances were remote. When she had finished summarising, Ky downed her whisky in one and winced at the ceiling.

Through the window, Fran watched a crow flapping on the roof of the tool-shed. Without taking her eyes away, she said to no one in particular, 'A pharmacy might have what we need.'

'The town's not safe,' said Ky blandly as though reading the words written on the ceiling.

Lugh frowned at Ky, trying to read her face. Her short sentences and long, cold words had meant little to him. Fran tugged at his sleeve and told him simply that Michael had been hurt very badly, that they had done their best for him and he was sleeping now. They would know in the next day or two if he would get any better.

After a pause, Fran said, 'Yes, it is possible he could die,' as though the boy had just asked her a question. She held his gaze. 'We can look in on him, but we have to be quiet as mice.'

LUGH SAT BESIDE HIS BROTHER's bed for three days and waited for the wounded man to open his eyes. On his lap, the boy cradled a bowl of cold apples stewed in sugar-water, spoon at the ready. Fran often sat next to him on the floor reading the herb book she had taken from the hallway bookshelf. Angelica, Bay, Calendula, Dill. She read the names aloud like a litany, a medicinal spell to conquer the silence, or aid healing, or banish negative thoughts. Elderflower, Fenugreek, Garlic, Hyssop. The boy did not seem to mind. He even seemed to take comfort from the sounds.

At certain times, Rhea came in and asked them to leave while she changed the wounded man's bandages or took care of his rehydration.

'No enema was ever enhanced by an audience,' she said.

Lugh did not understand the terminology, but he was wise enough to know when he should get out of the way. He sat cross-legged outside the door and stirred the mushy apples.

'They also serve who stir apples and wait,' said Ky, emerging from her bedroom. She crouched down, wearing the same black boiler-suit she always wore, and looked into his face.

'We've done our best with him. You do know that, don't you?' she said. 'It might help if we knew what happened to him. Like where did he go? Or what happened to your parents?'

The boy neither replied nor looked at her. They stayed on the landing in the dying light, listening to the crows outside. Ky sighed and left him alone to stir his apples, something to do. She went into the garden and tried the car key in the old Cortina. Unbelievably, on the third or fourth turn, the ignition kicked in and the car rattled to life. She turned the battle-scarred vehicle around the yard and reversed it back down to the house. One corner of the bodywork had been so badly damaged that it hung loose and scraped the ground. Ky was no mechanic, but the engine still seemed to run and with that she was satisfied.

At dawn on the third morning, Rhea went into the bedroom. Without electric lights, they had taken to rising with the sun and settling down at the fireside after dusk. The wounded man, Michael, had suffered another fever the night before. Rhea had sat with him until late, wiping the sweat from his body, the damp, chestnut-coloured hair from his brow, and soothing his unconscious mind with platitudes. She wanted to be the first to check on him in the morning, but the boy was already sitting there at the bedside when she entered. Rhea knew immediately, from the stillness of the room, the heavy emptiness of the body, that the young man had died in the night. She knew from her time in the camp what death did to the air of a room. She knelt beside the bed and put her fingers to his pale throat, knowing she would feel nothing.

The boy stared down at his bowl of cold apples, continued to stir the spoon.

CHAPTER THREE
ADVENT

T HEY BURIED MICHAEL IN THE orchard that same afternoon. Fran and Ky dug the hole as deep as they could, no more than half a metre because the ground was mostly clay, hard and unyielding through lack of rain. As they cracked and shovelled into the earth, the boy stood at the bedroom window watching them work. It was another clear December day and the sunlight illuminated the fields and mountains with coloured precision. Between the hills behind the farm, where the road led down to the town, he could see a blue seam of sparkling sea. The only sounds he could hear were the cawing of crows in the apple trees, the scraping of the earth from that hole in the ground.

'I've seen lots of people die in the last few months,' said Rhea behind him. She was leaning over Michael's body, fixing the top buttons on his white shirt. 'More than anyone should have to see, more than there ever needed to be. Sometimes I would overhear people say things to the relatives, you know, the ones left behind: wives and husbands, partners, children. Easy things, comforting things to make them feel better. Things like, she's at peace now, or she's gone to a much better place, or it was his time to go. Worst of all, it's god's will. Things that weren't true but sounded comforting and reassuring, mainly to the person saying them.'

Rhea sat down on the chair beside the bed and smoothed the long hair away from Michael's face. She had washed his body and dressed him in a suit she found hanging in the wardrobe, the only suit he owned. He was young, she thought. He looked much younger now than when they had first brought him in from the car, all bloody and cut up and half torn open.

'He does look like you,' she said to Lugh, though the boy was still looking out of the window. 'The thing is, dear, I don't think those easy things that people say are true. I don't think everything can be comforted with a few words, nice as they might sound. I don't think Michael did suffer at the end. He wasn't conscious, so he wouldn't have felt any pain, but he shouldn't be dead, and that's the truth of it. It wasn't his time, it's not part of some big plan, and he is too young to die. He shouldn't be lying here like this on his bed wearing his one and only suit, and we shouldn't have to bury him today. There's no sense in it and it is wrong, dear, it is.'

Lugh looked down at the crows in the orchard, at Fran and Ky struggling to dig, at the dirty hole they could make no deeper.

No one spoke when they carried the body down the stairs and into the garden. They laid him on the grass next to the hole and caught their breath, each one considering the next step. Fran took the boy by his hand and led him into house, upstairs to the immensely empty bedroom.

'What should he take with him?' asked Fran. She sat on the mattress, which had been cleaned and stripped bare, and looked around the room.

Lugh understood. Carefully, he peeled the band posters from the wall, rolled them up and gave them to Fran. He chose other items that had been sacred to his brother: a pair of trainers, a long-dead laptop and mobile phone, a hairbrush, bottle of cologne, old shoebox full of keyrings, pebbles, birthday and valentine cards, other curiosities that had been kept for reasons that no one else would ever know, no one but the dead. When he had finished collecting items, Lugh paused in the hallway and took down the book of herbs from the shelf. This he also handed to Fran.

They returned to the orchard to find that the body had been laid in the hole. Michael was facing the sky with his arms crossed neatly over his chest. His skin looked too clean, too pale against the red clay, thought Fran. She knelt down and helped Lugh place the grave goods around his brother. For a moment, she even wondered whether the clean black stitches in the dead man's brow would get infected under the dirt.

'What should we say?' asked Ky. She was watching the fields, the empty hills, the road to the town, always an eye out for danger.

'I think we should say, goodbye Michael O'Byrne,' said Rhea. 'Isn't that right, Lugh?'

Still kneeling beside the hole, the boy passed the book of herbs to Fran. She was about to place it with the other offerings in the grave, but Lugh lightly touched her arm and she understood. She opened the book and began to read aloud the properties of herbs. Aromatic rosemary, a flower of remembrance, anaesthetic sage to ward off the plague, thyme for courage and to cure nightmares, yarrow to purge fevers, soothe aches and pains.

When Fran had read enough, she closed the book and they listened to the chorus of crows for a while. They could have stayed longer, but Ky took the shovel and the ceremony was over.

The funeral must have stirred old memories for Rhea. Sitting in her armchair later that evening, she talked fondly and inconsequentially of the grandmother who had raised her, childhood Christmases, suet puddings and school holidays, trivial neighbourhood scandals, Mrs-so-and-so who lived next door and gave her strawberries from an allotment.

Fran sat beside the fireplace with Lugh's head on her lap, and drifted in and out of attention to the older woman's tales. It was like listening to a radio play in the old days, thought Fran, the comfort of a background narrative to banish the creeping silence of night. In the spaces between stories, Fran imagined that ten-year-old Rhea looked identical to her present-day self: grey-haired and bespectacled and calling everyone *dear*, just a smaller, daintier, primary-school version. She wondered if Rhea had been bullied back then for being an infant senior-citizen, knitting on the playground steps, offering sweets to new kids and patching-up scrapped knees. Fran felt a surge of irrational fury at the bullies she had conjured in her own imagination. How dare they laugh at her, she thought, waving her fist at the little bastards who had formed a taunting circle around ten-year-old Rhea in the playground. The bullies jeered, so Fran threw her fists at their grotesque faces and cast them into clouds of smoke, sparks rising from a fallen log in the fireplace. Lugh sensed her tension and raised his head to look at her. Fran smiled reassuringly back at him.

'I am sorry, my dears,' said Rhea, not for the first time that evening. 'I do go on about such a load of old nonsense, don't I? It's not of the slightest interest to anyone else, I know.'

Just as Fran was reassuring her that they were listening, Ky walked into the sitting room. She sat down in the empty armchair, wiped her tired eyes and looked at each of them in turn.

'We're leaving this house,' Ky declared. 'We have to leave tonight.'

At times like this, she thought, a pinch of tobacco would make it all more bearable.

CANDLES, CANNED FOOD, DOZENS OF boxes of matches. Dried food, blankets, more matches, water bottles, jerry cans, a tent. Everything that was not essential was stripped away from Ky's ruthless stocktaking on the kitchen table. First-aid kit, detergent, kettle, cups, a pot and a pan, a strict allowance of clothes for each person.

'Looks like the saddest camping trip ever,' observed Rhea. 'Can I take my suitcase?'

'No room for that suitcase, sorry,' said Ky, tying string around a roll of blankets

'And what about my knitting?'

'Of course you can take your knitting.'

'And how much wool exactly?' Rhea laughed at Ky's frosty expression. 'Sorry, dear, it's just that I'm still knitting that jumper for the boy. If we are coming back, I don't want to take too much wool in case it all gets ruined. You do understand, don't you?'

'Are we coming back?' asked Fran. She was half-way through loading up the car and had stopped in the doorway to overhear this exchange.

'I don't know.' Ky threw the bundle of blankets onto the table and ran her fingers through her hair. She froze suddenly at a noise, the sound of distant engines, and pointed triumphantly at the ceiling. 'You hear that? That's coming this way and it's coming now. Perhaps we can discuss suitcases and wool and wheat seeds when we're not in imminent danger?'

'Mea culpa, dear,' Rhea apologised, and she helped Fran carry boxes into the car.

The night was cloudless, moonless and intensely black. Since the lights had gone out down below, it felt like the voltage of the stars had been turned on full. If there was one thing for which Fran was grateful to the troubles, it was this – that she could now see the constellations as clearly as the ancients had seen them. Not quite the same, for she knew that some stars had grown fainter while others had flared up over the past thousand years or so. Still, when the lamp-lit cities, towns and motorways had all been snuffed out, the stars had reclaimed the night. Since she was a little girl, Fran had been able to recognise a couple of the figures up there. With the help of illustrations in Ky's encyclopaedia, she was beginning to join more of the dots: the horns of Taurus above the shoulder of Orion, the Gemini twins leaping ahead of the bull, the brighter-than-ever Milky Way flowing down the back of the black mountains. In time, she hoped to map the entire universe, or at least the little patch of it that she could see of it.

Tonight, however, there were other lights in the sky. Above the small seaside town where they had arrived on the mainland, machines hovered in the air and poured white floodlights over the empty streets and houses. It was these that Ky had seen from the bedroom window. When the floodlights twitched along roads out of the town and the murmur of engines grew nearer, Ky had come downstairs and said that they must leave. There had been a discussion, of course, questions about why they should abandon this house that was so far from the town, or where they would find another safe place, or even who was driving those machines.

'They could be ours,' Rhea had said reasonably. 'We don't know they're not ours. Besides, whoever they are, why on Earth would they want to bother with us?'

'You remember what they did at the camp, I know you do,' Ky said. 'They were supposed to be ours, weren't they? Besides, there is no ours anymore. They're all the same, all of them. It's just us now. And I know you're not seriously asking why they would bother with three women.'

'Oh, damn and fuck them all,' Rhea had said, and she meant it. 'But weren't we waiting for something like this, for some kind of order to be restored? Francesca, dear, what do you say?'

'I reckon Ky's going to ask us if we trust her,' Fran replied in measured tones. As she spoke, she looked into the boy's worried eyes. 'And, I'm going to tell her the same as I did last time. Yes, Zachariadou. I trust you.'

Lugh lowered his gaze and let go of Fran's hand.

'After that, I'm going to ask Lugh if he trusts us,' Fran continued, taking up the boy's listless hand once more. 'And, if he does, I'll ask if he'd like to come with us and keep us company.'

Standing outside now, Fran loaded her box into the car, smuggled the chess set and a bag of seeds under the seat, and watched the lights circling above the town. There were other lights down there on the lower ground too, intense white glares from ships or patrol boats or landing craft on the shore, or perhaps there were floodlights stationed in the streets. All she knew for certain was that the strange glow of machines behind the hill was killing the stars. There were other sounds now too, not just the engines in the sky but something more substantial. To Fran, it sounded like something was raking loose earth and boulders in the distance, like the ground was being combed on a colossal scale. There was also a sporadic, deep-bass peal that thundered underground as though a giant, iron, primordial door was being slammed repeatedly beneath the earth. She wondered if the machines had opened an underground gate that could not now be closed. Perhaps, while it had been swinging free, something had bolted out.

'I think Ky might be right after all,' said Rhea. She loaded another box into the car and stood beside Fran. The glow from the town was so intense that they could see each other's faces. 'What on Earth can be making all that racket?'

'Nothing good,' said Fran.

Though she did not hear him, Fran sensed that Lugh had arrived quietly at her side. She reached out and felt the bag on his shoulder, which he had packed with his allowance of clothes. Against his chest he clasped a book, which she guessed must be their bible of herbs.

'All set?' she asked, though she knew that he was.

Ky was the last to leave the house. She took one last sweep of the rooms to ensure that nothing vaguely useful had been left behind, jammed the back door shut with a chair and left by the front. Although there had been no discussion about who should drive, Ky accepted the empty driver's seat without a word. No one had said anything about where they would go. The lane at the end of the farm track went only two ways: right to the town or left to the mountains. Ky started the car and rolled down the track without lights. In the back, Lugh sat next to Fran. He did not look up as she stroked his arm. Nor did he look back through the rear window as the car rolled past the grave in the orchard and stopped at the gateposts. Ky switched on the low headlights and turned left towards the mountains. Even then, the boy did not look back.

THERE WAS A MAN STANDING in her room. Fran knew it was a man because he was breathing like a bull or a horse, like a feverish beast that was struggling for air. She could smell him too, damp armpits and thick neck and old piss stains on the underclothes that had not been washed in months. And though it was dark and she could see nothing, she knew that his brown eyes bulged and that his hair was soiled with mud or dung, and that his front teeth were broken and his molars had turned black with infection, which is why the steaming air reeked like hell. And as he stamped the floorboards, Fran knew that he would charge at any moment because he could, because the sensation of shattering wood and bone and plaster would be satisfying to him, because he was the flaming, plague-ridden apocalypse and nothing and no one could stand in his way.

Fran closed her eyes and, thinking of what came after, whispered, 'She's behind you.'

When she opened her eyes, the sun had almost risen and the world was grey stone and splintered tree. On either side of the mountain road, the pine forest had been devastated by the windstorm. Amid the wreckage of fallen canopies, a few upright tree trunks stood here and there like white pillars stripped bare and pointing accusations at the sky. Looking out of the car window, Fran at first thought that these white trunks were bodies standing to attention. As the car slowed down to take another sharp bend on the single-lane track, she saw that the bodies were just different forms of the broken forest, incidental survivors.

If there was birdsong or the cough of a common crow, if a dog had barked in the distance or the wind had made some unremarkable sound, that would have helped Fran feel more at ease. But the cemetery silence of trees, broken only by the clatter of a loose underpart of the car, led her to think that she was still asleep, that they were travelling through some shadow of the valley of her dreams. She turned to Lugh. He was the one who was sleeping, his head resting lightly against her arm and the herb book still held in his hands. Do you trust me, she had asked him. Though he had not replied, he had followed her as she had followed Ky. That was enough of an answer. And that was why he could sleep beside her now. Which must mean, she thought, that this wounded landscape was not her dream. This, as Ky had said, was the new natural.

Another tight bend and the track became a mere ledge with a wall of mountain rock rising on one side and a steep drop down the other. A row of stones and occasional boulders marked the edge of the narrow road. Although there was no wind, cold air flowed into the car through the windowless door of the front passenger seat where Rhea sat with a blanket over her head. Another bend and Ky stopped the car in the middle of the track. As she climbed out to survey the landscape below, Rhea and Lugh both woke up. Rhea uncovered the blanket from her face and asked if they had arrived somewhere.

'Somewhere,' confirmed Fran. It was so cold that she could see her breath in the air. She stroked the hair away from Lugh's face while he yawned, stretched and blinked sleepily up at her. 'Let's go outside and see what only the eagles can see.'

On the edge of the road, Ky was rummaging through her rucksack for a pair of binoculars. Now that the sun had risen over the hills in the east, they could clearly see the way they had come. The gravel track appeared and disappeared around the folds of the mountain below, snaking between contours of grey rock and hectares of fallen forest. Much further down where the bare stone crags levelled into shrubland and brush, the track became a respectable-looking black asphalt lane meandering between patchworks of green farmland that had been left fallow and unharvested for the first time in more than two or three thousand years. The road disappeared behind hedges, coppices, geometries of woodland, clusters of houses, merged with a main road and ran into the small town on the coast, beyond which the blue sea dissolved into a hazy horizon.

'They've reached the house,' said Ky, looking through the binoculars. 'Some kind of vehicle in the yard. And see, down at the coast. There's a heavy cruiser or something just off the shore.'

'Can you see any markings?' asked Rhea. 'Any idea who they are?'

'Too far to tell. Besides, does it make any difference?'

'There is no ours anymore,' said Fran. 'They're all the same.'

'Agreed,' said Ky. She took a deep sigh and asked Lugh if he knew where this road led, if it crossed the mountains, and what lay on the other side. As she had expected, the boy frowned into the distance and said nothing. Ky cast a meaningful look at Fran, handed the binoculars to her and walked away from the edge to inspect the damaged mudguard on the car. Fran accepted the challenge. Standing next to Lugh, she held the binoculars to his eyes and asked what he could see.

'Blue. Blue. More blue,' he said.

'Sea blue or sky blue?' asked Fran.

'Sea blue.'

'Curious,' she said and then, gently turning him around so that he was facing the mountain, she asked what he could see now.

'Now it's just grey,' he said, squinting through the binoculars.

'Mountain grey or sky grey?'

'Mountain grey. Tonnes of mountain grey.'

'And behind that mountain grey, what's on the other side?'

Lugh twitched a smile. 'More mountain grey.'

Fran took the binoculars, pretended to breathe on the lenses and to scrub them vigorously, then she handed them back to him with a confident smile. Lugh looked again.

'There's this road that goes on and on and down to the big forest,' he said.

'This road?' she asked, pointing at the gravel track they were standing on. The boy nodded. 'Are there any towns or houses, or maybe someone you know that lives down there?'

'Only the forest,' he said. He let her try the binoculars for herself.

'I see,' she agreed. 'It does seem to go on forever.'

'To the end of the world.'

'Curiouser and curiouser.'

They climbed back into the car just as Rhea disappeared around the corner with a bundle of tissue paper. While they waited, Ky flicked through her encyclopaedia in search of maps while Fran explained that the road led over the mountain to a forest that never ended. In the distance, faint at first but growing louder, they heard the dull drone of engines. Ky took the binoculars and scoured the landscape through her open window.

'We need to go,' she said, counting up to five helicopters over the fields. 'Where is Rhea?'

'They don't know about us, so they're not looking for us,' Fran reassured the boy.

'No, but they are looking,' said Ky. 'Where is she?'

Rhea apologised when she returned to the car and said she was not feeling well. Ky drove quickly now, accelerating along straight stretches of the track though the car rattled noisily in protest. After a while, there were no more steep ledges or panoramic views of the fields or the sea. Instead, the road turned into a narrow crevice through the mountain, a passage strewn with rocks and boulders. The summits still appeared to be some way above them, for all sides of the granite corridor rose higher than anyone could see. There was, however, a distinct sense of atmospheric change as they left the clear morning behind and drove through the sunless, winding canyon path. Now that they were concealed, Rhea asked if she could stop for another toilet break. Ky leaned forward to check the narrow cleft of sky above and agreed.

'That's another one finished,' said Ky as she emptied the last drops of petrol from a jerry can into the fuel tank. 'The last one should have got us a lot further than this.'

She noticed Rhea's face as the older woman returned, and said, 'You're not feeling okay.'

'A little upset with all the changes probably,' Rhea replied, though she would not look at Ky.

'Finish the flask of tea, what's left of it. And go and lie down in the back with the boy. Fran can keep me company up front. And, Rhea, I am sorry.'

'What are you sorry for now, dear?'

'For pushing. I know I push a lot. All the time, in fact. Sorry for being a pushy cow.'

Rhea looked tired and pale and out of her usual humour. She was shivering in the cold, but she managed a smile and said, 'There's times when people need to be told what to do. Isn't that right? Cometh the hour, cometh the pushy cow.'

Back on the road, they followed the mountain pass between sheer grey walls that rose steeply on either side of the track. Fran could see more of what lay ahead now she sat in the front. She wondered who or what had created this silent path through rock, whether it had been carved by a glacier during the last ice age or by men with lamps and dynamite during an age of expansion. Now that the world was in full retreat, she could not imagine anyone blasting through a mountain to lay a road now, least of all one so rarely travelled. Must have been built by something else, a secret race of gnomes, she thought, or a tribe of mountain nymphs. She had read about those in the encyclopaedia, the mountain nymphs—oreads. They were good spirits, patron spirits, said to guide lost travellers away from danger, down to safe paths or occasionally, mischievously, to some high, sacred spot with a god's eye view of the whole world. And then to turn a stone corner and suddenly encounter the abundance of everything on the other side of the mountain, a rich carpet of treetops as far as could be seen.

'Must be the oreads,' Fran said aloud, smiling at the beauty of the unexpected scenery, the return of open, blue sky. Now that they had emerged from the claustrophobic passage through rock, the track followed a meandering ledge down the north side of the mountain. Below them, as Lugh had promised, the forest did appear to go on forever. The low winter sunlight cast a golden sheen over a landscape of canopies, dense evergreens and stripped-bare deciduous alike.

'You're turning into Rhea,' Ky laughed, 'coming out with random shit. Oreads? Seriously, what are oreads?'

'Look at this, O'Byrne,' Fran said excitedly, ignoring Ky's question. 'Here's your forest.'

The boy did not reply, so Fran turned to the back seat. She saw Rhea lying on her side, her arms wrapped around her stomach. The blanket covered half of her face and, where it lay open, Fran could see where the older woman had vomited. Lugh sat as far away from Rhea as he could, his fingers held tightly between his thighs so as not to touch the sick. He returned Fran's gaze with wide eyes, looking both guilty and afraid.

When they stopped to clean the mess, Rhea was shivering and appeared more fragile than ever. Fran helped her onto the roadside to relieve herself again, washed her and changed the blanket. She asked Lugh to sit in the front and navigate while she sat in the back and minded Rhea.

'You hear that?' Fran asked as she closed Rhea's door. Lugh cocked his head and nodded. Somewhere on the mountainside, they heard what could have been music. Concentrating on the sound, Fran recognised it as the faint tinkling of bells.

'Sheep, or maybe goat bells?' she asked.

Lugh shrugged and frowned at the road ahead.

The rough track led down the mountain and came to a three-way crossroads on the edge of the forest. There were no road signs, only an old wooden pole from which a rotten branch, tied to a twist of rope, dangled in the breeze. One way turned right and appeared to follow the foot of the mountain. After a moment's consideration, Ky chose the road that led straight ahead into the forest as though that had always been their intention.

The windstorm had stripped the last leaves from the trees and, though the branches arched above the road like the roof of a tunnel, there were still clear patches of sky overhead. Fran lay her arm over Rhea and stroked patterns on the blanket, until the sick woman touched her fingers to say both, thank-you and stop-it-now. When Rhea's breathing fell into the measured rhythm of sleep, Fran caught Ky's eye in the rear-view mirror.

'Something she ate?' Fran asked in a low voice.

'No, my love, not food poisoning,' Ky replied. 'She hasn't eaten anything suspect. None of us have. Let's hope it's stomach flu.'

'And if it's not?'

'If it's not, then we should think about why that town was deserted, and who might have been there recently.' Ky glanced at the boy in the seat beside her. He was gazing at the road but listening to every word, so Ky encoded her next ones. 'Pathogens. Biological. Possible exposure?'

'No,' Fran said firmly. 'No, I don't think it's that. I don't think it's that at all.'

Ky let the subject drop. After a moment's pause, she remembered their conversation on the mountain pass, and said, 'You still didn't tell me about the orrids.'

Oreads, Fran corrected her. Mountain nymphs, spirits that guide lost travellers to safety.

'Right. And what do we call the spirits of the forest?'

Before receiving an answer, Ky braked and parked the car in the road. She peered through the rear window at a long wooden pole she had seen standing on the roadside. A bare branch hung loosely from a rope tied to the top of the pole.

'Second one like that we've seen today,' said Ky. 'That's not a coincidence.'

She and Fran left the car and went to inspect the sign. There were no obvious markings on the stick, nothing to indicate its purpose, but it was clear that it had been planted intentionally. Ky warned against touching the thing and circled it warily. To Fran, it had the look of a crude totem that some primitive mind had loaded with meaning. It made her afraid.

Neither of them noticed that Lugh had also left the car, but they looked up when he uttered a cry of discovery. He had found a small, partially overgrown footpath leading through the undergrowth from the other side of the road.

'Good man,' Ky said with admiration. 'While we're busy looking at the cheese, he's inspecting the whole mousetrap.'

'Not everything is a mousetrap,' said Fran as she went after Lugh.

'No, but every mousetrap is a thing. Wait,' Ky called after them, but they had already started down the track. Ky hesitated, glanced back at the car and thought about grabbing her knife from the front seat. Fran and Lugh were now out of sight, so she hurried after them instead.

The path had been concealed from the road by loose branches that the boy had kicked aside. It was a narrow track, possibly nothing more than an ancient way for deer or wild boar to cross the forest, so Ky and Fran had to walk in single file behind the boy. After a few minutes of silence, Ky said they should return to the car, but just at that moment the path widened out and passed alongside a dry stream. On the other side of the stream was a clearing, a well-kept vegetable patch, a small wooden shack with windows and a chimney, water barrels and a stack of chopped wood. As far as they could see, there was no one about. Instinctively, the three of them crouched down behind a cover of ferns to observe the smallholding.

'Fuck it, I should go back for the knife,' Ky whispered.

'Why don't I just knock on the door?' asked Fran. 'That's what we would do in normal times, isn't it? That's the normal thing to do. Not every cabin in the woods is a mousetrap.'

'And say what?'

'I don't know. Do you have any cheese?'

They both smothered their laughter. Fran closed her eyes until the fit passed. When she opened them, she caught Lugh's shy, awkward smile that suggested he would never understand silliness between grown-ups. She would have asked him what he thought they should do, but Lugh lifted his finger and cocked his head to listen to something on the air. In the distance but growing closer, they heard the sound of a man's voice, a deep baritone singing a slow, mournful melody. Through the trees on the other side of the clearing, a man lurched into the open carrying a long wooden stick over his shoulder and dragging a dead goat behind him. He wore nothing but long-johns and unlaced boots; his chest was bare and his torso so thin that they could see the shadows between his ribs. Of his face, all they could make out were the dark hollows of his eyes and the ridge of a bone-sharp nose. In contrast to his skeletal body, the unkempt beard and wild emanation of hair made his head seem disproportionately large. Hunger and hardship made it impossible to guess his age: he could have been thirty or sixty. Strangest of all, he wore a ring of green leaves on his head, woven into an autumn crown.

'*Adam tried to hide himself, when he heard God say,*' he sang as he strolled in an unsteady line towards the wooden cabin. '*Why are you so frightened, why are you afraid? You have brought the winter in, made the flowers fade.*'

The man halted at the vegetable patch, let the goat fall to the earth and then smiled at some amusing thought for a minute or more. Without warning, he took the branch from his shoulders and pointed it at the three figures hiding behind the ferns. It was only now that they noticed that the stick was shaped like a shepherd's crook, with a twisted root for a hook at the end. Only Ky saw that blood was dripping from the end.

'He's waiting for you,' the man called in a singsong, hide-and-seek voice. He repeated the phrase four or five times, each time varying the stress of the words. It was unnerving to hear him speak without seeing a mouth move within his beard.

Ky tugged Fran's sleeve to lead her back down the path, but Fran shook her head and whispered that they could outrun him. The man raised his staff with both hands above his head and took an unsteady step towards them. Ky pulled on Fran's arm and insisted that they leave, but Fran stood up and revealed herself to him.

'Who's waiting for me?' Fran shouted across the clearing.

The man crouched down in alarm and pulled a variety of expressions, mostly of disbelief and distrust.

'Knows you're there, he does. Knows everything, everything there is to know. Now he's waiting for you. Waiting and watching you,' he replied dangerously.

'If he's watching then he must know that we don't mean any harm.'

'Seen you, he has. But now he's thinking whether or not to come out,' the man pondered.

Fran glanced up at the sky and said, 'If he's seen us, then he must know we've got a sick woman with us. She needs somewhere to rest. Perhaps he can let her rest in this house?'

'Can she cook? Can she clean?' he asked in a different, surprisingly rational voice.

'No, she's sick. She needs a place to rest.'

The thin man jumped to his feet and stumbled a few steps forward, dragging his shepherd's crook behind him. This sudden move surprised everyone, including the man. Ky and Lugh stood up from their hiding place and prepared to run, but Fran stood her ground.

'She's not sick,' the man scoffed, jabbing an accusatory finger towards Ky. Then he pointed at Lugh. 'Oh, knows you, he does. Seen you before, he has. Been waiting for you to come back. Knows those eyes, those fox's eyes, bastard eyes. Thief in the night running off with your tail between your legs. Become a boy again, boy. Thief-thief in the night-night.'

The man's voice rose in fury as he staggered towards them and poked his finger towards Lugh, dragging his bloody crook behind him. When he was half-way across the clearing, Fran decided it was time to leave and shoved Lugh ahead of her down the path. Ky ran behind them and looked back frequently to see if the man was following. They were making so much noise that she could not be sure. When they reached the car, Ky grabbed her knife from the dashboard and confronted the forest while the others climbed quickly inside.

Rhea was still asleep on the back seat, though she had vomited again on the blanket. Fran reached forward to reassure Lugh with a squeeze on his shoulder, though he flinched at the touch. Outside, Ky stood with her back against the car door and listened. From somewhere within the trees, they could hear the melodious baritone of the man singing, '*Walking in a garden at the close of day, Adam tried to hide him when heard God say –*'

THE TENT KIT WAS INCOMPLETE. It lacked the correct poles, so Ky had fashioned her own version of a shelter against the side of the car using the flysheet, guide ropes and branches. They had parked off the road, hidden well enough behind undergrowth so as not to be seen by some passing goat-killer with a shepherd's crook, and Ky had improvised a makeshift intruder alarm around the camp using string and dangling glass bottles.

Rhea's bed was the back seat of the car, which was considered the warmest and most comfortable spot, while Ky slept in the front to keep watch on her throughout the night. Wrapped in blankets, Fran spooned against Lugh inside the tent and listened to the sounds of the night-time forest. She was not afraid of the hunter-prey footfalls, the tinkling of distant goat bells or the screech of flying nightbirds. Fox, deer or hare, wild boar or bear, or maybe even the wolves had returned. She did not know which creatures were calling—except that one, she knew, was obviously an owl—but she did feel safer among the trees and darkness than within any house. Walls and windows did not stop monsters coming inside. At least out here you could climb up high among the branches, or twist your body around hard roots in the earth, or screech like a vixen-roe-bitch until the threat ran away. If it were not for the cold, she could live here forever. If it were not for Rhea growing weaker by the hour, and Ky fearing traps, and the boy grieving—if it were not for the others, she could live here contentedly until she died.

As if sensing this twist in her affections, Lugh pressed his body closer to Fran and slipped his cold fingers between her thighs. They lay like this for minutes, hours, listening to the creaks and sighs of the night. When the boy moved his fingers again, exploring the dark, Fran pulled his hand away sharply and held it firmly, safely, against his own chest.

Ky dug a firepit in the morning. She made a tripod from three metal rods and hung a pot over the fire to cook lentils for breakfast. Rhea had not been sick all night, but she was still feeling fragile and they had to support her through the trees so she could empty what was left inside.

'It wasn't what you thought,' Fran said to Ky, 'that biological-exposure-pathogen thing. It's not that at all. When everything's uncertain, we should take care not to get too paranoid.'

'No, but we should think about that goat-man's garden,' said Ky. They were sitting around the firepit in the evening, eating their third meal of lentils that day. 'We need fresh vegetables.'

'The goat-man needs fresh vegetables too,' said Fran. 'That's why he planted them.'

'We need them too. Rhea needs them. Or are you worried that, he is watching you, thief-thief in the night-night,' said Ky, mimicking the man with the shepherd's crook.

'I'm watching you, Zachariadou.' Fran reached out her fist and pretended to place a delicate object into Ky's open palm. 'Here, take this.'

'Animal, vegetable or mineral?' asked Ky, carefully examining the nothing in her hand.

'Mineral, I imagine.' Fran thought for a moment, then added, 'but it doesn't really matter.'

'Vegetable would have been more useful. Do I get a clue?'

'It's a magical ring of invisibility,' said Fran. 'Let's see what you do with it.'

'It's not much of a fucking game if you tell me the answer straight away.'

'Well played, Francesca,' said Rhea, who was feeling well enough to sit beside the fire with them. She saw Ky's confusion, so she added, 'Plato's question, dear. Will a just person still behave justly if they have a ring of invisibility, if there are no consequences?'

'Ah, what is justice?' Ky said, narrowing her eyes on the imaginary ring. 'Is it justice that a madman can dine on cabbages and goats while three women and a boy starve—?'

'We're not starving,' Fran interrupted.

'We're not starving yet,' Ky corrected her, 'but give it a week or two.'

'Maybe Plato says it's justice for a madman to eat the food he himself has sown,' said Fran.

'Plato's dead. What does he know?'

'But that goat-man is still alive,' said Fran, 'though barely. I could count his ribs.'

They sat in silence, each one staring into the fire. After a while, Ky threw the magic ring of invisibility into the flames with one dismissive gesture, and that was an end to the debate.

Another raw morning, another early evening. The frost stayed silver on the roof of the car all day until the setting of the sun. Fran returned late from the forest bearing an armful of herbs, thyme and dandelions. Something to flavour the lentils, she said. Rhea seemed to have recovered from her sickness, but she had gained a stubborn cough that made it hard for her to breathe.

'We need to get you somewhere warm,' Ky said to her as they sat around the fire.

'Nonsense,' Rhea replied when she had stopped coughing. 'I'll be fine after a little gin.'

'I'll just pop to the off-licence in town for a bottle, shall I?' offered Ky.

'No one's going to that town,' said Lugh unexpectedly. 'No one. That's what you said.'

They all turned to stare at the boy who rarely uttered more than a syllable. Fran sensed some dark, unfathomable anger in him just simmering below the surface. She touched his arm, but he shook her away and stood up quickly.

'I was only joking,' Ky called after Lugh as he disappeared inside the tent and zipped it up behind him. 'What just happened there?'

'The last time you said that, about not going to town,' said Fran, remembering back to the day Michael had arrived, 'I'd offered to go to the pharmacy.'

'And I said no one's going to the town. He's angry at me for that?' Ky thought for a moment. 'He blames me for what happened to his brother?'

'I blame you for getting us this far in one piece, more or less,' said Fran.

'I second that,' added Rhea. 'Pushy cow.'

When Fran emerged from the tent into cold, broken sunlight the next morning, she found Ky packing their things into the boot of the car. Most of the camp had been dismantled, only the tent and cooking pots remained. Rhea was sitting by the fire and brewing a saucepan of tea.

'Don't bother, Francesca, dear. I've already tried to reason with her,' said Rhea. She glanced at Ky and shook her head. 'She says we're to leave this morning. Says we're to find better accommodation. And, get this, she says we ought to go looking for a pharmacy.'

Fran sighed and washed her face in the cold-water bucket. She sat down beside the firepit and accepted a mug of tea from Rhea.

'There's a million reasons why you were right, Zachariadou,' Fran said, 'about me not going to look for a pharmacy in that town. I talked to Lugh last night. I think he understands.'

'And a million reasons why we need medical supplies now,' Ky said without looking up.

'And is misplaced guilt one of those reasons?'

'Misplaced guilt.' Rhea chuckled. 'We covered that in training. Week one, day one. We can't save everyone, dear. Remember?'

Ky made a muted sound like a cat's meow and continued packing. Fran exchanged a meaningful glance with Rhea and they decided to leave the conversation there. Instead, they listened to the cry of indignant crows, the wind rising in the trees. Fran heard, or thought she heard, the tinkling of bells in the distance.

Back on the road, Ky drove them further into the forest that never ended, leaving the mountains and the goat-man further behind. Rhea sat in the back and coughed vigorously every few minutes, ending each fit with a sigh of apology. Fran sat beside her and idly watched the colours of passing trees, light-browns running beside the road, darker bodies skulking behind and a domain of cluttered black in the deep beyond. She thought about what Lugh had said last night. It had been a rare effort for him, a complete, premeditated sentence brimming with stifled anger. She had not seen that coming. She had not been sensitive to his resentment. She had tried to reason with him in the tent afterwards, but he had said nothing more. Now he sat in the front passenger seat beside Ky, staring ahead at the ever-oncoming road, unflinching.

In the early afternoon, Ky slowed down as they approached a small junction. Their road-tunnel through the forest continued straight ahead but another, unmarked lane appeared out of the trees from the right. There were no signs, no town names or distances to tell them where they were or what lay in any direction. A round mirror was nailed to a tree trunk opposite the turning, reflecting the subsidiary lane back on itself.

'What says my navigator?' Ky asked the boy. 'Shall we try it?'

Lugh peered down the turn-off and shrugged.

'I have confirmation from my navigator, it's okay to go right,' said Ky, turning onto the lane.

The road was narrower than the one they had left behind, wide enough for only one vehicle to pass up or down. Old branches interlocked overhead, masking more of the sky and making the day darker. Ky drove carefully now that the trees were so much closer to either side of the car. The rattling mudguard and other loose underparts sounded louder and more intentional now they were travelling so slowly. Even Rhea's cough seemed deliberately designed to draw the sullen attention of the forest. Ky watched the fuel gauge creep lower. She considered the options. There was nowhere suitable to turn around, there was nothing to stop for, there was only the lane ahead. It must lead somewhere and that, she decided, was as good or as bad as any other way. I trust you, Ky, she thought to herself. Someone fucking has to.

It was dusk when Ky parked the car at the end of the road. Fran had slipped in and out of sleep, seen the trees drift past and dreamed of beds, wolves, baskets of apples. Now that the noise of the engine had ceased, she opened her eyes and saw what the others had already seen. The trunk of an ancient tree lying across the lane. A derelict cottage half-buried in ivy and brambles. In the overgrown garden of the cottage, a young woman and a teenage boy, both dark haired and wide eyed and wearing identical checked shirts, sat at a table and poured tea from an imaginary teapot into broken cups. The two figures stared at the unexpected arrival of the car, a statuesque picnic tableau frozen in fear.

CHAPTER FOUR
ARCADIA

THERE HAD BEEN A LIBRARY of sorts in the relief camp. It had held an odd collection of titles, mostly beauty magazines, books of already-completed crosswords, trashy romances and detective novels in various languages that had been donated or discarded in the belief that the less-fortunate but no less literate would be grateful for anything to read. The people who had donated these books had packed them in cardboard boxes with socks, blankets, tampons, scarves, bobble hats and baby clothes along with tins of baked beans, and waved them off to the camps with a sense of having done something good in a world that was steadily going bad. After a while, the delivery trucks stopped bringing *Cosmopolitan* and *Hola!* magazines to the camps, and brought only people and desperation. That marked the second wave of the troubles when the predictions started coming true, when the weather pushed people over borders and borders back over people, and acts and substances that had previously been banned began to be employed with impunity.

When the trucks stopped bearing goodwill gifts altogether, Ky had idly wondered if any of the newly arrived evacuees had ever given their own boxes of donations to the camps. Now that circumstances had been reversed, she imagined their faces if chance should reunite them with their old goods at the Destitution Warehouse. It would be ironic if they were presented with a pair of their old socks or knickers, a crossword book or beauty magazine, she thought. Then she had thought about those who had never sent anything at all, not even a tin of baked-beans, and her thoughts turned less charitable. If there was some way for her to know who had given when they had plenty and who had not, then she might behave like some petty god on Judgement Day, dividing the camp into deserving and undeserving, sheep and goats, distributing bread or stones, medicine or placebos accordingly. She decided that it was just as well she would never know.

It was in the camp's library that Ky had first seen Fran. Ky had been volunteering in the medical centre for four or five months when the second wave, the real movement of displaced people, began to flow. This new influx of evacuees had coincided with the downing of the satellites and the servers. Ky sometimes suspected that the former might have had some impact on the latter, although she knew there were other factors—climatic, biological and chemical—to blame. Once the communications had gone down, once people could no longer see and share the small reassurances of daily existence on the devices in their hands, that was when the real panic set in. Perhaps people felt safe so long as they could scroll through the mundane and the catastrophic, know which was which and where. But when the screens went blank, there was no way to tell when one would turn into the other. Like the unseen dangers on the wind, thought Ky, it was always the unknown that generated the most fear and paranoia.

Ky had gone to that library to overcome the unknown. She was in the dark about the present, much more about the future, so had turned to history for a little light. The books were unsorted, unpacked and then re-packed into bigger boxes that had to be browsed with a casual, interdisciplinary attitude. She had picked up a promising volume—a *History of Modern Europe*, published some sixty years earlier—when she saw Fran sitting cross-legged on the corner carpet where the children were put for storytime on Friday afternoons. Fran held a book on her lap, though she was staring through the window at the pink sunset sky. Her mouth was slightly ajar as though she had just read something extraordinarily beautiful and was musing on its afterglow. She looked like a pre-Raphaelite subject, entirely elsewhere. Ky could not take her eyes off her.

'I should never come in here to find something specific,' Fran had said when she realised she was being observed. She did not turn to see who was watching her, but continued to gaze out of the window at the last colours of the day. 'I'm always, always disappointed.'

'You were looking for a particular book?'

'Yes, something flower-related. I want to start a garden. I grew up in a house with a large garden, my father's garden. I miss the greenery. Everything's so grey and sterile here, so concrete.' Fran turned and held up her paperback for Ky to see the cover. 'All I could find was this.'

'Baudelaire, *Flowers of Evil.*' Ky laughed as she read the title. 'I know it. I have a copy. I mean, I used to have a copy. Not quite what you were looking for?'

'Not entirely. Listen.' Fran recited some lines at random, all thighs, lips, deadly sins, damnation, and finally a fragment that Ky had heard before and would now always remember, *'My heart, burning like a volcano and deep as the void. Nothing will satiate that wailing monster, nor cool the thirst of the Eumenides.* Who are the Eumenides when they're at home?'

'The Furies,' Ky answered quickly. 'Old hags, spirits of vengeance. So deadly that you should never name them aloud in case you accidentally summon them.'

'All well and good, but how is that going to help me with sweat-peas and honeysuckle? Seriously, *Flowers of Evil?* Who had the idea to send a book like this here?'

'I did, actually. That was my copy.'

Fran looked horrified and apologised at once, but Ky laughed and admitted that she was joking. She sat down beside Fran on the carpet and introduced herself.

'Kynane Zachariadou?' Fran repeated her name incredulously. 'Another joke, surely?'

'Trust me, it is my name. If I'd wanted to be clever, I would have said Baudelaire. I should have said I'm Baudelaire.'

They sat side by side on the library carpet talking about books, names, origins, anything and everything except the troubles. When the dining-room bell rang for the evening meal, they walked together to the canteen queue and their conversation cooled. Something had happened when they crossed the line between the library and the canteen. Without a word, they each understood that a chance book-browsing acquaintance had transitioned abruptly, unexpectedly and without invitation, into a dining companion. Ky felt self-conscious about her earlier flirtation, which she had assumed would be a passing diversion. Now she could think of nothing appropriate to say for this new phase in their relationship, so she concentrated on rolling a cigarette. Fran, on the other hand, was comfortable with silences. In very different ways, they were each content to see wherever this friendship led.

KY HAD LEARNED TO TRUST Fran's silences: she always seemed to use them wisely. Now, for example, outside the derelict cottage, Fran was crouching down to tie her boot lace. When she had finished, she stayed close to the ground to appear small, unthreatening, and smiled at nothing in the far distance. The brother and sister were gradually edging away from the cottage garden and had got as far as the open gate. They looked scared enough to run into the woods at any moment, but they were equally curious to see new people and seemed not unwilling to talk. To Fran, they resembled feral animals who had lingering, unerased memories of early domestication.

'And there's another house, you say?' Fran asked after a pause, still gazing away.

'More than one, like an old village,' replied the young woman who said her name was Ruth. Fran reckoned her to be about seventeen or eighteen years old, but hunger and a defensive naivety made her seem much younger.

'And there's a library in the big house,' said the boy that Ruth had introduced as Abel, her younger brother. 'We've not been inside, not yet, but we did look through the window.'

Fran could not guess how old this boy was. He was about the same height as his sister, but had the awkward, lanky look of an adolescent puppy. His voice had broken, but he talked with the guileless enthusiasm of a child and did not flinch at holding his sister's hand. He could be ten or sixteen. Hunger, she reflected, distorted people's ages.

'Really? A library?' said Fran. She exchanged a smile with Ky, genuinely delighted.

Ky had left the car and was also moving slowly so as not to scare the brother and sister. She sat down on the tree trunk that lay across the lane and turned to the sky to show that they could run if they wanted, it was all the same to her. Now would be a perfect time to roll a casual cigarette, she thought, if only she had some tobacco. Besides, frightened children and lame animals were Fran's thing. Not for the first time, Ky would sit back and let her friend do her magic.

'Aye, a library,' the boy continued, sensing that this information pleased the strangers. 'We looked in the window and saw loads of books, like the walls were made of books, but we didn't go in because, you know, it might be where someone really-bad lives, even though all the god-haters are supposed to be in the bottomless pit. But it might be where one of the people-that-we-hide-from lives—though I don't know why they're not at the bottomless pit, too—so we thought it's best not to go in, not until our Enoch has a look around. Enoch has an axe, so it's probably best he has a look first, just in case. So we did look in the window, but we didn't go in, did we?'

Abel glanced anxiously at his sister to make sure he had not said anything out of turn. Her face revealed nothing new, but she put her hand on his shoulder and made a shush-now noise.

'We should be getting back,' she said, taking the boy's hand as though he were a toddler.

'Sure, if you have to,' agreed Fran. 'We're looking for somewhere to stay. An empty house like this looks perfect. We might end up being your neighbours?'

'Oh, we don't know if we'll be here staying because our Enoch hasn't seen it yet,' said Abel. He pulled against Ruth to stay with the strangers and explain as much as possible. 'Enoch's my brother, our brother. In fact, none of them have seen this place yet, not even Mother. She's in the camp and she's not feeling well because she's got the morning sickness again.'

'Morning sickness?' asked Fran. 'Your mum's pregnant?'

'A bit, and she said that we shouldn't go too far on our own because of what happened last time, and because of what could happen if we meet anyone…'

Ruth tugged her brother's hand sharply to silence him and took another step closer to the trees. Fran smiled her understanding.

'It's strange for us too, you know, meeting you. We haven't seen anyone for weeks. We thought you might be ghosts, sitting there drinking tea in the garden. That's our friend Rhea in the back seat.' Fran gestured towards the car. 'She's not very well either. That's why we need to find somewhere to stay. It's not nice sleeping out in the cold if you're not feeling well, is it?'

'Is that your brother?' asked Abel. He craned his neck for a clearer view of the serious-looking boy in the front seat of the car. Abel raised his free hand to give a half-hearted wave, but the boy in the car just frowned back at him.

'That's Lugh. He's a friend too.'

'Is he a believer? Are all of you believers?'

'Abel,' Ruth said sharply, pulling her brother away. 'We really have to go now.'

Fran nodded. 'I understand.' She stood up carefully and backed away to demonstrate that she was not going to pursue them. 'Listen, if your mum needs help, tell her that we have nurses here. Rhea and Ky, both of them are medically trained. Will you tell her that?'

'We have to go,' Ruth repeated, too anxious now to hear what Fran was saying.

'I will, I'll tell her,' said Abel, still half-waving as he was pulled into the woods.

THE COTTAGE AT THE END of the lane was a decrepit shell. The rafters had collapsed in places where the weak old wood could no longer hold out against the heavy limbs of ivy that engulfed the house. Where the roof had broken inwards, the ivy had trespassed and sent fingers in exploration of the empty rooms, creeping along skirting boards and underneath doors, pushing against windows until the frames split and the glass had shattered over the overgrown lawn. In time, the vines had poured down the stairs and prised apart the floorboards to reunite with the damp soil beneath the foundations. The ivy was a house-snatcher that had taken the body of a cottage.

In the front garden, between whips and hoops of thorny bramble, stood a stone plinth where Ruth and Abel had taken their pretend afternoon tea with broken cups. Ky had thought it was some kind of flat tombstone but, glancing at it on her way to the house, she could see no inscription and assumed it was an ornamental bench or stone table. Peering through the open windows of the cottage, it did not take her long to assess the dark, rooty interior as unfit for habitation. Still, the front door had been prised open by ancient ivy, and the house afforded some shelter against the coming night. Ky returned to the car and said that Rhea and the boy should wait in the ivy cottage, while she and Fran investigated what Ruth had described as an old village.

'That girl and her brother, you think they'll turn up again?' asked Fran, as she and Ky climbed over the moss-covered trunk that lay across the lane.

'Your new little friends, Hansel and Gretel?' Ky laughed and shook her head. 'You shouldn't give so much away to strangers. Not till we know who we're dealing with.'

'Do children really terrify you so much?'

'It's not them, but what comes with them that worries me: the unknown. Look,' Ky pointed her knife towards the tree stump on other side of the grass verge. They could still see the marks where it had been hacked repeatedly with a sharp blade. It had not been felled recently because the old stump had thrown up a fleet of young stems in an attempt to live again. 'It didn't fall naturally. Someone cut it down on purpose.'

'Those kids, you think? They said their brother has an axe.'

'No.' Ky frowned. 'This was cut down ages ago, maybe years.'

'To keep the world out?'

'Or to keep something in.'

'It's not exactly insurmountable,' said Fran as they continued down the lane.

'Maybe it was just a gesture, like a symbolic act.'

After the fallen trunk, the lane became even narrower. Thistles had cracked through the surface of the concrete, and other weeds and wildflowers encroached between the trees to overcome the verges, take possession of the road. The forest felt entirely silent except for the occasional ring of a distant animal bell, so distant, thought Fran, as to be merely in the mind, a ripple of her imagination.

'Dryads,' she said unexpectedly. 'That's what they're called, the spirits of the forest. Don't you remember, you'd asked me what they were.'

'Did I? Like a fucking century ago, at least. What made you think of that?'

'I wonder.' Fran gestured towards the trees. 'It doesn't feel dangerous here, does it?'

'We shouldn't trust our feelings, my love. They usually let us down. Everything's dangerous, everything, until we can be sure it's not.'

'It doesn't feel dangerous to me, not in the slightest. Besides, you ask me to trust you. Do you trust me, Fran? You ask all the time. How could I tell you I trust you if I didn't feel it?'

'Because you know I'm always right,' said Ky, laughing uncomfortably.

'And why are you always right? Because you trust your feelings.'

'I hate to disenchant you, but my decision-making is much more empirical than that.'

They followed the lane around a bend and came suddenly upon two rows of grey-stone houses which had been built among the trees or which the forest was in the act of reclaiming. The two terraces faced each other across the road, which was now little more than a stony footpath. Fran counted five front doors on the left-hand terrace and seven on the right. Although the trees had grown up against the ends of the terrace walls, these houses looked much more intact than the ivy cottage they had just left behind.

'Workers' cottages?' asked Ky.

'What work would they have found here?' asked Fran, peering through the windows.

'Fuck knows. Logging? Maybe we'll find a mill or a factory or something.'

'I don't think anyone's been home for a long, long time.'

Fran rattled the chain of an old bell that hung outside the first house and put her ear to the letter box to listen to the untroubled silence within. Ky watched with a secret smile as her friend moved from one front door to the next, ringing and listening, ringing and listening—or perhaps not even listening at all, but feeling whether there was anybody at home or not.

Still smiling to herself, Ky followed the path around the side of the terrace into the rear yards. She found a broken window at the back of one house which she crawled through and landed inside a pantry. The kitchen was filled with pots and pans, china plates stacked on a dresser, a clothes rack hanging over a wood-burning stove, an oil-lamp on a table. It was getting dark, but she could see that a thick layer of dust coated every surface. Feathers and bird droppings had long lain undisturbed over the stone tiles of the floor. She stepped gingerly through the hallway, the sitting room, and up a wooden staircase that creaked with decades of disuse to the landing. There was a metal bed frame and mattress in each of the three small bedrooms and the ghost of a scent of oil-lamps and eiderdowns, lavender mothballs and the jaundiced pages of old books. Ky wondered if she could really smell these things or if her imagination was colouring in the gaps. Neither true nor necessary, she thought, as the door bell rattled and she ran downstairs.

'I don't think electricity had been invented the last time anyone lived here,' she said to Fran at the front door, 'which suits us well now that it's been lost again.'

'Was electricity invented? Who did that then?'

'Discovered then, or harnessed or whatever. You know what I mean, Miss Pedantic,' said Ky, closing the door behind her. 'There's a fireplace, oil lamps, a real-fire-stove-thing we can use to cook and heat water on, even an old tin bath—every luxury you could wish for in the new Dark Ages. Home-sweet-fucking-home. And security too. No one will be kicking these doors in.' Ky held up a large iron key she had taken from the back door.

'How did you break in?' asked Fran. They walked the path between the empty houses towards another twist at the end of the lane.

'I was a cat burglar in a past life.'

'Or just a cat. You were definitely a cat.'

Fran stopped to read an old street sign screwed to the wall of the last house. Although it was getting too dark to see much, she could just make out of the shape of the words.

'Usquam Mews,' she said. 'What a funny name. You know, this might be the last street sign left anywhere in the world. I heard that people were taking down all the street names and road signs when the troubles started, after the satellites came down. They said it would confuse an invasion, if there was ever going to be an invasion. If some army or other had to rely on old maps to get around, they wouldn't know where they were. Did you hear about that? So there might be no streets with names anywhere in the world except here, this one little street. Usquam Mews.'

'That's like rearranging furniture on the Titanic,' Ky scoffed. 'Would that have made any difference to an invasion, taking down road signs?'

'I wonder. It might have. It's probably easier to obliterate streets if they don't have names. Same as with people.'

Neither of them wanted to follow that thought, so they followed the lane in sombre silence. Having come so far, they were curious to see what lay at the end. Around the bend, the road passed through an open gate and up towards the front steps of a large white manor house. Their eyes had grown accustomed to the growing darkness as the daylight faded, and now they could just make out the outlines of walls, window frames, ledges and chimneys. At the front entrance in the centre of the building, four columns supported the stone roof of a portico and, above that, a square tower rose into the darkening sky. They could see no lights in any of the windows, though they did catch the fresh scent of woodsmoke as though a fire had been burning nearby recently.

So there it is, thought Fran, that's the big house.

'You want to take a peek in at the library before we head back?' asked Ky. She reached into the darkness to take hold of Fran's cold hand, but felt resistance when she tried to lead her up the driveway towards the entrance.

'You don't feel it?' said Fran, pulling back.

'Feel what? That your hands are freezing?'

'That the house is watching, like it's been waiting.'

'It's just old bricks and mortar, nothing more,' said Ky, though she sounded less confident than she had a moment before. 'What did I say about not trusting our feelings?'

'You said that everything's dangerous. You did, you just said that.'

They stood at the open gate and looked up at the bulk of the building against the bruised evening sky, the first kindling of stars. There was no wind, no sound from the forest, not even the chatter of the last birds settling down for the night. The house is watching, thought Ky and she hated the way Fran's suggestion had crept inside her own bones. It was the first time she and Fran had been alone like this in weeks, possibly months, and she had wanted to prolong their twilight adventure. It would have meant something to have ended this rare moment in a library of all places, but the big house was watching them and everything was dangerous, and Ky could not allow her own sentimentality to put them in danger. Besides, it was dark and she could smell that woodsmoke, which meant someone else was around. They would have to come back in the morning, take the castle by daylight.

RHEA WAS LATE. THE OTHERS were already in their places, crowded by the darkness onto wooden pews or kneeling on cushioned prayer stools as old as the chapel itself. Candlelight exaggerated the faces of the congregation, hollowed their cheekbones and gave each of their brows an accusatory glow. Damn and fuck it, thought Rhea, as she hurried down the aisle and sat on the last empty seat. She took off her long black winter scarf, which she had not worn since primary school, and the green bobble hat that she had picked up recently at the Destitution Warehouse in the relief camp, and settled against the back rest. The wooden pew ends were more decorative than she remembered, carved with leaves and roots and the eyes of the Green Man, vigilant hares and deer running under a mysterious moon. Odd that she had never noticed these patterns before, and odder still that some craftsman had been allowed to carve such pagan images in a chapel. They spoke of a secret nature, these living landscapes, creation before a creator.

The music began, a sweet woodwind thread, the sound of creeping bassoons that made her forget whatever she had been thinking. She closed her eyes with tear-filled recognition and clenched her hands on her lap. The adagio march grew achingly familiar, rose in heart-breaking clarinets and basset horns and profound end-of-days titans' voices crying, *requiem aeternam*, and silently she cried with them, *requiem, requiem*, in the imminent knowledge of the forever-loss of love. And when she opened her eyes, he was there again as she knew he would be, sitting on the bench in the opposite choir, all scarfed-up for the winter and unshaven and blue-eyed and so typically Joshua-like with that awkward, guilty smile he so often wore at that bastard age of twenty-three. And she knew he would speak to her at the end of the performance because it was too much of a coincidence that they should see each other here after all this time, and surely they must have forgiven each other by now.

The deer had run, the hares in the woodwork had all gone underground and the mysterious moon had set. Now the pews looked plain and puritan as the Introit played into the pitiless Kyrie. Rhea closed her eyes again and felt exhausted with the well-worn tragedy that must inevitably follow: the packing of her books and boxes, the leaving of the old, cold college bedsit she had shared with Joshua, with the freezing bathroom and the electricity meter that was always running out, but she had to go through that awful, purgatorial phase one more time if only to learn that she could soldier on alone through the coming year and the year after that, and through all those other years that must inevitably come after.

Kyrie eleison, they sang, the choir, demanding mercy as though marching to war against an unmerciful god. Rhea could not bear to sit through the intensity of this entire movement, waiting to speak to an unshaven Joshua who was now too ashamed to even look at her across the aisle of her dream. Instead, she yearned to be at home again, eating marzipan strips in the kitchen while her grandmother stirred a bowl of mincemeat and muttered for the umpteenth time about how much she hated Christmas. And that was the thing that really outraged the conscience of the choir: not the monumentally unforgivable things that she and Joshua had done to each other and which they now could barely remember, but all the time that had been stolen between her in her grandmother's kitchen and her in that chapel. At twelve, at fourteen, at sixteen, at some point she must have lost concentration for a second or two, and when she had looked up she was twenty-three and choking back tears at a public recital of Mozart's Requiem, or thirty-eight and playing that same Kyrie on a wind-up gramophone alone in her apartment, or sixty-something and waking up with a bad cough on an unknown bed in neither her grandmother's house nor Joshua's cold bedsit, but in a stranger's house in a world that had turned against itself. And her first thought on waking was the realisation that the clarinets and the horns had never finished playing and the choir had never attained mercy, so she never did get to speak to Joshua again, the sanctimonious bastard, though she knew, she *knew*, she would have done if she had had the decency to dream until the end of the performance.

Rhea rolled onto her side and coughed so hard that her throat felt raw. When she opened her eyes, she saw Ky sitting in the armchair beside her bed.

'That cough's sounding better,' said Ky with overdone optimism. 'It's loosening up at last.'

'I've no doubt it is. And all the troubles are over and the weather is back to normal and faeries are making breakfast in the kitchen too, I suppose? Oh, breakfast, what I wouldn't give for a bacon sandwich. I swear I could eat an entire pig. What do we have instead? Acorns and grass?'

'Obviously that, although Lugh's also been stewing apples to make you feel better.'

'Oh, I am sorry, dear.' Rhea sighed and wiped the leftover tears from her eyes. 'You've been so kind and considerate, sitting there like an angel, and I've woken up all bitchy. I am sorry.'

'Bitchy is good. Bitchy means you're feeling better. Look, we found something for you.' Ky lay a handful of old records in cardboard sleeves on Rhea's blanket.

The older woman took her glasses from the bedside table and sat up on her pillows to read the album covers.

'You shouldn't get too excited,' said Ky, 'there's nothing to play them on, but we thought they would cheer you up anyway. Happy Midwinter.'

Rhea held the sleeves in both hands and stroked the faded colours, the old-fashioned fonts and the frayed cardboard edges with her thumbs. The covers were dark and of the same classically sombre style as those two records she had loved and lost: large blocks of browns, greens or purples, photographs of conductors, flautists, violin sections, entire orchestras or the blurry portraits of long-dead composers. Tchaikovsky, Mahler, Beethoven, Monteverdi, Holst, Wagner, symphonies and cycles and operas. Though she did not know any of the works, the names were as comforting as old uncles, friends of the family who had somehow survived the troubles and shown up at her sickbed to wish her a speedy recovery. At least something has been saved, she thought.

'Well?' asked Ky when the older woman had mulled over each of the covers. 'Do we have any of those soul-of-humanity pieces your gramophone guy talked about?'

Rhea shook her head and laid her fingers over Ky's hand.

'It's a shame we don't have anything to play them on,' said Ky. She stood up and looked out of the window to give Rhea a moment to regain composure. 'Fran's been out foraging in the back gardens. It's a wilderness out there, she says, but she did find a heap of old vegetable plots that have gone to seed: onions, potatoes, carrots, peas, leeks, some berry-bushes— what else? Oh, apple trees and even a plum, can you believe? So we shan't starve, not just yet. No bacon sandwiches I'm afraid, but Fran swears she keeps hearing goat bells in the forest. Don't know what she'd do if she came face to face with a goat. Doubt she could kill it. And I thought she wanted this brave new world to be vegetarian.'

'Thank you, my dear,' said Rhea in a hushed voice, reaching up again for her friend's hand.

Ky squeezed her fingers in return and gazed out of the window. The midday sun had done its best, but it would soon sink again beneath the dark roots of the surrounding forest. For now, for a clear, fearless, lucent moment on the shortest day of the year, Ky could keep watch over the concrete yards, the gardens overgrown with brambles and thistles and, beyond that, the fruit trees where Fran knelt down to discuss wild salad leaves and edible and poisonous mushrooms with the silent, attentive boy.

AFTER A LUNCH OF SELF-SEEDED vegetables that had been harvested from the garden, Fran asked Lugh if he would like to come with them to the big house. Ky looked away, hoping that the boy would decline the invitation and allow her to have another private moment with Fran. Lugh shrugged and gave his half-hearted consent.

'You'd better cover your ears if we find any Baudelaire in the library,' said Ky, trying to disguise her disappointment. Lugh frowned, sensing Ky's insincerity.

The lane to the manor house felt different in daylight, the trees less clustered in close suspicion and the forest more receptive to strangers. Turning the corner up to the open gate, Fran imitated the reiterative calling of wood pigeons, which she always found comforting if slightly ridiculous. Passing the stone gatepost, they saw a single word that had been etched a long time ago in large letters, Usquam, which they presumed was also the name of the big house. The low afternoon sun was hiding behind the tower and they climbed the driveway in cold shadow. A gang of common magpies lined the path up to the steps of the white house, hopping and squawking in mock outrage at the approach of three humans.

'Five for silver, six for gold,' said Fran, counting the birds. 'Seven for a secret never to be told. But eight—what's eight? Do we have to go back to the beginning, back to one?'

'I have absolutely no idea what you're talking about,' said Ky, shooing the magpies away.

'Really, Zachariadou,' laughed Fran, 'with that cosmopolitan education of yours, you never heard of the magpie thing? One for sorrow, two for joy?'

'Three for a girl, four for a boy,' said Lugh. Surprising himself, he blushed and smiled shyly at the ground.

'No, my cosmopolitan education never covered that,' said Ky, evidently uninterested.

'I am surprised. You do know that Ky had a very interesting upbringing, don't you?' Fran said to Lugh with a mischievous smile. 'She grew up in a circus. Her mother was a famous and very beautiful trapeze-artist. They travelled all around the world: Paris, Athens, Jerusalem, China, Siberia. She learned all kinds of things, languages, local customs, how to skin rabbits, how to make Molotov cocktails. Then one day, when she had had enough of that life, she decided to give it all up and settle down in a little library by the sea. And that's where I met her.'

'A very amusing story,' said Ky, unamused. She left them behind and marched up to the house, peered through the ground-floor windows and then disappeared around the corner of the building. Fran and the boy exchanged a glance and followed slowly behind. Some days, thought Fran, without any obvious cause or explanation, Ky's moods could turn just like that.

There was a wide blue breathing-space of sky behind the house where acres of wild forest had long-ago been cut down and the land cultivated into ornamental lawns, rose gardens, occasional fruit trees and herbaceous borders with a small, decorative fountain in the centre. Although grass and weeds had grown over the paths, Fran could still discern the layout of the gardens. A Victorian glasshouse, iron-framed and with most of the window panes still intact, stretched at least one hundred metres down one length of the lawn. At the far end of the garden, a stone wall divided the aesthetic grounds from what would once have been a small-scale working farmyard with a barn, milking shed, duck pond and—to Fran's delight—boxes of wooden beehives.

Ky had taken the path around the house to a paved patio at the rear, where she was shielding the sun from her eyes to peer through the French windows into the dark interior.

'Who's been looking through my window?' Fran asked in a baritone bear's voice as she and Lugh joined Ky on the patio. 'What can you spy?'

'It's locked, but there is a key on the inside,' Ky said without looking up.

'How the other half lived.' Fran joined her at the glass. 'Is that an actual harpsichord?'

Through the French doors she could see a scene from another age: a drawing room filled with an abundance of dark furniture, deep colours and glittering surfaces. In the corner of the room, underneath a hanging chandelier that resembled a glass-beaded birdcage, stood the mahogany harpsichord. The floors were carpeted with black, red and ochre patterns, wall-to-wall rugs that Fran guessed were Persian. A sofa and two chaises longues stood before an impressive open fireplace, on one side of which was a tea-table with a laid-out set of china cups and saucers, silver teaspoons at the ready. Gilt-framed mirrors of various shapes and sizes hung on the walls alongside oil paintings of landscapes, horses, greyhounds, pheasants, a fox hunt, a hapless trout. At the end of the room, a pair of embroidered curtains had been draped open to reveal an archway into an inner room, the hallway perhaps, or the library. And, seemingly on the surface of every cabinet or dresser or writing bureau, the afternoon sun made prisms of light on silverware and glassware, decanters, candlesticks, a crystal bell, flower vases, an ashtray, a music box.

'Yes, it is an actual harpsichord,' said Ky without interest. 'But, even with my cosmopolitan upbringing, I never learnt to play one.'

Fran withdrew from the glass doors and looked at the back of her friend's head. Ky's short black hair had been cut badly, blindly, and was growing unevenly. I need to sort that out for her, thought Fran. It would be a small gesture to smooth over whatever upset had soured their friendship today and made Ky tetchy. She could not think of anything she had said or done or omitted to do, but Ky was clearly pissed off about something, and even now she was walking away from the French doors without a word.

Fran called after her but, before she could think of what to say to lighten her mood, she heard a curious, high-pitched reedy noise coming from nearby. It sounded like a bird's call, but the single repetitive note was too regular and too monotonous to be anything natural. Ky also heard the noise, which she took as some kind of warning signal and she cocked her head to listen. Cautiously, she continued around the corner in pursuit of the noise and found Abel sitting on a wall, half-hidden beneath the canopy of an overhanging apple tree. In his fingers he clasped a recorder on which he was blowing a single high note with such concentration that he had closed his eyes. Ky knew that the boy was not conscious of her arrival. She knelt down as Fran had done with Abel and Ruth the day before, and waited for him to catch his breath before she spoke.

'Jingle-Bells, am I right?'

'Oh, heck,' cried the boy. He jumped to the ground and was ready to sprint away, but he froze when he saw who she was.

'It was Jingle-Bells, wasn't it?'

'Well, it was supposed to be London's Burning,' he said, almost smiling though his body still tended towards flight, 'but I can't get the high bit near the end. You know, *fire-fire.*'

'*Fire-fire,* of course,' Ky agreed. 'I always had difficulty reaching that bit too.'

'You play the pipe-flute too?' he asked excitedly.

'The pipe-flute? No,' Ky shook her head seriously, 'but I did play a recorder just like this one at school. Every Friday afternoon everyone had to. It was the law.'

'Recorder, recorder,' Abel repeated, looking anew at the instrument in his hands. 'I'm not supposed to play it at all ever because Mother says that someone might hear and it could attract the attention of someone really-bad, but I thought it would be all right to play it here because the big house is in the way so the sound won't get very far and there's no one around. And Ruth says I can as long as we don't tell, and—oh, is that nice lady with you, and the boy in the car? And did you see the library where the walls are made of books?'

'That nice lady?' queried Ky. 'So, am I not a nice lady too?'

'Well, yesterday I thought you might be a boy. But today I know you're a lady.'

'Charming.'

Fran had been listening to this conversation behind the corner. She waited until this moment to turn the corner and greet Abel. Lugh followed behind, frowning and saying nothing.

'There she is, your nice lady,' said Ky, standing up and sinking her hands deep into the pockets of her boiler-suit. 'Now, you fancy showing us where that library is?'

Abel was accustomed to following Enoch wherever the firstborn led, or doing whatever Ruth told him, or listening in silence as his parents talked over prophecies and revelations when everyone else had gone to bed, or mostly being looked through if he should ever have something to say, but he could never remember being a subject of interest to others in his own right. It was a new sensation for him, as though he had been invisible all his life and now, for the first time, someone had actually seen him and, moreover, recognised something of interest. He beamed with pleasure and took them around the back of the house to the last window on the ground floor.

'Here it is,' said Abel proudly. He stood on tiptoe to lean against the ledge and peered through the window. Lugh took up the same stance beside him.

The library was darker than the drawing room, though they could see that bookshelves did indeed cover all the walls from floor to ceiling. The books themselves looked like grand hardbacks from previous centuries, serious tomes with black covers or marbled jackets and gold lettering, not a beauty magazine, cheap romance or used crossword book amongst them. Two leather reading chairs stood before a small fireplace and, hanging from the ceiling in the centre of the room, was another glass chandelier that resembled a birdcage.

'I would have found it,' Ky said to Abel. 'I was standing right here when I heard you playing London's Burning. I'll have to teach you how to reach that high note. Secret's in the thumb.'

'Was it really the law that you had to play the recorder every Friday afternoon?' he asked.

Before Ky had time to answer, they heard the click of old metal as a key was turned in a lock and one of the French doors further down the patio creaked open. The door swung back and forth in a slight breeze, as though the house had unlocked itself to let in some air. Instinctively, Ky took the hunting knife from the holder in her belt and stood in front of the others. Seconds of expectancy passed with nothing happening. Ky tried to rationalise the occurrence. She considered how the door, which she had tried and which she knew for certain had been locked, could have opened itself at that particular moment. She took a cautious step forward and then another, but stopped when she saw a hand reach out and hold the glass door open. The man, when he eventually emerged from the drawing room, appeared very old and almost entirely bald except for a rim of grey hair around the back of his head. He wore a pair of small, gold-rimmed spectacles and a simple grey gown, the likes of which Ky had never seen before: a plain habit or a robe that a clergyman from another century might have worn. He did not seem to notice them immediately, but tottered uncertainly forward to scrutinise the gardens. Slowly, he turned his head and, on seeing Ky and the knife in her hand, broke into a wide and unconvincing smile.

'Have you come to take all the silver?' he said in a clear, high-pitched voice that sounded altogether too childish to suit his age. He made a pretence of laughing, shaking his shoulders and guffawing heavily, though he kept his unblinking eyes fixed on Ky.

'We can't do much with silver,' she replied, placing her knife back into its holder, 'but we wouldn't mind taking a look at those books.'

'Gosh,' the old man said, rubbing the bald crown of his head with an open palm, 'I would say yes right away, no hesitation, but I really don't think the Gentleman would agree to that. The library is his pride and joy, you know. Nothing much of value, of course, but enormously sentimental to him. You know what these funny old families are like.' He made another laughing noise, though his pale blue eyes remained steely. 'And you're just passing through, are you?'

'Not at all, we're practically neighbours,' said Ky with a tight smile. She knew she should probably feel more sympathy for an elderly man who was merely alarmed by strangers in his garden and defending his property but, behind his obsequious charm, she sensed a cold, calculating mind. Everything is dangerous, she reminded herself.

'How wonderful,' he grinned, though his eyes narrowed on Ky's face. 'Would you believe, I thought you might be gypsies or something. Have you come far?'

'Just there,' Ky pointed down the lane. 'We've requisitioned one of those empty houses.'

'Goodness, are you Bolsheviks then?' He guffawed again and rubbed his head as though stirring the thoughts inside. His eyes moved from one face to another, lingering on Lugh's and settling finally on Abel's. 'And there are just the four of you, are there?'

Abel returned the smile, though he quickly felt uncomfortable with the old man's profound attention. The boy lowered his gaze and shifted his feet so that he was standing further behind Fran and rubbing shoulders with Lugh. When Abel looked up again, the old man was still staring at him with that intense gaze, a hungry grin of too many teeth.

It was those prominent teeth in particular that most unnerved Abel. He remembered what Mother had told him about not going too far on his own, though she did not go into the details of what could happen if he met someone really-bad, a god-hater perhaps who had avoided the bottomless pit. That was the thing that scared Abel the most. He could not believe that Ky and her friends were god-haters because they had been so nice to him, but he was afraid of the old man in the funny dress. Besides, if he really thought about it, this was all Ruth's fault for leaving him alone when she should have been keeping an eye on him. She had repented for weeks after that last time and they had prayed so hard for her not be so careless as to lose him again. She ought to have known better.

The old man was still asking Ky questions about how many children were with them, but his eyes were fixed on Abel the whole time. Abel considered when would be a polite time to slip away without anyone noticing. He prayed that some quick and unexpected miracle would occur so that he could leave without offending anyone and then, praise be, something did.

'Abel,' cried Ruth, appearing around the corner of the house. She looked pale and tired as though she had been crying. She was scratching her wrists, which was something she always did when she was anxious.

As Abel made to leave, he realised that he had been holding lightly on to Lugh: one hand on his arm and one touching his shoulder. Abel apologised and let go at once. They looked at each other for a moment, as though seeing each other for the first time. Abel knew that there was not the slightest trace of evildoing or god-hating or anything really-bad in the younger boy's blue eyes. He was merely curious, intrigued.

'Abel,' Ruth called again, and this time her brother came running.

CHAPTER FIVE
EPIPHANY

THE FOLLOWING HAD TAKEN THIS way and that through a wilderness of trees that conspired overhead to close out the sky, and thorns that tore at their knuckles and cut their clothes, and cold earth that burned the soles of their feet until Mother could walk no further because she was still being sick even when she had eaten nothing. Sometimes they heard whispers of footfalls over the next embankment, or hooves circling around them and then thundering away on the hard, dry earth. The dogs barked but would not follow Enoch in pursuit of whatever the beast or beasts were. When Enoch returned, he said he had seen nothing but trees. When they closed their eyes at dusk, they dreamed of bark and branches that flowed overhead all through the night. When they woke with the first light of morning, the trees stopped dancing.

They had camped beside a stream for fresh water, tied the tarpaulin sheet between three old oak trees with one tall stick in the middle that gave it a circus tent feel, and killed the last chicken because it never laid any eggs. Enoch had sat alone outside and stared for days at nothing, said nothing, ate little. One morning, he pointed his axe in the direction he had been contemplating and said, this way. Father and Uncle Joe, Matthew and Mark followed him with their machetes, and the dogs too, into the forest. They went looking for meat because Enoch had seen the hoof prints of an animal. Enoch had said only god-haters abjured meat. Enoch had said that the Lord was testing them.

Luke was named the man of the camp and left behind to guard it. He sharpened sticks all day with a knife, as Matthew had shown him, and built a palisade fence around the circus tent. Mother was always sick in the mornings but this, she said with satisfaction, was only to be expected. She caressed her belly and never left her bed until after midday. Ruth was told to keep an eye on Abel; neither of them were to stray too far from the camp.

'We have to tell Mother now,' Abel said to his sister. 'What happens if she finds out?'

They were sitting at the stone table in the front garden of the ivy cottage. The broken cups lay empty before them because Ruth was not in the mood to play a game of tea. She pressed her hands tightly together on her lap to prevent herself from scratching.

'What if those people come looking for us,' Abel continued with rising panic, 'or they find the camp and they speak to Mother and they say that they've seen us and they know our names and everything, and we haven't told her anything already? Then we'll both have to do penance.'

'She'll ask questions,' said Ruth. 'Mother always asks questions. She'll know.'

'Then let's say that we found those people today for the first time, and the houses today too and not yesterday, and that we ran off as soon as we could and came back to tell her at once. Then she won't be upset. Or she might still be sick and not she'll not want to ask questions because, you know, she doesn't like to talk when she's got the morning sickness.'

'Mother will know.'

'You should have kept an eye on me,' Abel sighed hopelessly. 'Wait till our Enoch hears.'

Ruth stared at the empty cups on the stone table and began to rock back and forth. She dug her hands deeper between her thighs to keep them still. A pair of magpies chattered noisily to each other along the garden wall and flew off to the roof of the ivy cottage for a better view of the human melodrama.

'We could always run away and live in this house,' said Abel, 'and never-ever go back.'

Ruth smiled for the first time that day, though she still stared at the empty cups.

LUKE HAD FINISHED BUILDING HIS fence around the tent and was now whittling a long stick into a spear. Every now and then, he lifted it over his shoulder and pretended to throw it in slow motion, whistling to create the effect of wind and speed. Inside the tent, he could hear Abel talking rapidly, telling Mother about the cups he had found. Mother had been sick all day and was in no mood to listen or to talk.

'You shouldn't light the fire until after dark,' Luke said to Ruth, who was collecting kindling. 'You know you're not supposed to do that.'

'Does it look like I'm lighting the fire?' asked Ruth, dropping the sticks beside the firepit.

Luke shrugged and continued to sharpen the point of his spear. Ruth sat cross-legged on the ground, away from the entrance to the tent so that she could not be seen from within, and eavesdropped on the end of Abel's tale. Mother was telling him to speak quietly because she had a headache. Abel lowered his voice and said that he and Ruth had found a house that was covered in plants today. Also today, they had found other houses nearby and there was one big house in particular that had a room full of books. He did not mention the other people until the very end.

'We ran off as soon as we saw them,' he said. 'When our Ruth called me, then we ran.'

There was silence for a while and then Mother asked him to fetch her a cup of water. 'And tell your sister I want a word,' she added.

Ruth did not look at Abel when he crawled through the tent flap and passed on Mother's summons. He seemed relieved that his story had gone so well, though Ruth knew that her own ordeal was about to begin. She stared down at the red fingernail marks on the back of her hands. Some had begun to scab over, others were flowering with bright beads of blood.

Mother was lying on her nest of blankets on the groundsheet, her head resting against the only pillow they had brought with them. She held a damp flannel over her eyes and did not say anything for several long seconds, though she knew that her daughter had crawled into the airless tent and was sitting near her feet. She could hear Ruth's shallow breathing, the rustling of skin and fabric as the girl fidgeted nervously with her sleeves.

'You lost your brother,' Mother sighed eventually. 'Aye, you did it yet again.'

Outside the tent, Luke continued to whittle the tip of his wooden spear. Abel returned from the stream with the glass of water. The two boys glanced at each other when they heard Ruth's voice inside the tent, high-pitched and anxious, explaining herself to Mother. Abel sat down next to his brother. They stared at the ground and listened.

'You're a *liar*,' said Mother, cutting Ruth's explanation short with a ferocity that made the two boys outside flinch. Mother emphasised the last word as though it was the most awful thing she had ever said in her life, the worst sin she could accuse anyone of. 'A liar. I asked you to do one thing, one good thing, to keep an eye on your little brother, and you lost him again. And don't tell me you didn't, don't you dare. I can't think what's wrong with you, girl. You're not a real woman: you don't have the right instincts. You're not normal. You're unnatural.'

Ruth tried to interrupt, but Mother said firmly, 'No. No. We'll not be going to your rotten houses. And I'll not be wanting to see you for some time. You're a liar. A liar.'

Ruth crawled out through the tent flap and ran away through the trees, holding back her tears until she was well out of sight. Luke shook his head and resumed the sharpening of his spear.

When Abel crept inside the tent with Mother's glass of water, he saw that she had also been crying. Her expression was still as hard as granite, but tinged with the sorrow of ages. She reached out her arm and invited him to lie beside her on the nest of blankets.

'I can't get my head around that girl.' She wiped her face with the flannel. 'I'm her mother and not even I can understand her. I carried you all in here,' she said as she stroked her rounded belly, 'for nine months, each and every one of you. How anyone can look their mother in the eye and lie, I'll never know, never. It's not normal behaviour. She's not normal. I'll never understand it.'

Abel lay down on the blankets with his back to his mother. She reached one hand over his chest and with the other she stroked his hair. She stopped crying and soon her breathing grew calm as she drifted into a light, untroubled sleep. Tears have a special smell, thought Abel. They made him feel safe and they made him feel ashamed. He stared at the broken cups that he had brought back from the ivy cottage with Ruth.

THE WATER IN THE STREAM flowed quickly over grey stones and old roots with a light song that never ended. The meandering banks became steeper the further away from the tent that Ruth ran and she found it harder to move through the thicker vegetation. She kicked her way through a blanket of wild garlic and the leaves released a pungent scent that Ruth thought for a dreadful moment might be gas, like that cloud of orange death on the Last Day. She stopped running and looked up to see if an aircraft had flown overhead. She could see little through the trees and there was certainly no sound of an engine. Only cuttings of blue sky between the branches, the piping of distant wood-pigeons and the stream rippling away from the tent and towards the rotten houses that Mother did not want to see. Ruth sat down on the riverbank and let herself cry.

She would have to do penance, that much was inevitable. This time she might be cast out for months. There was less food than ever to share so she would be spared hardly anything, and she was already feeling hungry. She was always feeling hungry. The unfairness of it all itched like hell and scattered her thoughts. Ruth could no longer say if she had lost Abel at the big house or not. Whatever she had done or not done, said or not said, she knew Mother would have blamed her regardless. And that was the thing that tore at her arms, her armpits, her breasts, her belly, her pubic hair and thighs and down to her ankles with jagged, red fingernail lines. Penance could take many forms. Being cast out was the worst. But at least Enoch was not around.

The beast, when it came, made no noise at all. Ruth did not know how long she had been sobbing with her face pressed into her arms, her arms folded against her knees. She imagined it must have been hours, but it could equally have been just a few seconds. She did not hear it approach, but she knew before looking up that she was no longer alone. Slowly, she lifted her head and stared across the banks of the stream into the eyes of an animal she had no name for. It was standing behind undergrowth so she could not see its body or be sure of its height, but she imagined it must be almost as tall as her, taller perhaps. Its face was long and whiskered, and its cheeks were patterned with spirals of creamy fur. Ruth thought that it must be male because he was crowned with two short horns. The Adversary has horns too, Ruth knew that for a fact, but so did many of God's creatures. Cows and deer she was sure had horns, and probably gazelles and antelopes, too. She did not know what manner of creature this was, but she was convinced it could not be the Adversary. He stared at her with vivid eyes, neither alarmed nor threatening, merely interested and taking a sympathetic look at her. He opened his mouth as though about to laugh, revealed a set of large off-white teeth and spoke to her. It was just a word, a simple, throaty, pebbly sound, but Ruth felt both fear and wonder at the miracle. The beast nodded once, twice, making sure that he had been both heard and understood, and then he was gone.

The forest looked just the same as it had before. The wood-pigeons continued to murmur and the water continued to ripple over stones, but things had changed. The trees no longer felt like strangers and everything, the tiny wildflowers and the pungent weeds and even the long-fallen autumn leaves, felt alive with a secret, internal vitality that she had never noticed before. And maybe this, thought Ruth, was her inheritance. Maybe this, at long last, was her new Heaven and her new Earth.

She wiped her eyes on her sleeve and stood up. Her hands smelled strongly of the wild garlic, but now she knew it was nothing to be afraid of because it came from the rubbery plant leaves. Below her, the stream played and splashed in one resolute direction, away from the tent of Mother's blame and towards the empty cottage of ivy.

'Go,' the beast with gentle eyes had told her before he had disappeared in the undergrowth. Ruth pulled her shirt sleeves over her sore wrists and followed the current of water.

⌣

THEY HAD MOVED THE OLD Cortina. The car had been driven off the lane, over the grass verge and parked behind a tree. One of them, the woman with dark skin and short hair who looked like a boy, had used a piece of hosepipe to syphon petrol from the car and into a metal can. Ruth had wondered if the woman was going to set fire to something, but she just took the can of petrol away. Peeking over the ledge of a window in the ivy cottage, Ruth had watched them cover the car with branches. Now it resembled a car-shaped pile of sticks. The undergrowth would eventually overwhelm it. Nature had a way of reclaiming things here.

It looked like those people were here to stay. They had settled into one of the houses down the lane and were making themselves at home. Ruth would sometimes follow the stream at the back of the ivy cottage to spy on the gardens behind the Mews. The other woman, the nicer lady with long light-coloured hair, was usually digging up weeds with the boy or planting seeds or explaining the shapes of leaves that they could eat raw or cooked in a soup. Ruth recognised some of these plants, the strong-smelling wild garlic on the riverbank for sure, and dandelions and mint, and even the hazelnuts which she picked for herself though none of these was fully satisfying. Sometimes she would creep down the lane and watch from behind a tree as the darker woman with short hair came and went with useful things from the other houses: brooms, buckets, pots and pans, glass jars and bottles, candles, blankets. Ruth wished she had found a way into these other houses first. One time, while she was spying on the comings and goings in the lane, Ruth herself had been spotted by the older woman with the cough.

'Hello, poppet,' the older woman had called, waving at her from an upstairs window.

Ruth had panicked and run back to the ivy cottage. For the rest of that day, she remained hidden in the back bedroom that she had made her home, and in which she had gathered a few belongings. Mismatched cups and saucers, spoons, a broken clock and a large metal pot sat on top of the mantelpiece. A stack of black hardback ledgers or notebooks lay on a wooden box to the side of the fireplace. Thick limbs of ivy occluded the window of that room, keeping out the sunlight but also the worst of the winter cold. On the few nightly occasions when the trick of rubbing sticks together had worked, Ruth managed to warm herself beside a fire in the bedroom hearth and had even heated pans of water in which to wash or make wild garlic soup. There were no blankets, but she had made a comfortable bed of sorts out of old coats from the wardrobe. Other clothes, shirts mostly, she had torn into rags and boiled for the next time she bled.

'When a woman bleeds down there, she's as sure to die as night follows day,' Mother had told her countless times before she did actually bleed. Back then, that first time she had bled, night did follow day, and then more nights and more days and still she did not die, though she knew she probably would soon. She had taught herself how to manage those days and to reckon when the next time would come around again, how long the danger would last. Mother bled too; this Ruth had discovered by chance when once she had washed the unsorted clothes by hand. Mother had been furious with Ruth that day, but no one could figure out why. Night followed day and Mother did not die either. That was a thing to remember.

The morning after the old woman with the cough had seen Ruth and called her poppet, a wicker basket appeared outside the ivy cottage. It had been left on the stone table in the front garden, the place where Ruth and Abel had taken pretend tea all those days ago. Ruth watched the basket from the upstairs window for hours before she convinced herself that there was no one around and it was not some kind of trap. She ran outside to collect it and brought it back to her secret room. Inside the basket, she found plums, nuts, some kind of deep-fried flatbread, and even oranges, which she had not seen for years. She split the oranges open with her thumbs and ate them at once, peel included, then licked her fingers and started on the crispy flatbread. At the bottom of the basket, she found an envelope addressed simply to, 'Our Dear Neighbour'. There was nothing inside, but on the back was written a short message.

You are cordially invited to tea at No. 4 Usquam Mews at any time that suits you.

It was signed by Rhea, and underneath was a postscript: *Honestly, dear, we don't bite.*

Ruth leaned back against the ivy-covered wall, took a bite of a plum and closed her eyes.

IN THE LOFT OF THEIR house on Usquam Mews, Ky had made a discovery. The walls on either side of the central chimney stack were largely cosmetic and, by scraping away the cement and removing a few bricks from the alcove, she could crawl into the attics of the houses next door. It was a simple enough trick and one that meant she did not have to break any more pantry windows to gain access. It was while she was hiding the two petrol cans in the neighbouring loft that she heard Rhea call her name. Rhea's voice sounded unusually bright, like she was up to mischief or play-acting a role, excessively polite and well-spoken. Ky replaced the bricks in the wall, climbed down the stepladder from the loft and hurried downstairs.

Rhea had taken the kitchen table and chairs into the back yard, where she was drinking tea with a strange young girl. It took Ky a few minutes to recognise Ruth, who was wearing a heavy, black duffel coat that made her look skinnier and paler than ever. Rhea had laid a platter of food on the table, some fruit, boiled eggs and the fried potato bread.

'I thought you must be entertaining someone,' Ky said with a sly smile to Rhea. She sat at the empty chair and poured herself a cup of mint tea from the teapot. 'It was the way you put on airs and graces when you called my name. "Oh, Ky, do come down, dear," like you were the queen or something. Hello, Ruth. How's your brother?'

Ruth looked from Ky to Rhea and back again with large brown eyes. She took a slice of the potato bread and, while she was still eating that, took another piece and nodded. Ky understood this to mean that her brother was well but that she did not want to talk about him.

'I was just asking Ruth here about that funny old man at the big house,' said Rhea, still using her sociable, best-mannered voice. 'Because everyone's seen him, apparently; everyone except me. And wasn't he wearing an old frock or something? And wasn't he behaving very oddly?'

As the older woman talked on, sometimes coughing, cajoling and asking questions but never explicitly requiring answers, Ruth began to relax and feel the comfort of cooked food inside her stomach. Rhea said that their other friends, Fran and Lugh, were doing jobs for the old man in exchange for food at the big house. In return for a few hours' work on his small farmyard each day, they could bring home eggs, honey, potatoes, even oranges from the large greenhouse.

'As it happens, that funny old clergyman was asking after your young brother, wondering if he would like to come up to the big house and give a hand too,' said Rhea. 'And he keeps mentioning someone else who lives upstairs in the tower. The Gentleman, he calls him…. But we don't think the Gentleman really exists, do we, Ky? We think the old man made him up for company. Must be lonely for him, living up there all alone, mustn't it?'

'The Gentleman,' Ky scoffed. 'There was that old rhyme, wasn't there, a revolutionary song from—was it the time of the Levellers? How does it go—Who then was the Gentleman?'

'Oh no, dear, I wouldn't know anything about that,' Rhea said.

Sometimes Ruth stopped listening to the other women altogether and simply enjoyed the novelty of a conversation that lacked any concealed threat of blame or accusation. She accepted another cup of mint tea from the pot, a real china teapot painted with blue willow trees and bridges over rivers, and she was reminded of all those imaginary teatimes with Abel. She was canny enough to know that there was still something make-believe about this whole contrived occasion, but it was a harmless pretence that these people were playing to get to know her. It was a grown-up game and it involved real tea and real food. And neither of them was asking difficult questions about Mother or why Ruth was living alone in the ivy cottage.

Ruth was looking at the freshly cultivated back gardens that had been cleared and dug into neat, parallel lines of seed beds. She was pondering what food they would be growing when she realised that Ky had just asked her a question and was patiently waiting for a response. Ruth blinked apologetically and bit her lip. She felt that she had spoiled the whole game.

'Writing paper,' Ky repeated, graciously overlooking Ruth's lapse in concentration, and the game was back on. 'Well, paper of any kind, really. There's none in any of these houses. Everything else you can imagine— pens, ink, desks, chairs, buckets and spades—plenty of those. There's even an antique telescope and an old globe, but no paper. Don't suppose you've got any lying around your place? I'd swap you something if you have. The telescope or globe perhaps.'

Ruth did not know what she would do with a telescope, or what the globe might be about, but her eyes fell on the china teapot decorated with blue willow trees. 'There's notebooks,' Ruth said, taking another slice of potato-bread from the platter, 'like you might write numbers in for selling things or keeping a record of money. You can have those.'

'And I was just thinking about that old cottage of yours,' said Rhea.

'No doors, no windows, bleeding great hole in the roof. Whereas these,' she gestured across the lane at the row of houses opposite. 'Well, they've all got roofs for a start. Seems a crying shame to let them stand empty.'

'Careful, Ruth,' said Ky, biting into the last boiled egg. 'If you move into one of these empty houses, you'll be accused of being a Bolshevik too.'

SOMETIMES RUTH PUT HER NEW teapot on the mantelpiece over the hearth in her sitting room, sometimes on the windowsill in the front bedroom, her bedroom. There were curtains hanging at all the windows in her new home, thin yellow curtains embroidered with green hawthorn leaves and white may blossom, but Ruth liked to leave the bedroom ones open so that the first rays of the rising sun would highlight the teapot, revealing the blue-painted patterns of willow and water. It was an act of creation that happened each day, the rising sun: nature revealing fine china.

The sun would not always rise in the same place over the teapot on her windowsill. That was something she had learned from Francesca. The nice lady, Ruth used to call her, though now she simply called her Fran. Fran had also tried to explain how the sun does not actually move, that it only appears to move because the Earth is turning. Ruth did not believe her at all and became sullen when she thought Fran was teasing her.

'I'm being deadly serious,' Fran had said. After a pause, she asked, 'Tell me, did you go to a school or did your parents—were you taught at home?'

'We had lessons at home, all of us,' Ruth shrugged. 'Mother said that the schools taught lies and the teachers were all god-haters, so we learnt everything we needed at home.'

'Like what?'

'Like everything. Like the creation, the flood, ten commandments. Everything.'

'Jesus Christ,' Fran said quietly.

'Him too, of course. Bethlehem, three kings, crucifixion. Everything.'

Fran stared into the distance and muttered, more to herself than to Ruth, 'There are more things in Heaven and Earth, Horatio.'

After that conversation, Fran had instituted Philosophy Night. Each evening, she said, they would take it in turns to choose a subject from the encyclopaedia and explain it as best they could to the others. It could be on any theme that took their fancy and be over as quickly they wanted. Ruth and Lugh were both reluctant to participate. After dinner on that first night, Fran had stood up from her seat at the kitchen table and announced her topic with an elaborate bow.

'The most important subject of all,' she had said. 'Our home, the Earth.'

With the flourish of a magician's assistant, Ky had produced the globe from under her chair so that she and Fran could demonstrate sunrise and sunset, axial tilt and seasons, equinoxes and solstices. Ruth had never seen the Earth as a globe before, all those oceans and mountains and continents and cities clinging to a sphere in the blackness of space. That thought had terrified her, the imminent danger of things falling apart and dropping off, so Ky had explained gravity.

'But what happens if gravity stops?' Ruth had asked.

Ky laughed. 'Then you end up living near us.' No one else found that amusing, so Ky became serious and said that gravity would never stop as long as a thing, any thing, the planet, say, had mass. Ruth did not understand mass or gravity, but she felt reassured that somebody else did. Then Fran announced that the sun was the orange that she placed in Lugh's hand, and the Earth was the globe that they each took turns to spin around the sun. Ruth had never laughed so much in her all life.

The location of the real sunrise did not change much from one day to the next. Ruth lay in her bed, a real bed with blankets and pillows, and watched the arrival of each dawn with interest. It took a couple of weeks before she suspected that there might be some difference. After a fortnight of heavy snow in late February and early March in which there were no dawns at all, Ruth woke to find that the morning sky had at last cleared and the sun was rising noticeably further to the left of the teapot than ever before. She was so pleased with this first-hand evidence of axial tilt that she could not wait to tell Fran and Ky that they might be right after all.

Ruth buttoned-up her black duffel coat and pulled the hood overhead. It was an old coat that she had taken from the ivy cottage. Although it was ludicrously too long for her and she frequently tripped over its hem, it was soft on the inside, tough on the out, and shielded her well against the winter weather. It was also the only piece of clothing she had ever chosen for herself.

Laying her basket on the doorstep for a moment, she closed the front door behind her and locked it with the key. It was something she always did, not because she considered it likely that someone would try to enter the house in her absence, but because it signified the authenticity of her own space. The weight of the iron key in her hand, the sound of the secret mechanisms clicking within the wooden door, these solid things substantiated her security. The threat of banishment had always been present, in the silences, in the questions, in a smile at the wrong time or a faraway melancholy when she should have been rejoicing. But now she was a keyholder to her own refuge, and she could never again be banished or cast out. Unless, of course, she banished herself.

Early morning sunlight glistened like crystals on the snow that had fallen during the night. Across the lane, the curtains in the house opposite were still closed. Her neighbours must still be in bed, Ruth thought, all except for Rhea who hardly slept and was probably making another cup of tea in the kitchen. Instead of going directly into their backyard, Ruth made a fresh path through the snow down the lane towards the ivy cottage. Over the fallen tree trunk and up the garden path, she found what she had expected to see: a single set of footprints around the stone table, last night's basket sitting empty. It was as though she were feeding the faeries, she thought, a real imaginary tea-party. She exchanged last night's empty basket for the full one she had brought with her this morning, and looked around the overgrown garden, at the dark ivy-choked windows of the cottage. There was no sign of Abel now, of course. Even if he were hiding somewhere, watching from behind brambles or peering between ivy fingers, he would never come out and speak to her, not while she was doing her penance, not until Mother decreed otherwise. Ruth's face remained unchanged, her eyebrows arched in perpetual, unfaltering surprise as she left the basket behind and walked carefully back through the snow.

As Ruth had suspected, she found Rhea brewing a kettle on her kitchen stove. Ruth hung her duffel coat on a hook in the hallway and told the older woman about the sunrise.

'They were right about it moving a little every day,' said Ruth. 'All this time, I never knew.'

'Hallelujah,' said Rhea, 'or would it be more appropriate to say eureka? Now, my dear, tell me. What's that empty basket all about?'

Ruth shook her head and shrugged as though she had no idea why she had brought it. Rhea said nothing for a while, fussed about with the fire in the stove, laid another cup and saucer on the table and then turned to the window, to the forest of white, frozen trees outside.

'I am sorry, dear,' Rhea said with a sigh. 'Francesca tells me not to say anything, and I know I shouldn't as it's really none of my business. But I am silly and these things do worry me. Did I ever tell you what I used to do, what I did for a job, before the troubles started?'

Ruth had been told several times before, but she let the older woman tell her again how she had been some kind of counsellor at a university.

'A bit like a chaplain, but not a religious one,' Rhea added quickly. 'Someone for people to talk to in difficult times, like bereavements or relationship breakups—and, believe me, there were plenty of student breakups, every bleeding day—or problems at home. Because sometimes it really does help to talk to someone about these things. It makes them feel so much less – immense. And all I do is sit and listen. No judgement, no telling you what you should or shouldn't do. I just listen, unconditionally. And tea, I also make tea.'

Rhea took the kettle off the stove and filled the teapot with steaming water. The kitchen filled with the scent of mint. She sat down at the table and took Ruth's hand.

'Least said, soonest mended,' said Ruth, repeating one of Mother's favourite maxims.

'Oh, I've heard that old chestnut before. Last person who said that to me swelled up like a balloon, physically, right in front of me, with the gas of all the unsaid things inside. And then, you know what happened? They exploded. Left a bleeding great mess on my walls.'

Ruth stared at Rhea with wide, gullible eyes and then flinched into a laugh that was utterly silent and lasted for several minutes. Rhea chuckled and poured out their tea.

'Now, is there really any harm in me asking about your basket, dear?' she said.

Ruth wiped her eyes and fiddled with the cup of tea.

THE SUN ALSO SET IN a fractionally different place each evening: that was something else Ruth had begun to notice. Now that they were rolling towards the spring equinox, the evenings were becoming lighter and the curtains did not need to be pulled until later each day. Ruth was lighting the candles in her sitting room when she heard a knock at the front door. After she had offloaded so many things at Rhea's kitchen table that morning—a tale-telling, Mother would have called it—she knew who it was and what it would be about.

'Now, dear,' Rhea said to her as soon as Ruth had opened the door, 'you're absolutely sure you're happy for us to go ahead with this?'

'Yes,' Ruth replied, hesitantly at first and then more resolutely, 'yes'.

'And you'll not be coming with us?'

Ruth shook her head and handed over the basket of food she had prepared.

'There anything else you want me to say to your little brother, anything special?'

'Just,' Ruth began and she stopped to think. She looked at Fran and Ky, who were standing a little further behind Rhea, each of them offering a sympathetic smile. Ky carried a small oil-lamp that lit their faces eerily from below. 'Just that I hope he's okay.'

'Will do. And I almost forgot, you've got this one tonight.' Rhea ushered Lugh through the front door. 'He's heavy with encyclopaedia. One of you will be doing the philosophy tomorrow night. Can't put it off forever, so we'll leave it up to you to work out who. Ta-ta, my dears.'

Rhea gave her a kiss on the cheek and headed off towards the ivy cottage.

'Remind me again why this is a good idea,' Ky whispered to Fran as they followed the older woman down the lane.

'A question for Philosophy Night,' said Fran. 'Why do we do kind things for other people?'

Ky laughed but did not reply. Their shoes crunched on the frozen snow and they could see their breath in the lamplight. An incomplete moon hung above the trees, though they lost sight of it as soon as they turned the corner and climbed over the fallen tree towards the cottage.

From where he was crouching underneath the window, Abel could not see the moon at all. He had not seen her white face for months, not since the forest had swallowed them up. Sometimes he dreamed that the moon was watching him sleep, though she was never there when he awoke. Abel closed his eyes now. He pulled the rug over his head and breathed against the rough fabric to warm his nose. He had never in his life felt so cold before. Apart from last night, perhaps. Yes, that really was the coldest night ever because Luke could not get the fire going at all. Whereas here, in this cottage—Abel turned to the large, empty fireplace—well, there was every chance they could start a fire here. But Mother would never hear of coming to Ruth's rotten houses, not even after today when her pain got so bad that she cried. There was even blood on her blankets, though she tried to hide it. And all she had to do was take a look at this rotten cottage with its rotten fireplace. Besides, a fire might set all this ivy alight too. And that would be something, that would be spectacular. Abel was imagining the incredible heat that such a house fire would generate when he heard someone calling his name from the garden below.

'Moon?' he replied. He said it so quietly that not even he could hear the sound.

'Abel, dear,' again came the voice, a voice he did not recognise. 'Ruth knows you're not supposed to speak to her because of all that penance nonsense going on, but she said you'd be allowed to speak to us, if you wanted to. Abel, dear, are you in there?'

Lifting the rug from his head, Abel peered over the window ledge and saw what looked like a firelit procession coming down the path towards the stone table. He did not recognise the older woman at the front, the one who was laying Ruth's basket of food on the table, but the other two he knew: the nice-lady and the recorder-woman. In addition to food, they brought fire.

'There he is,' Fran said as Abel walked warily, unsteadily, down the path towards them. He looked more like a long-legged puppy than ever, she thought, a stray with residual trust of humans. As he approached the oil-lamp, she saw that his cheeks had hollowed with hunger since she had first seen him drinking imaginary tea with his sister in this garden. Darkness now circled his large eyes. He had become a wraith, attracted by the flickering lamplight.

Rhea brushed the layer of snow off the stone table and laid out parcels of food wrapped in old newspapers. She spoke in that confident, playful way she did to put strangers at ease, as if she and Abel needed no introduction at all because they had always known each other. He smiled appreciatively in return and pressed his fingers against the heated glass chimney of the oil-lamp.

'Your sister's settled nicely into her new house,' Rhea said as she unscrewed a glass bottle and poured a cup of steaming herb tea for the boy to drink, 'though she misses you very much and says you must visit her whenever you can. In the meantime, we'll be here twice a day at least, with breakfast and supper laid on, and pass any messages between you two. And that is allowed,' this she said emphatically, 'because I know it to be so. And it's nobody else's business who you speak to, and don't let anyone tell you otherwise. Now, young man, how is life in the wild? How's your mum doing? I hear she's expecting another little one?'

Abel, who had been basking in the mindless exultation of warm tea and lamplight, struggled to sort his thoughts of the horrific day into words.

'Mother's bleeding. She shouted at me to get out.'

He put the empty cup on the table and glared at it as though it had led him into temptation. He thought of all the potato-bread and boiled eggs and plums that he had taken from the baskets here and eaten by himself. Of course, he had taken most of it back to the tent and told Mother that he found it near the houses. But there were some days when he was so hungry that he had gorged on everything, even the crumbs at the bottom of the basket. And now Mother was bleeding and here he was, drinking warm tea with strangers.

ABEL WAS ALLOWED TO CARRY the oil-lamp so long as he was careful and watched where he was treading. He led the three women along the riverbank, through snow so deep that it sometimes came up to their knees, and over the shallow stream towards the tarpaulin shelter that looked like a circus tent. The lamp did not provide much illumination—more than starlight, less than the full moon—just enough to see a metre or two around the boy, whose thin face looked even more spectral in the underglow. Several times, Ky had to tell him to slow down as he scurried ahead like a flighty will-o'-the-wisp. They each heard the woman's cries long before they saw the camp.

Abel slowed his pace as he approached the wood-fire blazing outside the snow-covered tent. Around the firepit, three hunger-pinched young men were sitting on the ground, each one staring grimly into the flames. Ky, whose eyes were sharp, was the first to recognise the striking family resemblance between Abel and his older brothers. She had expected to meet only one, but here there were three of them, each with the same long dark hair covering their ears, the same arched eyebrows and forlorn expression as they listened to their mother howling within the tent.

'You're back,' cried Abel. He ran up to greet Mark and Matthew, who had been gone for months, but stopped when he saw the look on their faces. 'Where's our Enoch? Where's Father?'

'Who's this?' asked Matthew. He jumped to his feet and stood between the tent and the three strange women. 'Abel, what have you gone and done?'

Rhea entered the firelight with the authority of one who knows exactly when it is time for people to be told what to do. She took the oil-lamp from Abel and said she had been called to attend to a sick woman and that was what she was here to do. 'Move aside, dear.'

'She is a nurse,' Abel explained.

'Mother's not sick,' said Matthew, though he was sufficiently awed by Rhea's temerity to stand aside and let her pass into the tent.

'Yeah, she sounds perfectly well,' Ky quipped as she entered behind.

Fran smiled and touched Matthew's arm briefly, kindly, as she followed the others.

The effect of the oil-lamp within the tent was dramatic. Outside, the light had been lost in the open air, squandered on distance. Inside, the flame reflected off the tarpaulin roof to illuminate the terrible scene in red, vivid detail. Mother half-sat, half-lay with one white, naked leg exposed over a bed of blankets that were soaked with blood. She looked up at Rhea, at Ky, at Fran, seeing but not seeing each of their unknown faces, her mouth twisted into a raging, primaeval o. Her cry was as unforgiving as the windstorm that had howled for days and days and dared never to end, never to rain, only to sound because that was all it could do. She gaped down in revulsion, in adoration, at the bloody mess between her legs, the mess that was her firstborn, her eldest son, Enoch, whose body had been torn open and whose blood flowed and mingled with the blood of her own miscarriage. She cradled Enoch's head against her belly as though he were the thing, fully formed and monstrous, that she had somehow just delivered. First and last, beginning and end.

Rhea passed the oil-lamp to Ky and knelt beside the bed. She put her fingers to the artery on the side of the young man's neck and felt a weak but distinct pulse.

'He's alive,' said Rhea, taking the mother's hand in her own and squeezing it until it hurt, until the woman turned and their eyes met. 'Your son, he's still alive.'

Mother did not hear Rhea speak, did not hear anything at all above her own continuous moan. She stared at Rhea, through her and through the world with a fury that was deeper than loss, thicker than blood.

CHAPTER SIX

REPUBLIC

THERE WAS A MAN STANDING in her room. Fran knew it was a man because she could hear his voice. He asked her something, a question she had heard before but could not for the life of her remember what it was. The man removed his coat and laid it carefully over the back of a chair as though he was biding his time, as though he owned time and everything that happened within it. Even in the darkness, Fran could sense it was a heavy coat. It smelled heavy, of thick blankets left outside on damp nights, of pallid slugs that had never seen the sun and had swollen fat inside the folds and creases where they hide from the moon. The man rolled up the sleeves of his shirt and at last Fran could discern something of his substance: the skin of his arms, just his arms, pale and disembodied at the end of her bed. It was then that she remembered the question.

'I don't know.' She sat up and covered her chest, her neck with the sheet, though she knew it would be of no use against him. 'I don't know what justice is.'

'It is whatever I say it is.' His voice was the breath of a bull, of a horse, the voice of the barnyard after dark, the nicker of a dreaming stable.

Why, she wanted to ask. Why whatever you say it is?

'Because I'm stronger than you,' he replied, though she had not spoken. 'Because I'm right.'

She heard the wooden floorboards clench and exhale beneath the weight of hooves as he walked slowly around the bed and came to stand beside the headboard. He had crossed his arms, and now she could see the contours of his strength. His fingers were hidden in the armpits of his shirt, but the thumbs stood tall, unnaturally long, and were tipped with sharp, horn-hard nails. He bent down to her face, so close that all she knew were the ice whites of his eyes. Through his nostrils, he breathed the stench of a slaughterhouse.

'Now, praise me,' he whispered.

Fran struggled against the mattress and pushed herself against the other side of the headboard, but he was there too, his presence a property of the air. She wanted to shout, 'She's behind you,' before he smothered her, before he pressed those horn-hard thumbnails into her skin, but she could not move her mouth. There was no space for her to do or to say anything.

She awoke to the sound of her name being shouted, not by the man who stood at the end of her dreams, but by Lugh. She had kicked the boy out of the bed they shared and he was kneeling on the floor with both of his hands cupped around his bleeding nose.

'Oh, Jesus,' she said when she realised what had happened. 'Again? I'm so sorry.'

'No blood on the bed,' he said.

'I know, sweetheart. I know.'

She grabbed a handkerchief from the drawer to stem the blood flow and led him carefully downstairs. Rhea was asleep in the sitting-room; they could hear the steady rhythm of her snores as they crept along the hallway and closed the kitchen door behind them. It was still night-time, though the gibbous moon was bright on the snowy ground outside. The first cockerels had begun to crow in the farmyard behind the big house so Fran guessed it would be at least four o'clock. Until the dawn, they could never be sure of the time. Dawn, midday and dusk: these were the only measures of time now. She lighted a scrap of paper on the kitchen stove which they always kept burning, and transferred the flame to an oil-lamp. Lugh sat on the table and swung his legs back and forth. He put his hand on Fran's book of herbs beside him, for balance or for reassurance.

'Let's get a proper look at you, wounded soldier.' Fran gently held his head back and raised the lamp to his face. 'Don't think I've done your nose any permanent damage. Still a handsome devil, even with all that blood up your nostrils. But,' she released his chin and rinsed the handkerchief in the sink, 'maybe it's time for us to think about different sleeping arrangements before I really do spoil your good looks. Keep your head back.'

Lugh kicked his heels against the table leg and said nothing.

'Perhaps now's not the right time,' Fran added after a pause, 'what with everything that's been going on.'

She glanced though the window at the moonlit trees. It was three days since they had met with that scene in the forest. Ky and Rhea had done what they could with Enoch in the tent, washed the deep wounds in his chest and leg, bandaged him tightly, tied a tourniquet around his thigh. Ky had argued against moving him, but Rhea was adamant that he must be brought inside to a decent bed in a warm house where they could care for him properly. It had been down to his brothers, Matthew and Mark, to fashion a stretcher from blankets and bear him painstakingly through the snow and along the stream to the Mews. Luke had followed behind carrying Enoch's axe. If anything, the distraught mother had been the most challenging burden, but the three women had managed to cajole, bully and at times physically carry her to the first house in the terrace, two doors down from Ruth's. Lugh had run into the lane to stare in wonder at the sudden, tumultuous arrival of so many strangers, but Ruth was nowhere to be seen. It was not until afterwards that Fran considered what the effect might have been on Lugh: the grisly procession, a bloody young man carried in blankets. The similarities with what had happened at the farmhouse were too raw to overlook. Perhaps that, Fran wondered, was the thing that had also prompted her dream to return.

She wrung the handkerchief dry and returned it to Lugh. 'It's understandable if all this has brought back memories of Michael.'

'I do know that man's not Michael.'

'Of course he's not. I'm just saying, it would be perfectly normal if it brought up the past.' She sat next to Lugh on the table top and swung her legs in time with his, left and right, back and forth. 'I know you think of your brother often. I do too. Those last days, when he came home so badly hurt, it was tough, really tough. We all hoped he would get better, Lugh, all of us. And Ky and Rhea did absolutely everything they could to make him well again. Sometimes having hope is the hardest thing, especially when the thing we desperately need to happen doesn't.'

'Michael was dead by now.' Lugh frowned at her as though she did not understand something fundamental and obvious.

'By now?' she asked, struggling to solve his riddle. 'You mean, after three days?'

Lugh nodded and turned his gaze to the ceiling, though his nose had stopped bleeding.

'And, after three days, this man, this Enoch, he hasn't died?'

Lugh blinked his long eyelashes to indicate yes, that is precisely what he meant. Fran carefully considered what her next move should be. All the questions that came to mind sounded too harsh, too accusatory, and could violate the delicate relationship she had with the boy. For a rare moment, however, he was trying to verbalise the mysterious, shadowy state of his mind and she knew she must follow with caution whichever way the maze led. She almost asked if Lugh wanted this man to die. Sensing a deeper, gentler way, she tried another tack.

'Why did your brother die after three days, whereas this man we don't know is still alive?'

Hearing his own thoughts laid out so starkly, Lugh fiddled with the bloody handkerchief in his hands. Fran sighed and laid her arm over his shoulders. Because the universe is meaningless and empty and has no sense of fairness, she wanted to tell him. Because we have to press on together through the darkness as best we can. Not very reassuring, but who deserves to be lied to? She kicked playfully against his legs to get them swinging again. Perhaps he wanted specifics.

'You're right, it's not fair, not in the slightest,' she said at length. 'But Michael's wounds were very much worse than Enoch's. When somebody gets injured deep inside, it's more difficult for the body to heal itself, even with all the skill and care that Ky and Rhea can offer. Whereas this man, this Enoch, well, he didn't have a bullet that went into his body. Rhea says it's a clean cut, like a knife or something, though his brothers say he was attacked by an animal. He's bled a lot but his injuries aren't very deep. That's the reason he's still alive after three days.'

'So why does she want to go to a pharmacy?' Lugh emphasised the *she* with an unexpected malevolence. It took a moment for Fran to realise that he was referring to Ky. After the first day of nursing Enoch, Ky had said that they needed better medical supplies and should look for a town.

'If this man's not dying, why does she want a pharmacy now?' Lugh demanded. 'And why didn't she let you go to one before, when Michael needed one?'

'Ky feels guilty about your brother. She shouldn't, but she does. Towns are dangerous. Towns are where the troubles are worse. You understand that. I know you're not stupid.' Fran slipped down from the table and put more wood into the stove. She was not going to humour this nonsense against Ky. 'Regardless of why, we mustn't let her go. You understand?'

They did not talk much after that. Lugh flicked absently through the book of herbs. Fran made tea from the geranium leaves they had gathered from pots outside the big house. The sky above the back gardens was beginning to grow pale with the early expectation of dawn. The blackbirds and others had begun to sing loudly, each in its own language with its own urgent announcements to make. Two of the cockerels were duelling vocally, both claiming victory for the ending of the night. Maybe six o'clock, Fran estimated, and the Morning Star was out too.

Sitting outside on the doorstep of their new home, Abel had also noticed that bright star in the sky but he did not know its name. His attention was on the moon, which looked far more remote than he remembered. Perhaps even a different moon, one not so much a friend as the distant relative of a friend; they had never encountered each other before and therefore had nothing to say. In the dark belly of the forest, he had re-created her face into a myth, pieced her tin-beaten fragments together in his dreams until she became something entirely perfect, entirely his. She would wait for him, she had promised, and she would sing and play hide-and-seek and keeping-an-eye-on-each-other when the time of testing was finally over, when the wilderness came to an end. And the forest had opened up and the sky had flooded in, but the moon was a broken remnant of her past fullness: she had forgotten him. Perhaps some part of her had been swept away by the windstorm after all. Perhaps there was nothing that could not be extinguished.

'We shouldn't light the fire during daytime,' said Luke, who was sitting beside Abel on the doorstep. 'They can see where we are from the smoke. It gives us away.'

Luke was not looking at the moon but at the length of fishing rod in his hand. The pole unscrewed into three sections and, with the handle, he was scratching the shape of a fish in the snow. Over and over, the eternal loop of a fish, invoking what he would catch later that day.

'They have their fire alight all day,' said Abel, meaning those people in the house opposite. 'They've lived here for ages and they always have the fire alight and it's not given them away. And that older woman, the nurse, she said Enoch must be kept warm if he's to get better, so maybe –'

'Maybe you shouldn't ask so many questions,' said Luke, though Abel could not remember asking any questions. 'If Enoch were awake, he'd make sure they didn't have a fire alight in the daytime. And Father, if he were still with us, he'd do the same.'

Neither of them said anything after that mention of Father. Abel stared dolefully at the fish that his brother had etched in the snow. It was not that he felt any deep grief, but a searing shame that he had forgotten about Father again. No one had mentioned him for days, not since that night only three of the five men had returned from the forest. Abel could not even remember the colour of Father's eyes. He could remember the outline of his features, the receding hairline, the hollow cheeks, the eyebrows raised in perpetual surprise or disdain or beseeching Mother for attention, but he could not remember the colour of his eyes. Nor, for that matter, could he remember Father looking at him. Through him, yes, and over his head, but Abel could not recall a time their eyes had met. Maybe they had never actually seen each other. Maybe that was why he did not miss him. If anything, Abel missed Uncle Joe more, and he had always worn sunglasses.

While Abel was grieving about not grieving enough, the front door opened and Matthew leaned out to look at the sky above the houses. He did not notice his younger brothers on the step and unwittingly knocked them both into the snow. Luke's hands scattered his fish into powder.

'Why you creeping about like that?' Luke complained, brushing himself down.

'Like what?' asked Matthew.

'Like a thief in the night.'

'No one's creeping about,' Matthew replied, closing the door quietly behind him. 'Have they left for the farm yet, that blonde woman and the boy?'

'Not seen a soul. Why? Why do you care what that blonde woman does?'

'She's been good to us.' Matthew scrutinised each of windows in the house opposite, the closed curtains that showed no signs of life. 'Got to do our bit in return. Give and take. Can't be all take-take-take, fish-boy.'

'Did Mother say you could go?'

'Mother's got other things on her mind. Later, fish-boy.' Matthew nodded an indifferent farewell and strolled up the lane, whistling as he went.

'Later, fish-boy,' said Abel. He jumped up from the step and ran to keep up with Matthew.

AFTER BREAKFAST, FRAN AND LUGH also headed to the farmyard. They no longer knocked at the big house to announce their arrival. The old man had grown accustomed to their comings and goings. He sometimes came down to watch them work or to pass inane observations about the weather, but he always insisted on inspecting the contents of their baskets before they left.

'Just to make sure I'm not short-changing you,' he would say with an unconvincing laugh.

This morning, there were fresh footprints in the snow that had fallen overnight. Following the tracks around the house and over the white, glistening expanse of the ornamental gardens, Fran was surprised to hear the gravelly rasp and heave of shovelling coming from the farmyard.

'I hope you're not taking our jobs away from us,' she teased when she saw Matthew clearing snow from the ground of the enclosure. 'That wouldn't be very neighbourly of you.'

Matthew straightened up and smiled at Fran. His expression was as warm and open, she thought, as that of a playful dog who was genuinely pleased to see her. He was the tallest of the brothers, taller even than Enoch, but he was also the leanest and his shirt and jeans hung loosely on his body like clothes on a scarecrow. Like his brothers, Matthew had a beard that was as thick, black and unkempt as the hair on his head. He wiped his brow with the back of his hand, paused thoughtfully, and then the smile faded as he registered what Fran had said to him.

'Oh heck, no, not at all,' he said, his brown eyes darting anxiously from Fran to Lugh to the shovel in his hand. 'We came to give you a hand, that's all, I swear. We thought, well, what with you coming here every day and doing all this heavy lifting and digging and you-know,' he mimed several inscrutable activities that involved bending his knees and reaching for the ground, a performance that lasted a surprising length of time, 'and we're all just sitting back and enjoying the fruits of your labour and not lifting a finger to help. So here we are. Lifting a finger to help. I swear, I swear on my life, we're not after your jobs.'

Fran had covered her mouth during the miming sequence but, by the end of Matthew's endearing speech, she was openly laughing. It was a liberating thing after so long to laugh like that. The absurd noises she produced shocked herself even as she was making them. She giggled often with Ky, of course, but the fit that took hold of her now was different. Matthew's eyes flitted uncertainly from the ground to Fran to Lugh—who was himself looking at her oddly.

'I am sorry,' said Fran, regaining control. 'You made me laugh.'

'Aye, so it seems,' he replied, smiling broadly again.

'Who's with you?' she said matter-of-factly, making up for her lapse into the ridiculous. 'You kept saying we. We thought this, here we are. Whose fingers are doing all the lifting?'

Abel was already in the chicken coop collecting eggs. He emerged from the shed with a full basket just as Fran opened the gate into the yard. The hens, at least twenty of them, rushed out in a flood of riotous clucking. Fran shooed the birds away from the gate and said she ought to show her new helpers the ropes before they lost the golden goose too.

'There's a golden goose?' Abel cried in astonishment.

'No, sweetheart, it's just a metaphor. It means the thing that meets all your needs. You know, the golden goose, Jack and the beanstalk, the giant and all that?'

Neither Abel nor Matthew had heard of these things, so Fran introduced them to fairytales while she showed them the routines she had established in the farmyard: the chuck-chuck noises she made to draw the chickens away from the coop before she collected their eggs; the root vegetable plots that were ready to be harvested now and the brassicas she was saving for seeds later; the hives that could be left until the bees woke from their hibernation in the spring, and the Victorian greenhouse with its tomatoes and grape vines and exotic collection of citruses, apricot, fig and olive trees from the

Mediterranean. Lugh sat on the stone wall, watching morosely as Matthew asked serious questions about magic beans and Fran, laughing frequently, tried her best to explain how the inexplicable always occurs in stories. It was only later in the morning, when their baskets were full, that Fran realised Lugh was missing and called abstractedly for him to join them. From his perch on the wall, Lugh dropped to the ground and followed at a distance.

'Truthfully?' asked Matthew, bending down to brush snow from the leaves of a herb from which Fran claimed that she made soap. 'What with beanstalks and talking bears, I've no idea when you're being straight-up and when you're telling stories.'

'Straight up, it's soapwort,' she said, stooping down beside him to rub a leaf between her fingers. She brought the scent to her nose and then to his. 'When it's ripe, they'll be a crop of pink soap bars growing like potatoes underneath every plant.'

'Crikey,' said Matthew, shaking his head in wonder.

'Oh, come on,' Fran cried as she elbowed him off balance. 'Surely you know that's too absurd to be true.'

Standing behind them and attending to every word, Abel snorted and turned to Lugh. 'She said soap grows underground like pink potatoes,' Abel explained as though Lugh had not been present.

'I know,' Lugh replied irritably. He could not understand why Abel had taken it upon himself to repeat what his own friend had just said. He could hear perfectly well for himself: he did not need a mediator. Besides, he knew all about that herb. 'It is soapwort,' he added petulantly.

The two boys blinked warily at each other.

At the end of the morning, Fran showed them where the thermometer hung on the wall of the milking shed and told them to keep a record of the daily temperature. No cows were kept in the milking shed now, she said, but she had heard bells in the forest and was convinced that a herd of goats had been left to roam free. If they should ever see one, a nanny goat in particular, preferably pregnant and with full udders, they should capture it and bring it here.

'So, the golden goose story,' mused Abel as they locked the gate behind them and headed up towards the big house, 'that's just a lie, then?'

'Well, no, not a lie exactly. It's a story, like any other story that's passed down through the generations,' she replied. 'When stories like that are told over and over again, they become reference points, like signposts or landmarks, that we can use to understand the world better. Or they help to give meaning to a situation. So, if you ever said to me something like magic beans or beanstalk or golden goose, it would trigger off a whole bunch of images in my head. Come on, surely you must know some stories? I know you do. What about the flood and the ark?'

'That's not a story,' Abel laughed incredulously and then, turning serious, asked, 'is it?'

'Well, some people believe it happened. And others think it's just a story.'

'Are you a believer?' Abel slowed his pace and fell behind even Lugh, who had been sullenly dragging his feet. 'Or are you—one of those others?'

Fran and Matthew stopped walking at the same moment and looked at each other. They both felt awkward at the sudden turn in the conversation, as though a chasm had opened up and all the morning's playfulness had drained into it, never to be repeated again.

'I think that all stories can have important meanings,' replied Fran, carefully measuring the weight of each word, 'regardless of whether or not they actually happened.'

'Aye, like parables,' said Matthew, smiling again.

'Yes, I suppose like parables,' she agreed.

They kicked through the snow on their way towards the big house but the extravagant sense of fun that had brightened their morning was over.

The old man took his time answering their knock on the front door, as was his custom. Fran was convinced that he intentionally left them waiting outside, counted to a thousand or took another book down from his shelf to peruse, solely to reinforce some feudal sense of authority over them, his peasantry. When he did eventually appear, he accepted his morning bundle of firewood and basket of produce from Fran with declarations of gratitude and offered, as a kindness, to examine what she had packed in her own.

'Golly, there are a lot of you today. Have you been breeding?' he chuckled, evidently pleased by his naughtiness. His eyes passed briefly over each of their faces, lingering on Abel's with a flicker of recognition though he did not comment on the youth's reappearance.

'It's too cold for such shenanigans today,' Fran replied with forced bonhomie. 'Has the Gentleman made a decision about the library yet? You did say you would ask him.'

The old man raised his eyebrows expectantly, indulgently, as though this was the first he had heard of the subject. He waited with extreme politeness for the favour to be asked again. Fran took a deep breath and obliged.

'We talked to you before about using the library in the house,' Fran explained patiently. 'You very kindly said you would ask the Gentleman if it would be okay. Don't you remember?'

'I did? Oh, I did, I did.' He clapped his hands gleefully like a wonderful thing had just been achieved. 'Yes, naturally the Gentleman would not be pleased if an army of muddy clodhoppers came traipsing all over his expensive drawing-room carpets, would he? Can you imagine his face? But, yes, he did say he'd consider your request most carefully. Most carefully. Of course, those books are his pride and joy, enormously sentimental. And I've no doubt he'd grant your request in a jiffy if some truly helpful little person could be called upon to keep his reading room spick and span.' Here, the old man's gaze drifted towards Abel. 'Someone to dust the books occasionally, perhaps polish the shelves and skirting boards for an hour or two each day? But yes, absolutely. The Gentleman will consider your request most carefully. Thank you so much.'

'Fucking Rumpelstiltskin,' Fran hissed under her breath after the old man had closed the door on them.

Matthew nodded in agreement, laughed a little too long and loud, and finally confessed, 'I don't know what that means.'

'You don't know Rumpelstiltskin either?'

'Never heard of no Rumping-Stilting.'

Fran shook her head and, sighing, briefly introduced them to another fairytale. 'Once upon a time, there was a miller who was very poor but who had a beautiful daughter...'

Behind the front door of the manor house, the old man listened to the conversation until their voices disappeared down the lane. 'Rumpelstiltskin,' he repeated sourly to himself as he gave up eavesdropping and walked down the hallway towards the kitchen. 'Father Ambrose to you.'

At the foot of the staircase, he paused and glanced at the basket of vegetables, eggs and salad leaves he carried in his hand. 'We'll have a spot of lunch after communion,' he said quietly to himself. Then, turning to the staircase that curved upwards to the landing above, he said more loudly so as to be heard in the attic, 'Perhaps a spot of lunch after communion, yes?'

There was, of course, no reply. The old man's voice echoed through the house and returned empty-handed. No matter, he would prepare two plates as usual—perhaps fried eggs today for a change—and carry them both up to that room in the tower. The old man, Father Ambrose, always took his lunch with the Gentleman upstairs. It was a regular custom, one of those small daily pleasures of living together with an old chum. Their friendship stretched back more than sixty years—or was it seventy now? —back to the mists of a distinguished preparatory school where they had both suffered the same unspeakable treatment in the dormitories at the hands of senior boys. In time, naturally enough, they themselves had become senior boys and the boot was on the other foot, so to speak. So long ago, so much water under the bridge. And later, when the Diocese had to move him quickly and with as little fuss as possible, first from one parish and then from another— and for the most trifling of reasons—he had always been supported by the Gentleman, always. In the end, it made perfect sense for him to accept his old friend's invitation and retire to this remote house. Besides, they had always shared the same tastes, enjoyed the same diversions. It did make things so much simpler.

Chuckling to himself, the old man called upstairs, 'You don't want an army of muddy clodhoppers traipsing across the drawing-room carpets, do you? Do you? Gosh, no.'

In the kitchen, Father Ambrose laid a frying pan on the stove and waited for the iron to heat up. One egg each should be sufficient, he thought as he prepared a salad. He would probably have to polish off both of their servings again because the Gentleman never touched a thing on his own plate, not nowadays. The Gentleman never did much at all since he had died naturally, so peacefully, in his armchair some three—or possibly four— years ago. The Gentleman was still good company nonetheless. He still seemed to possess the same old tastes, enjoy the same old diversions. That, at least, was some consolation for the old man.

THE CURTAINS IN THE SICKROOM were always closed; Mother made sure of that. She had laid cushions on the floor beside the bed where she spent most of the time on her knees, either whispering for a miracle or holding Enoch's hand in her own tight grasp. Throughout her night-time vigil, she watched her son's placid face for a sign that her prayers were being answered. When Rhea arrived in the mornings, always with two cups of tea and some comment on how improved Enoch looked, Mother stood up slowly and rubbed the pins-and-needles from her legs. She would only then visit the bathroom, as though she had endured discomfort all night long just waiting for someone to relieve her shift. She was determined that Enoch should never be left alone. When she returned to the sickroom, she invariably found that Rhea had opened a window.

'Just to let a little fresh air in,' Rhea explained each day. 'Gets so stuffy here, doesn't it? So long as he's all rugged up, won't do him the slightest harm.'

Without a word, Mother would close the window, re-draw the curtains and return to her station on the bedside cushion. After that one night of inconsolable anguish in the forest, her face had hardened back into its customary stoniness, never to be cracked again. It had taken several days for Rhea to elicit more than a monosyllabic response from the woman to offers of food, tea, more tea, and enquiries about her own health. Eventually, Rhea's indefatigable chatter and my-dearing had worn her down and they had reached a truce of sorts.

'Isn't it odd,' Rhea had said one evening, 'I still don't know your name. It wouldn't be very appropriate for me to call you Mother, would it? I must be more than ten years older than you.'

Rhea had laughed warmly. Mother had stared in cold silence at her son's unconscious face.

'And Mrs Mann sounds far too formal and distant, don't you agree?' Rhea had persisted. 'What about your husband, what does he call you?'

'He would call me Mother and I would call him Father. But now he's been taken.' She turned to Rhea with a look of absolute triumph on her face. 'My husband has gone to the Lord. So now he can't call me anything at all, can he?'

'Come now, dear, we don't know what's happened to him for sure, do we?'

'Yes, we do. I do. Mother knows.'

There was a great deal of confusion over what exactly had occurred in the forest. Matthew and Mark were the only ones close to knowing, but even their versions conflicted. Matthew was open, Mark said little. Everyone agreed that it had been Enoch's idea to go hunting. They had all heard the rustlings in the undergrowth at night, observed hoof tracks in the dirt during the day. Enoch said that the beasts of the forest had been put there to provide them with meat. Enoch said that Father, Uncle Joe, Matthew, Mark and himself would gather what the Lord had provided and they would not return empty-handed. Enoch said they would be gone for a few days. They were gone for months.

They had lost the stream on the second day and never found it again until the last, that day they returned to the camp. There were other bodies of water, black pools, red rapids, rivers that ran in hungry circles and ate their own tails in an endless loop, leading the men back to places they had been lost before. They dug traps and laid in wait. Matthew said they never caught a living thing; Mark said they killed plenty. Matthew said they lived on berries, leaves and bitter-tasting mushrooms; Mark said they divided tough meat. Matthew said the dogs disappeared early on; Mark said they lasted until the end. Matthew said their fingers turned into white icicles at night; Mark said they scorched their hands on fire. They ran from a black boar that spoke their names backwards; they chased a hairless goat that ran on two legs. Uncle Joe was the first to be killed; Father was the first to die. Enoch tried to save them both; Enoch claimed that he tried to save them both. It was the boar that staked Enoch. No, it was the goat, the goat that turned.

'The Lord took my husband away, my brother Joe, and my unborn child,' Mother had said. 'The Lord planted a miracle inside me, such a precious, little sacred thing. And it was miraculous, it was, to be bearing fruit at my age when the tree is all but bare. He put it there to prove his love and then he took it away to test mine. I must have passed, mustn't I? Aye, I must have. He brought Enoch back to me, like he was the one I'd been carrying all along. My firstborn, born again. And that is a comfort. That's the miracle. You're not married, are you?'

'No, dear. I almost was once, once upon a time.' Rhea smiled and was about to say more but Mother cut her short.

'So you don't have children.' This time, it was not so much a question as an accusation. 'Aye, thought so. If you did, you'd know.'

'Know what, dear?'

'What love is. Real love. What it does to you. How it changes you, gives you intuition and insights that no barren woman could ever understand. It's a terrible, terrible gift, motherhood, but a blessing too. Aye, it's a blessing. Them that are too selfish to have children will never know what a blessing it is. I pity them, I do, that lack such love. I do, I pity you.'

Rhea had looked down at the knitting in her hands and thought for a long time about what she should say. For once, she decided to say nothing.

One morning, a week or more after Enoch had been brought to the house, Rhea followed her usual routine of examining the young man's wounds, changing his bandages and seeing to his hydration. Mother's eyes were closed throughout the process, her lips pressed against her knuckles as she murmured words only she could hear. When they had each finished their rituals, Rhea sat down in the corner chair and took up her knitting. Mother whispered her fierce amens and settled into a less uncomfortable position on the cushion.

'Nippy as anything out there today,' Rhea observed. 'Had a terrible night with this cough.'

Mother nodded her approval.

'Francesca says it'll be the equinox soon, then we'll all notice the lighter evenings, longer days. She wants to hold a little shindig to celebrate, bless her.'

'God save us.' Mother took hold of Enoch's hand in both of hers as though to keep his dreams safe from such talk.

'Oh no, dear, it's all natural. It's just the seasons doing what they do. Happens every year.'

'When the people went whoring after strange gods, the Lord turned his face against them.'

'I'm not sure it's got very much to do with strange gods. Or whoring for that matter,' Rhea speculated. She was constantly bewildered by the other woman's vexations. Nothing she ever said seemed to satisfy or placate or, at a bare minimum, not offend Mother. Rhea shrugged and concentrated on knitting Lugh's jumper for a while, finished one row, swapped needles, began on another. Outside, they could hear the blackbirds singing. Someone was digging in the gardens behind the house, probably Matthew now that Fran had shown him how to prepare the ground for spring vegetables.

'I heard about this meeting of yours,' Mother said suddenly with unexpected interest.

'Yes, dear. I told you about it yesterday. Don't you remember?'

'Luke told me about it last night.'

Rhea lay down her needles and, leaning forward to share a confidence, said, 'Well, there's been some silly disagreement about the fire being alight during the daytime. And Fran wanted a tree or two cut down for firewood but, well, let's just say that Mark is very possessive about the axe. Now there's so many of us living side by side, it would be nice to agree some common rules so we can all get on with each other, don't you agree?'

'The only laws we need are those of the Lord.'

Rhea wanted to ask what the Lord had ordained about lighting fires during the day or neighbours sharing an axe. Instead, she sat back in the chair and cleaned the lenses of her spectacles on her cardigan sleeve.

'I shall not be there,' Mother added, raising her chin and smiling slightly as though she had won an argument. 'I shan't be leaving my son's bedside till my prayers are answered.'

Rhea attempted to persuade her to attend, but Mother's mind was made up.

'Ruth will be there,' said Rhea, trying an alternative strategy, 'and I know she'd be so pleased to see you. You must be very proud of her. She really is such a wonderful young woman.'

'Woman?' Mother laughed. 'A woman's not a real woman until she's given birth.'

'Now I have to disagree with you, my dear. That's not actually true, anatomically speaking.'

'Anatomically,' Mother scoffed as though to say, what would you know? She did not speak again for the rest of that day.

❧

THE SUNSET WAS HIDDEN BY clouds, a dense swathe of pink and grey that promised to unload yet more snow. Walking home after locking the chickens in the coop for the night, Fran drew the rim of her woollen scarf over her nose and stopped to look up at a great bird of prey that was circling slowly overhead. If she had access to Rumpelstiltskin's library, she would be sure to find some book that would help her identify this raptor. She knew by sight and song most basic garden birds, blackbirds and song thrushes, crows and starlings, but birds of prey were beyond her knowledge. The wingspan of this one was spectacular, and she wondered whether it was perhaps an eagle from the mountains, if there were eagles on those mountains, that had ventured down for a taste of forest meat. She was glad to have locked the chickens up for the night.

Coming home through the back door, she found Ky sitting at the kitchen table scribbling away in one of the notebooks. Since Ruth had provided them with writing paper, they had sorted the ledgers into various functions. Ky had taken one book for herself to write up their first-hand account of the troubles, which she wryly referred to as *A Herstory of the Modern World*. Fran had taken two notebooks, one for use as a herbal in which she penned sketches, descriptions and the medicinal and culinary uses of plants that she found growing in the forest. The other book she used as an almanac, keeping detailed records of her sowings and reapings, crop yields and seed production, weather observations and the like. She hoped this approach would improve their harvests in the years to come. The fourth ledger had been put aside for tonight's meeting, and it was this book that Ky was now assiduously writing in.

'How's the magnus opus coming along, Herodotus?' Fran asked as she hung up her coat and unlaced her boots.

'Herodotus?' Ky chewed the end of her ink pen for a moment and then announced, 'I think I prefer Herodota, Mother of Herstory. Herodota… that is a title I could live with.'

'Are you writing about how ravishing I am?'

'Invariably. It's an epic about your pre-Raphaelite hair and Rossetti looks, and those bee-stung lips always slightly ajar like you're swallowing flies. The face that broke a thousand hearts. No ordinary mortal can resist.' Ky laid down her pen and rubbed her tired eyes. 'Talking of breaking hearts, how's your toy boy? Not Lugh, the other one.'

'Here's a thing. I'm not even going to dignify that with a response.'

'You're right, I'm sorry.' Ky folded her arms on the table and shook her head as though she were truly penitent. 'How's Saint Matthew the Perpetually Erect?'

'Fuck off, Zachariadou,' Fran sang in a don't-get-me-angry voice.

'I know, I know. That was childish and I'm out of order. I really am sorry, my love. I promise not to make fun of your boyfriend until his balls have dropped.'

'What's sad is that you spent your whole day practising this.' Fran lifted the lid from the pot on the stove, inhaled the steam and gave the stew a stir. 'Just for the record...'

'Yes, yes, you've said it all before. He's not your boyfriend and he's twenty-three and a half years old or whatever,' Ky paused to re-open her ledger, 'and his balls have already dropped. Probably. As it happens, I've actually been working on something interesting for tonight. Basic rules for the assembly: respecting other speakers, not interrupting, submitting a motion and the like. You want to add something? Oh, and—please Miss— can I be Scribe?'

'Scribe, not secretary?'

'Scribe sounds so much more Herodota, don't you think?'

'You can be whatever you like, Zachariadou,' said Fran, leaning over Ky's shoulder to see her notes. 'I get the feeling you've done this before.'

'I do have previous experience in organised dissent.'

While Fran was reading and making favourable noises, Rhea opened the back door and ushered Lugh and Ruth into the kitchen. Rhea fussed with their coats and scarves, and told Ruth to go and make herself comfortable in the sitting room.

'Poor dear Ruth, she almost didn't come,' Rhea whispered over the kitchen table. 'Took some persuading. Not easy being the only girl in a litter of so many boys. And, really, what is all that penance nonsense about?'

Ky considered this statement for a moment and then scribbled something else in her ledger.

Outside, the heavy bank of cloud had eclipsed the sunset and a few feathers of snow were already swirling in the air. The flakes latched onto Abel's black hair and the downy fur that darkened his chin, melting instantly. Standing with Matthew at the front door of Fran's house, Abel raised his knuckle but did not knock. Both brothers had been eager to attend but, now they had arrived, each felt reluctant to enter.

'What's wrong? Are you Abel or unable,' said Matthew, using the old family taunt.

'Abel. What's your excuse?' he said, knocking on the door.

Rhea flapped the two brothers inside and, peering through the thickening blizzard, caught sight of Luke and Mark loitering in the lane. She scolded them for picking their noses and ordered them to make up their minds: in or out. Harried into a decision, they entered. To accommodate nine bodies in the front room, Ky removed most of the furniture and laid cushions on the floor. It was still overcrowded and, during the first few minutes of settling down, Abel could sense that everyone felt ill at ease.

'No one should light fires during the day,' Luke declared with an impatient, barely contained anger. It was an unexpected eruption that caused everyone to stare at him in wonder, except for Mark who was nodding in prearranged agreement. The meeting could have broken down into disorder before it had even begun, had not Ky instantly agreed with him.

'And I do agree, wholeheartedly,' she said. 'I'm only sorry that I didn't recognise the danger first. Anyone can see the smoke from the chimneys for miles around, right?'

'Aye,' Luke nodded, though he was so taken aback he could think of nothing more to add.

Ky said she looked forward to supporting him when this important issue was raised at the appropriate time. First, she said, the terms of the assembly needed to be agreed. Briskly, she rattled through the code she had prepared: protocols and etiquette, rights and responsibilities, duties of the chair, the scribe, simple majorities and so on.

'One final thing,' said Ky. 'Penance is suspended during the session of an assembly. All those in favour of adopting this code?'

She raised her own hand, as did Fran, Rhea and Lugh. One by one, the others in the room put their hands in the air because that seemed to be the action expected of everybody.

'Comrades,' Ky announced with a slap on the floor, 'we have ourselves a constitution.'

Abel did not fully understand the procedures of the evening. He signed his name in the ledger when it was passed around the room because Ky asserted that they had all agreed the code and should all put their names to it. Most of the time, he watched Matthew and raised his hand whenever his older brother did, which was always in accordance with Fran. Sometimes Abel put his hand up with Luke and Mark because he felt sorry that no one ever agreed with them. He was mystified by the heated exchange about the axe and common ownership, so he abstained on that one. The discussion on daytime fires was interesting because it was the only time that Ky and Luke agreed with each other. Rhea, however, became distressed when she argued that the stove had been alight all winter without incident, and she would not have recovered from her illness without it, and why couldn't each household decide for itself whether or not to light its own fires? Abel liked Rhea and it was a sad thing to see her upset so he raised his hand when she did. He was relieved when she was permitted to keep her stove alight all day if that was what she wanted.

When there seemed nothing more to discuss and Ky was ready to close the book, Mark, who had barely spoken a word all evening, interrupted and said that there was one last thing.

'Mother doesn't want you telling any more lies,' he said, pointing his finger at Fran. Mark glared at her with such a deep and unexpected abhorrence that Fran reacted instinctively by laughing. Sitting cross-legged on the floor beside her, however, Matthew's face hardened.

'You can laugh, but Mother knows exactly what you are,' Mark continued. All the frustrations and defeats that he and Luke had suffered throughout the evening seemed to have crystallised around this one last fiery outburst at Fran. 'You're to tell no more wicked stories to Abel, no more magic and beans. And no one should be even sitting in the same room with our Ruth while she's doing penance. And you,' this time Mark aimed his finger at Matthew, 'you're the eldest here, Matthew Mann, and you should be ashamed—*ashamed*—to side with god-haters against your own flesh and blood.'

Matthew jumped to his feet with such ferocity that everyone thought he would kick Mark where he sat. Abel flinched in expectation and grabbed Ruth's arm. There was a moment of awful silence when anything could have happened, had not the sound of a woman's voice been heard in the street.

One by one they stood up and went to see what was happening outside, a collective retreat from the scene of imminent violence, leaving Matthew standing and Mark waiting.

The snow had fallen heavily during the assembly, and now everything in the lane had become a smooth, anonymous white. Mother was also in white for she had draped a sheet over her head and shoulders against the blizzard and was leaning out of her upstairs window, crying in an albatross voice, 'God is great.'

And the snow continued to fall as she called. And all those who had come outside at the sound of that voice, those who were standing in the lane with their faces upturned to Mother, knew that Enoch had finally woken from his sleep.

CHAPTER SEVEN
PENTECOST

ALL MORNING, THERE HAD BEEN noises coming from the house next door. Ruth sat in her own kitchen and listened to the scraping of table and chair legs on kitchen tiles, the lifting of bed frames upstairs, and the deep, barked sentences of her brothers who were forbidden to even look at her. The family that had cast her out now occupied the space on the other side of her wall. They had arrived at the house on the far end of the terrace, Number One, and now Number Three had fallen into their hands too. For reassurance, Ruth clutched the key to her own front door, Number Five, in the pocket of her jeans.

She looked around the room at the few artefacts she had accumulated during her months of precious independence. The willow-patterned teapot on the kitchen table, the yellow curtains embroidered with hawthorn leaves and white blossom, the mismatched cups that she had lined up neatly in a row beside the clock that did not work on the wooden dresser: all talismans of her new life. Most impressive of all, standing on the mantelpiece in her sitting room, was the globe that Fran had lent to her, with its blue oceans and green continents and grey mountains bound together by the mysteries of mass and gravity. And yet now, listening to the bangings coming from next door, Ruth realised just how fragile were all these pieces of her new Heaven and Earth.

The fire in the stove had gone out overnight, but she would not relight it. She knew that she could let it burn all day if she wanted. At the assembly, she had raised her hand with Rhea and most of the others, and that question had been decided. Still, she did not want to draw attention to herself. There were enough reasons why she was at fault without adding to them. The smoke would give her away. Listening to the thuds and the voices next door, she took the key from her pocket and, with its sharpest edge, began to rake pale indentations on her forearm.

THE METAL BLADE CUT EASILY through the earth. There had been no heavy rain for weeks, but the snow had melted with the promise of spring and now the black, peaty soil was well saturated, pliable enough for Fran to dig into new seed beds. Much of the ground behind their terrace had already been prepared, shaped into rows with deep drainage channels between, and planted with onion, leek and carrot seeds from the old man's vegetable plot. Rhea was often out helping in the garden too; together they had planted a line of potatoes in the shadiest corner of the garden where Fran wanted to cut down more trees if only she were permitted to use the axe. There were no green shoots yet and it remained to be seen if she had sowed too precipitously. Fran suspected that she should have waited until after the last snow. With no one to guide her and no access to the library, she was cultivating their food production in the dark.

This new section of ground she was preparing, ploughing by hand and spade every afternoon, was destined for a more advanced crop. In their last few days at the farmhouse, the days after the windstorm had ended and before Lugh's brother had died, Fran had wandered the neighbouring fields of overripe grain and performed her own private harvest. She had filled a plastic bag with wheat and barley seed-heads, and brought these mixed grains on their journey over the mountain to the forest. If they were ever going to eat bread again, real bread not Rhea's fried potato cakes, then it all depended upon her success with these grains. The earliest farmers had managed to do it, this much Fran had gleaned from Ky's encyclopaedia. The cultivation of grains had accompanied the foundation of the first cities in Sumer, Mesopotamia, the Indus Valley. Without bread, there would be no civilization: the one was intimately bound to the other. With each cut and slice of the earth beneath her spade, the continuation of so much depended.

It was a heavy thought and one that was ridiculed instantly by a crow that had watched Fran turn the soil but now uttered a shocking laugh and abandoned the garden in a crack of black wings. Fran looked up from the furrows she had made and decided to leave the digging of Sumer for another day.

The sky was an unbroken grey with no sign of sun. She reckoned that it must be getting on towards dusk so she took off her gloves, wiped her brow and hesitated when she sensed that she was being observed. Not by the crow: she had been fully conscious of that bird's attention and had seen him fly the field in a fit of contempt. No, this was another pair of eyes altogether, though she could see no one around. If it were Matthew, she would have known at once. He would have strode towards her, tall and gangly and flailing his long arms as though he were climbing a steep hill to reach her. He would come with an open smile and an instinctive willingness to follow wherever she led, to fetch a ball or go for a walk. Matthew would not hide and skulk.

Perhaps it was Ky, who often watched her like a cat from the shadows, from a quiet window or sitting on the doorstep while whittling something sharp and practical. No, not her either, thought Fran as she squinted at the house. Not now, not lately. Ky's moods, unpredictable at the best of times, were becoming a permanent strain in the household. Her barbed comments about toy boys had turned from the playful to the spiteful to the downright sullen. A few weeks ago, Ky was a dependable digging companion in the garden; now she was rarely to be seen. Her daytime territory was out in the forest. She only came home to eat, lick her wounds and sleep.

Lugh had become equally elusive. The boy still accompanied Fran to the farmyard in the mornings to collect eggs and tend the vegetables, but he vanished after lunch and his whereabouts were a mystery. At least Fran's bed was her own domain once more. Without a word, Lugh had taken to sleeping in Rhea's empty bedroom, as the older woman inevitably slept in an armchair downstairs. It was a subtle, unannounced shift in household dynamics and one that seemed to have occurred naturally. Fran had been wanting to curl up alone or stretch beneath her own sheets for months, but she did feel the emptiness left by the boy's desertion. Development, she corrected herself. He was fast becoming a man. Wherever he was now, it was not Lugh who was watching her.

In the distance, either through or above the trees, came the clinking of a metal bell and then another and another, like a shower of coins falling on a tin plate, everywhere at once and yet nowhere to be held accountable. Fran could picture the shape and colour of the bells: beaten copper, hollowed bronze the size of a fist, weather-worn and rusted, but she could not tell what kind of animals were playing this march, whether cows or sheep or goats. Nor had she heard so many of them performing together before. It was a ponderous, chaotic ceremony of spoons, tins, triangles, begging bowls, any old iron processing through the forest. It felt like a twilight announcement, the arrival of the equinox, hoof-marched and cacophonic, wild, timely, ancient.

Fran forgot to think about who might be watching her. Leaving her spade standing upright in the earth, she entered the forest in search of the herd of bells. After she had gone, Mark stayed where he had been spying on her, lying hard on his belly among the apple trees. Fran had left before he could finish, but that did not stop him pushing slowly, rhythmically against the ground. Chewing a blade of grass, Mark shoved until the sap dripped over his teeth.

THE KITCHEN WAS FILLED WITH the fragrance of flowers, perfumed steam and the banishing of nightmares. Rhea had stripped the lavender heads from their stems and left the blossom to steep in a bowl of boiled water. In the absence of basic toiletries, lavender water had become a panacea for many intimate requirements. Sitting at her kitchen table, Rhea folded rags with Ruth and initiated the young woman into the arcana of her own body. Ruth blushed at what Rhea told her and would not have believed most of it if she had not seen those anatomies revealed within the pages of the encyclopaedia. Ruth glanced anxiously at the kitchen window to make sure no one was listening outside or, worse, was about to walk in on their discussion. But Rhea was unabashed and said there should be nothing secret or shameful about the human body.

When Fran came in from the back yard followed by Lugh and Abel, Ruth quickly closed the encyclopaedia. She was immensely relieved that none of them seemed to have overheard.

'I've lost my mind,' said Fran, taking off her boots and unbuttoning her jeans. 'There's a herd of something passing through the forest. Goats,

I think. I went looking for them but couldn't see anything. Only the sound, like an orchestra of bells, absolutely incredible. These two said they heard nothing. So I must have lost my mind. Has Matthew been over yet?'

Fran struggled out of her muddy jeans and slipped into the pyjama bottoms she had hung to warm on the rack above the stove. Abel and Ruth both coloured and stared at the floor, but no one else seemed to mind Fran's naked legs.

'Sorry, dear, not seen hide nor hair of that one for days,' said Rhea, discreetly packing the pile of folded rags into a bag for Ruth. 'Oh, but I am pleased to see young Abel here. He'd better stay for tea, else I'll start to think he's avoiding my cooking.'

'Mother said Enoch needs some peace and quiet because he needs to rest and he's still not himself yet,' Abel said rapidly, anxious to explain himself. 'And Mother asked if I could stay here, just for tonight, because Matthew and Mark and Luke are moving into the house next door, and Mother doesn't want me to get in their way. And tomorrow she's taking me to see the old man, you know, the pastor at the big house, so she asked if it's okay, just for tonight—'

'If you could be in our way instead?' said Rhea, finishing his sentence. 'Of course, dear. Nothing would give us greater pleasure. You'll cope with sharing Lugh's bed, I'm sure.'

The two boys looked at each other for an awkward moment until Lugh shrugged and sat down at the table. Abel sat opposite him, fiddled with the encyclopaedia and nodded uncertainly.

This was not how Fran had imagined they would celebrate the spring equinox. She had anticipated opening the nettle wine, which must surely now have finished fermenting, and had looked forward to seeing Matthew's reaction to alcohol. Matthew had already hinted that he may not be able to attend, but Fran was still disappointed not to see him. His mother probably disapproved. Fran was not entirely sure what it was that his mother disapproved of, but it was safe to assume that she disapproved of most things, homebrew and other women in particular. Still, Fran thought it odd that Abel had been allowed to show up whereas Matthew was denied.

At the kitchen table, Rhea asked Abel and Ruth about their lives before the troubles. As the brother and sister talked about prayer camps and

Bible studies and talking in tongues, interrupting each other and offering clarifications, the taboo of penance between them was tacitly worn away. Half-listening to their stories, Fran unscrewed the airlock on the glass demijohn of wine that had been left to brew all winter, and took a sniff. It smelled green, she thought. Not very strong, as was to be expected, but at least it was not repellent. She syphoned the wine into a couple of empty bottles and took a sip. It tasted green too, a soft green, nettles without the sting, low alcohol content, but with a subtle after-kick of lemon peel. Not quite the disaster she had feared. She stared through the outline of her face, the sad smile reflected in the window pane, and tried to penetrate the darkness without. Matthew still might come, she thought. He might.

'Well, that's not really how it happened at all,' said Rhea, recalling Fran's attention to the kitchen table. Rhea was talking about the beginnings of the troubles, the storms that had taken cities and droughts that shifted borders; the downing of planes, satellites and treaties; the poisoning of water supplies and bombings of nuclear power plants: evacuations, orange skies, fallout. 'It was people that did all those things. Actual people, men and women pushing buttons and following orders from other men and women. There was no Last Day, my dears, no end of days. And, really, what kind of mind would send anyone to a bottomless pit? We know plenty of good people that have gone, don't we, Lugh?' Rhea reached out and took Lugh's hand. 'And then there are those people still doing awful things out there now, like those soldiers at the camps. Francesca, I'm not wrong to tell them this, am I? Do you think it's wrong of me to say this?'

'I don't know,' said Fran, still staring out of the window. 'Maybe we shouldn't question their ideas. After all, we only know what we think we know. Their beliefs or ours: it's all the same in the end. None of it makes any real difference. We are where we are.'

'Bullshit,' said Ky suddenly. She had come home quietly through the front door and had been listening in the hallway while Fran's attention was fixed outside. 'Fucking bullshit.'

'Well, that was quite some entrance,' Rhea laughed and made a clownish gracious-me face at Ruth and Abel, though neither were reassured.

'It really makes no difference?' asked Ky. She glared at Fran with an expression of anger, hurt, even loss. 'So, you and me, we deserve to burn in some pit and that makes no difference?'

'Heck, no,' said Abel excitedly. 'You don't deserve to burn in the bottomless pit, not at all. It's only the unbelievers, the god-haters that get sent there.'

'There is no god, Abel,' Ky said without looking at the boy. 'I can't hate what doesn't exist.'

There was silence for a moment, heavy with tension and the boiling of lavender.

'I'm just saying, maybe we shouldn't rush to judgement on their ideas,' said Fran. She turned her back on Ky and observed the room reflected in the window, everyone in negative, reversed, outlined in distance. 'We have to live with them. That's the bottom line, isn't it? We have to tolerate each other. That's something I know that even you believe in, Zachariadou.'

'And what happens when the thing you tolerate doesn't tolerate you?'

'We have an understanding. It will never come to that.'

'You go that way, then,' Ky replied quietly after a pause. 'If it's all the same, if everything's relative, you go that way, my love. It will be interesting to see how you get on.'

The Ky in the window pane turned around and abandoned the reflected kitchen. Fran continued to stare at the glass until the outlines of the door, the oil-lamp, the figures at the table dissolved in lavender steam and she could only see grey, formless condensation.

⬤

THERE WAS NOT THE THINNEST splinter of a moon anywhere in the sky, though the night was cloudless and glittered with stars. Lugh angled the old brass telescope at one reddish star hovering above the forest. He peered through the eyepiece and played with the focus until he was satisfied. Then he sat on the edge of his bed and waited for Abel to take a look.

'What?' Abel asked with a half-smile. He stood beside the window with his hands in his pockets and rocked back and forth on his heels, not knowing what was expected of him.

'Just look,' said Lugh, touching the eyepiece. 'I dare you to look.'

'But what is it?'

'Mars.'

'What's Mars?'

'It is what it is.'

Abel did not understand, but he put his eye to the metal tube and said nothing for a long minute. Lugh sat patiently on the bed and stroked the spine of the encyclopaedia beside him.

'What is it?' Abel asked again, though this time he spoke quietly, awed.

'Look.' Lugh lay down on the bed and opened the book on a page that had a leaf as a marker. He shifted to make room for Abel beside him, but paused to ask, 'Are your jeans clean?'

'Of course,' said Abel affronted, but he still looked down to check. 'I think so. Why?'

'Because my bed is clean.'

Abel had never wondered whether his trousers were clean enough to lie on a bed before. He knew they were washed sometimes: they must have been. Lugh noticed him hesitating and, taking his own set of pyjamas from under his pillow, handed them to Abel.

'They're clean,' Lugh said simply.

Abel knew that he ought to be grateful but he did not feel it. As he turned his back and undressed in the corner, he only felt more ill at ease. They do things differently here, he thought. They look at strange red lights in the sky. They had rules about wearing pyjamas just to sit on a bed. And, for the first time in his life, there are no evening prayers.

'Look,' said Lugh when they were lying side by side on the blankets, the encyclopaedia propped open on the pillow in front of them. 'Mercury, Venus, Earth, and Mars. That's Mars. That's what we can see tonight. Sometimes we can see Jupiter too, but not tonight.'

The candle that stood on the window ledge gave just enough light to illuminate an elementary map of the solar system. Lugh read aloud fragments of the article that interested him, the clockwise rotation of Venus, the moons of Jupiter, dust storms on Mars. Little of this made any sense to Abel, but he was fascinated by a map of the skies that he had never imagined before, a row of coloured planets running smoothly on curved tracks around the sun, a tiny white moon that clung faithfully to the Earth.

'Does it say more about the moon?' Abel asked when the other boy had finished reading. They were now sitting so close that their shoulders were rubbing, though neither had noticed.

'The moon?'

'Aye, the moon,' said Abel excitedly. 'I dare you to find something about the moon.'

Lugh nodded and turned to a full-page map of the moon. Abel could barely breathe. It was like seeing the photograph of a ghost, or an angel, or a face from his dreams. Not from anybody else's dreams, only his. This is what she looked like in everyday life, in this real world, with all her scars and pockmarks and wrinkled skin. It was her, but it was not her. It was the moon without her make-up, a mythical beast caught in artificial light, in a cage. He thought he would never tear his eyes away. Distantly, he heard Lugh's voice reading more things aloud, but nothing really caught his attention until the other boy said the moon was drifting away from the Earth.

'She's leaving us?' Abel asked with an expression of abject sadness. 'She's going away?'

'Not yet,' said Lugh. He frowned at Abel, not unkindly but with concern. 'Not for tonnes of years. We'll all be dead by then. What do you want to look at now?'

Abel touched the moon's face: it felt neither hot nor cold. He traced the coastline of her eyes, the Sea of Tranquillity, Sea of Rains. Not forever, she had told him as much. She was here for now. Reluctantly, he let her go and told Lugh that he could choose what they looked at next.

'Antibiotics,' said Lugh quickly, as though he had been waiting for his turn to choose.

'Oh good,' Abel replied, though it was an alien-sounding word that he had never heard before. He understood less of antibiotics than he did of the planets, but he listened politely as Lugh read sentences that meant nothing to him. If there had been pictures, he thought that might have helped. He imagined it was something about prisons and war, possibly robots.

'My brother's dead,' Lugh said when he had finished reading. He did not look up from the book but kept his eyes on the single word, Antibody, at the top of the page. 'He died because she wouldn't let him have antibiotics.'

'Oh,' Abel nodded, finally understanding. He was right, it must be something to do with the war. 'Who wouldn't let him have the anti-robots?'

'Antibiotics,' Lugh said sharply. 'She wouldn't. Ky wouldn't. She said we weren't allowed to get antibiotics from the town. So Michael died and she buried him in the orchard. She killed him.'

'The unbeliever?'

'Yes,' said Lugh decisively. He was not entirely sure what that meant, but he knew it was something to do with the argument in the kitchen earlier. 'Her.'

'My brother died as well,' said Abel after a pause.

'Did he?' Lugh immediately thought of Enoch. Enoch was alive, he was sure. That one had recovered and woken from his sleep, whereas his own brother, Michael, had died. 'Which one?'

'Well, when I was born, I had another brother with me,' said Abel, talking freely as his eyes darted around the room, 'and he was born at the same time. Well, he was actually born a few minutes before me, but it was roughly at the same time on the same day, but Mother said he was dead when he came out but she still called him John. And then I was born a few minutes later and they didn't know I was there because they weren't expecting me as well, and Mother said it was a miracle that God made me to come out alive because it made up for our John who came out dead. So that's how I've got a dead brother too.'

The two boys looked at each other for a moment, shoulder to shoulder, one with an expression of permanent wonder and the other frowning darkly.

Leaning against the wall outside their bedroom, Ky raised her face and sighed. She had never heard Lugh say more than a handful of words before, and now she had overheard him reveal so much. They were whispering now, the boys, as though their dares had reached a different depth of intimacy. Ky did not need to know anymore. Carefully, so as not to make a noise on the floorboards, she crept into her own bedroom and quietly closed the door.

❤

EVERY BIRD IN THE FOREST seemed to be choiring the morning as Mother closed her front door and headed towards the house opposite. A month ago, the world was locked in ice and hard snow: now it was bathed in golden spring sunlight. Things could not be more different, thought Mother as she took the path around the back of the house and perched on the wall of the back yard.

Rhea noticed her through the window at once and came out to offer a cup of tea.

'Just here for my son, then we'll be off,' Mother replied with a nod and a difficult smile.

'An absolute pleasure, dear,' Rhea muttered to herself as she climbed the stairs to the landing. 'No need to thank me, he was no trouble at all. Stop it now, don't be silly.'

When she opened the bedroom door, Rhea noticed nothing out of the ordinary in the two boys curled up together. She told Abel that his mother was waiting for him in the back yard and left him to put his clothes on.

'Oh, heck,' Abel said after she had closed the door. He grabbed his underpants and, with his back to the bed, began to dress at once. He buttoned up his shirt and, looking down at himself, noticed just how dirty his jeans were in the sunlight.

Abel thought he had said goodbye to Lugh when he closed the bedroom door, but he would never be sure. He knew he had not even looked at the other boy. In fact, Lugh might still be asleep and would wake up alone and wonder what had happened. It was a bit like the Rapture, Abel thought as he ran down the stairs: one will be left sleeping in bed and one would be taken. He would have to tell Lugh about that when he saw him next, then they could look up Rapture in the encyclopaedia. Maybe Lugh would find it funny too. Maybe he wouldn't.

Abel was still smiling when he came outside and stood before Mother. She had tied back her hair and was wearing her smartest white blouse and a long, black skirt. The little crucifix around her neck glinted gold in the sunlight. At her feet lay a small, plastic bag.

'There you are,' she said after a moment's scrutiny. Something was on her mind but she was not yet ready to divulge it. Perhaps she never would. She picked up the bag and they set off down the lane. Abel flattened his unruly hair, tucked in his shirt, brushed down his trousers.

'Ants in your pants?' Mother teased. 'Not nervous, are you?'

'I don't know,' he replied with a shrug.

'He's a man of God, so there's no need to fear him. He's full of wisdom and comfort. I've talked with him often about your father and your uncle, God bless their souls. Prayed with him too in that chapel in the big house. The world is full of wolves, son, wolves, but Father Ambrose is a shepherd. He calls himself a priest, but to us he's a pastor and it all amounts to much the same thing. You're to stay with him for a while, like we talked about. You're to learn to be a man of God too. A man of God sees what's in your heart, knows all your secrets. Long as you've nothing to hide, you've no cause to be afraid of him. You've nothing to be ashamed of now, have you?'

Abel laughed uneasily and said nothing.

'You've a good soul, a clean soul,' she said. She glanced up and commented on the sunlight, the birdsong, the cloudless sky. Abel sensed that she was preparing him for something else, something cold and sharp, incisive. His stomach clenched in anticipation. 'Course, you wouldn't have done anything to be ashamed of last night, would you?'

'Nothing,' he said far too quickly. Or perhaps he uttered it too slowly and the word sounded exaggerated and off-key and not all convincing. Either way, he blushed and smiled blindly at the ground. It was taking them forever to reach the big house.

'Nothing?' Mother raised an eyebrow. She looked like she was about to smile, like she wanted to smile, but could not bring herself to perform the act if someone was lying to her. 'I see.'

They walked along in silence for a few steps more. Abel concentrated on the sound of their shoes on the broken concrete, kicking stones, clacking.

'Those people, those friends of yours, they said their prayers last night, didn't they?' Mother spoke with such contrived expectancy that Abel felt sorry for disappointing her. 'They didn't say their evening prayers? Now, that saddens me. That does make me sad. And no morning prayers neither? I see. And what sort of things would they have talked to you about?'

Mother flicked question after question at her son as though she were asking out of friendly curiosity, but Abel sensed that she was fly-fishing for specific sins. His mind became as knotted as his stomach and he could think of little to say in response. After a while, his little turned into nothing at all. Mother looked hurt, betrayed by the son that had once been her miracle.

'I see,' she said coldly when she accepted that he would give her nothing.

After an eternity of silence, they arrived at the big house. The paint on the immense front door was peeling in places, revealing dark, damp wood beneath. When Mother tugged on the doorbell chain, Abel watched more paint lift and disperse like dust in the air. Neither of them spoke while they waited underneath the portico. Mother stared down at her feet, stony faced with profound disappointment. Sometimes Abel made a noise in the back of his throat as though he had remembered how to speak but then, just as instantly, forgotten. Eventually, the boy heard the slow grinding of metal devices as a lock was unclasped and the front door opened.

Father Ambrose, wearing his grey habit and gold-rimmed spectacles, greeted them with delighted surprise and some confusion as though he had not expected their visit. The old man rubbed his bald head with exasperation, but he smiled and said that he had been taking a service with the Gentleman upstairs. He would be with them presently if they could make themselves comfortable in the drawing room. Although he was a small man and much older than Mother, he skipped ahead and led them through an unlit hallway towards the bright drawing room with French doors at the back of the house.

'Do make yourselves at home,' he said to Mother as he retreated up the staircase. 'And, really, I don't want you to blame yourself at all. I'm always getting my days in a muddle too. Gosh, happens all the time. Think nothing of it.'

Mother tightened her lips into a smile and alighted on the edge of the sofa cushion. Abel stood with his back to the French doors, his face a mask of unreadable blandness.

'Take your hands out your pockets,' Mother said when they were alone, though she did not look at the boy. Her eyes were fixed on the painting of a trout in the alcove beside the fireplace. 'Sit down, son. You're making me uncomfortable.'

Abel walked to the harpsichord in the corner of the room and lowered himself onto the stool. Mother sucked her teeth disapprovingly, so the boy changed his mind and sat beside her on the sofa instead. His eyes flitted across the large landscape painting that hung above the mantelpiece: a mountain, a forest, a pack of men in red jackets riding horses over a stream, somewhere a fox. They listened to the dull pulse of a grandfather clock, the last working timepiece in the world, its pendulum swinging the seconds of their discomfort.

'How wonderful of you to come, Marion,' the old man said, clapping his hands when he returned to the drawing room. He sat in an armchair next to the sofa and leaned attentively towards Mother. 'And how is your son? I mean the eldest, of course. How is poor dear Enoch?'

'The Lord answered our prayers,' said Mother. 'The Lord saw fit to bring my firstborn back to this world, where he is needed, where he has work to do. I sat at his bedside night and day, and I didn't leave until our prayers were answered. I watched the transfiguration, Father Ambrose. I watched it with my own eyes. Prayer and faith, that's what did it. Prayer and faith.'

'Of course, of course,' said Father Ambrose with deep feeling. In an instant, his face and his manner had shifted from the playful to the profoundly compassionate. He reached out to hold Mother's hand. She straightened her back but did not remove her hand from his touch. 'And you, you have endured so much. So very much. How are you?'

Mother answered each of the clergyman's questions firmly, with the same unshakeable belief in the rightness of things and the mystery of God's ways. Her iciness thawed under the old man's attention. As they conversed and the grandfather clock beat the seconds of the morning away, Abel thought about the name Marion. He had never heard anyone call his mother that before, not even Father. The boy's attention trickled over the curious objects in the drawing room: the brightly painted china cups and silver spoons on the tea-table, the crystal decanters filled with mysterious coloured liquids and potions, the silver candlesticks that were shaped like classical pillars and those that were muscled into the bodies of slaves bearing the weight of illumination. On a table in the alcove, an ancient record player with its brass horn raised in silent, perpetual expectation reminded him of Rhea, of the records she longed to play, of yesterday evening in her kitchen and yesterday night in Lugh's bed. There were so many fine and beautiful things that Abel had never seen before, so much to understand. It was while he was admiring the golden vine leaves that swirled around a vast mirror frame that he realised Father Ambrose had spoken his name. The old man was whispering in one of his intense voices now, his watery-blue eyes fixed on Abel for the first time since they had entered the house.

A vocation was a precious thing, the clergyman said, a sacred duty that requires extraction from the corporeal world and refining in the spiritual.

'It will be hard for him not to see you so often,' Father Ambrose said with great sympathy to Mother, though the old man's gaze had settled on Abel, reading his heart. 'And for you not to see him every day too. Naturally, you can come whenever you feel like it, but I do think—at this delicate stage in the boy's journey—it would be well to give space for the Spirit to act upon him. Though the Church does not consider it as such, I sometimes think of motherhood as a sacramental act, like baptism, say, or ordination. Preparing oneself for the sacrament of ordination is not an easy thing but, if it were easy, there would be no sacrifice. It is through sacrifice that we are purified. And you, Marion, who have sacrificed so much already, so very much, you do understand that, don't you? It takes a tremendous leap of faith, but you do get it, don't you?'

'The world is full of wolves,' Mother replied, nodding resolutely. 'Abel is a good soul, a clean soul. I've no doubt he will become a man of God in your good hands, Father. I carried him for nine months so that he could live. Now it's his turn to give back to the Lord.'

'It will take a little longer than nine months,' the old man chuckled, 'but he will be taken care of, I promise you. If the Lord has given him a vocation, I shall do all I can to help him realise it.'

'Aye, I've no doubt of that.' Mother paused and fiddled with her wedding ring. 'So, he'll be living here for more than a year?'

'More than year.' The old man gazed at the ceiling as though he were calculating fractions. 'I, for example, was in a seminary for three years.'

'Dear Lord. Three years?'

'Well, it is a matter of temperament,' Father Ambrose explained, taking Mother into his confidence. 'To be alone with God day and night, to fast and to pray and to keep the greater silence, immersed in the scriptures, naked in the Spirit... it's not an easy path, the holy life. Many are called, but few are chosen. There was that other boy I told you about, of course, but that was such a disappointment. He upped and left after only a few months, ran off to the woods. Turned completely wild, living like a goat. A sad outcome. You see, it does take a very special kind of soul to answer the call, to serve the Lord, to become Christlike.'

'So be it.' Mother stood up and brushed unseen specks of distraction from her long black skirt. 'It's done. It's agreed.'

Abel stood up as well, not entirely sure of what had just been done or agreed. Mother raised her chin and looked at him strangely. She was smaller than him now, he realised. She was no longer the tower of white iron that once reached to the clouds; she was just an older woman, greying, loosening, wearing her finest skirt and smartest blouse, saying goodbye to her youngest son for an unspecified length of time. She took him by the shoulders and brought him into a peculiar embrace, an adult embrace, a thing that she had never done with him before. He could smell that she had washed her hair this morning.

'Your things are in this bag, just what you need, underpants and whatnot,' she said resolutely. 'Now, you do as you're told and learn your lessons, and the Lord will bless your endeavours. I'll see myself out, Father Ambrose. God bless you.'

Abel watched his mother walk away without a backward glance, her exit played immaculately. The boy wanted to run after her. The drawing room felt too bright, too sterile, a museum of cold curios, empty of all comfort. The old man rose to his feet when he heard the front door close. He smiled at Abel, a secret smile, reassuring and unnerving in equal measure. If Abel's own father had never looked at him before, then this gaze contained an entire childhood of withheld attention. Abel looked down at his own dirty trousers, unable to endure the intensity.

It had not rained for weeks and now the ground felt as hard as rock. Fran was thankful that she had completed most of the hard digging during the thaw. If she had left it any later, it would have been impossible to cut the soil. She threw the weeds onto a heap and stood up to survey her orderly domain. The carrots, leeks and potatoes were already showing strong signs of growth, and the young wheat was like a green mist on the ground, but the onion shoots had only just made a tentative appearance. She must have planted them at the wrong time of year, too late or too early. She would make a note in her ledger to do it differently next time, but first she needed to bring more water from the stream. The taps in all the houses were running slowly of late, as though wherever the supply came from was dwindling, so she had taken to irrigating the garden with stream water. She dropped the weeds in the compost bin and crossed the lane to the back of Matthew's house. As she had anticipated, he was working in his own garden. More accurately, he was holding a fork in his hands and staring absent-mindedly into the trees. It was something that all the brothers did from time to time when no one else was around and there was nothing to disturb them. It was an endearing trait, thought Fran, as though they switched off the batteries when not in use, and came back to life when the world demanded. Or else, in a moment without obligations, simply entered a state of blissful emptiness. Even now, Matthew did not notice the sound of her approaching footsteps on the dry soil.

'Hey, daydreamer,' she called when she was close to him. 'I need someone with muscles to fetch water with me.'

'Francesca,' he said, turning in surprise. Rather than walking towards her with his usual delight, he seemed confused by her arrival and took a step back. 'I was just—'

'I know, you were away with the dryads. So then, muscles? I promise to cut your hair in return. I'm really quite good, so long as you want it short like Ky.'

Matthew did not reply but his deep brown eyes shifted from the dry earth to the trees to the upstairs window in the house behind her, but not at her.

'What is it?' Fran did not turn around but suspected that someone, probably his mother, was watching from the house. She was always watching from the house.

'Water?' he said with a belated smile, and he went to collect his barrel and a bucket.

Fran followed and glanced up at the row of terraced houses. Only the blank sky reflected in the windows, the blue and empty heavens.

'Jack and Jill,' said Fran, as she and Matthew carried the empty barrel between them towards the stream. They each held the rope handles on the side, swinging the barrel slightly. Unevenly too, because Matthew was so tall. 'Although I imagine their pail was smaller.'

Matthew did not know what she was talking about, so Fran sang him the nursery rhyme a couple of times until he picked up the words and tried it out too.

'Weren't you allowed to sing rhymes like that when you were a kid?' she asked.

'Course we were. Like—what's that one about a cradle, and the tree breaking?'

'Rock a-bye baby?'

'Aye, that's the one. And, there was that other that went, here comes a chopper – '

'To chop off your head?' Fran nodded approvingly. 'Oranges and lemons.'

'See, I wasn't brought up on some other planet. And we still do sing on Sundays, of course, though not daft songs like that, mind. Hymns and stuff. O Spirit of the Living God. Shine, Jesus, Shine—you'll know that one, surely. Everyone knows that.' He laughed when Fran shook her head. Now that they were under the trees, sheltered by light green canopies and away from the houses, he seemed to have relaxed into his natural self, at ease with her and with the world. 'But, I swear, we never sang about people falling down hills, breaking crowns. Can't for the life of me figure out the sense in that. You'll say it's a metaphor or something fancy.'

'Or just a rhyme, or a warning to watch where you're treading,' she said as he stumbled on a hidden root. 'Maybe Jack and Jill were two peasants who did all the hard work and ended up dying of exhaustion, ingratitude. Where are your brothers? What do they do all day long?'

'Mark does his fair share, sometimes, often. Aye, he does. And Luke goes hunting.'

'Hunting? Listen, if we broke our crowns, they'd soon have to fetch their own water.'

They walked in silence, listening to the sounds of spring in the forest. Fran was delighted to have caught the simple call of a cuckoo a few weeks ago. Now, amidst the songs of blackbirds and others she could not identify, she heard her first woodpecker drilling a hole in a tree.

'When you're doing that thing you do,' she said after she had enjoyed the music of the forest for a while, 'you know, staring into nothing like you've gone to sleep with your eyes open, like you were back there in the garden, what goes through your head?'

'What thing I do?' he asked as though she had just said the most ridiculous thing ever. Fran gave him a stern look, so he laughed and shrugged good-naturedly. 'I don't know. All sorts. Like I never thought I'd be living here, in a forest of all things. Like I'd never thought I'd have to fetch water from a stream. Like I never thought I'd be badgered so much by someone called Francesca. Francesca? What kind of name is that? And you do it too. Don't say that you don't, don't you dare. I've seen you gawping at the end of your nose, mouth wide open, tongue lolling out. You were just doing it back then. I saw you, I swear.'

'Catching flies, Ky calls it. Used to call it, back in the days when she was speaking to me.'

'Catching flies. Catching butterflies,' said Matthew, nodding approvingly. 'And you, what sort of creatures run through that head of yours when you're catching butterflies?'

'Now there's a question,' Fran said enigmatically. They had reached the stream, but the water here was shallow through lack of rain and so they continued walking along the riverbank to where they knew the channel was deeper and ran more slowly. 'Why, what do you think are the creatures that run through this head of mine, Mr Mann?'

'Elephants. Big, fat elephants in raincoats and wellies and umbrellas, jumping in puddles.'

'Fool.'

'Okay, maybe not elephants. But birds, lots of birds, like a – what do you call them big cages, like as big as a shed and they're full of birds flying around?'

'An aviary?'

'Aye, an aviary. That's what it's like inside your head, all feathers and whistles and singing daft songs about buckets of water and breaking crowns, and beanstalks too. And there's a bed with feather pillows. And a dressing table with, let's see. Aye, there's pots of make-up and creams and a mirror, and piles of books too. I know there'd be plenty of books because you went to college and you like your books. And there's a picture too, a picture of a boy and you're sitting at the table looking at this boy with your mouth hanging open, catching butterflies.'

'A fascinating insight,' said Fran, unimpressed. 'So, I must be vain if I think about doing make-up in front of a mirror all day, despite the cacophony of birdsong in my head. But at least I read a lot, is that right? But, tell me, who's this boy that I'm supposedly pining over?'

'The make-up's just a shot in the dark. You know, the sort of thing that women used to trouble themselves about, wasn't it? Before the Last Day? Make-up and clothes, wasn't it? I don't know. I didn't know that many girls outside prayer camp. Now don't be getting yourself offended, Francesca. I know you're not like that now, and I can tell you there's not a day goes by that even Mother doesn't miss her face cream, though she'd never say as much.'

'Some day we'll talk about a thing called misogynistic preconceptions, Matthew Mann. But I'm keen to know more about this boy. Who's that boy in the picture frame?'

'Well, I'm thinking there must have been some boy at one time or another, no?'

They walked along the riverbank without talking for a while, until Fran put her side of the barrel on the ground and bent down to examine the furry leaves of a plant that she recognised from her herb book. It could be comfrey: good for bruises and broken bones.

'There might have been once,' she said, concentrating on the leaves. 'There might have been two, perhaps. One at college. That didn't last long, ended within a year, but I suppose it must have meant something at the time. And there was another one, Dean, after that. Perhaps I lived with him. Perhaps the living together was hard, damaging. Perhaps it became like one of those houses that you do keep birds in, feathers in the air, all that cacophony. And perhaps I was the only person in the world who clapped when the satellites fell and the electricity went down and the sky turned orange. You call it the Last Day, don't you? Funny, I think of it as the first.'

Fran folded two of the comfrey leaves into her pocket and took up her handle of the barrel.

'Another funny thing,' she said as they followed the stream that had deepened from a shallow riffle into a dark, flowing run. 'Neither of those two boys are the one in the picture.'

They set the barrel down where the river became a deep pool, high enough to be reached from the bank. Matthew knelt beside the edge and used the lesser bucket to ladle water into the barrel. He did not say anything but watched the fragments of his own reflection shatter and reassemble upon the rippling surface.

Fran watched the other Matthew come and go on the dark water, the ghosts of thin fish fretting beneath his outline. Eventually, she asked, 'Is it now my turn to imagine what creatures are running through your head?'

'Ssh.' Matthew lifted his hand as he stared at the trees where he had heard a noise. They both peered at the abundant undergrowth, the mosaic of soft greens and hard browns, bramble flowers on the forest bed pierced by spears of sunlight. It was the azure flash of a kingfisher diving, lightning quick, that drew their attention about thirty metres further down the riverbank to where two faces coolly returned their gaze. Sitting cross-legged and absolutely still at the edge of the water, Ky and Luke were quietly watching them. Ky offered a faint nod of acknowledgement and then gave her full attention to the fishing rod in her hands, wound the spool a few turns and settled back to consider the float bobbing up and down in the river. Beside her, Luke continued to stare. When Matthew raised his hand in greeting, Luke twitched his lips into a tight smile and then leaned forward to whisper something against Ky's ear. Ky agreed with whatever Luke had said, but she kept her eyes on the water.

Fran considered this strange encounter for some time after they had left the stream. She never suspected that Ky was spending her days secretively fishing with Luke, or spending time with any of the Mann brothers for that matter. Menn, for the plural, she guessed she should call them, and she would have laughed aloud at that thought had the sloshing barrel been less of a struggle. Matthew had only half-filled the container with water but it was still a cumbersome weight for the two of them to carry. Breathless, they did not talk on the way back through the forest. More than anything, Fran wanted to know what was going on in Matthew's mind.

'We need an easy way of doing this, an alternative to muscle power,' Fran said as they both collapsed on the grass verge near the lane, panting heavily. Matthew rolled his head in agreement and stretched out flat on the ground, his eyes closed.

'It's a close call, but I think you did a fraction more of the carrying than me,' she added.

Matthew grunted, unable to say a word. Fran turned her face to the cloudless blue sky overhead and decided that she must broach the conversation they had left unfinished. If it was not done now, the moment would be lost and the summer soured forever.

'I think,' she began, 'that the creatures in your head are probably dogs: black, shaggy, friendly dogs that are probably running scared and a little disappointed right now. But they needn't be worried. Honestly, they needn't. We come from very different worlds, you and me, with very different backgrounds, but that is only a problem if we make it one. Thing is, Matthew Mann, if there is a picture frame in my head, then there's just one face in it. That face is yours.'

'Dogs?' said Matthew, his eyes still closed. 'That's funny. I do miss the dogs.'

'Which dogs?'

'Two black, shaggy dogs, just like you said. Lost them in the forest.'

'Oh, those. Ky's convinced that you ate them.'

'Lost in the forest,' he said distantly. He walked his fingers over the grass until he touched Fran's elbow, traced the length of her forearm, and clasped her warm hand within his own.

THE LAST HOUSE IN THE terrace had finally succumbed to the noise. Things dragged themselves places, paused for thought in an alcove or on a step, or hung suspended in the dusty air before limping off somewhere else. Floorboards contracted and exhaled, wood walked across wood and leaned against the wall, listening. Listening back, Ruth had retreated to a corner on her kitchen floor and only breathed when the things next door went to sleep. Her curtains were drawn all the time, but the fabric was so thin and worn that she could tell when it was day and when it was night. At night, she pulled on her black coat and became invisible, crossed the lane without fear of being seen and spent her evenings listening to strange stories and unimaginable ideas at Rhea's kitchen table. The days she spent hiding under her own.

The noise had risen like an inevitable tide, unforgiving and relentless. Somehow, it had passed by the walls and windows of her refuge to inundate the final house at the end of the terrace, Number Seven. Her front door had stood firm against the flood, a rock in the sea. The iron key burned safe and sore in her hand. But that which flows must also ebb, and nothing stands forever. Nothing untrue, she thought. Nothing fallen. It would come by her house again one day and when it did, when the tide swept back, something would give way, give her away.

Sundays were the hardest. On those days, the walls swelled with condemnation so loud that she had to retreat to the sitting room and slip into a crack behind the armchair. Even from the sanctuary of her hole, she could hear the floorboards clench next door, the thunder of feet and hands, of tongues vibrating fire in the air, the slap of wings against ceiling plaster, her brothers' deep voices remembering Zion by the rivers, the waters of exile, though even the kitchen taps had now run dry. Ruth made more holes and waited for the silence of the all-clear to ring out like an empty heaven, like a finger pointing at the darkness, at a black coat folded in a crack.

'For my soul received a flood of glory when the Lord sanctified me,' the walls and the woodwork thundered, rocking the globe on her mantelpiece, eclipsing the sun at the window. 'Oh, I never shall forget how the fire fell, how the fire fell. I never shall forget how the fire fell when the Lord sanctified me.'

The voices were still remembering how the fire fell when the knock came on her front door. Ruth held her breath and did not move for a long time. She could have imagined it. It might have just been something falling to the floor, the teapot from the kitchen table perhaps, or a brick from the wall. She pushed the key closer to home and twisted. The knock came again and again, deliberate and measured, the patient insistence of a will that had known the beginning and the end, the first and the last, and would never go away. Ruth pushed the key deeper and deeper until it slipped smoothly into place with the relief of old metal turning without resistance, turning as it ought to, and the front door opened and she was blinded by the evening sun.

'For on me his spirit fell with burning fire when the lord sanctified me,' they sang, the two figures standing on the doorstep, their eyes burning with grace.

Ruth closed the front door behind her and went with Luke and Mark, the brothers who had been waiting for her, to the house that thundered with feet, the air quivering with breath and the dust-lit falling of day. There were others in the room standing in corners or perched on the edge of perception, others like flames, and others that clapped with hands that she could hear rather than see. Surrounded by all this tumult, Mother sat on a simple chair against the wall, a white sheet draped over her shoulders. Her palms were laid open on her lap, ready to receive into the light the daughter that she had banished to the darkness.

'That's it,' said Mother as Ruth knelt beside the chair. Mother accepted her daughter's head onto her lap and gently smoothed the girl's hair, stroked the edge of her jawline, her pale neck. Beneath her hands, Mother could feel Ruth trembling as she sang or cried or tried not to cry and accepted the grace of forgiveness. 'Aye, girl, that's it.'

Satisfied with Ruth's meekness, Mother looked around at each of her sons. Not all of them were here, of course. Abel had been granted a seat in the grand house and would not be seen until he was ready to serve, until the time was right. A sensitive boy, it was fitting that Abel's path would be a softer one, a scholarly one. Scripture and prayer in a quiet place: he would come to know the Good Book better than any of them. Mother did not hold with all Father Ambrose's High-Church traditions, but he was a man of God nonetheless and he would school her youngest to be likewise. There was also the patronage of the Gentleman upstairs to be thankful for. And as for Abel's intimacy with the god-haters, well, his separation from them was a blessing.

Luke and Mark had performed their duty well, just as Mother had bidden them. They had brought their foolish sister back from her penance without any fuss, and now the two boys stood on either side of the door, two sentinels, two bright angels, raising their pleasant baritone voices to heaven. Faithful boys, the best of boys, they knew that they had done well.

Matthew sat cross-legged on the floor beside that girl, Francesca, to whom he had lately taken a fancy. Mother's instincts were sharp: she knew exactly what type of skirt this one wore. Still, the girl did put on a show of openness to the Spirit. This was not the first prayer meeting that Francesca had attended and she did make a sweet and joyful noise to the Lord. The girl would not do for Matthew, of course, but the Lord would put an end to all that nonsense.

And finally, sitting on the chair beside Mother was Enoch, her firstborn, he who had returned from the valley of death, baptised with blood and born again, burdened with the inheritance of the Earth. Enoch had been so pale and quiet since his sacrifice, since his suffering in the forest, but Mother knew that his bull-like strength was returning. Day by day, with each of her prayers, her son's gifts were returning. She closed her eyes and listened to Enoch's voice, a surprisingly light, melodic tenor, as he sang of fire and flood, and beat a rhythm on the floorboards with the axe that he now used to help him walk. A good voice, the best of voices.

When the last line of the hymn burned out in the air, Enoch leaned forward to speak. Injury had aged him. It was his birthright to bear a sterner countenance than his brothers, but pain had hardened him further. Whatever had happened to him in the forest, whatever he had endured or witnessed, had tempered him like iron in the furnace. The Beast that could not kill him had only made him stronger. He was the last to have seen Father and Uncle Joe alive and, because of that, something of those two departed souls lived on in him now. In some ways, thought Mother, her firstborn was more than one man: he was three. And that too was a blessed consolation.

When Enoch spoke in tongues, the sounds he made were uttered in his singing voice, softer and lighter than his common voice. It was a sibilant language that had never been spoken before, a tongue-flapping gibberish that babbled like a stream, both soothing and unnervingly primitive. He toyed with vowels and soft consonants until the strange message was finished, then he leaned contentedly back in his chair and waited for someone else to complete the miracle.

After a moment's consideration, Mother released her daughter's head from her lap and folded her hands together. Pressing her fingers to her forehead, she prepared herself and her audience for the performance. To one is given the gift of tongues, she said, to another the interpretation of tongues. Her gift, thank Heaven, was the lesser.

CHAPTER EIGHT
THE GARDEN

RHEA'S SORCERY HAD TAKEN A different turn. In the old days, the days before the troubles, she would cycle home from work on a fine summer's evening with a cake and a nice bottle of red wine in the basket on her handlebars. Her apartment was on the ground floor of a quiet house on a quiet street: bay windows, sandstone bricks, a wooden porch where she could leave the bike. If it was a warm evening, and the summers of memory are inevitably kind, she would open up the garden doors, crank the handle on the old gramophone and listen to the ghostly echoes of an orchestral storm while giving time for the wine to breathe. The garden was not much: a small lawn bordered by roses, a jasmine creeper that rarely flowered, night-scented stock, occasional marigolds. In those days, she did not consider plants for their practical, medicinal or culinary value. They were simply there to give colour, scent, contentment. An unsophisticated garden for sophisticated times. Magical evenings, sometimes with friends, often alone: sweet woodwind, creeping bassoons, a summer gale of brass and horns. *Requiem aeternam.*

There were no rituals of turntable and disc to perform anymore, no needles to lift nor handles to crank. The dead would never again be conjured to sing for her evening pleasure. Dead music, thought Rhea; the day the music died. She had owned that song too, of course. Bye, Bye Miss American Pie: a long-time favourite, knew all the words. Everyone had known all of those words, everyone in the college bar, even Joshua. Maybe owned was the wrong word. She had merely had access to that song when it existed in some virtual, gaseous form, a code in a cloud before all the clouds were busted. Access was a privilege, not a right: access could be denied. But when she had held those vinyls in her hands, she had owned them outright. Them good old boys were drinking whisky and rye and singing. I do miss listening to music, she thought, I really do.

Rhea's sorcery was simpler now, less potent. On the kitchen table in front of her lay her assortment of old, faded record sleeves, the classical albums that Ky had given her as a midwinter gift. One by one, she was saying the names of the composers and their compositions to Lugh. The boy was sitting beside her with the encyclopaedia open before him.

'There's a silent "h" in the middle of Mahler,' said Rhea. Lugh still could not find any such entry in the book, so Rhea spelled the name out for him. 'Symphony Number Two, dear. Is there nothing on this one either?'

Slowly, the frown lifted from Lugh's brow and his face softened in the candlelight. Since all the oil for the lamps had been used up, they were now using the candles. Lugh ran his finger underneath the sentences and read aloud the secrets of the mute sleeve in Rhea's hands. The symphony begins as a solemn march, he said, called Funeral Rites, followed by a delicate remembrance of lives lost. The tempo rises, cries, longing for relief from the suffering of the world, a final fanfare of resurrection. Rise again, my dust. Rise again, my heart. The German, he could not read. As the boy spoke, Rhea removed the disc from its cover and stroked the grooves in black vinyl with her fingernails as though she could conjure the music, as though she were the needle and the boy was the brass horn. Her magic was not strong enough. She could imagine but not summon these dead sounds.

'Thank you, my dear. That was lovely,' she said, replacing the record and selecting another. 'Now, what can we find on this one. Let's see, Gustav Holst. The Planets, an orchestral suite in seven movements. Well, that sounds right up your street, doesn't it, young Galileo?'

'What happened first?' asked Ky, who was sitting at the far end of the table. She was only half-listening to their conversation while writing in her ledger. She looked up inquisitively from her work and chewed the end of her pen. 'Was it that drought in eastern Europe or those Russian planes coming down in that storm in the Baltic? Or were they both around the same time?'

148

'Now, dear, don't go spoiling the evening with unpleasantness like that,' Rhea said with heartfelt disappointment. She removed her spectacles and rubbed her tired eyes. 'Why not ask Francesca in the morning. I never did pay much attention to those stories at the time. It was such a worry and everything happened so quickly. You ask Francesca. I've no doubt her memory's sharper than mine. And, besides, we were having such a lovely time tonight, weren't we, Lugh?'

'We were,' the boy replied sullenly, without looking up from the book.

'It is important,' said Ky. She returned to her page and continued to scribble.

'What's done is done. Now,' Rhea replaced her glasses and patted Lugh's arm, 'the Planets.'

There were only a few lines for Lugh to read on this composition. He had got as far as Saturn when the back door opened and Fran returned home. She did not take off her boots as usual but stood on the mat with her arms folded.

'Francesca,' said Rhea warmly, though she was unable to turn around fully because of the stiffness in her neck. 'Your ears must have been burning, dear. We were just talking about you. How did it go this evening? We could hear all that clapping from here.'

'Oh, it was illuminating,' said Fran. Her voice sounded too high, too piercing to be sincere. 'Yes, that's the word, illuminating. Enoch was there. He's on his feet again, seems much better. And Ruth was there too, which is nice for her because it means her penance is over. And, what else? Oh, that's right. While they were speaking in tongues, you can't imagine what the Holy Spirit let slip. Apparently, Ky's leaving us. That's right, that was the illuminating thing. Apparently, on Thursday, Ky's going to that town to bring back medical supplies. You know, that town behind the mountain and beside the sea, the one with an army crawling all over it. The one that Ky said was too dangerous for me to walk to when it was just down the fucking road.'

'Watch your language,' Ky said, coolly leaning back in her chair. 'God is watching you.'

'No, dear, no,' said Rhea, becoming distressed. 'Ky wouldn't be so foolhardy, would you?'

'But Ky couldn't tell us this herself, could she?' Fran's voice was dangerously playful. She sat down at the empty seat and leaned across the table, holding Ky's gaze. 'No, there are no revelations from Ky anymore. Ky's too busy hanging out with Luke in the woods to confide in us about her suicide schemes. It's funny, we're more likely to hear what she's up to from the Holy Spirit than we are from her. How's that for miraculous?'

Ky smiled grimly and went to the sink for a glass of water, forgetting that the pipes had run dry. When nothing came out of the taps, she disappeared into the pantry for a bottle of boiled water.

Rhea continued to lament the idea of Ky leaving. 'It's not as if you could just take the car, not without enough petrol,' she said. 'You'd have to go by foot and that could take days, weeks even. And when you get there, those soldiers... Oh no, dear, no. It's far too dangerous, Ky. It's ludicrous, in fact. I won't, no, I won't—'

'You won't what, Rhea? You won't allow it?' said Ky with a laugh. Leaning out of the pantry, she said to Fran, 'Can we crack open your green wine? If we're having this conversation now, I'd appreciate a drop of some holy spirit.'

'Wine is fermented. It's not spirit if it hasn't been distilled,' said Fran. She folded her arms and stared at the window, at the deepening red of the summer sunset sky.

'Because now is a perfect time to discuss the fermentation process?'

'Fine, help yourself. Get me a glass too,' Fran conceded. Ky returned with the bottle of green wine and four glasses. Lugh accepted his serving without a word, partly because he did not want to say thank you to Ky, but also because the others might deny him the drink if they noticed.

'*Yammas,*' said Ky, raising her glass. No one responded.

'It's so attention-seeking. It's so dramatic,' Fran said fiercely after taking a sip of her wine. 'You know, Rhea, the other illuminating thing I learned—'

'Please, can we kill the fucking illuminations,' cried Ky. 'And you call me dramatic?'

'The other illuminating thing I learned is that Ky's not going to town alone. Instead of talking to us, she's been scheming in the woods with Luke—'

'Fishing in the woods with Luke. He didn't know how to use his fishing tackle. I was showing him how to catch trout. We have to live with them, that's what you said.'

'So, where are all these fish you and Luke have been catching?' asked Fran.

'I thought it politic to let him take them all.'

'They've been eating trout?' Rhea cried in disbelief. Recovering herself, she added, 'I am sorry, my dears. I know it's unimportant but, really, it would have been neighbourly of them to at least offer a little bit of fish, wouldn't it?'

'Not if all the fish in the world are theirs to inherit,' said Ky. 'Wouldn't be right to share good trout with folk who ought to be burning in a bottomless pit.'

'Enough of the fish already.' Fran sighed. She finished her own wine and refilled their three glasses, for Lugh had concealed his beneath the table. They sat in silence, considering what had already been disclosed while, outside, the forest birds sang the last of the evening chorus. Eventually Fran asked, 'So, you asked Mark and Luke go with you to that town?'

'Listen,' Ky said calmly as she leaned forward on the table. 'We'll need another assembly soon: there's plenty to talk about, plenty to decide. There's the water situation for a start, which is dire, which might mean digging a well. And we could do with sharing their fishing tackle, couldn't we? And there's that axe they haven't let us use yet. Enoch's risen from his deathbed and Old Mother Mann is on the loose so, right now, when it comes to the numbers, we'd lose every vote. Mark and Luke were hardly cooperative at the last meeting, were they? You can bet they'll be less so at the next. If I can take those two with me, well, it evens the numbers up a bit.'

'And poor dear Abel,' Rhea added, shaking her head. 'How that woman can pack her youngest off to the big house is beyond me. Locked up with that peculiar old man, and for how long, I'll never understand. And we do miss Abel, don't we, Lugh?'

'She wants Abel to become a pastor or whatever. It's her faith.' Fran shrugged. 'I'm sorry, I'm still struggling to get my head around Ky's incredible mission. So, what's your plan? You steal medical supplies—even though no one is currently injured or ill—from a town occupied by an army. And Mark and Luke will accompany you so we can use their fishing sticks while they're away? Is that it? Is that your plan?'

'Fishing rods. Listen, do you trust me?' Ky asked, looking into each of their faces.

'The fuck I do, Zachariadou,' Fran laughed coldly. 'The fuck I do. You've lost already. Your plan's been foiled already. While they were talking in tongues, you want to know what the Holy Spirit revealed? Turns out, when Ky goes on her adventure, she will be accompanied by two of the brothers, but it won't be Mark and Luke. No, the Holy Spirit wants Matthew to go instead of Luke. So, that's great, isn't it? Ky and Matthew and Mark sneaking into a military camp to steal supplies that we don't actually need. Risking their lives unnecessarily.

'But, thinking about it, maybe you haven't failed,' Fran continued, addressing Ky directly. 'Maybe this is what you intended all along. Let's be honest, you've never been happy about me and Matthew, have you? Cards on the table time, why is that? What was it, jealousy or disappointment? And you dare to talk to me about trust. The fuck I trust you, Zachariadou.'

All eyes were now fixed on the table. The kitchen felt unnaturally quiet in the aftermath of Fran's outburst. None of them had heard her speak like this before, with such force and spite. Her hands were shaking with emotion. She hid her fingers beneath the table so no one would see.

After the silence, Ky filled all their glasses with the last of the green wine, even Lugh's, and said, 'I suppose that was illuminating. Am I allowed to guess which of them claimed to speak for the Holy Spirit?'

'The mother,' Fran said, without giving Ky a chance.

'Convenient.' Ky nodded. 'Just for the record, I didn't plan this. I didn't want Matthew to come with me. I'd feel better knowing he was here with you. And we do need medical supplies. When the next injury happens—and there will be one and it could be serious—we'll need everything close at hand. We won't have time to waste walking to town. I don't want another death on my conscience. What do you think, Lugh? What say you?'

'Don't lay this on Lugh,' said Fran quietly, dangerously. 'Don't you dare lay this on him.'

'I want her to go,' said the boy. He returned Ky's gaze with a cool assurance, almost a smile.

'The ayes have it.' Ky finished her glass of wine and left the room.

❧

THE MORNINGS WERE DRY AS the evenings were dry. The sky was always thirsty, though the profound blue gave an illusion of deep water, of Greek seas and swimming pools, a mirage of fluid coolness. From her bedroom window, Fran could see the forest suffering. The deciduous trees, the oak and ash and aspen and lime that had risen and stretched through many human lifetimes, had barely passed through the first flush of spring green before curling prematurely brown, anaemic yellow in June. The sun had turned her garden ceramic grey and the dawn into a plainsong of flies.

Fran thought of her father's garden, the garden of the house where she had grown up. That had been a garden full of trees, an enchanted forest: holly and oak, weeping willows, a cedar of Lebanon. On Sundays, her father would drive her to the garden centre and they would spend hours among herbs and hardy perennials and sapling trees in a sweltering greenhouse that always sounded of running water. Her father had known the Latin names of trees: Acer, Fraxinus, Quercus, Salix. He spoke it easily, that ancient, arboreal language of genus and species, the names of old friends flowing from his lips. Fran missed his voice, that garden, that greenhouse, the sound of running water.

Lugh was sitting at the table when Fran came down to the kitchen. He had already prepared scrambled eggs and seemed unusually keen to be off to the farmyard.

'How's the hangover this morning?' she asked him over breakfast. 'I see everything, even a sneaky glass of wine under the table.'

'Two glasses,' Lugh admitted. 'I'm fine. It wasn't as strong as my brother's beer.'

'Really, O'Byrne. I had no idea you were a hardened drinker.'

The boy shrugged. Impatient to be gone, he put on his trainers and waited outside.

Although it was early, the air felt thick and hazy with the conviction of another sweltering day. The rising sun blinded them as they walked down the lane and turned the bend, past the stone gatepost with the name of the house etched in sharp Gothic letters, and around the imposing white walls of the building. In the trees, the magpies scoffed as they passed.

'You go ahead, I'll catch up with you,' said Lugh when they reached the lawns at the back.

'Why, what other engagements do you have lined up?' Fran asked suspiciously. 'It's not Abel, is it? Do you have a secret tryst with Abel?'

Lugh frowned at the distant trees and made an indistinct sound of possibility, a perhaps.

'Where?' asked Fran excitedly. 'Can I see him too?'

'It's tricky. Sometimes he can't come at all, not if the old man's about. And he's not allowed to say anything either. He's taken a wow of silence.'

'A what?' Fran laughed.

'Look.' Lugh produced a sheet of notepaper, on which Abel had pencilled various sentences, innumerable yes and no responses in his last conversation with Lugh. At the top of the paper, probably his first message, he had scribbled: 'Cannot speak. Took wow of silence.'

'Wow,' said Fran, returning the paper. 'Can you give him my love? Oh, ask if he can smuggle any books out of the library.'

'I'll see what we can do,' Lugh replied, glancing shiftily around him and stuffing the note back into his pocket.

'You're full of surprises today, O'Byrne.' She brushed his shoulder lightly as a thank you and headed off towards the farmyard.

The lawns behind the big house had turned brown and patchy, baked dry by the relentless sun. There would be no reason to cut the grass for months, for nothing was growing as it ought to be. Although the old man had requested that the grass be watered and well maintained, Fran knew that was a waste of water and labour. All their efforts should be directed towards producing food, not manicuring a croquet lawn.

Fran marshalled the chickens out of the coop and scattered a little grass seed. When she went inside to collect eggs, she found the body of another dead hen, the second this week, a feast for the flies. She suspected the cause was malnutrition, not disease. The earth was so hard that the birds found it impossible to scratch for worms. Still, if Rhea did a nice job of cleaning any maggots out of the flesh, they could eat a skinny old chicken tonight.

By the time Matthew arrived, Fran had already seen to the watering of the vegetable garden. She heard his footsteps approach as she was trying to dig around the wilting potato plants. She did not turn around to greet him.

'Guess who?' he said cheerfully enough.

'Someone with the horse-sense to bring a bucket of water, I hope?' she replied without looking up, cracking at the parched earth with her trowel.

Matthew returned from the well in the farmyard with the sloshing bucket. 'The horse is back with water.'

'But you can't make him drink.' Fran smiled to herself and straightened up. 'I don't suppose you got that, did you?'

'I did, I got the water, see. Where's best place for it?'

'Oh, I don't know.' Slowly, she stood up and stretched her bare arms, her spine. The back of her t-shirt was already soaked through with sweat and the flies were a constant nuisance. 'Over the potatoes or over your own head. Or take it with you on Ky's suicide mission.'

Matthew looked down at the bucket, at his reflection in the water, and said nothing.

'I don't suppose you tried talking to your mother,' she said. A statement not a question.

'It's not Mother. You know it's not Mother. It's—'

'I know, it's the Holy Spirit.' Fran put her hands on her hips and kicked at the dry earth. 'But don't you ever wonder why someone's god has the exact same opinions as that person? You never get someone saying, for example, I don't agree with war but my god does, do you? Or vice versa? What if my god doesn't want you to go, but your mother's does? Whose god is right?'

'Francesca, there is only one God.'

'Maybe,' she said with a sigh. She knelt down beside the plants and tried to dig for potatoes again.

'So, where's best place for the water?'

'Wherever your god wants you to put it.'

Matthew thought for a moment and then tipped the bucket over Fran's back and bare shoulders. Her cries of shock and laughter echoed through the air and over the thirsty forest.

Walking across the lawns towards the farmyard, Lugh stopped when he heard the sound, thought for a terrible moment that the stolen goods had been missed, his crime discovered. He pushed the library books deeper down the front of his trousers and continued on his path.

⏑

THE CURTAINS IN RUTH'S KITCHEN had been pulled open. The morning sunlight poured over the room, imposing stark new colours on the wooden floorboards, the odd collection of cups on the dresser, the gaudy teapot on the table, and revealing the air to be a cosmos of swirling dust. Ruth had not opened the curtains herself. That was something Mother had done, her first act on occupying the house. Lifting the curtains to her nose, Mother sniffed the fabric, examined the embroidered hawthorn blossom and pulled a disappointed face. At least she did not say anything.

'The curtains were here already,' Ruth said.

'I see.' Mother walked around the table and came to a halt at the window, twisted the taps in the sink.

'We've not had any water for weeks,' said Ruth. 'I'd make a pot of tea, but—'

'You shouldn't light the stove during daytime.'

'I don't. I haven't.'

'You shouldn't do it anyway.'

'No, I shouldn't.'

'It's a big old house for just one person, isn't it?' Mother asked, her voice brightening as though a new thought had occurred to her while inspecting the ceilings. 'Do you really need all this space? I wouldn't need all this space. I'd feel bad having all this space. I'd feel selfish, self-loving, terribly proud, God forgive me. Aye, I wouldn't feel right. But I suppose I'm like that. Don't like to take more than is due. Just the way God made me.'

As Mother talked, she moved casually between the downstairs rooms, scrutinising the walls, corners, skirting boards, fireplace. When she noticed the globe on the mantelpiece, she put her finger on Africa, gave the continent a shove, watched the whole planet spin. 'Why in heaven's name would anyone keep such a thing in their house?'

'It's not mine,' said Ruth, hovering at the doorway to the sitting room. 'It's theirs.'

'Theirs, is it?' Mother nodded, her suspicions confirmed. She sat down on the armchair and folded her hands on her lap. 'I suppose you'd have been seeing a great deal of them, your friends, haven't you? Cosying up to strangers. Not how I would have spent my penance, but it's not my place to judge. I leave that to the good Lord. He knows the secrets of our hearts. Knows all your thoughts, Ruthy. Knows if you've been repenting your sins. Still, it's right and proper that you're back with your family now, back where you belong.'

Ruth followed her mother's example and sat down on the sofa.

'Aye, it's only family that matters,' Mother continued with a meagre smile. Leaning forward to share a confidence with her daughter, she said, 'I was beginning to worry about our Abel. I can tell you this now, Ruthy; I'll know you'll understand. He'd been hanging about with those strange people every hour God sends. And what sort of things they talked to him about, what nonsense they filled his head with, only heaven knows. I dread to think. Bad company ruins good morals. And can I tell you the worst thing?' Mother's voice had sunk to a whisper. 'He wouldn't tell me. Whatever it was they talked about, he wouldn't tell me, his own mother. Now that's not right, is it? That's not normal, Ruthy. I can't get my head around that boy. I simply can't understand him.'

'I can't either,' replied Ruth, lowering her gaze to the crucifix that rested on Mother's collar, the flash of gold on her restless fingers.

'I knew you would understand.' Mother settled back into her armchair and smiled benignly at her daughter. 'You're a good girl, Ruthy. I know I can trust you. It's such a blessing that we can talk like this again, isn't it? Mother to daughter. As it ought to be.'

'Aye, it is.' The silence stretched, twisted into an aching chasm that Ruth knew she would have to sacrifice something into, to feed it, to appease Mother's appetite for absolute loyalty. Sliding a fingernail down the dark comfort of her sleeve, Ruth spoke falteringly. 'Those people, they're strange. I think they're unbelievers. That one with the darker skin, Ky, she surely is. In fact, she said she was.'

'God help us,' Mother said with feeling. She leaned forward to take more.

'Maybe the older woman, Rhea, is too. She said there was no Last Day. Said no god would throw anyone, no matter how bad or how wicked, into a bottomless pit. That's what she said.'

'Oh, my girl. My poor girl.' Mother reached out and took Ruth's hand, clasped it tightly. 'And you sought friendship with these people? You turned to god-haters during your penance?'

Ruth lowered her eyes and stared at Mother's hand pressed over her own, felt the cold edge of her wedding ring, the hidden sting of a bitten, broken nail.

THE FIRST CLOUD APPEARED THE following morning, did not linger for long, dispersed by noon. Kneeling in the vegetable plot, Fran noticed it, but did not give it much attention. The weak little thing was too pale to carry rain, too modest to provide shade. She returned her attention to the wilting onions, tried to sow peas in the stone-hard earth. The next day there was a fleet of orange clouds above the eastern horizon. To Fran, they looked like a school of slender whales leaping across the rising sun. Within a couple of hours, they had plunged into some distant sea, but taken a little of the unbearable heat down with them. In the evening, Fran wrote her observances in her almanac: Midsummer Day, six thin clouds in the east, sunrise yellow-orange, midday temperature: thirty-four degrees centigrade (three lower than yesterday), sunrise and sunset times, bird sightings, etcetera.

When she had finished writing her notes, she closed the ledger, folded her arms on the cover and looked at Rhea who was reading next to Lugh at the other end of the table.

'What's your contraband knowledge today?' Fran asked her.

Rhea peered at the front title of the grey hardback book in her hands, the first of three similar volumes that Lugh had smuggled out of the big house.

'Let's see, we have the *Lives of the Eminent Philosophers*,' Rhea read slowly, 'by Diogenes La-Lae-Laertius. Quite a mouthful, isn't it, dear. Believe me, it gets no easier inside. There's a whole chapter about our old friend Plato, but I'm struggling to find an answer to the question.'

'Oh, on how to be just?' Fran asked. She lay her head on her arms and closed her eyes.

'What is justice. Listen, see if you can make head or tail of this.' Rhea cleared her throat and read aloud a few sample sentences. 'We must assume the existence of justice, existing in and for itself,' she said. 'The idea of justice is eternal: it stands in nature like an archetype.

'Well, why must we assume any such thing, I wonder?' she added in consternation. 'I wish we'd something else to go on, something plain and simple that an old fool like me could understand.'

'Did we get the wrong book?' asked Lugh. He looked up from his own reading and fidgeted with the sleeves of the black woollen jumper that Rhea had finally finished knitting for him.

'Oh, no, dear. It's a lovely book, very useful indeed, and you must tell Abel thank you very much from me. Just look at that, all those names,' she flicked through the contents pages, 'so many eminent philosophers. Honestly, you wouldn't have thought there was enough work in the philosophy industry to go round. And these are the just the ancient ones, Greeks mostly.'

'We are all Greeks now,' said Fran sleepily. 'Skip to the end. Might find your answers there.'

'Let's see,' Rhea turned to the last chapter and read occasional sentences. 'Epicurus, now I have heard of him. That's nice, his school was called The Garden. Pleasure is good, pain is bad. Now that's plain enough for even me to understand. Listen to this, "A wise man knows how to talk about music." That is a very pleasant thought, but I wonder why it should be so?'

'Music!' cried Lugh, suddenly remembering the thing that he had forgotten to tell Rhea. He dug inside his pocket and retrieved a scrap of notepaper which he passed to her. Rhea studied the note and suspected that the pencil scribbles must be the one-sided communication from Abel to Lugh. In the centre of the page, scratched in bold capital letters, she found the sentence: 'Tell Rhea—wind-up record player.'

'A gramophone? Really, dear?' She turned the paper in her hands as though the answer lay somewhere on the other side. 'Now where could it be?'

Lugh explained as much as he knew, that there was a wind-up record player in the drawing room of the big house, but there was no way of getting it outside unseen, even for a short while.

'We can ask the old man, can't we?' Rhea pleaded. 'There's no harm in asking, is there?'

'He'll speak to the Gentleman upstairs, but the Gentleman upstairs will never answer.'

'But if we take the records to him,' Rhea continued, pleading. 'If he sees the bleeding things in our hands, you never know, he might be open to sharing. He might have a taste for Mahler.'

'He might. No harm in asking.' Fran sighed, closing her eyes again. In the darkness, she saw cracked grey earth baked hard by the sun, thin stems of wheat wilting behind her eyelids.

When the back door opened and Ky entered the kitchen, Fran kept her eyes closed and her head resting on the table. Rhea made an effort at light-hearted small talk about philosophy and gramophones while Ky picked at a plate of mashed potatoes on the counter.

'And we did think, we were just saying, there's no harm in asking about the gramophone,' Rhea went on. 'You never know, the Gentleman upstairs might let us use it, mightn't he?'

'The Gentleman upstairs,' Ky mused thoughtfully. 'When Adam delved and Eve span, who then was the Gentleman? That's it, the rhyme I was trying to remember. You know it?'

'No, dear, can't say I've ever heard it before. But spinning, that reminds me.' Rhea tugged a slip of paper out of her book and handed it to Ky. 'Wool and thread. If you do happen to pass a haberdashery on your trip, it would be very handy if you could pick up a few extra bits and bobs.'

'I suspect haberdasheries were a key military target, but I'll see what I can do.' Ky smiled as she read through Rhea's shopping list. 'Toothpaste and toothbrushes? Well remembered, I didn't think of those. Well, only two more sleeps to go. Bedtime for me.'

If Fran was less tired, if she had the resources to feel anything except exhaustion, she would probably have said goodnight. Instead, feeling nothing, she drifted in closed-eye contemplation of cracks, kaleidoscopic dryness. Rhea said goodnight for them all and returned to her reading.

Gradually, goldenly, the midsummer sun set at its northernmost point on the horizon. It would be another twelve months before a day would last this long. Now, without oil for the lamps and a moratorium on the use of candles except in emergencies, there was not enough light to read by. Rhea removed her glasses, rubbed her eyes and asked Lugh what he had been studying in the encyclopaedia. Her eyes still closed, Fran only half listened as the boy spoke in small sentences, clipped phrases, about shooting stars, constellations, the hunter Orion and his clever dogs, the greater and the lesser. It had been weeks since they had been out together, Fran and the boy, to plot the map of the heavens. They had reached as far as the tip of Cassiopeia's toes and gone no further. These days were hard and Fran was tired. They would pick up the stars in a kinder season.

If Fran went outside now, she would have seen something more than the sunset, more than the Evening Star leading the charge of night. In the east, another cloud, this one rising like a purple wave over the parched forest. Some change in air pressure must have prickled Fran's skin, stirred ancestral memories of rain and flood, a need for shelter, for higher ground. In her bed that night, she dreamed of water running through the trees, sweeping away the desiccated fields of wheat and vegetables, transforming the dry lane into a river of raging white that rose against the walls of the house. Instead of her bed, she was lying on the floor of a cave and waiting for the water to subside, for the cascade of rain to stop streaming over the stony entrance to her shelter.

She shouted for Lugh, but the boy had gone away, would have called for Matthew but could not remember his name. Something in the storm must have heard her try, for its heavy feet stumbled on stones and came lumbering towards her cave. It was a colossal thing, hunched and ancient and had barely begun to walk on two limbs at all: a dim, dense outline behind the waterfall at the entrance. And this is how the world ends, Fran thought as the thing paused outside the curtain of water, a moment before it assumed clarity. Not with megastorms and droughts and planes falling over predatory borders, but with this primitive thing standing at the door, a shapeless, mindless, instinctive being from a time before good or evil, summoned by the primordial flood, and come to take and batter and maim whatever it will, whatever it wants.

It was still dark when Fran was woken by the sound of her name being spoken softly, a hand shaking her shoulder. She was no longer in a cave but lying in her own room, wrapped so tightly in her sheets that she could barely move. Lugh was crouching beside her bed.

'You called my name,' he said with concern. 'I heard you next door. You were shouting.'

'What time is it?'

'Later than you think. Look.' He opened the curtains and revealed the first day in months without a sunrise. The sky was grey with heavy clouds, a strange semi-darkness that made the room feel smaller. Fran untangled herself from the sheets and wiped her eyes.

'At last,' she said, reaching for her shirt. 'It's cooler too.'

She wore a cardigan on the way down to the farmyard, though she took it off by the time she said goodbye to Lugh at the corner of the big house.

'Give Abel my love, and thank him for the books,' she said.

'I'm giving him this,' he replied, taking the recorder out of his pocket.

'I see. Smuggling musical instruments in and books out. Will he be allowed to play it?'

'That's not the point.'

'What is the point?'

Lugh shrugged. 'That he could if he wanted to.'

Fran considered this answer while she performed her morning chores around the farmyard. The air was much cooler in the shade of the great cloud and a relief from the months of merciless sun. The dry plants in the vegetable plot seemed to revive at the drop in temperature, and the chickens were constantly craning their heads upwards in expectation of rain or else of the sky falling in. When Matthew arrived, later than usual, he was followed by Mark and Luke. Mark went directly to the milking shed without a glance at Fran. He emerged with one of the wheelbarrows.

'I'll be needing this tomorrow,' Mark mumbled as he wheeled it past her.

'Help yourself,' Fran replied and then, turning to Luke, said, 'So you're the new muscles?'

'Our Luke will be doing my share while I'm gone, won't you, fish-boy?' said Matthew, laying a hand on his younger brother's shoulder. Luke nudged it off and shifted a few steps away.

'I'm sure we'll get well acquainted over the coming years, won't we, Luke?' Fran gave him a small smile. 'Matthew can show you the ropes today.'

'Years, what years? I'll be back in under three weeks, Francesca,' said Matthew, but she had already turned away and was walking towards the vegetable garden.

When she checked the thermometer at midday, Fran was surprised to see how much the temperature had fallen with the arrival of the cloud. She wondered if it was natural to drop almost fifteen degrees centigrade in one day, or whether this was all part and parcel of the new natural. A few more years of record-keeping and she would have a more reliable idea of how nature was now behaving.

She did not say goodbye to Matthew when she and Lugh left the gardens. Walking beside her, the boy instinctively knew not to speak, not to draw Matthew's attention to their leaving until they had reached the big house and rattled the chain of the doorbell.

'Goodness, how generous,' the old man said when he finally opened the door and accepted his daily basket of vegetables from Fran. 'There was no time to water the lawn today again?'

'I expect this cloud will see to that much better than we can. Besides, I'm sure you'd prefer fruit and vegetables to a lush lawn.'

'I'm so glad we don't have to choose between the two,' the old man laughed, though his blue eyes remained cold. 'Not an either-or situation, food or lawn, is it? How lovely, cheerio.'

'Gramophone,' said Fran quickly before the door had closed on her completely. 'You have a gramophone. We have records. Lots of records, nice stuff, classical stuff, Mahler and all sorts. I'm sure you'd love them. We would like to use your gramophone, please.'

'My, you are audacious today,' he giggled though the crack in the door. 'You mean music? Here? Oh, I really don't think the Gentleman would agree to that. Not since his, you know,' the old man touched his ear and grimaced to indicate some kind of hearing disorder or injury. 'But, I'll tell you what. I shall ask the Gentleman on your behalf. You know what these funny old families are like about such trifles, but I shall ask him, that I promise. And I do know that the Gentleman will consider your request most carefully.'

'If he doesn't like music, then why does he keep a gramophone?' asked Lugh.

'Yes, thank you so much,' the old man said, though he had closed the door on them.

'That was brave of you,' Fran complimented the boy as they walked back to the house.

'He's wrong,' Lugh said in a low voice. 'That old man, he's really wrong.'

'Really, really wrong. Fucking Rumpelstiltskin. I don't trust him either.'

The temperature continued to drop throughout the afternoon. Fran needed to wear her cardigan outside to water the barley and wheat, clear weeds from the vegetables. She gave up after a short time, complained of a headache and left the last tasks to Rhea and Lugh.

'Must be sensitive to all this heaviness in the air, dear,' Rhea said, and told her to lie down.

Fran closed her bedroom curtains and lay down in the darkness, hoping she would not be troubled by any more dreams. The dull, aching pulse in her forehead had spread around the base of her skull, muting all thoughts and sensations other than pain. She longed for the days when a cheap, disposable packet of tablets in the bathroom cabinet would solve something so trite, so debilitating. She vaguely remembered a headache cure from her bible of herbs, was it fenugreek or feverfew? Must be feverfew, the clue was in the name, and did aspirin really come from the bark of young willow trees?

From the garden, fragments of broken conversation drifted in the air like ash from a bonfire: Rhea laughing so hard that she coughed and could barely breathe, and Lugh repeating a strange phrase about Cassiopeia dipping her toes in the Milky Way, something he would never say. Or perhaps it really was ash floating in the air and they had set fire to the dry wheat and barley, a bonfire of grain, the cities of Sumer and Mesopotamia burning. Fran wanted to go to the window and scream at them to stop, but Rhea pressed a cool, damp flannel over her forehead, gave her water to drink, put the bonfire out. The ash turned to stars, Cassiopeia reclined.

In the morning there were voices in the lane. Fran could not hear what they said, but she knew these ones were real. The dull, throbbing darkness still cradled her skull, heavy as the winter blankets that someone had placed over her in the night, but the fever had lifted. On some level, she knew that they were going now: Ky, Matthew and Mark, or was it Luke? One of the brothers, it did not matter which, was going with them, taking a wheelbarrow, back in three weeks. If she could open her eyes, if she could leave the coercive gravity of her bed, she would wrap the blanket over her shoulders and go outside to say goodbye. She wanted to say goodbye. She heard them saying goodbye. She imagined Matthew bending his knees and reaching for the wheelbarrow, saying, 'Here we go. Lifting a finger to help.' Fran whispered goodbye from her bed and seeped into the atoms of her blanket.

꧁

THE CLOUD SETTLED DENSELY OVER the forest as though it had made up its mind to stay. It came with an icy chill that muffled the air and made the house feel unnaturally quiet. Rhea opened the stove and threw another log onto the flames just to hear some noise. Careful now, she thought; she did not want to wake Francesca. Rhea had sat beside Fran's bed all night, listening to her dreamland whispers and cooling her fever with water and kind words.

It was a strange sickness that had struck the girl without warning. She had been working too hard under that sun, Rhea suspected. And Ky going this morning, and Matthew too, and now this sudden chill. It had all been too much for Fran to take: the poor dear was exhausted, that was the cause. But this cold spell, this uncanny drop in temperatures, how could she explain that? It made Rhea nervous. More than that, it scared her. A cold spell was the right phrase: it reminded her of some dark tale of childhood, a nightmare from when she was little. Nature turning upside down and doing what it should not; an unsettled Earth throwing a tantrum.

Rhea wished that Ky had not gone, not today of all days. At least Lugh would be home from the farmyard soon. She tried not to notice the cloud that her breath made in the cold air and took up her book, *Lives of the Eminent Philosophers*. She would face this moment philosophically.

Epicurus was reassuring: he seemed more human and less condescending than Plato. Moreover, he made much more sense to Rhea. After ten minutes or so of reading, she forgot her unease and found comfort in his simple proverbs, committed as many as she could to memory.

'It is impossible to live a pleasant life without living justly,' she said, looking up at the window and repeating the phrase as though this were the answer she had been looking for all along. It was no such thing, of course, for it told her nothing about the nature of justice, but she liked it nonetheless. She took up the ink pen and underlined that sentence. It was not her book and it would have to be returned to the old man's library one day, but she wanted the sentiment to be noticed by someone else, some idle reader in an unknown future. There were other phrases she liked too and, once she started underscoring, she realised she could not stop. Finally, she found what she thought she was looking for.

'Natural justice is to prevent one man from harming or being harmed by another,' she read aloud. It was such a pithy formulation that she wondered whether it could really be that simple, if that were all there was to it. She had harmed a man once, sharply, bloodily, in the back without seeing his face, and she had done it to prevent him from harming Francesca. When she thought about it now, that terrible night in the last house, she knew she had only done what was necessary. And she would not hesitate to do it again to prevent anyone from harming her girls or the boy, her true kin. It had not been revenge, not an eye for an eye, but she still felt that it had tainted her, spoiled her forever. She hated the man for that: not just for what he would have done to Francesca but for what he had driven her to do, in effect for what he had done to her. She read the consoling sentence again. To prevent one from harming another, that is justice. She sighed and put the book down. That would have to do for an answer today.

The freezing silence was fractured by the incisive, insistent, staccato cry of a crow in the garden. The bird must have flown right up to the back door or the window because it sounded so close and urgent. Rhea filled the kettle and, looking into the garden, saw a dark shape standing on the edge of the trees. It was a chilling sight, this thin, waiting thing that appeared as a shadow of her earlier fears. It took some seconds before she realised it was only Ruth wearing her hooded duffel-coat against the cold, her face turned down as though thinking, perhaps praying. Rhea had not seen the girl for days, not since her penance had ended and she had been accepted back into the fold of her family. With all the disputations going on in her own household, Rhea had had little time to worry about poor Ruth. She put the kettle on the stove and, grabbing her coat, went outside to see what was up with the girl.

Ruth was so immersed in her thoughts that she did not hear her name being called. It was only when Rhea reached her and took her arm that Ruth stirred from her dreaming and flinched at the older woman's touch.

'What on Earth have you done to yourself?' Rhea asked, seeing blood on the girl's hands.

'It's nothing. It's just a scratch,' said Ruth, hiding her fingers. 'I was praying.'

'For what, stigmata?' Rhea tried to see her hands, but the girl pulled away. 'What's wrong, my dear? What is it? Has something happened, something bad?'

'He said I'm to bring you,' Ruth said vacantly, as though she were still lost in her thoughts. She stared at the ground and took another step into the forest. 'He said you're to come with me.'

'Where to? Look at me, dear. Who said I'm to come? Was it Abel?'

'He did,' Ruth replied so quietly that she could hardly be heard.

'Don't go running off now, I can't keep up. It's Abel, is it? He's not hurt himself, has he?'

Rhea followed Ruth into the trees, stumbling through undergrowth and over hoops of thorny brambles. She did not know what to think, whether there was some kind of trouble or the girl was merely playing a game. Either way, she had never known Ruth to behave so strangely before. Struggling to think of an explanation, she asked, 'Does Abel want to show me something? It's not the gramophone, is it, dear? He didn't get his hands on that wind-up record player, did he?'

'He said I was to bring you before him.'

'Bless him. I bet he did, didn't he?'

'Aye, he did.'

It was still the middle of the afternoon, but the lowering cloud had cast the forest into an early, dismal twilight. Rhea was glad that she had brought her coat, but the icy air hurt her face and hands. Winter at the end of June, she thought, surely this was not right. Gramophone or no gramophone, she wanted to be back home, sitting beside the fire with Fran and Lugh, and Ky too if she would only be there, and the kettle would be boiling on the stove by now. Rhea pursued Ruth's black coat further along the riverbank until the girl disappeared among the shadows and the first white snowflakes began to fall. Rhea stopped to catch her breath and held out a palm, disbelieving what she saw. A little winter in the heart of summer, ice crystals drifting through the sun-baked, bone-dry trees, melting on her outstretched hand. Such a gentle end to nature as she had known it: silent and fearful, the blanching of reason.

No more hide-and-seek, she thought, turning back towards home. She did not know the forest, so she followed the meandering riverbank, thinking it must lead eventually back to the house. The air thickened quickly with snow. Soon she could see little more than the closest trees, the rest of the world was erased. In the distance, she heard or thought she heard the barking of a dog but, when she stopped walking, the dog fell quiet too. She did not know how long she walked, floundering over hidden roots and slipping on wet leaves, a blanket of wild garlic. Eventually, she caught sight of a solid black shape among the trees. At first she thought that Ruth had reappeared and she stumbled towards her, calling the girl's name. As she came closer, she realised it was just a sheet of black tarpaulin hanging between branches, an old weather-worn tent that she had seen once before in winter, the real winter, not this bastard midsummer winter. Rhea leaned against a tree, coughing for breath, exhausted and winded.

She did not know how long the voice had been speaking before she caught the sound, before the words broke through to her consciousness. It was a cold, impersonal voice, like a distant announcement or a radio play, or the voice of a phone in her pocket.

'And I looked, and behold a pale horse: and his name that sat on him was Death,' it said, and she did not catch the rest. Lifting her head, she peered through the white static of snow and saw him approach, Enoch leaning on his axe as if it were a walking stick, limping through the trees. She felt instantly relieved at the sight of him and called his name. He did not look up but continued towards her, his eyes set steadfastly on the ground.

'And power was given unto them over the Earth,' he continued, closer now.

Rhea wiped the melted ice from her cheeks, her brow, and called his name again. It was strange that he would not look at her, but perhaps he too was lost, perhaps he was suffering from the cold as much as she was. Once more, she thought she heard the distant yelping of a dog, or a fox, or a frightened deer calling forlornly through the snow.

'Enoch, dear,' she said as the man came to a standstill before her. He raised his face and she could see his expression, stern and merciless, seeing but not seeing her, and now she could hear him clearly.

'And power was given to kill with sword, and with hunger, and with death,' he said, heaving the axe into the air, over his head, onto hers, 'and to kill with the beasts of the Earth.'

CHAPTER NINE

CANAAN

THE FIRE IN THE BEDROOM hearth had burned so low that it was now nothing more than embers, a grate of dying stars. The constellations were not ones that Fran recognised: they flickered and receded and rekindled elsewhere, an inconstant game that she did not want to play. Turning away, she pulled the blanket over her cold face and wondered who had lit the fire and why. If it was winter again, then what had happened to the summer and the harvest, to the wheat and the barley that she had planted from seed, and would there now be bread?

Of course there was bread, she thought, sinking back beneath the sloe-black layers of viscous sleep. It was inconceivable that there would be no bread in the apartment. There was always bread in the cupboard over the toaster: bread and breadsticks, sometimes crumpets and muffins. She wondered if there were muffins today, and honey, and soft butter in the butter dish, perhaps peanut butter too. Her mouth watered at the thought of toasted muffins, melted butter. If it was a Sunday, and today felt like a Sunday, then she must have a hangover. And if she had a hangover, then Dean would have one too. She could not remember what had happened last night, not an uncommon occurrence if they had been drinking on a Saturday, or any other night for that matter, but she could be sure that Dean would be suffering too. He would be lying on the sofa in the lounge flicking through his messages with some film on the widescreen television in the background, a can of cold lager, hair of the dog, within his reach on the carpet. If she went into the lounge, he would not look at her but he would say something, bark something, inevitably unkind. She did not want to hear what it was, not when she was feeling this delicate, so she decided to stay in bed. If there was only some way to have toasted muffins without seeing Dean, without flinching from whatever he would say. And a mug of hot chocolate too.

The last logs gave up the illusion of solidity and disintegrated in the fireplace, a sigh of ash and sparks. There was no fireplace in the apartment with muffins and butter, so she must be in some other place. She pulled the blanket away from her ear and listened for clues. No buses, no cars, no high-pitched beeping of a pedestrian crossing outside, nothing but a solitary crow calling through the empty air. A winter sound, the sense of snow, and a man standing at the entrance to her room. Fran knew it was a man because she could hear him breathing heavily, with difficulty, as though he were wounded, as though he had been stumbling against trees and over wet grass to reach this moment, this bed, the stench of sweat and the backwoods on his skin.

Fran resurfaced through the weavings of wool and fevered dream, and slowly pulled the blanket from her face. She knew where she was now, which bed and which house: it was the man standing at her door who was out of place. From the way he was breathing, quick and nervous, he also knew that he should not be there. Fran would not speak to him, she would not say anything until there was light. If she spoke to him in the dark, if he answered while he was still a shadow, then he would become incarnate and nothing could ever dispel him, not even direct sunlight. Slowly, Fran raised herself up from the covers and reached to the bedside cabinet. She found the stub of a candle, but neither matches nor a lighter nearby. Feeling around the side of the cabinet, she pulled on a handle and opened the small drawer. That was empty too.

Fran closed her eyes and tried to stem the wave of dread that flushed over her and thundered a pulse in her ears. If she could not see him, then surely he could not see her either. He must have known she was there, but what did he want and what was he waiting for? If she moved imperceptibly and did not make a sound, if she put one hand on the floor and then the other, she could drag herself down and slip under the bed in slow motion. It was not much of a plan, nor much of a defence, but at least it was something. Quietly, she pulled the blankets off her shoulder and reached over to touch the cold wooden floorboards. As she put her weight on that hand, the floorboard gave out a loud tell-tale creak and she stopped dead. The man's breathing quickened and he stepped forward into the room. They stayed like this for an eternal moment, poised in the darkness, each of them waiting for the other to act. Tentatively, Fran reached her other hand down to the floor where her fingers touched upon an unexpected shape, a small box of matches lying beside the bed. The box rattled lightly as she picked it up and removed a match. She counted to three, held her breath and struck the match.

The match head flared brightly for an instant and then dimmed, giving just enough illumination to cast shadows on the walls and reveal the room as empty. Fran tried to keep her fingers from shaking as she lighted the bedside candle and raised it over the floor. The footprints were real. Glistening mud and wet leaves, an outline of boots that had tramped through the woods or the darkness of her dreams and come to a standstill at her open door. One footprint had breached the threshold.

THE LANDSCAPE OF EVENING WAS defined by a ghostly fluorescence. A thin layer of white covered the lane, the grass, the branches of trees, the ridges and the furrows of the vegetable gardens. In the right season, Lugh would have stepped on the cracks between the patches of snow to encourage more flakes to settle. But this was the wrong season and that frightened him. Holding the firewood close to his chest, he kicked through the fallen snow on his way back home. If he could erase it, then it would not have snowed at midsummer and nature would not be broken.

Late June had regressed to February. Perhaps the sun had burned itself out with the hard drought of the last few months. Perhaps they had lost track of the months and the seasons as they had of the hours. Now nothing was reliable, nothing could be known.

In the kitchen, he lay the branches on the floor and lit one of the last, emergency candles. The kettle had boiled dry on the stove and the fire had been left to burn low, lower than he had ever seen it before. Rhea must have neglected the stove, probably fallen asleep at Fran's bedside, so he emptied the tray of ash outside and fed fresh wood to the embers. The kitchen felt peculiarly empty as though it were the wrong kitchen, as though he had come to the wrong house. There were no vegetables on the chopping board, no saucepan of soup, no steaming pot of tea on the side. It felt as deserted as the farmhouse after his mum had gone, and then his brother. He stood still in the semi-darkness and listened for the sound of others: a cough, a sigh, the creak of an armchair. For a moment, he had the terrible sensation that he was back in that abandoned farmhouse. If nature could break, then so could time, so could his mind. But Fran's gardening boots were standing beside the back door, Rhea's knitting lay in a heap on the chair, the book she had been reading was resting on the table, and there was movement on the landing overhead, someone coming down the stairs. Not everything had been broken.

Lugh poured a jar of preserved apples into a saucepan, set the pan on the stove, and flicked through the pages of the book on the table. In the dim light of the candle, he found reassuring traces of Rhea, marks she had made in the last chapter, sentences she had underlined in black ink, although little that made sense to him. Laying the book on the table, Lugh turned to the stove and was startled to see a man standing in the doorway to the darkened hall.

Enoch's face was a mask of indifference. His long hair and curly black beard concealed any hint of an expression. He contemplated the boy impassively for a moment, and then limped into the kitchen leaning on his heavy stick for support. Before reaching the door, Enoch stopped at the table and touched the book that Lugh had just laid down, tracing the words on the cover with his finger. Whether the title meant anything to him or not was impossible to tell, but he picked up the book anyway and left by the back door.

'That's not yours,' said Lugh, following Enoch into the back yard. 'That book, it's not yours.'

'That book's not yours,' Enoch said, imitating the boy in a mocking, dangerous voice. He did not look back at Lugh but limped steadily away and disappeared around the corner.

Lugh listened to the thud of Enoch's stick on the ground, a dull, heavy metal sound that measured the distance of stones between their houses. When the noise faded into silence, Lugh locked the door against the cold and pushed the key deep into his pocket. In the candlelight, he saw Enoch's leafy footprints on the kitchen floor, the black outline left by the axehead, his walking stick. Lugh took his candle and followed the tracks into the hallway. He found Fran standing at the top of the stairs, a blanket draped over her shoulders.

'It wasn't you, was it?' she said, looking down at the boy. 'No, I know it wasn't you.'

'Where's Rhea?' asked Lugh.

Fran shook her head.

They stared at each other for a moment, two faces dimly lit by the last candles in each of their hands, above and below, darkness between and silence around them.

The cloud broke apart in the night, released a savage barrage of ice, not snow this time but torrential hail that roared as it battered earth, branch, brick and tile, stripping leaves and shattering on stone. Fran laid blankets on the kitchen floor, a bed of consolation in front of the stove, two bowls of stewed apples and a game of chess by firelight. They had been to the houses opposite, but the mother had said that no one had seen Rhea at all. In the woods, they had shouted her name for hours, stumbled over roots and bramble. Only an owl returned their call and, in the distance, a dog or a gekkering fox. At first light, if there was light, if the sun should ever return again, they would go back out to search for her. For now, Fran moved a pawn over the chessboard and listened to the clamouring hail.

'Was it my turn or yours?' she asked.

'Probably,' Lugh shrugged and continued to stare at the window, taking no interest in the game that was taking all night to go nowhere.

'What's going on in that head of yours, O'Byrne? Come on, better out than in.'

'Hail,' he replied after a pause. 'Rhea out there in this hail.'

'She would have found somewhere to shelter, I'm sure. She's not a fool.'

'She left her knitting.'

'Which must mean she'll be back soon.'

They both started at a sound outside, a different sound that each for a moment thought was Rhea coming home, but soon realised was something rolling on the ground, a bucket perhaps knocked over by the force of falling ice. It rocked back and forth, back and forth, the metal handle scratching against stone. Not for the first time, Lugh opened the back door to peer into the blackness outside and returned disappointed.

'We should keep the door locked,' he said. 'Should always keep it locked now.'

'But what if she comes back and we're not here?'

'You said she'd be back in the morning.'

'I said she should be,' said Fran and then, more confidently, 'She should be.'

'That man can't get inside if it's locked.'

That man has an axe, Fran was going to say, but she did not want to talk to Lugh about Enoch. Some boundary had been crossed, some unseen, infrared, gossamer-thin thread separating coexistence from chaos, civility from barbarism had been breached the instant that Enoch had entered their house unannounced, uninvited, stood at her door, one foot over the line. Invisible or not, he had broken an unspoken principle. Next time, it would take more than a match to dispel him. Next time, she would need her own ring of invisibility.

'I wish Ky were here, and Matthew,' she sighed, returning the pawn to its original position.

Lugh stared at the board and said nothing. There was another explosion of hail in the darkness, a thunderous torrent of ice that ricocheted against the walls and windows with a growing roar, drowning out all sound and thought.

In the lull between downpours, Fran and Lugh drifted into fitful sleep, taking turns to wake and lay more wood inside the glowing stove, or to stir suddenly at a noise outside, something breaking or falling over that sounded like an axehead clicking against stone.

The hail turned to heavy rain, the rain to occasional showers that smothered the unremarkable sunrise. When the dim underside of purple clouds could be discerned in the sky, Fran brewed a pot of tea and boiled eggs for breakfast. Lugh unlocked the back door and surveyed the gardens. To his relief, the snow had melted, but the vegetables had been battered by hail. The onions and leeks lay limply on the earth and not one of the thin strands of wheat was standing.

'Don't tell me,' said Fran, pouring tea into their mugs. 'I don't want to know.'

Without a real sunrise, it was impossible to know the time. Neither of them spoke as they walked to the big house, stepping carefully between rivulets of rainwater that flowed down the lane. It was so cold that they could see their breath in the air, and fragments of still-frozen hail lay scattered like shrapnel among the beaten grass and broken wildflowers. It was earlier than usual when they knocked at the big house. The old man eventually opened the front door wearing a pair of blue and white striped pyjamas and rubbing his bald head. Glaring over the rim of his spectacles, he listened to Fran with an air of disapproval and, for once, did not pretend to smile.

'Why do you suppose that I would have seen your friend, or anyone else for that matter, at this inglorious hour of the morning?' he replied crisply, a schoolteacher addressing his most troublesome pupils. He hummed impatiently, waiting for an answer.

'She's been missing since last night,' said Fran. 'She might be injured or ill. You see, it's not like Rhea to simply disappear. Please,' she put her hand against the door as the old man gestured her away. 'I only want to know if you've seen her.'

'And this couldn't have waited until a more decent hour?'

'No, it could not.'

'This really is… ' but the old man could not find sufficient words for what he thought it was.

'I just want to know if you've seen her.'

'It's your own fault, Ambrose,' he said, shaking his head as he addressed himself more kindly than he had spoken to Fran. 'You have a big heart, that's the root of the problem. You give these people a helping hand, though you know how troublesome they'll be, they always are, these types, and that it will all probably end up with a lot of bother. And sure enough, here we are. Terrible bother, and at this hour of the morning too.'

The old man closed and locked the door. He lingered for a moment to hear what they would say, the boy and that vexatious girl on the doorstep. As he expected, it was nothing complimentary. He broke into a toothy, mischievous grin, glad that he had stood for no more of their nonsense than was absolutely necessary. Best to nip it in the bud early, he thought, else they would start calling at every hour of the night and day, a complete disregard for the lives of real people. He padded across the parquet hallway in his slippers and up the winding wooden staircase to the first floor, a balconied landing overlooking the hall. Following the gallery past several empty bedrooms, he stopped at the dark, panelled door to the tower, the largest and most ornate entrance on the landing, removed a key from his pyjama pocket and slid it into the keyhole.

'Coo-ee. Are we awake?' he called up the unlit stairway. 'Haven't fallen asleep, have we?'

Something shifted in the dark room at the top of the stairs. The old man called again and now there was the sound of a body moving on the floorboards, muscles stretching, bones clicking.

'Nevertheless not what I will, but—' Abel called faintly from the room in the tower. 'Nevertheless not what I will, but—'

'Beloved boy, it really is a very simple verse to remember,' said the old man, mildly irritated.

'Nevertheless not what I will, but—' Abel shouted, his voice rising anxiously.

'Let's give it another day, shall we? Shall we?' the old man said as he locked the door.

M**OTHER STIRRED THE ASHES IN** the stove with an iron poker, scraping the hidden corners of the grate to make sure the last of the embers were dead. She removed the ash pan and stood up straight, sighing at the sudden pain in her knees, her aching spine. The water in the kettle was still lukewarm from last night; that would have to be sufficient for their needs until the fire was relit in the evening. If only these blessed summer days did not last so long, she thought as she cast the ashes into the garden, then they could have hot water in the morning. Still, her firstborn son knew best. If he said no fires during the daytime, then no fires during the daytime.

She sat down at the kitchen table and picked at the bones of last night's trout. The windows looked so much simpler and more decent without those old curtains hanging up gathering dust, she thought. No need for curtains if you've got nothing to hide. That globe had gone too; Enoch had seen to that. Why the girl wanted to clutter up the place she would never know. Of all her children, she found Ruth the most difficult to understand. A strange, secretive creature, always something going on behind those eyes, always hiding something. God forgive her for thinking so, but her daughter was not quite normal. There was something missing, some innate, familial instinct that was second nature to all her boys, her good boys, faithful boys. Like now, Ruth was still holed up in her bedroom, would not be down until past midday though there were chores to be done: Enoch's soiled clothes to be scrubbed for a start. Always reluctant to do what should come naturally. Aye, the girl was not quite right.

Mother's concerns for her children were interrupted when Luke came in from the garden and lay a bucket of the small fish he had caught, just a few minnows and a roach, on the table. He said that he had seen Fran in the woods.

'Still calling for that old woman, she is,' said Luke, sitting down opposite his mother. 'Asked me to go looking with her. You and me and all of us. Says we're to have another of those meeting-things. Quite angry she was. I didn't know what to say. Said I'd speak to you first.'

'You did well, son.' Mother nodded, her expression set in granite. 'Needs to be brought down a peg or two, that one. Needs to know her place. You tell that girl we'll be over this evening to settle things. No, sooner is better. Tell her we'll be there shortly. I'll pray with Enoch, then we'll be over. Best end this nonsense quickly, straighten things out so she knows what's what. And Luke, you're a good boy.'

The continuous, unbroken, sky-sized cloud rolled overhead, stirring but going nowhere, turning within and against itself and unleashing a steady cascade of rain. By the time Fran and Lugh returned from the forest, they were soaked through. They hung their dripping coats to dry on the rack above the stove.

'You shouldn't have gone out in this,' said Lugh, handing a tea-towel to Fran to dry her hair.

'You sound just like Rhea.' Fran smiled, but then felt the return of the stomach-hollowing fear that, for a careless, shameless moment, she had forgotten.

'Got to be careful,' he said. 'You only just got over that fever.'

'Wish I still had it.' She rubbed her hair dry with the towel. When she looked up, Lugh was frowning at her. 'I mean, I wish this were just some fevered hallucination. Don't look at me like that, O'Byrne. I'm not leaving you as well.'

'As well as who?'

'You're right. We don't know what's happened to Rhea, or when she'll be back.'

'You said she'd be back this morning.'

'I said I hoped she'd be back this morning.'

'You said—'

'Oh, Jesus, what do I know?' Fran shouted in exasperation, slapping the tea-towel against the table with a sharp crack. 'Honestly, what do I know? How can I possibly know more than you? If you're so wise, why don't you tell me what's happened to Rhea? Why don't you tell me when she's coming back?'

Fran pressed the towel against her face and breathed deeply, trying to recover herself, her shattered self-possession, feeling doubly guilty for yelling at the boy. 'That's unfair. I know it was unfair. I'm sorry.' She uncovered her face and reached for Lugh. She brought him into an embrace but felt his resistance. 'I'm sorry. I'm awful, I'm a terrible person. We're both worried; we shouldn't turn on each other. O'Byrne, I'm sorry.'

While she was holding him, stroking his hair and rocking him, there was a cursory knock on the window and Mother let herself in through the back door. Fran continued to hold the boy, though she stared at the woman who had walked into their kitchen.

'Come in?' said Fran, releasing the boy. 'That's the usual thing, isn't it? Knock-knock, who's there, come in.'

'Not interrupting anything, I trust,' said Mother with a sideways glance at Lugh. Her eye fell disapprovingly on the fire in the stove, though she stood close enough to warm herself beside it.

'Not if you've come to help.' Fran pulled a chair out for the older woman to sit down. 'Rhea's still missing; we can't find her anywhere. Bring some chairs from the sitting room, Lugh.'

'I can stand.' Mother nodded as Ruth, Luke and finally Enoch followed her into the kitchen. 'We'll all stand, thank you.'

'That's just going to make me uncomfortable, and I'm feeling uncomfortable enough as it is. Please,' Fran said wearily, indicating the chair again. 'Sit.'

Mother arched her eyebrows at Enoch, but sat down close to the stove nonetheless. After a moment's uncertainty, each of her children followed suit. Lugh returned from the front room with a chair for Fran, while he pulled himself up to sit on the counter. Fran related her concerns for Rhea, how nobody had seen her since yesterday afternoon.

'I'm sick with worry—we both are,' she said with a weak smile at Lugh. 'If she is lost in the forest, then we need—we would like your help to find her. We're asking for your help.'

'And what if she's not lost?' Enoch said just above a whisper. He did not look up but watched his own thumb running circles over the cover of the encyclopaedia on the table.

'What do you mean?'

'There's the Beast out there in them woods.' His brown eyes were fixed on the shapes that his thumbnail scratched on the book. 'I seen it there in the darkness. It took Father, took Uncle Joe. Damn near took me also.'

'I saw him too,' said Ruth unexpectedly.

'You did what?' Mother leaned forward to peer at her daughter's downturned face.

'I did, I saw him first day of my penance, out there in the forest.' Ruth closed her eyes and gestured at the door. 'Funny beard, horns on his head, and terrible, terrible eyes. He spoke to me too. I didn't think it could be him, the Beast, but it was, it must have been. Told me to go. Told me to leave you,' she said, finally opening her tear-filled eyes to stare intensely at her mother.

'My poor girl.' Mother reached out to take Ruth's hand. 'And you obeyed him?'

'Seriously, there is no devil running about in the forest,' Fran said with a reassuring glance at Lugh. 'All we want to know is whether you'll help us look for Rhea. That's it, that's all.'

'I agree with you,' Luke said in a strange tone, an insincere smile, triumphant eyes. 'And I'll say so when that issue's raised at the appropriate time. But first, best we all agree that no one will be lighting fires during the daytime.'

'Aye, agreed. And there'll be a book somewhere hereabouts, won't there?' Mother looked around the kitchen. 'Isn't there some fancy book where all those things get written down? You'll know its hiding place, Ruthy. You'll have seen it before.'

'Behind you, Mother.' Ruth nodded towards the pile of ledgers on the dresser. 'It'll be among those ones there, I'm sure.'

Mother took the four black notebooks from the shelf and lay them on her lap. She flicked briskly through the pages of each until she found what she was searching for.

'This looks like the one. Minutes, codes, constitution, all sorts of clever words and conceits going on in here. Aye, very clever things.'

'Can someone please tell me what is going on?' said Fran, unable to comprehend the ludicrous twist to events. She thought this had to be a dream, an absurdist, fevered nightmare in which Rhea had disappeared and no one appreciated the seriousness of the situation. Enoch would not look at her but stared at his thumbnail marks on the encyclopaedia, a closed expression on his face. Luke and Ruth kept their eyes on their mother as she read sentences aloud in a solemn, yet sarcastic voice. Only Lugh returned Fran's gaze, wide-eyed with fear and desperate for some sign of reassurance from her. She shook her head, unable to offer anything.

'Now, listen up,' said Mother as she ripped pages from the ledger and carefully folded each one into the burning stove. 'There's to be no more fires during daytime. No more wicked stories and nonsense about magic beans and such. And no more clever constitutions and books and whatnot. The word of the Lord is sufficient for our needs. For the Lord has promised, "I will give unto thee and to thy seed after thee the land wherein thou art a stranger, all the land of Canaan, for an everlasting possession; and I will be thy God." As it was promised, so it's come to pass, amen.'

Luke and Ruth echoed the amen. Enoch nodded and handed the encyclopaedia to Mother.

'Don't you dare,' Fran shouted as she scrambled to grab the book from the woman's hands.

'Uh-uh,' said Mother, holding it behind her back, out of Fran's reach. 'No clever books, else you won't be needing our help to look for your old woman now, will you.'

'But we need it,' said Fran, her face so close to the other's that she could have bitten or at least slapped her. 'We actually need it. Even you need it, for the garden, for everything.'

'Only one book we'll be needing, that's the Good Book.'

Fran resisted a little longer, one hand clutching Mother's wrist, the other on her shoulder. Behind her, she knew that one of the brothers was already on his feet, Luke probably, waiting to seize her the moment the woman gave him the nod. So many lines had been crossed in such a quick succession of seconds, such a rapid collapse into outrageous behaviour, that Fran sensed only one more boundary remained to be broken. And she was not ready to give them a reason to use violence on her, on Lugh, not yet.

'But why?' Fran asked, sounding like a child. As soon as she had uttered the question, so infantile and profound and all-encompassing, she knew that she had signalled her surrender.

'Because I say so, my girl,' said Mother. 'It's the right thing to do and must be done.'

Fran released her grip on the woman's wrist and slumped back into her chair, exhausted, defeated. Mother twitched a satisfied smile and carefully positioned the encyclopaedia among the dancing flames in the stove.

'That's it, that's sorted,' said Mother, standing to button her coat, brush down the memory of the scuffle from her clothes. She gestured for Luke to open the door. 'We'd best take a look for her now, that old woman. Can't promise it'll do any good, mind, not if the Beast took her, so you'd best start praying for her soul. God bless.'

Obedient as shadows, Luke and Ruth followed their mother out the back door and into the torrential rain. As Enoch limped behind Fran's chair, he paused and lightly touched her shoulder. Fran leaned back to glare at him and silently curse. The thick black hair and beard concealed all but his dark eyes, lips and sharp cheekbones. Though she had rarely seen Enoch before, and never at such close range, Fran was unnerved by his resemblance to Matthew. Physically, Enoch was much broader, stockier and built like a pit bull, but there was an unmistakable, unsettling familiarity in his features. Of course, all of the brothers shared a likeness, but this was different. Maybe, if she scratched at that beard and that hair and those eyebrows with her fingernails, she would uncover Matthew's face hidden beneath the differences. Fraternal archaeology, wishful digging.

'Don't be troubled,' said Enoch. His hand lingered on her shoulder, found a strand of loose hair that he looped around his finger, dispensed the ghost of a smile and then he was gone.

'They burned our encyclopaedia,' said Lugh in the silent aftermath.

'They did,' Fran agreed, 'in a fire that shouldn't be burning during daytime, apparently.'

She glanced inside the open stove at the blackened book, the flames licking the remains of the cover. Even now, if she retrieved it from the fire, some fragments might be salvaged: Plato or Mesopotamia, maybe bee-keeping. But the rest was cinders and the whole was spoiled. She closed the stove door, listened to the rain, the stream of water running down the lane.

The soil softened and released its grip on stones that rolled away in the running water. Leaves that had curled yellow in the relentless sun were stripped from the forest by the unending rain, carried away and deposited wherever the flood had taken the sun and the summer. Daylight was underwater grey, a ripple of reflections teeming down the morning windows, evening walls, while the percussion of a thousand drops stretched the night into a half-dream of heartbeats, footsteps, a knocking at the door.

'Who's there?' asked Fran.

'Never a trace of her,' said Mother, standing in the darkness outside. 'Beast most likely got her, just like we said. Same as it did Father and Uncle Joe. No sense looking for her now, putting us all in the way of danger. Best accept what it is. What's done is done.'

Fran locked the back door and sat down on the bed of blankets in front of the stove. Lugh said nothing as he lined up the pieces on the chessboard, took his first move in the flickering firelight. Another night came ticking the wet seconds on roof tiles, on attic floorboards, on concrete and puddles, a steady pulse of water torture knocking on wood.

'Who's there?' asked Fran. Nobody replied, though the tick-tapping persisted.

Lugh kept his eyes on Fran's boots splashing through the water ahead of him, walking against a tide of days that turned into a week and then another, into the third. Sometimes in the farmyard they saw Luke digging for potatoes in the flooded vegetable plot, picking strawberries in the greenhouse. Luke heard them approach but did not turn around.

'Mother says you're to give up looking for that old woman,' Luke said, raindrops dripping from his glistening fringe. 'No point tempting fate, is there?'

Fran walked straight past him as though he had not spoken, as though he were not there. In the forest, she called out Rhea's name louder than ever, loud enough to be heard by Luke. In the forest, she now carried a sharp scythe, as did Lugh. No point tempting fate.

The rain played the same tune night after night, high notes, heavy notes, occasional improvisations. Fran moved a rook across the chessboard, tapped its course to the rhythm of falling water, said, 'Knock knock.'

'Who's there?' asked Lugh.

'Enoch.'

'Enoch who?'

'E-knocks but e-can't come in.'

Lugh smiled a little, barely amused, and considered his next move. 'Knock knock,' he said after a long pause, taking her rook with a pawn.

'Who's there?' Fran replied.

'Mother.'

'Mother who?'

'Motherfucker burnt the encyclopaedia,' said Lugh, almost spitting the sentence.

'O'Byrne,' Fran cried, trying to sound appalled, but soon she was laughing. The more noises she made, the harder Lugh found it to quash his own laugh. Fran rolled back on the blanket and closed her eyes until the fit had passed.

'Seriously, O'Byrne, that must be the funniest thing you've ever said.'

As she sat up to take her next move, there was a real knock on the back door. Fran and Lugh looked at each other as the handle turned once, twice, but the door was locked.

'You better come over, see who's back,' said Luke on the outside.

'Who? Who's back?' said Fran. She leaped up and unlocked the door. 'Is it Rhea?'

'Better come see for yourself,' Luke replied, backing away into the wet darkness.

They slipped quickly into their boots and coats and caught up with Luke outside. Fran asked again who had returned, but Luke remained enigmatic, said they would soon see. He led them past a wheelbarrow that stood curiously empty in the middle of the lane, and into Ruth's house—the house that had once been Ruth's but was now firmly under Mother's occupation. Inside the flickering dimness of the firelit front room, it took time for Fran to distinguish between the shadowy figures seated around the fireplace: Enoch in the armchair, Ruth crouched on the floor beside the hearth, and Mother staring at her hands on the edge of the sofa. Another body, the one that had returned, sat cloaked in blankets beside Mother. He was thin-cheeked and glistening wet in the light. In a moment of blind relief, Fran believed the shivering silhouette was Matthew. Instinctively, she knelt down beside him and smiled into his face. But the resemblance soured, dissolved into difference, the familiar brown eyes turned strange and unresponsive, unfocused with poor vision. It was the other brother, Mark, gazing back at her.

'Where are the others?' Fran asked, retreating from the transformation.

Mark stared at her without speaking, offered a slight shake of his head.

'They've been taken, just like they all get taken,' Enoch replied on his silent brother's behalf.

'Where are they?' Fran insisted, grabbing hold of Mark's arm. 'Where's Matthew and Ky?'

'Beast took them,' said Enoch. 'Beast took both of them before they even reached the mountain. Beast took them in the night, in the forest, while they slept. No point asking. That's all there is to it.'

'Will you, please,' said Fran turning, pausing between each word, 'shut the fuck up and let him speak for himself. I want to know what's happened to Ky and to Matthew.'

'You'll not speak to him in that tone,' said Luke, stepping forward to lay his hands on Fran. Enoch shrugged indifferently to allow this offence to pass unpunished.

'Beast took them before we reached the mountain.' Mark was shivering so much that his lips trembled, but he kept his eyes fixed on Fran. 'Set upon us when we camped down for the night, while we were sleeping. It came for Ky first. Matthew did his bit for her, but—fool, he should have stayed out the way. Nothing he could have done. Nothing nobody could do.'

'No,' said Fran, shaking her head, 'that doesn't make sense. Why were you sleeping in the forest? The mountain isn't that far away. And where have you been for the last three weeks? It doesn't make sense, Mark, it doesn't. I don't believe you. Why are you lying?'

'Like I said, no point asking for more,' said Enoch. He nodded at Mark to comfort or to hush him. 'That's all there is to it. What's done is done.'

'I ran off in the dark, got lost in the forest.' Mark lowered his gaze. 'Nothing I could do. Nothing nobody could do. Beast took them, both of them.'

Fran gripped his arm, 'You're lying. I know you're lying.'

'Enough now,' Enoch said decisively. 'Lord's will be done.'

'And you,' said Fran, turning to Mother, 'are you not saying anything? Have you got so many sons that one more or less doesn't matter? It's Matthew we're talking about. Matthew.'

Mother continued to stare down at her clenched hands, her face etched in firelit marble.

'Lord's will be done,' she said finally, echoing her firstborn in a cracked voice.

After a moment, Mother raised her eyes to the quickening torrent of rain outside, an intense roar of water against the uncurtained window.

CHAPTER TEN
DIONYSIA

THE FOREST BORE RIVERS INSTEAD of leaves. Stripped barren before their time, the trees nursed bottomless pools among the cradles of their roots, drip-fed a fruitless waterland of puddle and pond, sodden mulch and mushrooms out of season. Lugh was wearing an old, broad-rimmed farm-labourer's hat against the incessant rain. He had found it among the boxes of farm tools and farmers' coats and bee-keepers' veils in the milking shed. It was a size too large and it reeked of musty old sweat, but he was grateful for the protection it provided as he tramped down the lane. He fought the saturated soil for possession of his boots, one sucking step after another, until he reached the solid concrete at the gate to Usquam House. After he climbed the rippling surface of the driveway and followed the path to the library window, he stood on tiptoe to peer inside.

There was no one inside the room today, no Abel leaning on the window ledge and pretending to study Augustine or Aquinas while surreptitiously reading the pages of a different book hidden beneath, some Brontë or Hardy, a Joyce or a Woolf. Thursdays were pointless. Abel was never in the library on a Thursday, nor a Friday morning for that matter, and Sundays were out of the question. Lugh was not entirely sure what day it was, but he suspected it was none of those. The days were all the same, nameless and anaemic, seeping from grey dawn to sunless dusk to damp blackness, except for Sundays which were marked by hymn-singing across the road, a violence of hands, babble of tongues. It had been a couple of days since Lugh had last heard that racket, so he assumed today must be Tuesday.

Just as Lugh was about to leave and walk across the waterlogged lawns to the farmyard, the library door opened and the details of the dim room—the books on the bookshelves, the patterns on the carpet, the birdcage chandelier hanging above two armchairs by the fireplace—became clear in a momentary burst of light. Abel crept into the library with a heavy book under one arm. He was barefooted and wearing his grey habit, a similar vestment to that worn by the old man, though frayed and more threadbare. Abel saw Lugh at the window at once, gave a small smile of relief and closed the door behind him. Instead of coming directly to the window, he placed his book on one of the armchairs, positioned the chair against the door and remained listening for a short while to make sure that he had not been followed, that the floorboards outside the room were not creaking with the footsteps of Father Ambrose. When he was certain the old man was elsewhere, he leapt lightly up to the ledge and unlatched the window.

'Where were you?' Lugh asked.

Abel put his finger to his lips and gestured towards the ceiling. He spoke with his hands and eyes in a language they had concocted between themselves. Now that Abel could play the alphabet on his fingers, naming people with a quick, indicative sign, he relied less on writing his answers on paper and more on signing. He indicated that Father Ambrose was upstairs and that he could be listening. They had to be quiet.

'It's a big house. Besides, he can't hear a thing in this,' Lugh replied in a lower voice as the rainwater dripped steadily off the rim of his hat. 'What does it matter anyhow?'

Abel sighed and shrugged to show that, even if he could speak, he could not explain. Instead, he absent-mindedly harvested specks of dust and raindrops from Lugh's sleeve. Lugh leaned closer and opened his palm, allowing Abel's fingers to pick gently, comfortingly at his skin.

'What day is it?' Lugh asked. 'I thought it might be Thursday when you weren't here.'

Wednesday, seven o'clock, Abel indicated with his fingers. One of his first chores of the day, the first thing Abel did every morning after prayers, was to wind up the grandfather clock in the drawing room. The day and the time were things he could share with Lugh, items of knowledge that he took pleasure in smuggling through the window in addition to contraband books. Remembering something, Abel smiled excitedly and began to sign with his hands, spelling an unusual word that Lugh had never heard before.

'Today is August, first of August. Today is L-A-M-M-A-S, Lammas?' Lugh read aloud, frowning as he struggled to interpret Abel's charade. 'Before, in times before, in old times, people digging, people working—farmers? — brought something in a bowl, they brought bread and fruit – brought food here to the big house at Lammas. Like a gift, a present for the Gentleman upstairs?'

Abel nodded, pleased that he had communicated so effectively.

'But me and Fran, we take food to the old man every day.'

Yes, Abel indicated half-heartedly, but this was different.

'Okay,' said Lugh, though he did not understand. There were so many special days and strange ceremonies and mysterious rites that went on in the big house, none of which made any sense to Lugh on the outside. He would never know why Abel had to live with the old man in the first place, why he was not allowed to speak, and what happened on those days he did not come to the library window. These were all just things for Lugh to accept, like the death of his brother, no fires during daylight hours and the endlessly falling rain. No point asking anything if the answers were more confusing than the question.

'I dare you to do this instead.' Lugh rolled up his other sleeve and demonstrated to Abel how he wanted to be stroked gently over the golden-red hair on his arms and, on the underside, the faint blue veins on his wrist.

Abel watched and willingly obliged. Lugh closed his eyes and lost himself in the sensation.

Tell me, Abel gestured after a few minutes of stroking Lugh's forearm while listening to the rain on the lawn, the leaking gutters, the trickle from Lugh's hat.

'What should I tell you?' asked Lugh.

Abel shrugged and indicated with his free hand: anything, everything. Tell me something.

'Nothing new to tell.'

Fran? Abel asked with a gesture of long, flowing hair. Is she not here again today?

'Not today,' Lugh said.

Why doesn't she come anymore?

'No point her coming, not in this rain.' Lugh presented his other wrist for Abel to stroke and changed the subject. 'So, this Lammas thing, should I take a bigger basket than normal to the old man today? Is that what I'm supposed to do?'

Maybe, Abel smiled mysteriously. If you like.

'Why are you smiling? Is it something else?'

It might be, Abel shrugged. You have to guess.

'Guess what?' Lugh did not like this particular game. It was difficult enough trying to communicate with someone who had taken a wow of silence. On top of that, he could make no sense of the cloistered otherworld of feast days Abel inhabited on that side of the window. It was like trying to communicate with a goldfish in a bowl, with a boy who had been turned into a goldfish and now lived by impossible-to-translate goldfish rules, though something recognisably human remained. His touch for a start. Lugh pulled his sleeve up to his elbow and indicated where he wanted to be stroked.

'If it's a riddle, give me a clue,' Lugh demanded. 'It's no fun if you don't give me a clue.'

Abel agreed and pointed at himself. Me.

'It's about you? Do you get to see the Gentleman today? Something like that?'

Abel shifted uncomfortably, a vague, non-committal response.

'Have you seen him already?' Lugh opened his eyes fully and withdrew his arms. 'Fran didn't think he was real, none of us did. What's he like? What does he look like?'

Abel shook his head, either to indicate that he had not seen the Gentleman or else, if he had, he did not want to talk about him. Instead, he held out his hand like a beggar and gestured for Lugh to run his fingers over his palm. I dare you to do this, he signalled.

'When Adam delved and Eve span, who then was the Gentleman?' said Lugh, drawing delicate lines over Abel's hand, up and down his fingers.

What does that mean? Abel asked.

'Not sure. Something Ky once said. I think what it means is, is there really a Gentleman? Like for real, like as real as you and me.' Lugh paused and looked up from the lines he was drawing on Abel's hand. 'Do you like this? Am I doing it right?'

Yes, I do. Yes, you are.

'Good,' said Lugh. He followed the same pattern up Abel's thumb, up each of his fingers and concluded by drawing a warm circle around the palm, sewing a path of touch from his outside world into Abel's interior world. The window was a portal, the only opening into that strange, closed, esoteric dimension behind the walls of the big house, ajar for only a few minutes on occasional days of the week, constantly at risk of being forever sealed should the old man discover their encounters. The patterns they drew on each other's skin were an invisible thread. They would each feel the mark long after the portal had been shut and they had each gone back to their own worlds. It was a subtle warmth that lasted until the next fugitive contact.

Another clue, a big one, said Abel. He rocked his arms as though cradling a baby, pointed at his own chest and then gestured, today.

'You're having a baby?' Lugh asked without considering the meaning of his words.

Abel arched his eyebrows in surprise and laughed aloud, shocking himself with the sudden noise. Instantly ashamed, he withdrew both of his hands and covered his mouth.

'It's okay, it was just a laugh,' said Lugh, reaching to take the other's hand. 'It doesn't count if it's not a word. It's like if you coughed. If you coughed, that wouldn't count either.'

Abel relaxed but kept his hands folded close to his chest. He looked at the ceiling as though some entity had shifted in the house. There was no movement anywhere, nothing but the steady, endless rhythm of the rain, but something was listening, an awareness had been raised. The house was attentive; its ears were pricked. Abel gestured that he had to leave, that he had to close the window and retreat back into the shadows of his world.

'But I never solved your riddle,' said Lugh.

Abel shook his head and reached for the window latch. They held each other's eyes for a moment, one look of contrition and one of reproach, then Abel closed and locked the portal. He waved slightly, disappointed that Lugh had never managed to guess that today was his birthday, then he repositioned the armchair in front of the empty fireplace and sat down to open his heavy, hardback book, *Lives of the Saints*, his back towards the window.

Lugh's legs were aching from standing so long on tiptoe. He crouched down among the flowerpots to ease the discomfort in his calves and sheltered from the rain beneath his hat. A cold trickle still found a way to flow down his neck. Between the lines of water streaming off the rim, he watched the garden twitch in the downpour, listened to the never-ending splash of a thousand droplets falling to earth. Was it a thousand, he wondered, or was it more? If he listened carefully, if he made an effort to distinguish between each individual splash, he might be able to count them all. The regular drips from the broken guttering were easy to isolate: they were close and deep-sounding, predictable as a pulse, as was the trickle from his hat. But there were dozens of splashes on the paving-stone path around the house, more than dozens, hundreds of dozens, and a different chorus of softer voices on the grass, on the ponds that had formed on the lawns. Beyond that, the roar of a sea falling on the tortured forest, the sound of a paper world crumpling.

Just as Lugh gave up trying to count the splashes of rain, he heard the sound of footsteps coming around the path. He did not move when he saw Luke stride out from behind the house and set off across the lawn towards the farmyard, his boots squelching in the saturated soil. Lugh stayed where he was, frowning at the disappearing figure. If he stayed small and still in the rain, a thing of no interest among the flowerpots, he knew instinctively that he could not be seen. It was a useful skill, but one to which he barely gave any thought. When the coast was clear, Lugh stood up and made his own way to the farmyard, skirting along the garden wall, the edge of the trees, keeping to his solitude.

Later that day, around midday Lugh guessed, although there was no way of being sure without seeing a glimpse of the sun, he returned to the big house with firewood and a large basket of produce. The old man opened the front door after the customary waiting period and rubbed his hands delightedly when he saw Lugh.

'Gosh, you are good,' he said, accepting the basket that was offered and inspecting the contents. 'A bumper crop indeed, parsnips and all sorts. You're all on your own again today, are you? Your audacious comrade decided that this work is all a bit much for her, has she?'

'I've brought more for Lammas.' Lugh shrugged. 'Like in the old days, for the Gentleman upstairs.'

'Well, now, what a revelation you are.' Father Ambrose looked at Lugh curiously, as though assessing him for the first time. Lugh did not flinch or withdraw from the old man's penetrating attention but frowned defiantly back. The old man appeared to be on the verge of saying something more, something sly and mysterious but, whatever it was, whatever request or proposal he had tentatively considered, he thought better of it, perhaps deterred by the boy's attitude of solid self-possession. Instead, Father Ambrose grinned, revealing the full condition of his unruly teeth. 'You are good, so very good.' And then he closed the door.

The magpies sat hunched in twos and threes on the wall of the front garden, seemingly too rain-drenched and wretched to comment on Lugh's passing. After he had reached the gate and set off down the lane, first one bird and then another shifted its glance and took to the air to pursue him, flying short distances between overhanging branches with an eye on his basket and occasionally, impertinently, on him. Lugh was conscious of this shadowy following: it had become a regular occurrence on his walk home. Drought and deluge had unbalanced the old normal. The magpies, amongst others, were having to adapt to the new. As long as he did not run, Lugh told himself, as long as he kept his pace steady and did not show his fear, nothing would happen.

Nothing did happen until he reached the path to his house, turned the corner of the terrace and discovered, perched casually on the backyard wall, a hooded figure in a black coat seemingly waiting for him. Lugh recognised the duffel coat at once: it was the one Ruth wore, used to wear when she dared to leave her house. But she had not been seen outside in weeks, and this figure sat with an air of insolence, of casual threat, his very presence outside Lugh's back door an act of incursion. At the sound of Lugh's footsteps, Mark lifted the hood from his face and peered short-sightedly through the rain, nodded a vague greeting of sorts. He had grown thinner during his month-long disappearance in the forest. Even beneath the beard, Lugh could see that his cheeks were gaunt, the sockets of his eyes deep and dark. He had the look of a famished animal.

'She'll have been in there all day, your girlfriend, all on her ownsome,' he said, chewing on a blade of grass. He grinned at Lugh and gestured towards the back door. 'Won't answer though, will she, that Francesca? Won't open that door, not to nobody. Nobody but you, I reckon.'

Mark chuckled to himself, a cold, clacking sound as though his mouth were dry, as though he had not had a drink of water in days, despite the endless rain. He nodded his head towards the door, then conspiratorially at Lugh, and back towards the door. It was a strange movement, this insistent, repetitive, prurient twitch that made Lugh feel uncomfortable though he chose not to show it. Instead, Lugh knocked three times on the back door and, in his deepest, most stolid voice, shouted the password, 'Motherfucker', to Fran.

'Mother—fucker,' Mark repeated slowly. He looked at the ground and said the word again, curiously, deliberately, as though tasting the sound for the very first time, pondering its meaning. He looked up in time to see Fran open the back door, usher Lugh inside and then slam it shut.

'How long has that one been sitting out there?' Lugh asked. He hung his coat and dripping hat on the rack above the stove, though the fire was unlit and would remain so until the grey light faded and the night set it. Fran turned the key in the lock but kept her hand pressed on the door.

'Not so long today,' she said distractedly, her mind elsewhere. 'Half an hour tops.'

'He's been there before?'

'Mm, some.' Without looking at Lugh, she went into the pantry and emerged with the glass demijohn of green wine. 'Good thing about all this rain is the nettles. Have you noticed, they love it. Can't get enough of it. Only thing that does. *For the rain it raineth every day.*'

'Is this one ready to drink?' Lugh unpacked his basket of vegetables on the table and glanced at the window, wondering why the curtains had still not been opened.

'Guess we'll soon find out.'

Lugh washed the salad leaves, thin onions and a cucumber in the sink. Now that the deluge had come, the taps were flowing with water again. He supposed that the pipes must be connected to an underground well or a reservoir or something like that, though the particulars of the waterworks remained a mystery. Whether the taps were running or not was as unpredictable and inexplicable as whether the sun shone, the wind blew or the rain ever stopped falling.

'We need a new password,' Lugh mused as he prepared their lunch.

'Did he hear it? I suppose he would have done.'

194

'And he repeated it. Don't think he'd ever heard the word before.'

'He actually said motherfucker?' Fran stopped pouring the nettle wine into their glasses and laughed aloud like she used to, like she had not laughed in ages. 'I would love to have witnessed that, I really would, just to see it. I don't suppose they say it much in Bible camp or wherever, motherfucker. Still, you're right. We need a new word, something they could never bring themselves to say.' She paused for a moment, the glass raised to her slightly parted lips. 'Mother sucks cocks in hell. That's it, the new password. They'll never ever say that.'

'I don't think he knows what a cock is either,' said Lugh.

'Oh, I think he does. He's had his out all morning.'

'He's what?' Lugh turned around, the kitchen knife still in his hand. 'In the garden?'

Fran shrugged and finished her drink, poured herself another glass.

'Why would he do that?' Lugh asked incredulously. 'Did he know you could see?'

'That's why he was doing it. Like a threat, I suppose. Not a very big threat.'

'Was it...?' Lugh gestured with his hands.

'See for yourself. He's probably still at it.'

Lugh crept into the pantry and peered out of the small, side window. He was silent for a long time, watching the man outside with a curious, thrilling fascination.

'It's not nice, O'Byrne,' Fran said quietly, seriously, her earlier humour now dissipated. She watched the green wine swirl around the glass as she moved her hand in circles, and added, 'You may like it, but I don't. I don't like it at all. It's—dangerous.'

'Hang on.' He crept out of the pantry and crouched down beneath the curtains of the kitchen window. He smiled impishly at Fran for a moment, but her downturned face had never seemed so sad, and he felt ashamed for having taken the whole thing so lightly.

'Fran, look at this,' he whispered.

'I've seen it already,' she said, still staring at her glass.

'No, this,' he said. Standing up suddenly, he pulled the curtains open, banged against the glass and shouted, 'What's that tiny thing in your hand, Mark Mann? Look out, the magpies will think it's a worm and eat it. See, they're coming for it.'

Mark jumped off the wall and scurried away, tugging at his trouser zip as he disappeared around the corner. Fran stood beside Lugh at the window and, shaking her head, smiled again.

'Where did you learn that? You're full of surprises, O'Byrne.'

'It's something my brother taught me to say if I should ever see a man with his cock out, like that, somewhere he shouldn't.'

'Your brother was a wise man.'

'I made up the bit about the magpies.'

'The magpie bit was the best.' Fran smiled. 'You're a wise man too.'

❧

IF YOU LEAVE THE BIG house, the wow doesn't work. The wow only works inside the house. So if you come outside, if you come, you can speak. Lugh repeated the reasoning over and over to himself as he walked down the damp lane and climbed the driveway to the big house. It was late autumn and the morning was dark, but the eastern sky was beginning to bleed a deep crimson shepherd's warning and the blackbirds were in an improvisational mood. The sun might even make an appearance, thought Lugh. Just a glimpse of it would be something, though the rain would return, inevitably, at some point. It always did. Rain was the only certainty. Rain was the new normal.

The library window was becoming easier for him to reach as the weeks and months went by. He could just about comfortably rest his arms on the window ledge now without standing on tiptoe and straining his calf muscles. On the other side of the glass portal, the library was in shadows and empty, but it was still early, there was still time. The problem with the darker mornings was that he could never be sure of what time it actually was until, of course, Abel appeared and told him. Same with the days. He should write the days down in one of those ledgers. That way, he would not waste his time coming to the library on Thursdays, Fridays or a Sunday morning. He suspected that today might be another Thursday.

The sky in the east grew tentatively lighter, accompanied by a cacophony of birdsong from the forest. Behind Lugh's reflection in the window pane, the clouds burned a paler red. While he waited, he studied the face that looked back at him from the glass. There were no mirrors at home, so he seldom thought about how he looked. Confronted by himself now, he turned his head from side to side, raised and lowered his chin, smiled exuberantly and grimaced horribly. Fran often said that he had long eyelashes. Luxuriously long light-brown lashes was how she put it. He turned again to the side and blinked several times. Perhaps, he thought. His eyelashes were much longer than Abel's, that was for certain, but Abel's were a deep brown, dark like his eyes. Smiling and grimacing, Lugh could see that his face had changed, that the shape was longer than he remembered, his neck was broader with a pronounced Adam's apple, and a soft, chestnut down had begun to grow above his top lip. The face that looked back at him was a stranger, more man than boy. He really did not recognise himself at all.

When Abel did not appear, Lugh assumed that it had to be a Thursday. He decided to take advantage of the dry spell to explore the forest. He had barely entered the forest during the last few months of endless downpour, but the sunrise was clear and bright, and it had been ages since he had heard so many birds singing in the morning. From the back of the farmyard, he followed the flooded banks of the fast-flowing stream until he found an abundance of wild garlic leaves. Kneeling down on the damp ground to cut and gather the leaves into his basket, he raised his head at a faint sound, a primitive rhythm of simple metal, of tin on tin tinkling a playful commotion somewhere in the forest. The music seemed to come and go, a hundred bells jangling far away and then swelling so close as to be just behind the next thicket of brambles or drove of old oaks. Among the tinny bells, Lugh also heard the murmur of occasional voices, bass words sung low and long, *come* or *run, where* or *dare:* he could not quite catch the meat of the word.

The brambles prevented him from following the music any deeper into the forest, so he gathered blackberries until his fingers turned purple, all the time peering through the trees for a sight of the orchestra. Further along, as the bells faded altogether and the voices dissolved into birdsong, he came upon the hazel trees that he remembered from last winter, though this year the nuts were few and still unripe. Almost leaving his boots behind in the marshy, mulchy forest floor, he took great strides along the riverbank until he saw the shredded remains of the tarpaulin tent hanging loosely from the oak trees just a few metres ahead of him. There was no wind to speak of, but the grim sheets shifted slightly as though animated with a life of their own. Lugh stood still and considered whether to turn back to the farmyard. There was something sinister about the scene; the dangling black fabric shreds resembled figures moving among the trunks, a coven of faceless shrouds convening in a secret, malevolent place. Lugh would have gone back, was about to leave, when he noticed the round white heads of familiar mushrooms, common puffball he suspected, gleaming on the forest floor that had once been covered by the tarpaulin.

Lugh collected the mushrooms rapidly, nervously, keen to be away as soon as he could. When he thought he had all the puffballs, he saw a half-dozen more pale-green, egg-like toadstools emerging from their small, sticky veils near the base of one of the oak trees. He did not recognise these caps but gathered them also into his basket. It was here, scratching among the leaf mulch beneath the drooping black sheet, that his fingernails uncovered something hard, a circle of glass in a gold metal frame, a pair of spectacles. One of the lenses was missing, presumed broken, but Lugh recognised them at once as Rhea's. He jumped to his feet and held the glasses up to the sunlight. His movement was so sudden that the clearing broke into life and three scandalised crows, unseen among the hanging trails of tarpaulin, cried in outrage and took to the air. Lugh grabbed his basket and fled the clearing, not looking back once as he ran along the riverbank towards the sanctuary of home.

When he arrived at the back door, panting and out of breath, Lugh tried to knock calmly so as not to distress Fran. The oddest things had begun to agitate her lately, often the most commonplace and unremarkable. A quickening in the rhythm of rain, say, or some animal barking in the distance. Whereas the things that troubled Lugh the most—the epidemic that had killed off the bees in the hives, the failure of the wheat and barley harvest, or Mark lurking behind trees in the garden—these things Fran shrugged off with seeming indifference, an air of not quite understanding why things like that would bother anyone. It is what it is, she would say.

Lugh knocked again and leaned against the wall, tried to regain his composure. He slipped the broken spectacles into the pocket of his jeans. Best not mention them to her, he decided.

'Were you upstairs?' he asked when Fran eventually opened the back door.

She made a muted noise of assent, looked outside to check both sides of the path behind the terrace, a quick glance over the empty garden, then closed and locked the door behind him.

'I found mushrooms in the forest.' He set the basket on the table and removed the wild garlic leaves. 'Puffball and something else, not sure what.'

'Do you know that Ky left her rucksack behind?' Fran listlessly picked through the leaves and blackberries that he unpacked. 'That army one. She never went anywhere without it. All her medical kit's still inside, you know. Bandages, iodine, needles, scissors. What do you think that means, the fact that she left it?'

'You've been up in her room?'

'Mm. I wonder what it means, the fact she left it here. What do you think that means?'

'That she was going to come back?'

'Yes, I think that too,' Fran said emphatically. 'I do think she intended to come back.'

Lugh continued to take out his foraged goods from the basket, but more measuredly now as he struggled to grasp the threads of Fran's thoughts. Not for the first time in recent weeks, he was at a loss to understand the things she half said but never quite finished, or why she had begun to turn the obvious into the momentous.

'We know she intended to come back,' said Lugh carefully. 'She'd said so.'

'Yes, but maybe it—the rucksack—maybe she left it like some kind of clue. Maybe, and this is what I've been wondering, maybe she still intends to come back. Maybe they all do.'

'But Mark said that the Beast—'

'Lugh,' Fran cried suddenly, shaking his wrist so that he dropped the toadstools he had been placing on the tabletop. 'That's not puffball, that's death-cap. This one and this one, all of these are death-caps, Lugh. They're deadly. What were you thinking picking these?'

'I knew these ones weren't puffball, I just didn't know what they were,' he said, quietly wounded, and went to the sink to scrub his hands. 'I do know what puffball looks like.'

'But these are bad, very bad.' She poked at the pale yellow-green caps with a spoon.

'I'll chuck them outside in a minute.'

'No, don't do that, not yet,' Fran said more calmly. 'Maybe we should keep them after all. Dry them out and keep them somewhere safe, somewhere we won't accidentally eat them. Not unless we have to.'

'But they're poisonous?'

'Mm, but we can keep them out of harm's way. Somewhere safe.'

Fran used a spoon and a fork to transport the death-caps, one by one, to a baking tray on the windowsill. The morning sun, which had shone so unexpectedly brightly and golden-red at sunrise, had disappeared once more behind the bank of cloud, and now the first few beads of daily rain were spattering against the pane. Fran admired the arrangement she had made of the six deadly toadstools beneath the window, each one freshly hatched with a limp birth-veil hanging from their stems. Without direct sunlight, she would probably have to roast them a little in the evening when the stove was lit. She remembered reading that half a death-cap could kill a man. With six, she could wipe out an entire family. They smelled sweet too, vaguely reminding her of warm honey, sugar water.

'Oh, honey,' she said without turning around, still enthralled. 'Must remember to extract more honey from the hives this week. We're completely out. Need to stock up before winter.'

'The bees are all dead. I told you,' said Lugh. He had sat down at the table and was staring at the back of Fran's head, wondering how she could have forgotten. 'I swept out their bodies, hundreds of them. Don't you remember me telling you?'

'Are they? Did you?' She turned and sat at the table, cupping her chin in her hands. 'No honey. Damn and fuck it, as Rhea would say. We need the glucose for the wine. Is it glucose or fructose? Which is it? Whatever it is, we need sugar for the brewing.'

'I can ask Abel. They've got tonnes of stuff, sugar and that, up at the big house. Abel says they've even got a wine cellar, though he thought that cellar was spelled with an 'S'—like seller, like there was actually somebody selling wine under the house. A wine-seller.'

'Yes, ask him,' Fran agreed contemplatively, a faraway look in her eye. If she did catch the pun, she did not feel the need to show it. 'Ask him about the wine too. Wouldn't it be something if he could smuggle us out a nice bottle of wine? Jesus, imagine that. Will you ask him today?'

Lugh explained that he would not see Abel for another couple of days, not if today was Thursday, but that he would ask him next time he saw him. If today was Thursday. If it was, which he thought it must be, then he should write it down, keep track of the days. Taking the four black ledgers from the dresser, he lay the books on the table and opened the first one. It was Ky's book, her herstory of the troubles. He flicked through the pages, read some sentences. Floods in the low-lying cities of southern Asia, northern Europe, the storms that brought down planes, panic at the borders, a rash of acts, defensive and belligerent, of states of emergency. The tick-by-tock countdown of events, each one subtle and seemingly unconnected in the thick of day-to-day details, that led inexorably to the here and now. Lugh skipped to the last page of writing, to the last sentence that had been left incomplete, an untied threat of ink suspended over lines that would never now be filled. An unfinished tale in a relief camp, a loose clause in a library of sorts, of beauty magazines and crossword puzzles, a woman with pre-Raphaelite looks reading French poetry on the corner carpet where the children were put for storytime, Fridays, afternoons, sunset.

'I'm sorry,' said Lugh when he had read the description several times.

Fran made a vague quizzical sound. When she focused on Lugh's face, she saw that his long eyelashes were glistening with tears. She had never known him to cry before.

'What for?' she asked, reaching out to take his hand in both of hers. 'What is it?'

Lugh shook his head and watched his teardrops fall on the unwritten expanse of paper.

ABBA, FATHER, ALL THINGS ARE possible unto thee, take away this cup from me. Nevertheless not what I will, but what thou wilt. Nevertheless not what I will, but what thou wilt. Nevertheless—Abel repeated the sentences over and over in his mind, making every effort to ensure that his lips did not move as he surreptitiously practised each word. Father Ambrose was pained whenever he saw Abel's lips move. Even in prayer with his eyes closed and his hands clasped over his anguished face, the old man knew whether Abel's lips were moving. The old man would know if Abel was practising those words again. The verses should spring naturally from Abel's mouth, he should not have to think about them at all. He should not have to think. Nevertheless not what I will, but what thou wilt. Nevertheless—

Abel opened his eyes the merest fraction, hoping that the old man was too preoccupied in his own conversation with God to notice. The midwinter sun had set during the past hour, and now the sky outside the solitary window was as black as the Bible in his hands. Two orange beeswax candles, one flickering on a polished silver holder on the altar and a lesser one in front of the tabernacle, provided the only illumination in the small chapel. It was the simplest room in the house, the most austere and the least cluttered with such ornaments as adorned the drawing room next door. The chapel was almost entirely bare except for the altar with its plain white altar cloth, the silver crucifix and candlestick, the mahogany tabernacle that was currently tenanted by the Lord in the form of a thin wafer, a statue of the Virgin in the corner, and the wooden benches on which Abel, the old man and Mother sat in prayer. Even the walls, plain bricks and mortar, had been stripped of extravagant plaster. The chapel was the room that Abel liked most in the house, at least when he was allowed to be here on his own. This and the library. The library because it was where he met with Lugh, and the chapel because, when it was empty, it felt utterly empty and he could simply exist without being scrutinised by anyone. It was not empty now. Father Ambrose shifted his position on the bench, gave a slight sigh of discomfort or grievance. Abel closed his eyes and prayed. Mother straightened her posture with a cracking of bones. Somebody's stomach sang a long hollow plainsong of dissatisfaction. It was probably his own because he had been fasting since yesterday. He pushed his Bible against his stomach muscles and the song of yearning came to an end.

Eventually, dismally, the grandfather clock in the drawing room next door chimed six o'clock, and everyone exhaled and stretched their limbs with relief. Father Ambrose stood up slowly, his knee joints cracking as he made his way to the altar to prepare to say communion. Mother adjusted her dress and shared a sad, secretive smile with Abel. Fearing the act may have broken some rule, she turned to face the wall. High-Church conventions were still largely a mystery to her but, since she had handed Abel into the care of Father Ambrose, she was warming to customs that she would once have derided as papist idolatry. The loss of Matthew had hit her unspeakably hard, harder than either the passing of her husband or Uncle Joe. This new grief was an indescribable thing, and she was increasingly turning to the priest both for the questions she should ask and for the answers. Grief had also inclined her to be more tolerant of the Mother of God, whose sufferings she now saw in a more sympathetic, less competitive light. She had learned to recite the Hail Mary, she attended chapel for communion on the various feast days of the Blessed Virgin, most recently the Immaculate Conception, and her preferred seat was the bench nearest the statue of the blue-cloaked Virgin. It was also an opportunity to see Abel, though she was not allowed to speak to him. Kneeling beside him now at the steps of the altar, she received a flavourless wafer, a cut of her god, from the hand of Father Ambrose. A moment later, a sip of sweet, warming blood from the silver chalice that her youngest son's lips had just touched: a kiss deferred but no less real for that. She savoured the taste on her tongue, crossed herself, and returned to her bench for the final prayer of thanksgiving.

After the old man had given the dismissal, Mother genuflected, threw one last ambivalent glance at the statue of the grieving Virgin, and then left the chapel. Abel remained sitting on his bench, bowed in prayer with his head in his hands. He thought of the times he had leaned against his mother in the front of the pickup truck and watched the gold crucifix dangling on the chain around her neck, her hands fidgeting over some irritation or resting lightly on his shoulder; the briefest exchange of a secret smile. He listened to the receding echo of her footsteps now as she walked briskly down the hall, opened the front door and let herself out. That was the sound he dreaded to hear most of all, that closing of the door, the reverberating toll of Thursday evening. Now for the vigil, now Gethsemane. He remained bent over, dissembling prayer for as long as possible until the old man coughed his impatience, rustled his robes.

'Are we ready for Gethsemane, my love?' Father Ambrose asked gently.

Abel counted slowly to three and opened his eyes. He could not postpone the inevitable any longer. Abba, Father, all things are possible unto thee: take away this cup from me.

'Nevertheless not what I will, but what thou wilt.' Abel crossed himself.

The staircase played tricks with time and space. It stretched impossibly far into the teeming darkness above, an illusion of terraced distance that pulsated in the dim glow of the candle that the old man carried behind Abel. The wooden steps shifted in the unsteady light, dilating and contracting with each sway of the candle, seeming never to end until all too soon they finished and Abel found himself standing before the open door to the tower.

'Hammer and tongs for Christ,' the priest said encouragingly when he saw Abel hesitate at the bottom of the unlit stairs.

Abel took another deep breath and ascended the final staircase. He stood for a moment in complete blackness, inhaling the stale, putrid air of the attic room in the tower. As the old man followed him up, the dusty shapes in the room were dimly traced by candlelight. Abel kept his eyes lowered and tried to concentrate on the threadbare carpet beneath his bare feet.

'Off with it, then,' said Father Ambrose with playful impatience, embarrassed perhaps that he should still have to goad the young man into the routine.

Abel slipped out of his habit, folded it neatly on the carpet, and then stood with his back pressed against the tall wooden cross that dominated the attic room. He kept his hands covering his genitals for as long as he dared, until the old man had put the candle on a desk and turned around to contemplate the naked youth with a look of bitter disappointment. Abel did not need to see Father Ambrose's expression to know that the priest was displeased. Haltingly, reluctantly, Abel stretched out his arms and pressed his knuckles against either end of the crossbeam, exposing his body to the cold. He lowered his head and closed his eyes, listening to every dreadful creak in the floorboards as the old man moved here and there, collecting his tools before coming to stand before him. Abel could feel the priest's breath on his goose-bumped skin.

There was a pinch of cold iron as the sharp tip of a nail was pressed against the palm of Abel's left hand, causing his fingers to clench partially. An oppressive pause, and then the old man groaned as he struck the end of the nail with his hammer. Abel flinched, though he knew full well that the nail would not pierce his hand. Father Ambrose cried out again and again as he held the nail firmly in his fist and pretended to pound it into the youth's palm. When he had finished with the left hand, he moved on to the right and performed the same pantomime ritual, hammering and groaning in imagined agony, though the nail only made a superficial dent on Abel's skin.

'Now we are Christlike,' said Father Ambrose, panting with the effort of his labour. He smiled and stroked Abel's cheek with the back of his hand, the one that still clasped the metal hammer. 'Open your eyes, my love. Open up, that's it. Now the Gentleman can see you.'

The old man backed away from the youth on the cross and retreated down the stairs, grinning as he disappeared below. Abel wanted to lower his gaze and stare at the floor, to close his eyes and shut out the figure in the dimly lit room. He wanted to let his trembling arms fall to his side, to curl into a warm ball on the floor, but he could do none of these things. Father Ambrose would know at once if he changed his posture, if he looked away from the rotten armchair that stood facing him across the attic. Involuntarily, Abel's eyes flickered to the skylight in the ceiling, to the raindrops running down the black glass. Another night without the moon, he thought. Yes, think of the moon, the hide-and-seek moon: she must be smiling down at him now. Hidden somewhere behind the veil of clouds, but always there like a promise, his tin-beaten, cratered archangel.

Thinking of the moon gave him courage. He could look at the old armchair and almost not see it. Without quite closing his eyes, he could picture the moon as a pockmarked shield suspended in front of him, trace the Seas of Tranquillity, Serenity. But then the candlelight flickered in a wintry draught, the shadows rose and fell against the wall, and the cadaver in the armchair reappeared more vividly than ever. The Gentleman sat slouched to one side in his chair. He had been dead for many years, had mostly decomposed, but he continued to stare blindly from deep-set holes in his tight leathered face, baring his teeth in a grimace of aristocratic delight.

Abel tried not to look directly at that face. Instead, he focused on the Gentleman's clothes, the powdery stains on his ancient black trousers, the blanket draped around his shoulder bones. Strands of the Gentleman's long white hair fluttered in a cold draught from the cracked glass in the skylight. Abel watched as a handful of fine threads teased themselves free from their mooring, floated ethereally across the room and settled in an unlit corner.

THE MOON DID MAKE OCCASIONAL, fragmentary appearances through gashes in the winter sky—a piece of silver at Epiphany, flash of full at Candlemas— but such sightings were rare and only emphasised how relentless were the weeks of rain between such breaks in the cloud. Lugh caught a glimpse of the fattening crescent moon at the spring equinox, an omen, he said, of a good summer to come.

Abel nodded politely and held his hand out, pauper-like. He signed the words, I dare you.

'What's that?' said Lugh, circling his thumb around the small black scab in the middle of Abel's palm. 'How did you get this?'

Abel gestured indistinctly. Something happened, an accident. He motioned again to have his fingers stroked, but Lugh grabbed his other hand and found an identical wound there.

'Funny accident to happen on both palms.'

Forget it then, Abel signed impatiently and withdrew both of his hands.

'Can't. You dared me,' said Lugh. He took hold of Abel's hand again and carefully examined the scab while drawing delicate circles around it. 'Don't you want to tell me what happened?'

Sorry, Abel shook his head.

'Suit yourself,' said Lugh, good-naturedly rather than in any way unkindly. He continued to massage the other's palm, taking care to avoid rubbing the wound. 'You know, if you come outside, the wow of silence doesn't work. The wow only works inside the house. So if you come outside, you can speak. Just a thought.'

Don't start all that again, said Abel, though he could not repress his smile.

'It's true, though. And I've thought of a way I could make you, if I really wanted to.'

Abel looked sceptical. How? he gestured.

'Like this,' said Lugh solemnly. 'Abel Mann, I dare you to come outside.'

Abel was aghast and shook his head vehemently, but Lugh insisted that he must because a dare was a dare. There was something exhilarating in the certainty of this principle, the absolute sanctity of dares. They both felt aroused by unimaginable possibilities that had not existed a moment earlier. They looked into each other's eyes and recognised that the other was equally stimulated, a mutual realisation which only charged their excitement further.

Abel felt his heart pounding fiercely. He folded his hands over his mouth, thinking of what must happen next. Whatever he did, he had to be outside with Lugh. The dare had awakened something within him, a necessity he had never experienced before. His mind worked fluidly over and under the various obstacles like water around bedrock.

Tonight, after dark, Abel gestured. You be here.

'Seriously?' Lugh squinted, disbelieving the signs he read. 'How will you manage it?'

Because today is a feast day, Abel motioned quickly with his hands. The Annunciation.

Lugh read the letters of the strange word and asked, 'But what about the old man?'

It's a feast day, so—Abel raised his thumb to his lips as though he were drinking from a bottle and pulled an intoxicated face. They both had to smother their laughter.

The day passed unbearably slowly. Lugh weeded the vegetable plots, collected eggs and harvested potatoes with one eye always on the grey sky, trying to guess the position of the sun. He imagined that he must have spent most of the day in the farmyard but, when he took firewood and the food basket to the big house, the old man raised his eyebrows and said, 'What, giving up so early?' Abel asked him for the time, but the priest gave a nebulous shrug and closed the door.

Fran was not in a talkative mood. She sat at the kitchen table with her fingers tapping a large book, sometimes opening the cover but never really reading. The book was the latest contraband that had come from the big house, an illustrated guide to birds. Lugh thought that it might cheer her up, but she had accepted the volume with an abstracted, far-away look, her lips parted though she said nothing. She seldom said anything these days. Lugh sat opposite her and wrote notes in the back of the black ledger, the one that had been Ky's. He glanced often out of the window as the day shifted towards evening, the rain hushed and the sun finally broke through the clouds. There was a rare manifestation of colour at sunset, long shadows, tangerine luminance, a springtime miracle.

The colours turned rusty and darkness fell. Lugh closed his ledger and told Fran that he was going to see Abel. The immensity of the occasion was lost on her. Tapping her book, she nodded as though Lugh was always seeing Abel in the evening.

'You'll be sure to lock the door after me?' he asked.

'Of course.' She offered a slight smile. 'Mother sucks cocks in hell.'

'She sucks indeed,' he replied, giving the customary response.

Lugh waited underneath the library window at the big house for what felt like hours, listening to every creeping thing in the darkness: nightbirds in the forest, restless hens in the chicken coop. One time he saw the calligraphic flourish of a fox as it trotted along the path, its clever eyes holding his gaze for a second before disappearing around the corner. Eventually, after the night-time world had taken on the muted quality of eternity, the window creaked open above Lugh's head and time returned with a quick succession of sensations in the dark. The emergence of Abel into the vacuum, the immediate proximity of his excited breath, the scent of his skin and the rustle of his clothes, all these things fascinated Lugh. He could not resist drawing close, attending to his movements, committing each to memory. Abel reached out for Lugh's hand, steadied himself on the window ledge and touched down, barefooted, on the world outside. They faced each other like shy strangers now that they were both standing on the same ground in the same dimension, no wall or window between them. They could have stayed like this all night, hesitating at the first achievement, but Abel remembered the bottle he had put on the windowsill and presented it to Lugh, an offering of stolen wine.

'Let's go to the milking shed,' said Lugh, but Abel took hold of his arm and held him back. 'Where then? You can speak now. You're not in the house anymore.'

Abel gestured over the lawn, not towards the farmyard but to the corner of the garden, the gap in the wall that led to the forest, the back way around the houses.

'You're not wearing any shoes,' said Lugh, but Abel had already set off across the black expanse of the lawn, his feet whispering a path through wet grass.

By the time they reached the ivy cottage, Abel was limping and hanging onto Lugh's shoulder to walk. They rested at the stone table in the front garden, where Lugh uncorked the bottle of wine and Abel nursed his bloody feet.

'You deserve this, you fool,' said Lugh, handing the bottle over. The intense excitement of the dare, of Abel's heroic crossing over the portal, had gradually faded as they stumbled through the forest. Now all Lugh could think of was the pain that Abel must be feeling in his feet. Abel understood this and felt that he had spoiled everything.

'You'll go back to the house?' asked Lugh. 'I don't suppose you've left it for good.'

'No, I should go back in a bit,' said Abel.

'So now you can talk?'

'So now I can talk.' Abel grinned. He took a taste of the wine from the bottle, winced and returned it to Lugh. 'I told myself that it's all right here, that the vow doesn't matter once we get here because it's like the old man can't hear or won't know, or that it somehow doesn't count because the rules are different. Like when you said if I coughed, that it doesn't count. Does that sound daft? I think it sounds daft. Sorry if it sounds daft. Why are you smiling?'

'Because I haven't heard your voice in ages. It sounds strange. It sounds different to how I remember it. You sound deep, very deep,' Lugh said the words in a mocking baritone. 'You sound like your older brothers. My name's Abel Mann and I have a very deep voice.'

'My name's Lugh O'Byrne,' said Abel in a lower tone, 'and I'm very disappointed.'

'Why would I be disappointed?' Lugh wiped his lips after taking a swig of the wine.

'Because you called me a fool.' Abel pointed at his injured feet.

'Well, you are a fool. Do they hurt very much?'

'Not too much.'

'There'll be water inside. Let's get you inside, wash them.' Lugh bent down and placed his hand tentatively on Abel's shin, feeling the bone, the soft layer of hair, the heat of his body. Abel did not seem to mind so Lugh let his fingers explore the calf muscle beneath. There was still no resistance, nothing but Abel's quickening breath, so Lugh ran his fingers further into delicate territory, under the hem of the robe to the fur on the thighs. Here, he encountered trembling.

'Is this okay?' Lugh asked, pausing, preparing to retreat at the slightest demurral.

'Is it a dare?'

'I think so. Yes.'

'Then it's okay.'

Lugh ran his fingers back and forth over the fine hair on the thigh, wanting to explore further but concerned about the cuts in Abel's feet. After a moment, he withdrew his hand and helped Abel stand. Inside the ivy cottage, Lugh tried the taps in the kitchen, which gurgled and then spluttered with an eruption of water. When he had filled the metal wash-bowl in the sink, he carried it to the blanket on the floor where Abel was resting with his back against the ivy-coated wall, his legs stretched out in front of him.

'Here we go,' said Lugh, laying the bowl on the floor. He knelt down beside the blanket, soaked a rag in the water, rinsed it dry and gently began to wash Abel's feet.

'You've got a thing about being clean,' said Abel, wincing and then relaxing into the coolness of the water. 'You don't have to do this, you know.'

'I know, and I know.'

Although he could see little in the darkness, Lugh worked methodically, knowing intimately the bones, the contours and indents that he had already wiped down, soaking and rinsing the rag, feeling the sticky blackness of mud and unwashed blood around new curves and corners. The rhythm was mesmerising, soothing to them both. When Lugh had finished with the feet, he moved up to the shins, smoothing around the calf muscles, the tender cave behind the knee. The water trickled into the bowl as he wrung the rag dry, a ripple of notes that lingered in the air, changed timbre from major to minor, water to bronze, became a tinkling of distant bells that played with the edge of the forest and wandered curiously into the garden.

'You're cold,' Lugh said, a statement more than a question.

'No, not at all.'

'You are. I can feel you're trembling.'

'I am not. You're trembling.'

'Then I dare you to take this thing off,' Lugh said quietly, tugging at the hem of Abel's robe.

Abel leant forward and slipped out of his habit, sat naked on the blanket, breathing thickly.

'I dare you to get out of your things,' Abel replied in the darkness.

Lugh stripped down to nothing and knelt on the blanket, his bare knees lightly touching Abel's warm thigh. The moment lengthened, rich with expectancy. When he could take the waiting no longer, Lugh ventured in a broken voice, 'I dare you to kiss me.'

At first, there was nothing, no word or movement from Abel, only the thunder of a heartbeat that the whole forest must surely have heard. I did not say those words out aloud, Lugh thought – although he knew that he had, for the trace of that dare had turned cold on his lips. To warm them, Abel leaned forward and pressed his mouth softly against Lugh's. It was a breath they each held with shy uncertainty until, in its own time, certainty took over and they could breathe more freely an air that became flesh. No more need of dares, the turns became instinctive, an epiphany of touch.

Sometimes they heard voices outside, words that steered their own unpractised language, a deep-bass pebble-song of *come* or *run*, *where* or *dare*, the chroma of bells ringing in their ears. The forest goats flowed around the ivy cottage, teeming through the undergrowth and flowering brambles, proudly mounting the stone table to survey the garden. Leading, following or merely accompanying their passage, a bone-thin man with wild hair and a wilder beard, a shepherd's crook resting over one shoulder, moved among the midnight herd. The man paused for a moment at the door of the ivy cottage and caught the soft, instinctive, unseasoned sounds coming from within. As the herd flowed around him, he adjusted the crown of leaves on his head and then continued to keep pace with the current of animals, cream-whiskered and short-horned in waxing moonlight, a cacophonic spring ceremony of hoof and bell.

CHAPTER ELEVEN
PASSOVER

I RIDESCENCE ON THE ROOFTOPS, LIVID white and coat-tails of black, every stain of purple-blue in the slash of a wing, eye-blink of mischief. Ruth could hear the magpies insisting on something—quick-quick, look-look—a plague of scavenging. When she opened her eyes, all she could see was the morning lashing against her bedroom window, washing away the ghostly traces of past raindrops with present downpour. The act of sunrise had not happened again, only the rain, perpetual rain, the senseless monotony of falling water. A year or so ago, Ruth had woken every morning to watch the sun creep over the china teapot, bringing to colour the fine blue lines of willows and doves, oriental pavilions, faraway figures standing on a bridge. Now, the teapot was kept where Mother said it should be kept, in its rightful place on the kitchen dresser. Outside, the magpies laughed.

There was one forbidden relic left on the windowsill: a broken curve of painted plastic, a fragment of the globe that Enoch had shattered with his axe and which Ruth had salvaged when no one was looking. The remnant was no larger than her hand, a jagged shard of blue Pacific and white Antarctica, broken letters floating in ocean and snow. She had been disappointed to discover that the globe was hollow inside, the interior dome a dismal grey, colour of emptiness, but that had not surprised her. There was no reason why there should be anything within, any great secret or revelation of meaning. The beauty and mystery of latitudes and longitudes, tropics and poles, ragged coastlines and serrated mountain chains, all of that had merely been paint on the surface, an illusion of substance without any real essence. The whole thing had broken so easily into assorted pieces with one knock of the axe. Vanity of vanities, all is vanity.

Ruth had kept that fragment on the windowsill to measure the place of each sunrise, but she knew there was no point leaving it there if the sun was never going to rise again. Last year, she had seen for herself the gradually shifting position of the sun. It had risen further and further towards the north each day until, on midsummer's day, it appeared so far behind the edge of the window that it was out of sight, way beyond what she could see from her bed. Since then, that day that Enoch had told her to play with Rhea in the forest, the next day scrubbing Enoch's clothes, there had barely been any sun at all. Nor the days and the months ever since.

Reflections of the rain rippled over the windowsill, dappling the edges of the broken globe with shadows of falling water. Ruth thought about getting out of bed and hiding the thing under her blanket before Mother came into the room. If Mother caught sight of it, questions would be asked, had to be asked, and Ruth never had answers. Slowly, she raised the blanket and moved a leg, but the bed frame made a loud tell-tale creak that gave her away and must have been heard from downstairs. Horrified, Ruth lay still and listened for movement in the house. If Mother thought that Ruth was awake, she would be there in an instant. If Ruth stayed in bed and pretended to sleep until midday, Mother would still be there. Sooner or later, whatever she did or did not do, someone would appear and there was barely a crack in the wall or under the bed into which Ruth could slip, stash herself away, stitch the edges tightly behind her.

She stared at the sliver of broken globe, praying for it to be in her hand. The more she prayed, the more convinced she became that she could feel it in her palm, pressing soundly against her skin, the ragged edges of an impeccably white continent opening a tear into which she could fit, faultless, clean.

There was a stirring in the house downstairs, but it was not the sigh and creak of Mother standing up, making her pointed way upstairs. It was a frantic, male commotion of boots and voices, the front door banging hard in the hallway, of bodies falling against the wall or struggling to be let loose. Ruth forgot about staying inconspicuous in bed, about broken coastlines and the hole in her hand. She crept to the bedroom door and, opening it slightly, leaned out onto the landing. She could hear the voices more distinctly here. Mark and Enoch were shouting at each other, not words but animal expressions of strength and will. Mother was there too, crowing high-pitched questions or commands that went nowhere or were ignored. There was a fourth voice in the hallway too, someone that Ruth did not immediately recognise. Whoever it was said little and moaned occasionally as though being hurt or handled roughly. The clamour was brought to an abrupt end with the loud, unmistakable crack of a hand slapping a face.

'Why—why?' demanded the last, injured voice that was clearly Fran's. Ruth could not imagine why the nice lady was there, or what she had done to deserve to be punished.

'Thou shalt not take a wife among the daughters of Canaan,' said Mother, although it was not clear who she was addressing. Crossly, she added, 'Get her out of my sight.'

The front door slammed and the downstairs fell silent. Ruth moved to her bedroom window and reached instinctively for the fragment of globe. As she stroked the broken edge, she looked outside and saw Enoch leading Fran towards his own house at the end of the terrace. Fran was wearing a blanket around her shoulders. Her bare feet slipped on the mud and wet stones. Enoch held her arm tightly, but Ruth could not be sure if that was to prevent her from falling or from running away. Ruth retreated to her bed, made a hiding-hole with the coastline of Antarctica.

⌣

FRAN HAD BEEN DREAMING OF Rhea. She often dreamed of Rhea, and Ky, occasionally Matthew. It was the ones who had gone that she spent her most intimate hours with now. Her imagination was a privilege reserved for the dead, for the dead never disappointed or did anything unexpected, anything out of character. The dead could be relied upon to do as they had always done. It was the living that you could not trust to behave.

Fran had been dreaming of the earlier house, the house near the seaside town with the orchard and the surrounding fields of wheat: Lugh's old house. She had been thinking about the broken back door that would not close, though Rhea always slept in the kitchen chair armed with her knitting needles and the hunting knife on the shelf above the range. Rhea had been talking aimlessly about music, as she often did. This time she was musing on Holst and The Planets.

'He was the first person to go into outer space, was Holst. Did you know that, dear?' said Rhea, glancing naughtily over the rim of her spectacles. Fran did not know that at all and suspected, even in her dreaming, that this may not be entirely true, but she let Rhea continue. 'Well, he was. First modern person at any rate, for the Greek philosophers, of course, had got there first. And Beethoven had his own kingdom, a tiny principality like Lichtenstein only smaller, on the border between—where was it? —Netherlands and Romania. Very mountainous, black forest, wolves and whatnot, some say vampires. Delicate little country as big as my thimble.'

Fran had known for certain that all this was utter nonsense. She was on the verge of saying so when the back door was kicked open, or blew open in the windstorm that had returned to howl around the house, and a set of car headlights shone brightly through the opening. Fran covered her eyes, unable to stand the intensity of the blinding white light that engulfed the kitchen and had probably killed all the stars in the night sky too. She knew instantly what would happen next. It was so inevitable as to be almost tedious if it were not so ugly. This time, he entered, the Beast of her nightmares, in the dazzling beam of the headlights, stomping his hard, keratin feet on the kitchen tiles. Fran tried to open her eyes, but the light was too strong, a grotesquely cold whiteness that burned everything it touched, sterilising her will and holding her down on the kitchen floor, her blanket-bed in front of the stove.

'But the back door was locked. I locked it myself,' she cried out, outraged at the unfairness of the intrusion. Even as she spoke the words, she realised that she could be mistaken, that she might have forgotten to do that one little thing, a turn of the key. She had probably drifted off into sleep, gone to visit that other kitchen in that other house which was haunted by memories of the dependable dead, as soon as Lugh had closed the back door and gone out into the night. She had promised him that she would lock it and she had failed. Always the living that let you down.

A hard smack, surprisingly hard, of a palm across her left cheek; another with knuckles against her right. Outraged, she opened her eyes against the light, the dull, grey light of a sunless dawn, flinched at the clutter of instant sensations that demanded to be filtered, interpreted, digested. The faded, slightly stinking cotton of a red-white-blue shirt, buttons broken or undone revealing a pale, hairless chest. The thick, black beard so close to her own face that she could perceive individual wires of wayward hair. The spittle on teeth, sharp white teeth but rancid breath, and a small, red, angry tongue that poked at the corner of a spit-whitened mouth. She struggled against the weight of his knees, rock-sharp and painful, that were pushing down and into her arms, but was unable to free herself from the mountain of his will. As he blundered unsuccessfully with the zip on his trousers, he grew more frantic, a nervous, violent frenzy, almost a consuming fear that he would not be able to touch himself in time.

Fran struggled against his knees and tried to agitate her arms free, but he pressed down on her so hard that the pain was overwhelming. She stretched her neck, trying to distance herself from the hurting, and finally saw his eyes: black pools of dilated pupil, no colour, no consciousness. The primitive blindness of a rudimentary species, half-man, half-dog, a thing before language.

'Mark,' she cried at last, defining him, enclosing the limits of his violence within a name.

For a moment, he held her eye, a flicker of something recognisably sentient, hateful, afraid. But then his expression contorted, he removed his fist from his desperate fumbling and punched her once, twice, more times than either of them could count. The first blow burst with unimaginable pain against her cheek, but the feeling disappeared almost at once in a temporary grace of numbness. It returned in an instant, throbbing with angry blood and nerves as Mark threw his fists against her face. Fran tasted her own blood, raw iron from beneath her core, felt elements of herself drifting away, a piece of lip, particle of eye. As her fragments scattered, she became conscious of another presence in the kitchen, a hunched figure standing at the back door. A memory stirred, another night, another man bearing down on her. Now that Mark's hands had returned to his fumbling, Fran swallowed blood and twisted the remnants of her lips together.

'She's behind you,' she tried to say. The words sounded like nothing, like an ache in her throat, so she swallowed again and summoned all her strength to repeat, 'She's behind you.'

The dead never disappointed or did anything out of character. The dead do what they have always done. They hear a sound, something amiss, and up the stairs they come at the precise moment they are needed, knitting laid aside, hunting knife in hand. Cometh the hour, cometh the battle-axe. Oh, Rhea, thought Fran, the tears at last streaming down her raw cheeks. Rhea, where did you go? I missed you so much, I missed you.

Just as Mark turned doubtfully around, half expecting this to be a simple ruse such as Ruth or his younger brothers might have used in a moment of sibling torture, the figure at the door stepped forward and another sound cracked the air, another blow against another head. The mountain shifted from Fran's arms and Mark slumped to the floor.

It was not the sound that Fran had expected to hear. Last time, it had been different. Last time, there had been a cry, many cries and thick cuttings, before the body had slumped on top of her. But, this time, her arms were free of the intense piercing and she could put her hands to her estranged face, the face that reassembled itself into excruciating new shapes. She rolled onto her side, pieced herself together as a coil.

Things continued to happen differently this time. Somebody's hand, whose she did not know, took hold of her arm and pulled her from the floor. Gently but firmly, she was manoeuvred to the kitchen sink, where she found the taps and held her head under fast-running water. Every new swollen contour of her face throbbed with a pulse that roared in her ears, but the water was cold and distracted her from the pain. Behind her, she could hear Mark complaining, vindicating, blaming. Once in while, there was another voice that was not Rhea's, just as the hand holding the back of her neck now, hard nails squeezing the tendons, was not Rhea's.

'But you said she's fair game, you did,' Mark argued. He sounded exasperated but also cowed, pleading his case before a greater authority. 'And why bother telling Mother anything?'

'Get over there. Get,' he shouted, that other voice that Fran now recognised was not Rhea's at all but Enoch's.

There was a struggle behind her, hard movements cutting the air. She turned off the water just in time for someone to shove into her, knocking the back of her head against the tap. She was torn away from the sink and dragged outside into the cold morning rain.

'She's not got nothing on,' Mark said with a nervous laugh. 'You can't take her over there like that, can you? What would Mother think?'

'Go get her a blanket then,' Enoch snapped. He pulled Fran to her feet and held her naked body against his hip to prevent her from falling. She could only see through the tender slit of one eye and, though she was shivering and unable to feel much through the pounding in her head, she was aware of Enoch's thumbnail scratching deliberately against her nipple.

The blanket was thrown over her shoulders and she was hauled across the lane for a purpose she could not fathom. The cold air made her feel fainter than ever, and she was only partially sensible of her feet slipping and stumbling through puddles to the terrace opposite, a front door opening with a violent bang, raised voices in the hallway and Mark being thrown to his knees. Mother said something Biblical, nonsensical, and then slapped Fran sharply across her already aching face. Fran put her hand to her cheek and asked, Why—why? She thought there had to be some confusion, some grievous misunderstanding that she could put right if only they would let her speak, if she could only put things into words. But she was dragged away before she could think of what to say, staggering in a daze down the lane to another door in another house. As Enoch leaned against the wall and pushed her into his dim, damp-smelling hallway, he left a mark of fresh blood on the door frame, the red welt of a hand print, the painted language of caves.

IT WAS THE MAGPIES IN the garden that stirred Lugh from his fleecy sleep. Their bawdy clacking sounded so close that he thought they must be somewhere in the house, perched on the windowsill above his head, eyeing him with sideways intent. He slipped his fingers into the warm, furry niche between Abel's thighs and stretched out his other arm, which had been curled around Abel's neck and was now tingling with pins-and-needles. He pressed his nose against dense black hair, inhaled the uniqueness of the body in his arms.

'The magpies say it's morning,' Lugh said when Abel shifted and stretched, fitting the smooth back of his body neatly against the front of Lugh's. 'Listen. Mor-ning, mor-ning.'

'They're lying.' Abel buried his face against Lugh's arm. 'Magpies always lie.'

'The crows say it's morning too. Listen, those are crows. Are the crows also lying?'

'No, not the crows,' said Abel, his voice so muffled as to be barely understood. 'Crows are serious. But magpies tell lies. Don't be giving them the time of day.'

'But the time of day is morning.' Lugh nudged the blanket from his head and knitted his brows. 'Abel, listen, it's day already. It's light outside. Shouldn't you be back at the big house?'

'Mm. But I don't want to leave. If I leave, then I won't be here.'

'What if—' Lugh broke his question in half, threw away the clause that he suspected would be dismissed out of hand, considered variations on the theme. At length, he returned to the original proposition. 'What if you never went back and we stayed here?'

Abel tensed, opened his eyes widely and said that he should get back to the big house.

Walking along the riverbank in the rain, Abel wore the boots that Lugh had lent him. Lugh trudged behind in his wet socks, said he would be fine because he could see where to tread and where to avoid the thistles and nettles. Abel glanced shyly at him and reached out his hand.

'Take it,' he said, but Lugh shook his head. 'Take it, please.'

'I don't want to. It's hard enough walking in just socks.'

'Are you angry with me?'

Lugh brushed past Abel's outstretched hand and walked ahead, his hands dug deep in his pockets. In the branches over their heads, black wings kept the two youths company as they made their way through the forest. Occasionally a row broke out between magpie and crow, insults were exchanged and the two sides separated until the next confrontation at a later tree. Nearing the back gardens of the Mews, Lugh slowed down and turned to face Abel.

'Why? Why does it matter?' Lugh asked angrily. 'I'm in my socks, and your in your—whatever that stupid dress-thing is that you wear. We've only got one pair of boots between us because there are no other boots probably anywhere in the world, or candles or bread or sugar, or anything. So what's the point in you going back to the big house? Who really cares if we stay at the ivy-house? What does it matter anymore? What does any of it matter?'

'It's Mother,' said Abel with an apologetic shrug. 'I want to, I do, but she said—'

'Oh, motherfucker,'

Abel considered the strange word for a moment, then asked, 'What does that mean?'

'It means stop being a baby, Abel Mann.'

Lugh stomped away through the trees towards the back gardens of the terrace. Abel watched him go, wanting to follow him but he knew that he had already missed morning prayers in the chapel. He knew that the old man would smile disappointedly with that look in his eye. He knew that the old man would know.

Lugh kept his back to Abel and did not once turn around. As he approached his back yard, Lugh could see that the back door had been left wide open. Walking slowly alongside the weed-ridden plot where wheat and barley had once tried to grow, he eyed the dark windows of the house, the empty garden, one magpie loitering on the wall of the yard. It was painfully familiar, this dull foreknowledge of loss, this sense of impending abandonment. He quickened his pace and soon found himself running, ignoring the thorns that had worn through the thin skin of his saturated socks. When he reached the house, he lingered on the threshold, not daring to enter. The door creaked in a slight breeze, an empty sound full of meaning. The falling rain spoke softly all around. If he stayed outside, he would never know. He frowned back at the forest with a faraway look in his eye, seeing beyond the line of trees that moment he had left behind. If he went back the way he had come, if he returned to Abel, then he would never feel what he would feel if he entered. He looked back at the house and saw, smudged on the doorstep, a small red handprint, another and another. He crouched down on all fours and put his fingers over the hand of blood. The magpie hopped along the wall and then took off into the bruised sky, silent for once.

***

SOMEONE HAD LOCKED THE LIBRARY window, but it did not matter. The big house was just a house, the old man was just a man. The rainwater roared in fast-falling, incontinent streams from holes in the broken guttering. The white walls were not so white when looked at closely; they had aged yellow, piss-coloured stains where the rain overflowed the downpipes, and the paint was flaking all over, exposing simple plain bricks and mortar beneath. At one time, the house had seemed impregnable. Now, Abel understood its weaknesses.

Hiding Lugh's boots between flowerpots under the portico, Abel pulled on the doorbell chain and waited. He knew it would be awkward, lying to Father Ambrose about where he had been and what he had been up to all night but, precisely because of that night, he was no longer afraid. Until yesterday evening, Abel had been suffocated by the belief that the old man knew everything, his deepest thoughts and fears, his private acts, even his dreams. But now, as Lugh had said, what did it matter? Abel had passed through the portal, torn a rip in the skin of the house and slipped through the hole to an unimaginably rich other-life outside. Although he had parted badly with Lugh, he knew it was not over. It could never be over. That other-life was as potent and real as this house was pallid and weak, weather-worn and flaking apart. Some magic spell had been broken, a curse lifted. Abel felt calmer than ever, tall as a beanstalk.

'Oh, gosh, it's you,' said the old man with a delighted grin when he opened the front door. He ushered Abel inside with an energetic sweep of his arm as though welcoming home a long-awaited guest. 'Come in, come in. I expect you've been busy preparing for Holy Thursday, haven't you. Like the old ascetics, Saint Francis and that lot, taming the flesh in the wilderness, but in your own special Christlike way. Well, we're nearly there, nearly there. Almost ready, aren't we?'

Abel had completely forgotten that today was Holy Thursday and tomorrow was Good Friday. As he wiped his feet on the doormat, the priest laid a hand on his shoulder and leaned intimately close, so close that their noses were almost touching.

'You are such a good soul, Abel, so very good and pure,' Father Ambrose said, gripping the youth's shoulder. 'I trust you implicitly. I want you to know that. Implicitly.'

Abel spent the whole day in chapel, sitting on the hard wooden benches with his head in his hands, sometimes kneeling on a prayer-stool when the back-bent position became too tedious. At those times when the old man poked his head around the chapel door, he would have noticed nothing outwardly different in Abel's silent prayer. Inwardly, however, Abel was possessed by a new state of grace. The devotions that sprang naturally to his mind now were sensations of Lugh, of the night that had passed and of all the others yet to come. He devised a litany of things to recite to Lugh next time they met. Yes, he would say, what if I never do go back to the big house. And what if we stayed together in the ivy cottage. And what does any of it matter.

Consumed by these imaginings, Abel barely noticed the hours slip by and the watery grey daylight fade outside the arched window. When the grandfather clock in the drawing room chimed six o'clock and the chapel door opened, Abel could scarcely believe that he had dedicated a whole day of devotions to Lugh. The thought pleased him immensely and he did not try to hide his smile. He listened to his mother arranging herself, her clothes and her piety, on the bench opposite while the old man took his position behind the altar, stretched out his arms in greeting and began the service for Holy Thursday.

'Almighty God, unto whom all hearts be open, all desires known, and from whom no secrets are hid—'

Those opening words used to chill Abel to the bone. Every time he had heard them before, he imagined his secret, sinful desires being perused and scrutinised by an elderly man whose own desires had long been made obsolete by time and disuse, and who resented those who still possessed theirs. Almighty God had once looked like his grandfather. Abel had never met his maternal grandfather, but he had seen photographs. His face looked perpetually displeased, much like Mother's, though hidden behind a long white beard. Since Abel had lived in the big house, Almighty God's silky white hair had gradually thinned and He had taken to wearing gold-rimmed spectacles and a plain grey habit. Neither variation of the Almighty had been impressed with what they had unearthed while poking among Abel's thoughts. Now, however, for the first time in his life, those opening lines of the service carried no fear for Abel. His heart was open and his desires known: he had no secrets from Lugh, so what did the rest matter? The elderly figure who was once known as almighty, whether bald or with a fine head of white hair, recoiled from Abel's indifference, lost his edges and melted away in the flickering light of the altar candle.

After the service, Mother genuflected and briskly left the chapel, pointedly refusing to look at her son. Something was clearly bothering her. Either Abel must have slighted her in some mysterious, incomprehensible way or else one of her other children had. Once upon a time, that look from Mother—or look withheld—would have sent Abel's thoughts into a downward spiral of wretchedness, but not anymore. Something had slipped in the axis of the Earth; lines that had been vertical were now lying on their sides. Abel felt elated. He smiled as he watched the priest strip the altar for Holy Thursday, removing the cloth, silver cross and candlestick, evicting the wafer from the mahogany tabernacle and extinguishing the candles. When they were in complete darkness, the old man stood before him, perhaps a little more breathless than usual.

'Are we ready for Gethsemane, my love?' Father Ambrose asked.

Abel opened his mouth to speak, but the words refused to be spoken. They were not forgotten, he knew them off by heart, but he could not bring himself to utter them. Something in his will refused to comply, surprising himself as much as the priest.

'Please,' Father Ambrose pleaded. 'One last time, for me, for the Lord. It is Holy Thursday.'

It was strange to hear the old man beg. He sounded exhausted, thwarted, as though he sensed that he had lost whatever magic he once held over the youth. Prospero without his books. One last time, he had said, though Abel did not understand what he meant by the phrase. Perhaps he knew that Abel was going to leave. Perhaps this was his way of letting him go.

'Nevertheless,' said Abel, forcing the words to appear, 'not what I will, but what thou wilt.'

Abel followed his own faltering shadow up the staircase to the stale, sour-smelling attic room in the tower. The old man placed his candle on the writing desk and opened a drawer. He seemed to take longer than usual to retrieve his tools, perhaps reluctant to turn around and see Abel still in his robe, or else dragging out the seconds of this one-last-time for as long as possible. Without being prompted, Abel slipped out of his habit and lay it on the carpet. He kept his eyes on the folds of the grey material, never once looking up at the shadowy figure, grey-haired and eyeless, slouched in the armchair across the floor, though he could think of little else. Covering his nakedness, he pressed his back against the cold, wooden cross in the centre of the attic and waited for the old man to turn.

'Ready to take the kingdom of heaven by storm, are we?' said Father Ambrose. He turned around with an expression of immense pity, his face lit from beneath by the long flame of the candle. Abel raised his arms, exposing his body to the old man, to the hated figure in the hateful room, and pressed his knuckles against either side of the crossbeam. The priest walked towards him, shaking his head with sadness or disappointment, and pressed the sharp tip of a long iron nail against the open palm. Abel flinched at the unexpected pressure on the scab from last time.

'Now we shall at last become Christlike,' the old man said with intense pathos. He raised the hammer in the air and groaned as he brought it down hard against the head of the nail, driving it deep into Abel's left palm. Abel roared with shock and agony as the tissue was severed and the pain seared up his arm. The old man held the wrist firmly against the crossbeam and struck the nail again and again, hammering it through the tendons and into the wood.

With one palm fastened to the cross, Abel's body twisted and fell against the old man. His free hand scratched at the priest's robes, his arm, the hammer in his hand, desperate to prevent another blow from being struck. The old man took a step back, breathing with difficulty or excitement. He looked surprised as he touched the red fingernail weals that Abel had scraped down the side of his face, as though not comprehending how anyone could do such a thing to him. Staggering backwards, he reached for the second iron nail that lay on the desk.

Abel howled in pain. He pulled at the nail which pierced his bloody left palm, feeling it loosen but unable to release it from the crossbeam. Father Ambrose stumbled towards him again, swaying unsteadily on his feet as he approached. He paused for a moment, a look of dreadful confusion on his face, then he grabbed Abel's free hand. Using all of his strength, the old man succeeded in pressing the youth's wrist against the crossbeam, but he was unable to hold it there and hammer in the nail at the same time. Retreating out of Abel's reach, the old man considered what to do from a safe distance. He would not look into Abel's eyes but stared at parts of his naked body, smiling vaguely as though his mind were in some other place. When he did step forward, he raised the hammer intending to bring it down on Abel's head. The hammer hovered in the air between them, pitching this way and that in preparation to strike. Abel shrank back against the crossbeam as the old man came closer.

'We *shall* become Christlike,' Father Ambrose said, panting between each word. He brought the hammer down at the moment that Abel lashed out at him. The hammer nicked Abel's shoulder before dropping to the floor, but the old man was shoved violently away to the other side of the attic. There was a sickly cracking sound as he collided with the edge of the desk and then collapsed behind the shadows of the armchair.

Abel stared into the darkness where the old man lay motionless, listening to his ragged, gravelly breathing. The Gentleman stared blindly back at him, grinning absurdly in the candlelight as though unsure what to make of this unexpected performance. Abel half expected the body to raise its skeletal hands and clap slowly, genteelly, or else to stand up and stumble towards him to finish what the old man had started. Either way, Abel turned to his own mangled hand. He fumbled with the head of the nail, jerking it this way and that, and gasping as it grated within the open wound. Biting his lip, he was determined not to cry out too loudly lest he attract the attention of the old man and bring him back to his senses.

Eventually, the nail shifted more loosely in the wood, pulled free from the crossbeam and scraped through the hole in his hand with a final, excruciating tug. Freed from the cross, Abel took up his habit from the floor, pressed his bleeding hand within its folds and stumbled towards the stairs. As he passed the armchair, he saw the shadows stir and coalesce around a gasping shape. The old man rose to his knees, holding his head as though deep in prayer. Abel lurched down the stairs, slipping and missing steps, floundering against the walls. When he reached the landing, he slammed the attic door behind him and groped with the key in the lock.

'Gosh, Abel, what have we done?' said the old man in the attic, sounding surprised. He laughed a little, a light, sing-song sound. 'Abel? Where have we got to? A-bel. A-bel.'

Abel sat in the darkness with his bare back pressed against the door, nursing the bloody bundle against his stomach. He listened to sounds in the attic, on the roof, scrapings on floorboard and tile, the scratching of a talon or fingernail, hook or beak, flap of a wing or a robe.

MOTHER WAS STIRRING IN THE kitchen. From her hole in the wall upstairs, Ruth could hear the clatter of points being made emphatically downstairs: the teapot being rinsed out, chairs being straightened, things being done with resilience, determination. Mother sighed deeply as she combed her hair, collected her things, shoes from the cupboard, coat from the coat hook, stood at the front door and waited for somebody to notice.

'You off out somewhere?' Mark called out from relative calm of the sitting room.

'Chapel,' Mother replied sharply. 'It is Holy Thursday.'

'Never used to call it that, did we? Holy Thursday? Is that a papist thing you picked up?'

Mother sighed with exasperation and said, 'I just don't know what's wrong with you, boy.'

'Why? What have I done now?'

'You know full well what you've done. That—*girl*,' Mother spat the word out viciously, relieved at last to have the opportunity to vent her choler. 'What you were thinking I'll never understand. And now look what you've started with our Enoch. Him and that—*girl*. She's not to be trusted, that one. She's sly, she's not natural. She always wanted to get inside this family, always. Just think how she turned Matthew's head, God rest him. Why you had to go over there in the first place, tempting fate, I'll never know. And I don't want to know. Your instincts aren't right, son. It's not right and it's not normal.'

'Why not have a word with our Enoch, then? If she's trouble, why not—'

'That's enough. Enoch's his own man. He's head of this family now and he decides his own destiny. But you, son, I don't know what's gone wrong with you.' Mother opened the door and prepared to leave on that accusatory note, but she paused to glower at the house across the road.

'And he'll be coming over here soon, that boy, looking for her. You mark my words.'

'What do I tell him if he comes and you're out?'

'You put him in his place,' Mother said firmly. 'Do something right for once. Nip it in the bud.'

The front door closed behind her and the house was silent for a moment. In her hole in the bedroom wall, Ruth hugged her shins and rested her cheek on her knees. The blackness comforted her, hid her from the attention of others, returned all things to their broken-down essence. She listened to the rain pattering on tiles, trickling down edges and falling, falling. Sometimes a cough or an urgent here-here-look-look from the scavenging birds on the rooftop, but otherwise all else was falling, blackness, dissolution.

'Ruth?' The voice was muted, a secretive question that no one else could hear, offered at the bottom of the stairs. One stair creaked a telling response, here-here.

'Ruth, you up there?' Another step croaked, warmer-warmer.

Ruth tightened her grip on her arms, pulling her knees hard against her chest. The blackness would not hold forever: the attention of others would always find a way.

Another step sang, closer-closer. Another replied, coming-ready-or-not.

When Mark reached the top of the stairs, he opened the door to Ruth's bedroom and found it empty. She could hear his slow footsteps pacing around the floorboards, opening the wardrobe, looking under the bed. The smart magpies on the roof cried, look-look, and Mark stepped towards the hole in the wall. As he reached out his hand, there came a loud knocking on the front door and Mark retreated quickly from her room, scrambling down the stairs to be somewhere else, somewhere he ought to be.

Ruth released pieces of her held breath into the pores of her shirt sleeve. She did not pay much heed to the loud voices downstairs, the boy on the doorstep, Mark in the hallway shouting, shoving, slapping. The attention had ebbed to the lane, far from where she crouched in the blackness. She could hear them both shouting outside, and now Enoch too, but Enoch was not here and Mark was not here, none of them were here. She pinched her shirt sleeve between her teeth and knew that it would not last forever. Sooner or later, the tide of attention would return to creep up the stairs and flood her room, seeking her out in the hole in the wall. Something would give her away. Something always gave her away.

After a while, the lane sounded empty. Ruth thought there might have been running, stones thrown, curses too: cursed be Canaan, a servant of servants shall he be. It was deserted for now, but they would return. They always returned, and Mother too.

Carefully, Ruth broke the seal of her blackness and slipped outside the hole. Evening had fallen while she had been hiding and she could barely see a thing, but that was all to her advantage. Still, she would have to be quick before they came back. She felt under the blankets of her bed and retrieved the fragment, the shard of Pacific and sharp Antarctica, edges of ocean and snow. As she crept down the staircase, she noticed that the steps stayed quiet for her, no tell-tale wooden voice crying out, help-help, Mother-Mother. In the hallway, she paused to grab her duffel-coat and then ran through the front door, hooded and hidden, her head bent down and heart gasping in her throat. Across the lane and over the gardens, the wet earth opening beneath her trainers, the deep forest gaping red, closing black behind her.

CHAPTER TWELVE
LYRIDS

THEY HAD TAKEN THE KEY from the back door. Lugh sat on the kitchen table and swung his legs back and forth, back and forth, holding a damp rag against his aching, bloody nose. He had not noticed that they had taken the key until now, but it did not surprise him. It was all part of the new normal. It was just what they did. Earlier that evening, when he had returned to the house, there were other things that needed attending to, more urgent things, like his nose for a start. He had cleaned all that blood around the kitchen sink too, but that was not his. They had taken the key and they had taken the blanket. They had taken Fran and left handprints of blood. Not for the first time that evening, he was overwhelmed by a wave of intense, murderous rage. Just when he thought this fit of violence would suffocate him, the mist passed and he could see again, clear-headed and rational, frowning with impotence.

He looked down at the bible of herbs on his lap and flicked through the pages. It was too dark to read much in the dim light of the last emergency candle, but at least he could see the drawings of plants, the bold titles of herbs at the top of each page. The rest, he could more or less remember. Rosemary for remembrance, sage to ward off the plague, thyme for courage and the curing of nightmares, yarrow to soothe aches and pains. There might be some thyme, but he knew there was no yarrow. Only cold water and a rag. There might be some dried comfrey in a jar somewhere, but that was for broken bones. He did not think his nose was broken.

'Still a handsome devil, even with all that blood clotting your nostrils,' Fran had told him once. He smiled at the memory and then, suddenly, silently and without any warning, began to cry, his tears landing on the unreadable words. And you're still a beautiful devil too, he wanted to tell her, even with all that blood in the sink. She would have laughed at that. At least, Old Fran would have laughed at that. Old Fran would have known what to do. She would have stewed apples, or lined up the pieces on the chessboard, or found something useful in the encyclopaedia to read aloud. Rhea would have kindled the fire in the stove and brewed a pot of mint tea. And Ky would have sharpened her knife, rolled her eyes and asked, Do you trust me? I do now, thought Lugh. I know it's too late, but I do and I'm sorry. He wiped the tears off the page, slipped down from the table and prepared the kindling for a fire in the stove.

The bed he made on the kitchen floor was for Fran when she returned. New blankets and pillows from the empty bedrooms upstairs: at least that was something he could do for her. A thought, a gesture, if nothing else. He had tried with the brothers, with Mark and Enoch, but they had turned on him like wild animals, confirming what he already knew to be true: that they had taken Fran, were holding her against her will, and were not going to give her up. They were feral, the brothers, chasing him with fists and stones, barking in the woods. They were stronger than him, and stronger than Fran. He tried not to imagine what they were doing to her now. Instead, he sat beside the open stove and thought about fire, scythes and poisonous toadstools. There were many things that he could do. The wave of mindless violence clouded his mind again with visions of death, throats cut and faces burned. He poked the sticks, watched the flames until the fit passed, leaving him cold. There was nothing he could do.

Lugh knew that there was no point in trying to sleep this night, so he sat cross-legged on the makeshift bed and carefully laid objects around him: the handwritten ledgers, Rhea's unfinished knitting of another jumper for him, her classical albums. Reverentially, he created a candlelit circle of scribbles, images, memories: a conjuring. None of these artefacts had possessed special meaning before, but now, after the loss of each of their owners, they assumed a sacred aura. Fran, Ky, Rhea: they had each left something behind, a concentration of thoughts, intensities, passions. Fran with her lists of leaves, both medicinal and culinary, sowings and reapings, bird sightings and sky colours. Ky with her urgent flow of facts and happenings, boots and borders, cities in the sea, falling stars: a story that Ky was determined should not be forgotten. And Rhea with her orchestral suites and Ring sagas, solemn marches, fanfares of resurrection.

Enclosed within his circle, Lugh picked through the relics. It was comforting to have all their memories around him, a sense of their presence and a protection of sorts, but he also half-hoped that he might uncover some clue, an intimation of what action he should take in the scraps they had left behind. He browsed through the curling handwriting in Fran's almanac. This time last year there had been a clear sunrise, cirrus clouds, blackbirds digging and a robin on the wall, the planting of root vegetables, preparation of wheat and barley beds. Lugh flicked ahead, more days of the same or similar, of temperatures rising, cloudless skies, the Dog Star coming over the southern horizon. Another week went by and then a curious shape was sketched in the margins, dots joined into an angular almost-figure-of-eight, an explosion of tail-blazing dots beside it. Written alongside this shape were several mysterious sentences that filled Lugh with excitement, though he could not begin to decipher their meaning: *Lyra the harp, Look to Vega – Remember, same time next year. Awesome. Must tell Lugh.* That last sentence was underlined. She must tell Lugh what, he wondered. He knew that Lyra was a constellation and that Vega was a star within that constellation, one of the brightest in the night sky, but what did Fran mean, same time next year? He looked at the date of the entry, then flipped to his own book of days to find today's date. In less than two weeks it would be a year since she had written him that cryptic message. He convinced himself that she had purposefully left it for him to find, that she had known he would need her advice and that she would tell him something. He had cast a circle and summoned assistance, and a sign had appeared. He just did not know what it meant.

The rain ceased its soft drumming against the window an hour or so after midnight. Lugh preferred the silence because he could hear the sounds of the night. If someone came, if there were footsteps around the back of the house, he would know. He glanced up at the back door, the keyhole an empty black eye watching him. Its attention was unnerving, so Lugh wedged a chair firmly against the handle. The door would not hold for long if one of the brothers shoved against it, but at least he would have a few seconds' warning. As an additional precaution, he grabbed the garden scythe and brought it into his magic circle, laid it across his lap ready to use if he had to. He blew out the candle to preserve what remained of the diminishing wax stub, half-closed his eyes.

Look to Vega—it made no sense, but it gave him hope in the darkness. He would ask Abel what he thought it meant. Not that Abel knew much about stars or constellations, he did not even know Mars, but he had read many books in the library now and he probably knew lots about prophecies. There was no point going to the library window tomorrow, it being Friday, so Lugh would have to wait another day before asking, another night alone in this house.

The logs settled comfortably in the stove; the books made room for him to lie down. *Look to Vega.* The riddle calmed him, offered a mystery that the skies would unravel, some greater mind to set things right and all would be well. Lugh drifted into the scent of black hair, of all-over fur and fascinating skin, the sound of bells jangling in the distance. *I dare you to take this thing off*, and Abel had, offering the everything he owned. *I dare you to get out of those*, and there was nothing left to hide. Soft down, pelted shanks, shinbones and hooves whispering rings around a purple garden, smoothing a path through violet undergrowth, stars rippling down ivy. Abel reached out and took the brightest one, probably Vega, and said, 'Look, same time next year'. Lugh wondered what that meant but, before he could ask, the hooves thundered away in the garden and the bells clattered like hail against the window. Lugh sat bolt upright in his bed, immediately conscious of the urgent knocking on the back door.

'Who's there?' he shouted and stood up, holding the scythe in trembling hands.

'Me, of course,' said the voice outside. 'It's Abel.'

Lugh unlodged the chair from the handle and opened the back door, the scythe raised in his hand. Abel stumbled into the kitchen wearing Lugh's unlaced boots and breathing heavily. Lugh lit the candle and saw that Abel was no longer dressed in his grey habit, but had changed back into his old clothes, dirty jeans, that chequered shirt. The habit, no longer grey but black, was wrapped tightly around his left hand and pressed against his stomach. Lugh could see at once that he had been injured. His face was pale and his wide eyes were dark, unfocused with fear.

'Would it be all right if you came back to the big house with me?' Abel asked brightly despite his condition. He reached his good hand against the kitchen chair to steady himself and smiled apologetically. 'I think something happened and—well, something did happen and—' here he slumped abruptly into the chair, 'and I'm not quite sure what's best to do.'

Lugh knelt down and carefully unwrapped the habit from Abel's wounded hand. The thin fabric grew darker and more saturated with blood the deeper he went until, unravelling the whole and holding the wrist, he laid bare the grisly, lacerated, weeping palm.

'Don't go anywhere,' said Lugh, already running into the hallway and up the stairs for the army rucksack he knew that Ky had left in her bedroom. Bandages, iodine, needles, scissors. He did not know how to use any those things, but he knew they were needed.

'I didn't go anywhere,' Abel said with a weak smile when the other returned and set a kettle to boil on the stove. 'It's bad. It's really bad.'

'It's not so very bad,' Lugh replied, crouching down beside the chair. 'I've seen worse.'

'I mean at the house. And Mother will come for communion in a few hours.'

'So,' Lugh mused as he washed the injured hand, dabbed the hole with copious iodine, 'now the wow's broken and you can speak... '

'Vow,' said Abel, half-laughing, half-wincing. 'It's a vow of silence, not a wow of silence.'

'You wrote wow. In your first note, you said it was a wow. Anyway, now you can speak, you can tell me what happened. I saw that scab before. I saw it but you didn't want to tell me.'

Lugh frowned as he pressed the bandage against the gash and bound it tightly around the knuckles, between the thumb and forefinger, over and over the punctured hand. He worked calmly and deliberately, looping the dressing under and around time and again, just as he had seen Rhea and Ky binding and re-binding his own brother's wounds. As he weaved, Abel spoke of attics and crucifixes, hammers and nails, Gethsemane, Golgotha. Hesitatingly at first but growing more fluent, Abel talked until the winding ended, his wound was bound and clipped tightly with a pin.

MOTHER WATCHED THE SKY THROUGH the kitchen window turn pale, watery blue. She sipped her tea, tepid after being forgotten for so long, and thought about extinguishing the fire in the stove. It would soon be day and the fire had to be out before sunrise. This would be her last cup of tea until evening fell again, which she did not mind because she took no pleasure in the taste. Weeds and grass, not proper tea, not what she would call tea, but beggars can't be choosers. Must make do with what there is, as Matthew used to say. Such a good soul, a kind boy, Matthew. He was, he had been, she reminded herself. He was the one who introduced her to these concoctions, showed her which leaves and roots to pick from the garden. She knew mint, of course, and dandelions, but the rest she had forgotten. Blackberries and raspberry leaves, that was right, she could just about manage those. She smiled to herself, remembering all that time Matthew had wasted trying to explain garden plants to her, but then her smile twisted. She supposed it would have been that girl who taught Matthew about leaves and teas back when she had her eye on him, turned his head, trying to lead him astray. And now that girl had her hooks in Enoch.

'Tramp,' Mother said aloud, a quick, vicious curse. She glanced around to make sure no one had heard. The kitchen was empty, just as the house was empty. She could say what she liked, only God would hear and he always agreed with her. 'Well, that's what she is, isn't she? A tramp.'

Enoch had his work cut out for him with that one, for sure, but he was an altogether different kettle of fish to Matthew. Enoch had been born strong, a natural patriarch; he would suffer neither nonsense nor fools gladly. He would bring that girl down a peg or two, Mother had no doubt. As the firstborn, the Earth was his inheritance and every teeming thing within it, even tramps. But Matthew had been different. It can't have been easy, being the second son, always following in his older brother's footsteps, always in his shadow. But he had accepted his place with the grace of an angel, always good-naturedly, always obedient. Not that Mother had ever had a favourite child—she did not do favourites—but if there was one that had caused her the least trouble, it was Matthew. She could always rely on him to make her smile with his foolishness. He was too good for this world: that must have been why the Lord saw fit to take him away. Better to be in Heaven than tempted by tramps on Earth.

The sky was brightening and the tops of the trees had turned golden green. Must be a clear sunrise, Mother nodded, a rare blessing for a sacred day. She knelt by the stove to check that the fire was out. Poking among the last embers, she snuffed them through the grate and satisfied herself that the fire had well and truly died. Ruth should be the one doing this, of course, but Ruth was worse than useless. Ruth had not been seen since yesterday afternoon, had probably taken it into her head to go swanning off into the forest or heaven knew where. Only God knew what went on in that girl's head, and even He must throw his hands up in despair. Ruth had not come back for her tea either, so Mother had locked the back door and kept the key in her pocket all night. There was still no sight of the girl this morning, but she would learn her lesson soon enough.

As Mother combed her hair for chapel, she told herself again that she really did not have any favourites. On the other hand, she did not think there was anything amiss in wishing that all of her children had been boys. Locking the front door behind her, she caught a glimpse of Luke disappearing around the bend in the lane, carrying his fishing rods towards the big house. He would return later with a basketful of vegetables and a nice fish or two, maybe even a trout: he never came back empty-handed. Another good boy, a faithful boy. It had not always been easy but, all in all, she had not done too badly with her boys.

By the time Mother reached the big house, the early morning sun had bathed the trees, the portico and the top of the tower in a rich amber light. She pulled the chain of the doorbell and arranged her blouse and skirt, her gold crucifix, while waiting for the old man to appear. Father Ambrose always took his time to answer the door, but this morning in particular he seemed to take forever. She wondered if perhaps he had been at his vigil all night and was still kneeling with his head in his hands, sharing in the suffering of Christ on the day of the crucifixion. These traditions were so new for her that, for a moment, she felt a sickening dread that she should not be there, that she might have misunderstood some vital piece of information about the time of the Good Friday service. Just as she was thinking about slipping away, she heard footsteps in the hallway, the grinding of cogs as the lock was turned and the door opened. Instead of Father Ambrose, however, it was Abel who stood in the doorway. He looked pale and tired as though he too had been praying all night. He was wearing a different grey habit and holding out a letter to her.

'What's that on your hand, son?' she asked, seeing the blood-stained bandage at once. He shrugged, unable to answer, and she immediately felt ashamed for having spoken to Abel directly, knowing how difficult it must be for him to keep his vow of silence, especially with her. She mumbled an apology, crossed herself rapidly and then opened the letter.

'My dearest Marion,' she said, thinking it was permissible to read the letter aloud to herself, whether or not Abel was present. 'It is with the greatest sorrow that I must tell you that today's services have been cancelled. The strain of last night's vigil has brought me closer to God, but now I am very sick and verily I must rest greatly. I have instructed Abel to look after me, only Abel, which is very necessary for his training to become Christlike. Looking after the sick is almost a sacrament, almost like Motherhood, so I know you will understand. I will write to you when I am well again, but I do not expect to be well for several weeks; I will write to you when I am. Also and as well, all future services have been cancelled too until, God willing, I am well, and I will write to you soon, but not before. You are so good, so very good, I trust implicitly that you will understand. God bless you, good woman. Father Ambrose.'

Mother stared at the letter for a long time after she had finished reading it, an expression of anxious concern, and perhaps a little confusion, on her face. She folded it away and was about to say something to Abel when she remembered his vow of silence. She was never quite sure what this vow entailed, whether he was simply not allowed to speak or if it was also inappropriate for her to address him. She assumed that it was permissible for her to think aloud in his presence, and so she decided to take the same approach as she did with the letter.

'I hope Father Ambrose knows that I will pray for him to have a swift recovery,' she said ostentatiously, a theatrical aside, looking at the sky as though Abel were not standing there. 'I will pray that the Lord sees fit to bring him back to continue his work very soon. Prayer and faith, that's what will do it. Prayer and faith. I trust Father Ambrose will know that.'

Mother seemed hesitant to depart. She brushed down her skirt, plucked atoms from her coat sleeves, glanced briefly at Abel and gave him a little smile of encouragement before turning away. He watched her walk down the driveway and disappear behind the corner at the gateposts. As her brisk footsteps echoed away down the lane, he closed the door and breathed more freely than he had ever imagined possible.

Lugh was waiting in the library. It was the first time that he had been inside the room, and he browsed the shelves with a serious expression, knitted brows, a faraway look, occasionally taking titles that he thought would be of use, or that might interest Fran when she came home. She would come home, he was convinced of that. He had already stacked a pile of old volumes in front of the fireplace when Abel entered the room.

'Did she fall for it?' Lugh asked, though he could tell at once from the tangible relief in Abel's expression that she had. 'And she didn't ask any funny questions?'

'No point her asking anything to me if I can't reply.' Abel sat in one of the armchairs and held his bandaged hand against his chest. 'Now we need to think what to do with him.'

'Rumpelstiltskin in the attic? We'll just leave him there, won't we?'

'No, because… because I don't think that's right. Why do you call him that?'

'It's what Fran calls him. It's like a weird creature from a fairytale.' Lugh sat in the other armchair and nodded at Abel's wounded hand. 'You know that he tried to kill you, don't you?'

'Yes,' Abel replied. 'Well, crucify.'

'Is that any different?'

'No, it's the same.'

'So, you want to let him out of the attic,' Lugh said slowly, making an effort to understand, 'because he tried to crucify you rather than kill you in a less creepy way?'

'I don't even know if he did want to kill me. See, it's complicated. I really do think he wanted me to be Christlike, in his way. It's what he kept saying.'

'Christlike? Like dead, you mean? And hammer your head in, too?'

'Yes, that wasn't very nice.'

'Listen,' Lugh said, leaning forwards and speaking as slowly and tactfully as he could manage. 'If you let Rumpelstiltskin out, what do you think he'll do?'

'I think he'll try to...' Abel gestured a hammer against his head, 'again.'

'And you want that to happen?'

'No, I just don't want him to be up there—dying.' Abel arched his eyebrows and stared blankly at the fireplace. 'I don't want to do to him what he was going to do to me. Otherwise I'd be the same, do you see? Look, I'm already wearing his old habit. Can we not take him something to eat, at least? Some water, perhaps?'

'He doesn't know I'm here, does he?' asked Lugh. Abel shook his head, and they looked at each other for a long minute. 'Okay. But if he does try anything, I'll be the one to crucify him.'

As they climbed the stairs and approached the attic door, they could hear the old man's voice moaning like a distant, eerie wind. Lugh clutched the only weapon he could find in the house, an iron poker from the fireplace in the library. The floorboards creaked when Abel put the provisions he had brought, a bottle of water and a plate of fried eggs, on the floor.

'Abel? Is that you? A-bel,' the old man called feebly from behind the door. 'Oh, beloved boy, I am in hell, absolute hell. How can ever you forgive me? I wouldn't dream of insulting you by asking you to, but—oh, my love—if there is a hell, then I am in it. I don't know what I could have been thinking. I would be ready to die, I am ready to die, but first I should like to see your face, ask for your forgiveness. Please, pity me a little and grant this one thing. Open the door, Abel. Open it, so you can see me kneeling, so I can beg for your forgiveness. Just that, nothing more.'

Abel gestured for Lugh to stand beside the door and then, cautiously, he turned the key. There was a shuffling on the other side, an intake of breath followed by silence. Abel turned the handle and, as the door opened, the old man pushed against it with all his might and sent Abel tumbling backwards onto the floor. The priest stumbled forwards too and landed on his elbows with the hammer clenched in his fist. Grunting, he knelt over Abel and would have brought the hammer down forcefully, repeatedly, against the youth's face, but Lugh struck him hard with the poker, first on his arm and then against his neck. The old man crumpled in pain, rolling aside and unable to resist as Lugh dragged him back to the attic staircase.

Lugh kicked the bottle of water inside, then closed and locked the door. They could hear him groaning on the other side, a feeble voice like the wind through a crack, the petulant kick of a shoe against wood. Shocked by his own violence, Lugh raised his face and caught Abel's eye.

'He's surprisingly strong, your old man,' said Lugh. 'How old is he exactly?'

'I don't know,' said Abel, rising carefully to his feet so as not to knock his bandaged hand. 'Old. Maybe fifty? Or eighty? I think maybe we should leave him in the attic a little longer.'

ABEL'S BEDROOM WAS A SMALL bare cell above the library at the back of the house. It gave off a dank, empty smell, like a disused cupboard that had never been aired. There was one window, draped with a thin net curtain, that would not open but overlooked the lawns, the farmyard and, beyond that, the forest. Underneath the window was an old school writing-desk, in which names and mysterious words had long ago been etched into the wood with the needles of compasses, emboldened with ink. A row of faded books—a Bible, dictionary, Augustine and Aquinas, Julian of Norwich, The Little Flowers of Saint Francis—stood on the desk, propped neatly against the wall with a beeswax candle. A crucifix on the wall and an emaciated mattress, weighted by the memory of other bodies, lay on the floorboards, a blanket and thin eiderdown for comfort.

For the thousandth time, Abel read the secret letters scratched on the underside of the desk. Beside him, Lugh's naked body was pressed warmly against the length of his own.

'What's bollocks?' Abel asked, reading the word that had always puzzled him.

'Everything's bollocks,' said Lugh inattentively. He turned another page of the book in his hands, an encyclopaedia at least a hundred years old, and continued reading in the afternoon light.

'But what is it exactly? Bollocks, a bollock,' Abel mused, running his finger over the engraving in the wood. '*Lick my bollocks*. What can it mean?'

Lugh laughed and, cupping Abel's balls under the covers, said, 'These are bollocks.'

'Gosh, and somebody actually wrote that for people to see?'

'It's an insult too, but also a dare,' said Lugh, returning to his book. 'Like, if I said it to you in the days before, I dare you to lick my bollocks, it would be a sort-of way of asking for it. But if you didn't want to do it, I could pretend I didn't mean it and it was an insult. And don't say gosh. Don't ever say gosh. When you say gosh, you sound like him upstairs.'

'Did I say gosh?' Abel's attention was still on the underside of the desk, searching the wood for scratchings of other dares. 'What should I say instead?'

'Say bollocks.'

'Bollocks.' Abel liked the sound of it. He tried it out again, 'Bollocks, what are you reading?'

'About Lyra, the harp. It's a constellation.'

'Oh, like Mars, you mean? Bollocks, why are you reading that?'

Lugh lifted the book over Abel's shoulder and lay it open on the floor beside the mattress so they could both see the picture: a lyre of stars in the claws of an eagle, Vega, the Ring Nebula. *Look to Vega*, said Lugh and he explained the message that Fran had scribbled for him in the margins of her almanac. *Remember, same time next year. Awesome. Must tell Lugh.*

'But if she knew something bad was going to happen, why didn't she just tell you? Or why not stop it from happening in the first place?' Abel frowned at the diagram of the constellation. 'And what do you think will actually happen with this star? And how would she have known anyway?'

'Because she would,' said Lugh sharply. He closed the book and sat up from the blanket. 'It's the sort of thing she knew, she does know. She knows all about nature and stars, and –'

Lugh folded his arms and stared ahead at the simple crucifix on the plain bedroom wall. When he had first seen that strange message written in Fran's book, he was convinced that it had appeared at that precise moment for a reason, that it portended something momentous. Sitting alone among the shadows of the kitchen floor, bloody-nosed and powerless to do anything, he had looked for an answer and an answer had materialised. Now that he had spoken it aloud to Abel, he understood how ridiculous the whole concept sounded. And what exactly, he wondered, did he think would happen anyway? That some star would come down to rescue her? That, exactly one year after Fran had penned that note, a host of Furies would ride out of the night sky and throw their spears on his enemies? Lugh felt sick with his own stupidity. In his desperation for help, he had concocted a fantasy as hollow and as make-believe as—he glared at the crucifix—as that thing. And all the time that he had allowed himself to be distracted by a fiction, Fran had been locked inside that house with those motherfuckers.

'Bollocks, where are you off to?' Abel asked as Lugh pushed aside the blanket and hastily dressed himself. 'Are you angry with me? Was it something I said?'

'Yes, I'm angry,' said Lugh, pushing his head through the hole in his jumper, 'and yes, it was something you said. You were right. You were right about everything.'

Lugh's thoughts were dark and bloody as he closed the drawing-room door to the garden and pulled on his boots. The afternoon sun was shining on the leaves of the forest, sparking on puddles in the rain-drenched lawns, but Lugh could see nothing around him. He did not know what he would do, but he had to do something. As he marched down the path towards the farmyard, he was roused from his reverie by someone calling his name.

'Were you in the big house?' said Luke, walking towards him with a bucket, the fishing rod under his arm.

'No, I wasn't,' Lugh said defensively as they approached each other.

'You were too, I saw you. Saw you coming out them doors. What were you up to?'

'I said I wasn't. I was just looking through the door.' Lugh continued to walk on towards the farmyard, then stopped and turned with a frown. 'Have you seen her?'

'What, that friend of yours?' Luke put the bucket on the floor and wiped his brow. 'Aye, but I'm not getting mixed up in all that business. Mother says our Enoch can do what he likes, but I've got no time for any of it. Doesn't seem right, the way I see it.'

'How is she? What did he do to her?'

'Seems all right, though I've not seen her much, to be honest. Like I said, none of my business. Enoch's house, Enoch's rules.'

'But why is he doing it? Why won't he let her go?'

Luke picked up his bucket and said simply, 'He's the firstborn.'

'Can you give her a message? Can you tell her, if she needs anything –'

'I'll not be getting mixed up in anything,' Luke called over his shoulder. 'Won't say it again.'

When Lugh reached the farmyard, he sat for a long time brooding on the wall. He knew that Luke had not gone away at all, that he was lurking somewhere behind a tree or around some corner, keeping an eye on him. Luke could lurk all he liked. Lugh should have taken more care when he left the big house, should have used a different, more hidden way out. He would have to be more discreet in the future. He would have to think before doing anything.

The library window was the most sheltered way in and out of the house. Screened from the garden by climbing roses and apple trees in blossom, only someone skulking on the patio would have noticed Lugh slipping out before dawn, creeping in after dusk. He sometimes saw Luke digging in the vegetable plots or emerging from the trees with a bucketful of fish, but Lugh kept his distance, biding his time. The forest guarded Lugh's manoeuvres, camouflaged his passing around the Mews and his vigil at the back of Enoch's house. Hidden among the leaves of the undergrowth, he watched the dark windows for a glimpse of Fran, a cry for help, or for Enoch to leave. He had stones in his hands, the scythe slipped through his belt, but there was never a sound, nothing to sting him into action one way or the other. Since the key to their old house on Usquam Mews had been taken, he now regarded that territory as lost, occupied by the enemy. In secret hours, he made occasional forays back inside the empty rooms, coming back to Abel at the big house with curiosities: black ledgers, vinyl records, an envelope of dried toadstools.

'If you ate one of these, you'd die instantly, probably,' said Lugh, searching the kitchen for somewhere to hide the envelope. 'Even looking at them for too long can make you sick. Where's the most secret place we can hide them? Somewhere that no one would ever, ever go?'

'No one's ever here anyway,' Abel replied. 'What about the chapel? That's pretty secret.'

Abel followed Lugh into the chapel where the altar had remained stripped and godless, the room unused since Holy Thursday. Lugh held his candle up to the tabernacle, lay the envelope inside and closed the little wooden door. When he turned around, he saw Abel looking uneasy.

'What?' asked Lugh. 'You're not still thinking there's anything special about this place?'

'No, it just feels a bit weird. What will you do with them, the mushrooms?'

'Toadstools,' said Lugh, lighting the way back through the dark, echoing hallway to the drawing room. 'Not sure. Probably nothing. Suppose we can test them out on Rumpelstiltskin.'

'Are you serious?'

'No, I'm not serious,' Lugh laughed, though the notion had crossed his mind, as had the thought of somehow slipping them to Abel's brothers.

Late one evening, when they were convinced that no one else would be around, they tried one of Rhea's albums, Monteverdi, on the gramophone. Neither of them knew how to operate the machine but, by attempting first one way and then another, they eventually cranked the handle and laid the needle on the turning disc. They looked at each other as the first ghostly crackles crept out of the brass horn like whispers from another time, from a dead and buried civilization. Abel smiled and was about to speak, when the room was blasted with a fanfare of noise, the bray of trumpets announcing the onslaught of *L'Orfeo*. Lugh scrambled for the tone-arm and, in the process of lifting the needle, scratched the record. They did not try again for days, not until they had reasoned that the only way to lower the volume was by wedging a sock down the horn.

More often than not, Lugh knew when someone was watching him in the garden. When he was planting new potatoes or weeding between onions and leeks, it was the sudden hush of the blackbirds or the urgent warning of a crow that told him one of the brothers was lurking nearby. One day, a couple of weeks after they had last encountered each other, Luke approached him in the greenhouse. Lugh was spreading a layer of rotten leaf mulch, turning the soil over with a spade. He did not turn around.

'Our Enoch says you're to gather food for him,' Luke announced. 'Just a little of what you'd get for yourself anyway, vegetables and whatnot.'

'Why would I do that?' Lugh asked after a moment's consideration, still digging.

'It's what Enoch said.'

'Why would I do that?' Lugh repeated each word slowly, deliberately.

'It's not just for him, I guess, is it?' said Luke. 'It's him and that girl.'

'Fran?' Lugh was suddenly conscious of the sharp, metal edge of the tool in his hands. He turned to look at Luke. 'Will I get to see her?'

'Not likely,' Luke laughed, backing away, his message delivered.

'So why would I gather food for him?'

Luke shrugged. 'You know what our Enoch's like. *Cursed be Canaan, a servant of servants shall he be*—something like that. That's what he said.'

'Okay,' said Lugh, returning to his digging. 'Tell him okay.'

Lugh smiled as he pushed against the spade and twisted the dark mulch over the soil. In the chapel that evening, he carefully deposited half of the dried toadstools into a new envelope and wrote, 'Not Puffball,' in capital letters on the label. It was perhaps too much of a risk, so he added, 'Fran knows best how to prepare them'.

The following night, the sky was as clear as Lugh could have wished for. The rain had held off for a few days and now the pores of the earth were opening for air. As Lugh and Abel walked down the garden path, they could hear the soil clack and sigh in the darkness around them.

'There she is,' said Lugh, pointing at a bright star in the east. 'That's Lyra, the harp. And that bright star at the top, that's Vega.'

'What do you think will happen?' Abel asked as he sat on the ledge of the small, stone fountain in the middle of the lawn. He looked up at the night sky and tried, unsuccessfully, to make out the shape of a harp. There were traces of cloud, not enough to obscure their view of the stars, and a low, setting moon. Abel was still disappointed not to see her brilliant full height.

'I think the earth will open and the Furies will strike down our enemies,' Lugh whispered. Since that morning when he had delivered the basket of oranges, lemons and the envelope of toadstools at Enoch's front door, he had been in an animated mood, saying the strangest things.

'Bollocks,' said Abel politely. 'Who are our enemies? And what are the Furies?'

'Enoch is my enemy,' Lugh said coldly, though he was smiling in the darkness. There was nothing that Abel could say to that. 'The Furies are the Eumenides. They're awful. They're like these tormenting spirits of revenge that drive you mad. They're so bad that you shouldn't even say their name aloud in case you wake them up and they come for you. You have to call them something else, something nice instead, like the Kindly Ones.'

'Are they in the Bible?'

'I think they're in the Greek Bible, but I'll have to ask Fran,' Lugh said and then, leaping up suddenly as though he had been stung, he pointed towards the east, to the side of the bright star, Vega. 'There, did you see that?'

Abel stood up and stared into the blackness. He did not know what he was supposed to be looking for, but he felt uneasy. Lugh stood behind Abel and clasped one arm around his chest. The other, he laid over Abel's shoulder.

'Follow the line of my finger,' said Lugh, pointing at the sky.

They stayed in this embrace for one minute and then another, staring into the emptiness until the stars began to dance. The night was turning cold, but their bodies formed warmth where they blended together, overlapping rhythms of alternate pressing, push and refrain, kindling the unseen. At last, it appeared: a shot of fire burning across the sky. The trail flared for only a handful of seconds, searing the blackness before it was gone. Abel was about to speak but then another and another flashed into existence, quickening overhead and fading into nothing.

'Is that what she meant?' Abel asked, when the flurry of shooting stars had subsided. 'When Fran said that about Lyra the harp, look to Vega?'

Lugh shrugged and pressed his chin against Abel's shoulder. Must be, he thought. They looked to Vega for a few minutes more, but the meteor shower had eased off for the moment.

'I dare you to come inside with me,' said Lugh, releasing Abel from his embrace and taking him by the hand over the dewy lawn to the house. Abel closed the drawing-room door behind them and was about to pull the curtains, when Lugh pulled him away from the window and down to the floor, to the playful sensation of darkness.

In the garden, another darkness stirred, a different kind of shadow. A furtive commotion of leaves and blossom, then Luke emerged from beneath the apple tree. He stepped warily along the path behind the house, careful not to make the slightest noise, until he reached the drawing room doors. Kneeling down on the hard paving stones, he put his face to the glass and looked inside. The room was unlit but, because he had been outside for hours, Luke's eyes had grown accustomed to the dark. It took time for matter to take form in his mind, the smooth movement of limbs, soft-edged and black-fringed, a tentative but resolute knowing. He watched the two bodies merge into one unbroken, unselfconscious outline until, respiring unevenly at the end, they divided into separate entities once more. When it was over, Luke leaned against the wall, himself breathing heavily.

A falling star flared overhead, almost audible, though Luke did not notice it. Instead, he stared at the obscure density of the forest and thought of Mother, of her face in the morning when he told her what he had seen this night. He could not tell Mother in the morning, he realised after a moment's reflection. He could never tell Mother. But he would have to tell someone. It would have to be Enoch. He listened to the rustle of the curtains being drawn behind him, an almost-audible star overhead. Then he crept away from the house and back to the Mews to sleep, or not to sleep, on the telling or not telling.

The stars continued to fall all night, sometimes in herds, sometimes alone. When the library window opened in the first pale light before dawn, Lugh slipped out and looked upwards to see where the Lyre had gone. Arcturus, Deneb, Altair, and there was Vega, fainter now that the night was fading, a mere fragment of harp but still visible nonetheless. He knew it was unlikely he would see any shooting stars in this light, so he laced up his boots and headed around the house.

Already, Lugh could feel that the day was different. As he walked down the driveway, the air tasted clearer to him than it had in months, free of the curse of cloud and endless rain. He wondered what he would find when he reached the terrace, whether he would hear the sound of Mother sobbing over the poisoned body of her beloved firstborn, or whether the lane would be stricken by a deathly hush, utterly silent except for the morning chorus of blackbird, robin and thrush. Most of all, he wondered if Fran would be at home already.

Turning onto the lane, Lugh tasted the smell of fresh woodsmoke. He looked at the rooftops and almost choked with emotion when he saw smoke rising from the chimney of their house, a thin line of hope climbing straight up through the windless air. He began to run down the lane, stumbling in his impatience to be home, slipping on the path as he turned the last corner, opened the back door and came face-to-face with a strange woman sitting at his kitchen table.

The woman was young, no more than twenty-five. She was dark skinned, had large light-brown inquisitive eyes, and wore a khaki army jacket and matching cap. She stared at Lugh in astonishment, but then slowly her face relaxed into a smile, revealing a set of immaculately white teeth. Lugh saw that the woman's hand was resting on a knife on the table. It was a hunting knife. Lugh recognised it at once.

His eyes moved quickly over other objects in the room: matches, candles, toothpaste and toothbrushes, a packet of tobacco and cigarette papers on the table, a child's plastic drinking cup in the sink. Two large khaki rucksacks stood upright against the wall. One of the rucksacks was hanging open and, spilling out of it onto the kitchen tiles, Lugh saw an assortment of white medical boxes, bottles, packages. Before he could think of what to do or say, there was movement in the hallway and another figure appeared in the doorway, a woman with a feline, slightly boyish face. In her arms, she carried a young child, a toddler no more than two years old.

'Well, there you are,' this second woman said to him warmly, familiarly, as though she had always expected to find him there. She set the child down in the arms of the woman at the kitchen table and then looked Lugh up and down, shaking her head in amazement. 'Look at you, Lugh. Your face is all fur like you're a fucking man now or something. So where is everyone?'

Lugh stared at her, at her short hair, her almond-shaped eyes, the black boiler-suit and military boots. He tried to speak, to say her name, but he did not believe that she was really alive and standing there, that the dead could return to life.

'Come on, man, spill the beans,' said Ky, opening her arms. He still did not move so she walked towards him and pulled him into a quick, awkward embrace. 'Where are they? Where are Fran and Rhea?'

CHAPTER THIRTEEN
KINGDOM

FIND ME A WILLOW TREE, a young sapling no more than two or three years old. Find me a white willow, Salix alba, you will know it by the leaves, white on the underside, they grow by the stream. From the withies you can weave a basket or a crib, a cradle or a coffin. They wove it in Sumer when they first planted wheat, in Mesopotamia when they built cities on bread. If you find me a willow tree, a young one, white, by a stream, it will soothe the humours in my skull. Yellow bile, black bile, fumes of choler and melancholy. Phlegmatic water pooling in the lungs, bloating the body black-blue, a sickness of lasting apathy. The dull aching burning drying dying of skin and tissue, all blood spent. A young willow, find it white, you will know it by the leaves.

Fran thought that the man could not hear her: he did not move from his chair. Fran did not think that she could speak: the man left the room. Those first nights were cold; her face was on fire. The man covered her nakedness with his but she shivered all the more, pushed himself inside her until he came, almost instantly, and then he let her sleep. She dreamed of an apartment with a bathroom cabinet, packets of pills stronger than aspirin or willow bark. She reached out her hand to open the mirrored door and saw herself in the glass, a monstrous thing, a someone else. The eye that looked back from the mirror was not hers, had never been hers. It lowered its gaze, ashamed or appalled, looked away. Whoever it was, perhaps someone who had wandered in from another dream, turned and walked out of the bathroom, leaving her to open the cabinet without a reflection, without a hand. And when she got there, the cupboard was bare.

'And so the poor dog had none,' she said, or must have said, because the man leaned over and touched her bruised lip, pressed so hard that she thought it would cherry-burst.

'Sleep tight,' he said. 'Don't let them bedbugs bite.'

He was beating a nail into her head... no, into the window frame beside her head but it felt just the same—crack-crack-crack—a splitting of wood, honeycomb bone. She must have moaned or rolled onto her side, given him the cold shoulder or something equally offensive, because the banging stopped and he pressed his summer-warm mouth, a hive of hair, against her ear, breathed softly once, twice, then roared against her skin, scattering her into fragments over the floor.

'Now, why would you go and do that to yourself?' he said with deep sympathy, a father to a crying child, sweeping her up and putting the pieces together again. She must have hit her forehead against the wall because now he was cradling her in his arms, holding a damp cloth against the bruise, rinsing in cool water, wiping her down.

'She's taking a bath,' he said with a rough laugh to himself. 'She is, she's taking a bath. Who is? Bathsheba is. Bathsheba's taking a bath. Bathsheba in the bath tub.'

The wet cloth moved down her neck, between her breasts and over her pubes, wetting the bed but the man did not seem to mind. He climbed inside her and grunted, slapped the cloth against the window, locked the bedroom door behind him.

Fran tasted iron on her tongue. She spat it out and tried to remember other tastes, consoling tastes, real coffee with brown sugar, butter on toast, honey on muffins. If she could get into the kitchen, she would bake something sweet. If they let her go to the kitchen, she would make a cake, a carrot or a simple sponge, butterscotch icing, frosting. There was wheat flour in the kitchen cupboard, butter in the dish, sugar, eggs, everything she needed. She had been to Mesopotamia to buy some bread.

'And when she came back, the dog was dead,' she laughed aloud, coughing on something, the sharp fragment of a tooth. She explored her mouth with her tongue and touched upon the jagged edge of her broken canine. She opened her eyes and flinched at the afternoon light which pulsed with the same rhythm as the pain in her head.

Enoch watched her from the chair beside the bed, his dark eyebrows slightly raised, his chin resting on his knuckles. She could not see his mouth behind the mass of his curly black beard. He could have been smiling or sulking.

'My tooth is broken,' she said, sitting up and cautiously touching her swollen lip. She did not know how long she had been lying in that room in Enoch's house. Looking around, everything seemed familiar, the same four walls from a fitful dream. The maroon blankets, metal bed frame, small fireplace and bare floorboards with a bucket standing in the corner. Overhead, a dusty, brown lampshade hung like a dead or dying sun. And Enoch on the bedside chair, impassively watching her from behind a tangle of beard.

'How long have I been here?' she asked, instinctively pulling the blanket over her breasts.

Casually, Enoch reached out his hand and tugged the blanket down again. It was a simple gesture, a token of ownership, that brought back unconscious memories of his pressure on her skin, inside her skins. She fought back the urge to cover herself again and, instead, took the piece of broken tooth from her mouth.

'My tooth is broken,' she repeated, staring at the miniscule fragment of white on her fingertip. She wondered how something so small could leave such a colossal hole behind.

Without taking his eyes off her, Enoch reached down and picked up a bowl of soup that he had put beside his chair. He swallowed a mouthful himself and then, leaning forwards, held out the spoon for Fran. She tried to take the spoon from his hand, but Enoch shook his head and emptied the spoon on the blanket between her legs. He repeated the gesture, one spoonful for himself and one, from his own hand, for her. She opened her swollen lips and accepted it. The soup was cold, flavourless, gritty with dirt, but she was famished. She nodded appreciatively and endeavoured to make a smile, opened her mouth for another spoonful.

When he had finished feeding her, he returned the empty bowl to the floor and sat back in his chair, watching her silently with the expressionless face of an animal mask. His dark-brown unreadable eyes never seemed to blink. Fran stared at the stain of soup that he had spilled on her blanket and breathed deeply, assessing the boundaries of this situation, the things she could keep and the things he could take, the likelihood of more pain. He could have done away with her by now if that had been his intention. Instead, he was feeding her, keeping her alive, for the time being at least. The rest was a performance, a charade of power. As long as she took care not to challenge that charade, she reasoned, she might stand a chance. On the other hand, there was a risk in seeming too submissive. The abject he would find contemptible. It had been the same during all those years she had lived with Dean.

'I don't suppose there's any wine to go with the soup?' she asked.

Enoch made a slight noise in the back of his throat, which could have been a laugh, a rebuttal or a warning. His face remained unreadable.

'Thought not,' she said. She considered asking him something else, a question to lure him out of his reserve, to open a line of dialogue. On the other hand, she recognised the danger of being too talkative. Loquacity could undermine the charade of power. She wondered if he knew what loquacity meant.

There was the sound of digging in the garden behind the house. Mark, probably, working over the vegetable plots that Matthew had prepared last year. She remembered Matthew lying beside her on the grass, his hands as work-hardened and calloused as her own, his black shaggy-dog hair hanging over her face. And then she thought of Mark: of Mark's hands, Mark's hair, his red tongue and the rancid smell of old sweat, knees pushing painfully against her arms, the force of his fists as he laid into her. She touched her face and felt the still-tender swellings. Enoch took her wrist and dropped it on the blanket. Matthew, Mark, Luke and John, bless this bed that I lie on.

'I must look an absolute monster,' Fran said. She could hear her voice trembling.

Enoch shifted in his chair, leaned forwards slowly until the strands of his beard were touching her cheek. She resisted the impulse to brush them away.

'I must look an absolute monster,' he repeated, imitating the high tremor in her voice.

The sun pulsed behind the horizon, behind the curtain, the curtain that she was not permitted to open. Fran lay with her arms crossed over her chest like a body in a coffin, like a body purporting to rest in peace. Her mouth was dry. There was no water in the room and, even if there was, she could not have moved to reach it. Enoch slept beside her, snoring on each in-breath, his hand laid heavily across her stomach. Sometimes the long nails of his bare feet kicked against her legs as though he were dreaming of running, or dreaming of kicking. Fran closed her eyes and tried not to think of her dry mouth, the pounding darkness of the room.

'Imagine you're in a darkened room,' she said to him one morning. He had finished spoon-feeding her scrambled eggs and was now watching her closely. 'How would you get out of it?'

Enoch's dark eyes flitted to the closed curtain, the nailed-down window.

'No, I don't mean here. It's just a riddle, like a game,' she explained simply, harmlessly, a way to pass the time. 'Imagine you're in a darkened room. How do you get out?'

Fran could see him thinking behind the mask, considering either an answer to the riddle or else the likelihood that she was up to no good. Fearing the latter, she solved it for him.

'You stop imagining you're in a darkened room,' she said with a shrug. 'That's how.'

Enoch's expression did not change, though his eyes clouded over for a moment as though trying to understand her meaning. At last, there was the faintest nod and his gaze returned to her.

'Another one?' she asked. He merely stared, so she said, 'Right, a tricky one this time. How many of each animal did Moses take with him on the ark?'

This time, his eyebrows narrowed as though he knew the answer. There was movement behind the beard, but still he did not speak. Fran closed her eyes to show that he could take all the time in the world if he wanted, she was in no hurry, had nothing better to do, could wait all day.

'None,' Enoch growled eventually. 'Moses took no animals on the ark. It were Noah that took them, two by two. Noah on the ark.'

'Good. Well done,' she said, nodding slowly and managing to look impressed. She had made a connection with the creature at last, but she knew that she should not overplay the praise. The charade was fragile, could snap at any moment. He was canny enough, or sufficiently suspicious, to suspect if his power was being patronised.

'That were an easy one.' He folded his arms, the flicker of an expression behind the mask.

'It was not, it was tricky. You're not as daft as you look, are you?' She knew, as soon as she had spoken the words, that she had overstepped the boundary. Enoch smiled briefly, a flash of white within the beard, but then the look soured, turned judgement-day hard and he rose to his feet. Fran struggled to think of something else to say, anything to undo or bury those words, but thoughts fled from her mind. She closed her eyes and cowered, waiting for the blow to fall.

She went to the undertaker's to buy a coffin. When she came back, the dog was laughing.

'Have you seen yourself?' he laughed. 'You look like a whore. Like the Whore of Babylon.'

He pushed in his thumb: someone was grunting. It was not her because the withies had woven a case around her, a coffin of willow, black not white, dark as the underground.

'Know what Mother says? Mother says you're nothing but a tramp.'

He broke through the willow and she splintered open, broke apart in sudden daylight, the sky falling into the hole, bringing down rooftops, treetops, rubble.

Nothing happened until he was there. The nothing was almost as unbearable as the things that happened when he was. Sometimes she thought that she did not exist until he was there to summon her into being, dividing the light from the darkness, firmament from water.

'Water,' she said, and she must have weighed nothing, less than nothing, lighter than air, because he lifted her up and set her down on the bucket that stank of piss, her piss. The cold metal rim of the bucket bruised her skin.

'Water,' he said quietly, mocking her with a feeble echo of her own voice. 'Water.'

The curtain palpitated with sunset and sunrise, a flickering light-box of comings and goings, translucence exposing the room as a sharp edge of things: chair, bucket, fireplace, bucket, chair.

'What a face,' he said, slipping segments of an orange gently between her lips. 'Open wide. What a sight for sore eyes. Isn't she a beauty, eh? Isn't she something, my Bathsheba.'

There was a basket of oranges and lemons on the floor, a jug of water beside her bed. Her arms trembled as she reached out and poured herself a cup, lifted it with great effort to her dry lips. A fire was crackling comfortingly in the fireplace, a sound that reminded her of Rhea. The edges of things quivered in the firelight, cast long, hairy shadows on the walls. An open book was lying beside the hearth. Its pages had been torn out, probably used to start the fire.

'You've not said much in a while,' Enoch observed, leaning back in his chair.

Fran sipped her water, continued to stare at the fire.

'Cat got your tongue?'

Book, bucket, fire, bucket, book. Fran's eyes grazed the objects at the end of her bed. Enoch was right, she had not said much in a while. How long was a while? Maybe the cat had got her tongue. Maybe she had no tongue anymore. She shook her head a fraction to show that she had heard him, agreed with him.

'Like the fire?' he asked pleasantly enough. 'You'd like the fire on all evening? Trouble is, fire's dangerous. Can't leave it on, not when I'm not here. Might burn the house down, then where would you go? Couldn't go into the forest. Beast gets you in the forest. Couldn't go to your old house neither: Beast gets you there too. Beast gets everyone there, even that boy. Wouldn't like the Beast to get that boy, would you? So, I wonder, where could you go?'

Fran lowered her cup and stared at the flames. She did not want to speak. Speaking was dangerous. Staying quiet could be dangerous too. Enoch leaned forward, so she spoke.

'What does he look like?' Her voice sounded dry, gravelly, tasted old in her mouth.

'What does who look like?'

'The Beast. You've seen him. What does he look like?'

'You don't want to know,' Enoch laughed.

'I do. I do want to know. He gets everyone in the end. I want to know what he looks like.'

'Like the Devil,' he said in a quiet, pantomime-villain voice, the storyteller introducing the wolves, leaning so close to her that she could feel his breath.

'And like God,' she said, knowing better than to retreat from him. She kept her eyes fixed on the fire. 'He can take life or spare life. He decides who lives and who dies. Thou shalt, he says, and it is. Thou shalt not, and it isn't. So he must look like God too, mustn't he?'

Enoch sat back in his chair and folded his arms, contemplating her from behind his mask.

'I wonder why he does it,' she said lightly, wondering aloud more to herself than to Enoch. 'That Beast out there, all alone in the forest. I wonder why he does what he does.'

They sat in the firelight, each staring in a different direction, listening to the crackle of damp wood struggling to burn. After a minute, an hour or a day, Enoch stood up, stretched his arms wide and rolled his head until his neck clicked.

'Don't go burning the house down, now, Bathsheba,' he said, giving her a mock-severe look before leaving. She heard the key turning in the lock, the tread of his uneven, limping footsteps fading down the stairs.

On the small stone hearth beside the fireplace, the book lay open and revealed the jagged edges of pages that had been ripped out to start the fire. Next to her bed, the water jug reflected the flicker of flames, a dancing light that played on the floorboards. The basket of oranges and lemons lay in the shadows beneath Enoch's empty chair. Bathsheba was being tempted. Tempted or tested, thought Fran. In some distant part of the house, she heard a door slam, another key turn in another lock, footsteps in the lane. It would not be long before he came back for the night, slouched beside her, over her, in her, kicking in his dreams. Tempted or tested, she thought, perhaps rewarded for good behaviour. The dame made a curtsey, the dog made a bow.

Slowly, carefully, so as not to make a sound, she reached over the edge of the bed and hooked her fingertips over the handle of the basket. She had never felt so weak in her life, but she managed to tug the basket towards her and lift it onto the bed. Oranges and lemons. No knife though, nothing to break the skins: Enoch must have taken that with him. She could be tempted with fire but not with a knife. She felt between the contours of the fruit for the softest orange, the one that was least likely to resist her nails, and touched upon a fold of paper at the bottom of the basket. Slipping it out, she held the envelope up to the light and read the handwritten inscription.

Not puffball, it said. Fran knows best how to prepare them.

She put the envelope on her lap and gazed at the fire, her lips slightly ajar, catching butterflies, possibilities.

LUGH JABBED THE POKER INSIDE the stove to separate the burning logs. The largest pieces he knocked into the ash pan and carried them, still smoking, into the yard to drown in the water bucket. The glowing embers died with a demoniac hiss, a last gasp of steam. When the fire was extinguished, he returned to his seat at the kitchen table.

'You can't go over there,' Lugh said firmly, 'not yet. If you go now, he'll just—'

'He'll just what?' asked Ky. She did not look at Lugh but stared at her knife, the point pressed into the table top, one finger pushing down on the handle. 'Tell me, what will Enoch do?'

'It will just make things worse. If we're not clever, it will make things worse.'

'So that's why you've done nothing,' said Ky, a statement not a question.

'I did try, I told you. I told you what they did to me.'

'That's right. You said they gave you a bloody nose. I imagine Fran's had more than a bloody nose, don't you? Every day that's passed, they'd have given her more than a bloody nose.' Ky grunted humourlessly and glanced at her friend, the other woman who was holding the young girl in her arms. 'You know, Maya here, she was given more than a bloody nose when the soldiers in that relief camp got hold of her. Why don't you tell him about that episode, Maya?'

'Go easy on the young man, Comandanta,' Maya replied to Ky. She spoke with a rich, musical accent, intensifying the vowels, sharpening the consonants, a playful strain that weaved a thread between sincerity and sarcasm. 'He's just a kid. I'm sure he did his best. Isn't that right, guapo? You did your best.'

'Magic mushrooms,' Ky scoffed. 'That's his best, that's classic. What's Fran to do with a mushroom? Chuck it at somebody's mouth? Wave them off on a magical trip?'

Toadstools, Lugh wanted to correct her. Instead, he stared at the various articles on the table: the knife, boxes of matches, new toothbrushes, toothpaste, Ky's pouch of tobacco, the pair of broken spectacles that had once belonged to Rhea. Ky followed his gaze over the objects. She lay the knife down and idly lifted the glasses into the morning sunlight.

'And the Beast got Rhea too?' she said. 'That bloody Beast. Successful fucker, isn't it?'

'They said it got you and Matthew as well.'

'Who said that?'

'Mark did. Before you reached the mountain, he said it took you when you were sleeping.'

'Fucksake, Lugh,' Ky shouted, smacking her palm hard against the table. She stood up abruptly and made to leave the room. At the doorway, however, she turned and ran her fingers through her short hair, exasperated. 'Did you not realise all that was bullshit? Fucksake, a beast in the forest? What was it, a deer? A squirrel?'

'You didn't come back.' Lugh spoke so quietly that she could barely hear his words. 'You didn't come home and you weren't here. You've no idea what it's been like.'

'And whose fault is that?' Ky made a mean face, a caricature of Lugh's scowl, and hissed, 'I want her to go. Who was it that said that? Tell me, who said that?'

'Easy now, Sofia,' said Maya, ostensibly to the child who was growing agitated on her lap. 'The Comandanta's acting all crazy, but it will pass quick enough. She knows this act is no good for no one. You will see, she's going to put it away any time now and remember that Francesca needs her help, just like we did. Watch the Comandanta, Sofia. See, there it goes.'

Returning to her chair, Ky told Maya, 'There's only so many times you can play that card.'

'Now, these two need to get their heads together,' Maya said with a nod at Ky. 'You and I, Sofia, we'll take a look around that garden out there, see what beasties are lurking in the long grass.'

'Comandanta?' asked Lugh, after Maya had taken her daughter into the garden.

'I know, it's dreadful, isn't it?' Ky smiled vaguely. 'She thinks I'm bossy. It's a long story.'

'Too long to tell me what happened?'

'Not if I keep it short.' Ky took a deep breath and looked out of the window at the sunlit trees, the clear blue sky above the forest. It was easy enough to start with the weather. There had been months like this, she began, days and days of blue sky, a drought they thought would last all summer. The clouds had come, of course, but they never imagined it would snow at midsummer. They did not pack wisely or prepare well. Mark complained every step of the way, abandoned his wheelbarrow on the roadside not long after they had set off. He said they should turn back for better supplies, winter coats, blankets and the like, but Ky insisted that they continue and Matthew was compliant. After walking all night through the blizzard, they reached the mountain on the second day and sheltered in a cave, waiting for the midsummer snow to end.

'But this is the new natural, isn't it?' Ky said matter-of-factly. 'The new normal is abnormal. We should have learned that by now. The windstorm, drought, midsummer snow and now this rain, almost a year of it. What the fuck comes after this? Still, we stayed in that cave and thought it would end, the snow, the cold, just one more day and it would all be over, back to summer as normal. It was in there, waiting for the weather to change, that Mark lost it. Must have been the third or fourth night, I suppose. I was asleep, woke up with his hands around my throat. Almost didn't wake up at all. In that sense, I suppose Mark didn't lie to you: the Beast did come while we were sleeping. Thank fuck for Matthew, that's all I can say.'

'What did Matthew do?'

'Intervened,' Ky said simply. After a thoughtful pause, she added, 'It's possible that Mark had planned it all along, was biding his time for the right moment. But Matthew wasn't in on it. They were so different, Matthew and Mark, chalk and cheese. I got close to Matthew in those few days. I liked him. He was decent. He would have been good for Fran. That's why I told him to come back here, to be with you all, keep an eye on things.'

'What happened in the cave?' Lugh had been fiddling with the pouch of tobacco on the table. Ky removed it from his hands and rolled herself a cigarette.

'Oh, you can guess. A fight, a struggle. Mark ran off into the night with his tail between his legs, shouting the usual: "You should be ashamed of yourself, Matthew Mann, siding with god-haters against your own flesh and blood." Bullshit like that. We didn't know what he would do or where he would go, so I told Matthew to get back here quickly. I wanted him to be here before the Beast returned. But Matthew never made it. Poor kid. Fucking, fucking flesh and blood.'

'He still might. You came back.'

'He won't, Lugh. Not after all this time.'

'There's more than one Beast.' Lugh stroked the frame of the broken spectacles on the table. 'Rhea went missing the same day you left, that first day of snow.'

Ky opened her mouth to speak but there was nothing to say, or else too much.

'You didn't come back after the cave,' Lugh said after a moment's reflection. 'Why not?'

'It's complicated.'

'I can do complicated.'

'I know.' Fran nodded. 'Complicated is your middle name. I never know what's going on behind that frown of yours, sphinx with a frown.'

'Don't change the subject,' said Lugh with a half-smile.

'Okay.' Ky lit her cigarette, inhaled and breathed a cloud of smoke at the ceiling. 'I didn't want to come back. Rhea was capable of looking after you all. Fran looked set to live happy-ever-after with Matthew. And you were such a shit to me, Lugh. Really, a complete little shit. I suppose I felt superfluous. I didn't want to hang around doing nothing. I don't like feeling useless. And we did need medical supplies. So, off I went to see what was left of the world.'

'And you found Maya and Sofia?'

'And I found Maya and Sofia. They were in a jam and needed help. I do that, I know now. I have a need to be needed. Is that a good or bad thing?'

Lugh shrugged the question off and asked, 'What is left of the world?'

'Oh, it's pretty much the same as here except the stage is bigger. Bigger beasts in a bigger forest.' Ky looked through the kitchen window at Maya playing with her daughter in the garden, pointing at crows, blowing dandelion seeds. 'There's still some good folk about, of course. Pockets of them, here and there. I suppose you could call it a resistance of sorts.'

'A resistance to what? The army?'

'Not exactly. I honestly can't say,' she replied evasively. She tried to think of some way to describe the uncoiling of old concepts and schemas, the thickening of emergent formations. She wanted to say chaos, but that word was not quite adequate when orders were still being given and taken. 'No, there are still armies—militias would be a more adequate description—but it's difficult to say who or what they're working for. You can see what one militia has done. That seaside town has been completely levelled, erased, nothing remains. Other cities along the coast, all gone. It's like the edges of the land have been sterilised. No one can live on the borders now.'

'But where have the people gone,' Lugh asked quietly, 'all those people in that town?'

'Ask Maya, she's full of grim theories, though some are more than theories. In her case, she was staying in a relief camp when one militia came and—let's just say they reduced the numbers. Later, another militia showed up and put the evacuees, the ones that were left, on coaches. Maya didn't know where they were being taken, just that they were being herded inland, away from the edges. Maya calls it her Black-Hole theory. She says fear, like gravity, is pulling everything into some cluster or other in the centre. And isn't that what is predicted at the end of the universe? Instead of expansion, everything collapsing again into a big crunch? Anyway, Maya jumped the coach at a roadblock before the point of no return. She's edgy, you can see that.'

'But she still needs her Comandanta,' said Lugh. Ky flicked her ash into the sink and shrugged. 'So you met them, Maya and Sofia, somewhere else, somewhere safe?'

'It was safe for a while,' Ky said. 'But it's not safe anymore. That's one thing they got right, Mark and Luke, about not lighting fires during daylight. The smoke does attract attention. It was our fires that gave us away. They came in helicopters, whoever they were, whichever faction. They saw our houses, greenhouses, the poly-tunnels. Nothing left of it now. Maya and I got away.'

'So there's nowhere else to go?' asked Lugh, raising his eyes to hers.

'I don't know anywhere else.' Ky turned to the window.

'Damn and fuck it.'

'Damn and fuck it, as Rhea would say.'

After a pause, Lugh added, 'I'm sorry I was a complete shit.'

They sat in awkward silence for few moments before Ky added, 'You know, I don't think you'd said more than five words to me before today.'

'Maybe I had nothing to say.'

'Maybe too much.' Ky thought of Lugh's brother, the hole in the orchard, of Fran's soothing voice as she recited the liturgy of herbs at his graveside.

'We will get her out,' said Lugh, his thoughts keeping pace with her own.

'I know. I just don't know how.'

'We can use the big house,' said Lugh, brightening at the thought. 'There's no one there, only me and Abel. They don't know about it, Enoch and the others. Why don't we all go there?'

'How the fuck did that happen? Did you lock old Rumpelstiltskin in the cellar?'

'No, not in the cellar,' Lugh replied evasively. 'See, that's also complicated.'

Before Ky could probe any deeper, they were interrupted by voices in the garden. Maya was answering questions in a steady, careful tone. A man was interrogating, demanding.

'Stay out of sight,' Lugh said to Ky as they both rose quickly from the table.

'Fuck that,' she said, taking her knife.

'Stay out of sight for now. If they know you're back, it'll be harder to get Fran.'

Ky's expression was defiant, but she backed into the hallway, knife at the ready.

'We just minding our business out here,' Maya was saying casually in the garden, though she had picked up Sofia and was retreating to the back door. 'We seeing the birds and the butterflies, all the bees. It's a beautiful day, no?'

'Why are you here? What are you doing here?' It was Luke's voice, barking questions, taking no answers. 'You have to go. There's nothing for you here.'

'Why, all these empty houses?' Maya replied playfully. 'No room for me and the little girl to stay for one night? That is funny.'

'It's private property,' said Luke, clenching his fists. Despite his posturing, his voice trembled unconvincingly. 'You're trespassing. You have to leave.'

'Oh, it's private property, is it? We didn't know it was private property, did we, Sofia? Private property, the chico says. All these empty houses, empty rooms, private property.'

'You have to leave, go back to your own home. There's nothing for you here.'

'I've said she can stay,' said Lugh, standing in the doorway, his hands dug deep into his pockets. Maya passed unhurriedly behind him. She cast one last sly smile at Luke before disappearing into the house. 'It's just her and her baby. She can stay with me tonight.'

Luke took a step along the path towards him, stopped and clenched his fists. He glared at Lugh in a different way, a look of absolute disgust and barely contained rage but something else too, something more unsettling. You wait, Luke seemed to say. You wait just a little longer.

'Best you tell your little friend to go home,' Luke said before he turned and walked away.

Lugh stayed in the back yard for a moment longer, listening to the birds in the sunlit forest, the magpies laughing on the rooftops, the quick tread of Luke's footsteps crossing the lane to Enoch's house, a secret message clenched between his teeth.

THE SENSATION OF PAGES WAS still on her fingertips. Fran had felt the letters tingling over her skin all night long, the taste of old typeface, older than generations, a font piece missing here and there, but the landscape of meanings was clear and cloudless: the sharp spires of consonants, smooth openings of vowels. The dead had underscored messages in ink, and Fran had harvested these thoughts like gems from a sacred stream, buried them deep in a secret hole that no one else, not even Enoch with his spoon, could prise out.

'Open wide,' he said, stirring the bowl of morning feed, possibly soup, possibly tea, grass-green and cold as a damp, daytime stove.

She opened her mouth. The dame said, your servant. The dog said bow-wow.

Rhea had been a wise old bird. She had knitted threads of wisdom under, over and around the sayings of Epicurus; the back of the book was a treasury of the old woman's last thoughts. Knit one, purl one, casting off an aphorism or two for someone to discover by chance and try on for size, someone kneeling beside a bucket of piss, a fireplace, behind a locked door in a boarded-up bedroom. How Enoch had come across the *Lives of Eminent Philosophers* Fran could not fathom, but she was glad that he had, glad that he had only torn paper from the front of the book to get his nightly fires going, not from the preciously annotated back pages.

Fran still did not open her lips wide enough, so Enoch dripped another spoonful of soupy tea over her breasts, shook his head in disappointment.

Natural justice is to prevent one man from harming or being harmed by another.

Enoch opened his own mouth and swallowed a spoonful, made a deep sound of contentment from the back of his throat, a rumble from the nether-parts of his beard.

The feel of the pages, cotton-rough and fibrously thick, still smouldered on Fran's fingers. Last night, after she had etched the underlined sentences in her memory and laid the book aside, after she had ripped the thin, leathery toadstools apart with her nails, slipped the shredded flakes down the side of her mattress and washed the toxins from her fingers in the piss-bucket, the impression of the words still played on her hands, a magic music, Rhea's last requiem.

Death is nothing to us; for the body, when it has been resolved into its elements, has no feeling, and that which has no feeling is nothing to us.

Fran had barely been able to sleep with the sensation of her old friend, so kind, so close, whispering at the end of her fingertips. When she did fall asleep, she dreamed of dissolution. The bed-chair-bucket-chair-bed had disbanded into their constituent dust, returned to their primeval states and drifted harmlessly in the air. Fran too had dissolved with them: her folded arms, her swollen parts resolved into their original elements and glittered unconsciously in the darkness. Butterfly dust dreaming that she was whole; a whole butterfly dreaming that she was dust.

It had been a simple enough thing to do, to slip the delicate flakes of death-cap into the breakfast bowl while Enoch had been kneeling at the hearth with his back towards her. By the time he had finished killing the embers, Fran was sitting up in bed and smiling vaguely, a look of distant enlightenment on her face. *That which has no feeling is nothing to us.*

'Open wide,' he said, holding out another spoonful for her to take. He would not ask again.

Fran opened her mouth and accepted the spoon as a sacrament. Take, eat.

'Good girl,' he said. He nodded agreeably and fed himself another mouthful. 'Though not much of a girl today, are you, Bathsheba? Looking old and haggard, old like an old shoe. Like some old tramp's old shoe, frayed at the edges, falling apart, stinking. I shouldn't have to look at a face like that in the morning. No one should. Not nice, looking at some old tramp's old shoe.'

As he stirred the weak soup and prepared to feed her another dose, they heard an urgent knocking at the front door, Luke in the lane shouting for his elder brother. Enoch fed the last mouthful to himself, smiled with satisfaction and gently stroked Fran's cheek with the back of his hand. Fran did not flinch from the touch but stared ahead of her, almost but not quite smiling.

'Don't go nowhere, now, old shoe,' Enoch said as he left the room.

ABEL SAT CROSS-LEGGED ON THE floor outside the attic door and tried again to reach the high note, *fire-fire*, on his recorder. He knew now that it was all something to do with pressing the thumb or not pressing the thumb over the hole on the underside but, whichever way he tried it, it sounded flat and never quite right. Besides, his left hand was still bandaged and he could barely move the fingers. Every morning after Lugh slipped out of the library window, Abel had sat on the landing and attempted to play London's Burning. At first, he had taken up the recorder to drown out the unending lament of the old man calling, 'A-bel, A-bel, time to let me out now.' As the days had passed, the priest's words had grown so faint as to be barely indistinguishable from the draught whispering beneath the door. Even now, while concentrating on that high note, Abel still thought he could hear the old man singing his name—A-bel, A-bel—an antique breath whistling through the cracks. And if he was still calling, then he was still alive. Lugh had laughed when he heard Abel playing the same tune over and over again outside the attic. He said it was a form of torture. Abel did not see it that way, though his left hand did ache as he played, *Pour on water, pour on water.*

Abel removed the stale mouthpiece from his lips and listened. This time, he was convinced that he had heard his name being called. Not just whispered under the door, but thundered urgently, a wind blowing through the house. Now there was nothing, no sound at all. He took a deep breath in preparation for the next round of the tune.

'Are you Abel or unable?' the hard, sharp, taunting voice echoed through the hallway and drifted up the stairs. Abel did not move. He knew instantly whose voice it was, but he did not think Enoch had ever said his name before.

'I've heard you've been very able, our Abel,' called Enoch.

There was another voice downstairs, Mark laughing enthusiastically and repeating the tail-end of Enoch's joke. Abel could not imagine why either of them would be in the big house or how they had got inside. For a moment, he thought it must be a dream, that the emptiness of the house had finally broken his mind, driving his senses to invent the company of voices.

'He must be upstairs,' said a third voice that was Luke's. 'I said he'd be up there.'

As the heavy footsteps began to climb the staircase, Abel stood up and looked around him. He was struck by an overwhelming sense of wrongdoing, of having been found out, though he could not think which of his sins had been unearthed. The balconied landing stretched around the open hallway, a dark wooden gallery that ran on either side of him, both ways meeting one point: the inevitable top of the stairs. Abel reached for the key in the attic door behind him.

'There he is,' Luke said when he saw Abel. They climbed slowly, Luke and Mark, following Enoch's limping pace up the stairs. The elder brother leaned against his stick for support.

'Aye, there he is,' said Enoch, panting as he reached the landing and turned along the gallery. 'Tell me, Abel, what have we done to offend the Lord?'

Abel turned the key and opened the attic door slightly. The skylight at the top of the tower had been broken. Although the old man could not have reached it, he must have thrown something hard at the window and now shards of glass lay glittering like morning dew down the attic stairs. A single shoe, a black brogue, sat halfway up the stairs. The sole of the other shoe was just visible around the edge of the door where the body of the priest had slumped at the bottom of the stairway. Abel could not push the door open any further against the obstruction.

'Cat got your tongue?' Enoch asked as he proceeded around the gallery, the clump of his stick beating against the floorboards. 'Luke, looks like your little brother's gone and lost his voice again. You'd best tell me what mischief he's been getting himself into.'

'Thou shalt not lie with mankind as with womankind,' Mark replied when Luke said nothing. 'It's a commandment, written there in black and white.'

'Not sure it's one of the commandments, is it?' Enoch asked when he reached Abel.

'Thou shalt not? Sounds like a commandment,' said Mark sullenly. 'Thou shalt not murder. Thou shalt not bear false witness. Thou shalt not lie with mankind. It's a commandment.'

'Aye, well it's an abomination any road,' Enoch agreed. 'And how does the Lord answer them that commit abominations?'

'He rained fire on Sodom and Gomorrah, that's what he did,' Mark replied brightly, reverting to his earlier enthusiasm. 'That's what the Good Book says.'

'He did indeed. So, how shall we answer our Abel?'

Abel left the attic door ajar and turned to face Enoch. Although almost the same height, the younger brother looked insubstantial beside the immensely solid muscle and breadth of the elder. Abel opened his mouth to speak, but could think of nothing to say. Instead, he smiled awkwardly and shook his head.

'Don't go trying that old chestnut,' said Enoch, as though he were weary of enough nonsense for one day. 'We know you're done with that silence. Our Luke here says he's heard you wittering on these past few nights, haven't you, Luke? Heard you making all manner of noises, you with that other animal, so don't be taking us for fools. You get your kicks from behaving like an animal? You like to be treated like an animal?'

Enoch stepped away from his younger brother and, with a nod at Mark, muttered, 'If he wants to be an animal, we'd best take him to the woods.'

Mark grabbed Abel by the wrist and pulled him roughly along the gallery and down the stairs. Although he did not try to resist, Abel tripped and stumbled, only to be hauled up again and dragged towards the sunlit drawing room.

'What will you be doing with him?' Luke asked as he and Enoch followed along behind. The firstborn said nothing.

Abel was pulled through the drawing room, inadvertently knocking aside a silver candlestick and an ashtray, and out into the garden. He found his voice, but all he could stutter was his brother's name—not Mark's nor Enoch's, but Luke's—which he asked as a question, laughing occasionally, embarrassed by the unnecessary force with which he was taken.

'What will happen to him in the woods?' Luke repeated. He lingered at the French doors and watched Mark dragging Abel across the grass, through the gap in the wall, into the trees.

'If it's a Beast he wants,' said Enoch, slowing his pace towards the forest but neither stopping nor turning, 'then it's a Beast he'll get.'

Luke watched Enoch walk away, leaning on his axe for support as he passed through the gap in the wall and disappeared into the misty forest. Luke considered going after them to make sure things did not get out of hand. He knew that they would and there was nothing he could do to stop it. Not with Enoch, not with the Beast. He hesitated uncertainly, gazing at the empty lawn, the dry fountain, the silent trees beyond the wall. The leaves still twitched after the passage of the dark carnival though there was not the slightest breeze to stir them.

Luke knew there was still work to do in the farmyard. If he took the path down the lawn, he could sweep out the chicken coop, or collect seeds from the lettuces, or push his fingers deep into the damp earth and feel blindly underground for young white potatoes. Or he could lean against the tool-shed and draw shapes in the dirt until evening, a box-house with a chimney, a body without a head. There were many ways to think of nothing, to not think at all and let all be done. He listened to the dull, repetitive queries of wood-pigeons in the forest, the memory of Abel's embarrassed laugh as he had been dragged through the drawing room, stuttering, 'Luke? Luke?'—as though asking for the punchline. 'Luke?'—a question too open, too obvious, to require further words. And, at that time, Luke had thought, could not help thinking, of replying, 'You can ask me stuff. Of course you can ask me stuff.'

After a moment's indecision, Luke turned away from the farmyard, from the gap in the wall where his brothers had passed, from the leaves in the forest that still twitched although there was no wind. Instead, he followed the path around the side of the house, his pace quickening to a jog as he hurried down the driveway to the lane, breathless by the time he reached his mother's house. He paused for a moment to catch his breath and then knocked urgently on the front door, loud enough to be heard by the whole neighbourhood.

CHAPTER FOURTEEN
EUMENIDES

WINTER RETURNED TO THE ROOM with a cold white light behind the shadow-play curtain, a crystallisation of the air and a cracking of sheets. Fine threads of frost perforated the walls, the sky-above ceiling with its lampshade hanging like a dead sun overhead, the dark plain of floorboards below. Contracting within the shell of her blanket, Fran tried to keep an eye on the ice spores that generated spontaneously from the surface of matter, spinning outwards from the edge of the elements— bed, chair, bucket and fireplace—to fill the aching emptiness. She could feel the winter creeping towards her, its static electricity drawing the hairs on her arms to stand on end as it tentatively approached and tried to touch, to infect her skin with the absence of heat. When the gossamer frost reached that patch of breakfast which she had forced herself to regurgitate over the sheets, she closed her eyes and listened. The dark stain of undigested fluid crackled, hardened, splintered, became diamond dust.

Here it comes, she thought at last: this is it. The ice crystals found her lips, filled her mouth with a painful cold that reached down her throat and flooded the hollow corridors of her body. She knew she was nothing, less than nothing, the husk of a body without defences. It would take no time at all for the traces of death-cap still in her system to take full possession. *Death is nothing to us*, she reminded herself, *for the body, when it has been resolved into its elements, has no feeling and that which has no feeling is nothing to us.*

But she did feel the cold and that was something. No nausea, no involuntary retching, none of those sensations that she had expected to feel, only the cold and now the room spinning. It was not the nothing after death that she was afraid of, but those things that happened on the threshold, a threshold that had lasted for weeks, possibly months. She reassured herself that there was not much more that could happen.

And now there was that noise, a knock-knock-knocking that was probably caused by the room spinning, by the hard edge of something catching rhythmically, predictably, on insensible wood as gravity lost its grip: a corner of the bed hitting the skirting board, perhaps, or a chair leg smacking against the wall. Fran tried to curl deeper within the contours of her blanket, but the knocking followed her down the hole, echoed within the spirals inside her. Here it comes, she thought again; this must be it now. But the knocking was merely a continuation of the cold that had taken possession of her bones, chattering seconds like the teeth of a clock, counting not-yet, not-yet through the pulse of her blood, the valves of her heart. This threshold could go on forever. She gave herself up to the sensation and let it all happen. The room revolved, wood beat against the walls, the door splintered into crystal powder and, weightless, she was lifted into the air. Not yet, my love, not yet, said someone, probably the voice of winter: there is still more to come. She gave herself up and was carried into a confusion of light.

LUGH LEANED AROUND THE CORNER and peered down the lane. He could see nothing but the trees reaching over the road, an arch of spring greenery, shadows beneath. Nothing to know what was happening around the bend, why Enoch and Mark, and later Luke and their mother, had taken off with such urgency towards the big house. It must be something to do with Abel, he knew it must. Lugh wondered if they had found the old man in the attic, if the priest had somehow broken free and now everything was in the open. The mother would not be pleased, but Abel would not be in any danger, Lugh reassured himself. All he need do was show her his palm, that corpse in the attic. Besides, Abel was a flesh-and-blood Mann and that counted for everything with them. Matthew had also been a flesh-and-blood Mann, little good it had done him.

Lugh fought the urge to leave his station and creep down the road, see for himself what was happening at the big house. Instead, he glanced back at Enoch's house opposite and wished that Ky would hurry up. She had been in there for ages, long enough to break through the pantry window, find Fran and bring her out. It was a simple enough plan: they should be out by now. Enoch and the others could return at any moment.

A wordless cry echoed in the air. Lugh lifted the scythe in his hand and stared expectantly at the bend in the lane. He imagined movement in the shadows beneath the trees, a silhouette taking shape in the sun-dappled shade. Ky had told him to raise the alarm if the brothers should return, but Lugh had not considered what signal to make until now. Another cry broke the afternoon silence, possibly animal, possibly human, possibly coming from the forest. Lugh struck the blade of his scythe against the corner of the house, sending out a clear, ringing chime like that of a small bell. Beneath the trees at the bend of the lane, from the direction of the big house, the shadows twitched in reaction to the noise. There was a ripple of black wings as first one and then more magpies materialised from the trees, flew erratically down the length of the road and soared to perch on the eaves of the terrace. Lugh was so startled by the movement that he rung his blade against the wall a couple more times.

'You ringing the dinner bell, guapo?' Maya asked as she arrived behind him, casually rested one arm on his shoulder. She wore her army cap backwards and was sweating from some exercise.

'Ky said to raise the alarm if something happened.'

'And what happened?' Maya nodded as she counted the birds on the roof. 'Three for a girl, four for a boy. I wouldn't ring my bell for a boy. But I'm not you, am I?'

'You know that magpie rhyme?' Lugh asked, though he did not lift his gaze from the shadows at the end of the lane. 'One for sorrow, two for joy?'

'I do know some things,' Maya said, amused though pretending to take offence. 'But I don't know what the Comandanta is doing over there all this time. There's not so many rooms, so many places for your friend to be. What can she be doing?'

'It's not good, whatever it is,' said Lugh. 'If it were good, they would be here by now.'

He looked at the windows of the silent house opposite, the dark panes blindly reflecting the shredded clouds in the sky. He had watched those windows night after night, crouched in the garden or stalking the street, and he never once had the slightest intimation that Fran was still inside. He only had Luke's word that she was there. He had imagined the worst happening to her and he had imagined the best and still, each night, he had gone back to the safety of the big house, the comfort of Abel's warm bed. He thought of the old man in the attic, wondered whether Fran had suffered similar treatment here, and instantly dismissed the idea that the two were somehow correlated. The universe just did not work like that. And besides, there was no similarity at all. The old man deserved what happened to him, Lugh told himself, he did.

'We don't know it's not good yet,' said Maya, squeezing his shoulder. 'We don't know nothing until the Comandanta comes out that house and tells us what it is.'

'She's not my Comandanta,' Lugh said absent-mindedly. 'You think I should go and see?'

'I think you should have more faith in the Comandanta, that's what I think. She's a clever woman, more clever than anyone. She got me and Sofia out of such bad places you can't imagine. Now, she told us we have things to do, no? I finished my thing, making that loft upstairs nice and ready, just like she wanted. Have you finished watching this road and making sure no one comes till she gets out? No, I don't think you have.'

'But someone shouted,' said Lugh. 'She didn't say what to do if I heard someone shout.'

'Someone shouted,' Maya repeated to herself. 'This shout, it comes from that house?'

'From the forest, I think.' Lugh gestured towards the trees.

'You're doing a fine thing here, watching this road,' Maya said decisively after a moment's reflection. 'I done my thing in that loft. Sofia's taking her nap and all's quiet, just like the Comandanta wanted. You keep your eyes open here, guapo. You watch out, make sure there's no trouble. I'll go see what the Comandanta is up to.'

'Maya,' Lugh called after her when she was already halfway across the lane. 'You will bring Fran out, won't you? However she is, you will—'

'We'll be out in no time, don't you worry,' she replied.

At the corner, just before she took the path around the back of Enoch's house, Maya turned to add, 'I know how is that feeling. That, that—' she could not think of a translation for the word she wanted to say, and so she gestured with her hands a wringing, tearing motion, 'like this inside. There's plenty people in the world doing that shit to others, things you can't imagine. Better we don't do it to ourselves too. Remember, you see the boys, you ring your dinner-bell.'

After Maya had disappeared around the corner, Lugh turned to the shadows at the end of the lane and wondered what could be happening down there. There was nothing to see and nothing to hear, no more cries from the forest, only the occasional cooing of a wood-pigeon in the trees. Even the magpies on the roof were silent, though Lugh could feel them observing him with intent. It was a mild spring day, calm and almost completely clear except for a hazy mist that clung to the forest like a thin layer of smoke. There was an air of eerie normality too, like a school day—in the days when there were schools—in which Lugh had managed to miss the bus again and everyone else was where they were supposed to be, sitting in their seats inside the classroom, whereas he alone was free to explore the world outside of rules. Except now the whole world was playing outside the rules. Scythes at corners were the new normal.

A stumble of footsteps brought Lugh's attention back to the terrace. Ky appeared first around the corner of Enoch's house, hard-faced and fierce as she glared down the lane and refused to look at Lugh. Maya followed behind holding a blanket against her body, a tangle of dank hair hanging over her shoulder. It took a while for Lugh to register that the insubstantial thing in Maya's arms, the weightless shape being carried across the lane, was Fran.

Lugh asked a question as Ky marched past him without a glance. He was not sure what his question was, if he had finished speaking or had even spoken the words aloud. His eyes were on Fran's unconscious face, on the face that had once been Fran's but was now bruised and twisted and distorted into someone else: an older relative, a primitive ancestor.

'Yes, she is,' Ky replied as she walked to the back door. 'As I said, more than a bloody nose.'

'The Comandanta's doing that crazy thing again,' said Maya with a kindly smile as she carried Fran down the path. 'You'll see, she'll stop that act any time now.'

Lugh took a last glance down the empty lane, then followed them into the house.

The kitchen had been cleared of all evidence of their presence: Maya had seen to that. The rucksacks, medical supplies, toothbrushes and tobacco, everything that they had brought with them was now hidden in the loft space upstairs. Maya rested Fran's body gently on the kitchen table while Ky pulled the blanket around her.

'You go up there first,' Ky said to Lugh. 'There's a white container in my rucksack, a bottle about so big. It says charcoal something—activated charcoal—on the label. Read the instructions then prepare it with water. I need it ready by the time we bring her up. There water up there?'

'You ask if there's water up there?' said Maya, shaking her head. 'Like I'd forget the water?'

After Lugh had gone upstairs, Maya added quietly, 'Charcoal?'

'Fran's eaten the toadstools herself,' said Ky, knotting the ends of the blanket around her fists. 'She's vomited what she can. Barely anything left in her stomach. The charcoal will absorb some of the toxins, but it may be too late to be effective. She's not got much resistance left.'

'She's no more heavy than Sofia, pobrecita. How long before we know?'

Ky shook her head. 'In a day or two perhaps. It all depends on her kidneys and the liver. It's a case of wait-and-see. You ready to lift?'

'You know, you shouldn't be so antipático – so disagreeable with the young man,' Maya said as she raised her end of the blanket and they manoeuvred Fran's sleeping body through the doorway. 'I think there's times when fear makes us do nothing. Don't be antipático with the young man for being afraid. That's no good for nothing.'

'I'm not. I'm trying not to. I keep thinking about the toadstools. I wonder if Fran managed to slip any toadstools to those other fuckers.'

'The man that did this,' said Maya, heaving her end of the blanket high as she climbed backwards up the stairs, 'if she slipped any toadstools to him, that's good enough.'

INSIDE THE FOREST, THE MIST trailed between the trees, sometimes condensing into profound clusters like the smoke of localised fires in which nothing could be discerned beyond the next few steps. Mother was constantly becoming entangled in brambles, her coat and long skirt pulled back by thorns. Once, she slipped on wet leaves and fell forwards, cutting her palm on something sharp and hidden in the undergrowth, a rock or the bitten edge of a bone perhaps. She released a belated cry of indignation and looked up in the expectation that Luke would come to her aid, but her son was already so far ahead that he could no longer be seen. Wiping the mud and moisture from her hands, she examined the open cut down the side of her palm. Though it was bleeding freely, it was not too deep. Still, it stung like hell and she should really return home to wash the wound under a tap before the Adversary took the opportunity to infect it.

'The Lord is my shepherd,' she said for protection, climbing to her feet. 'I shall not want. He maketh me to lie down in green pastures. He leadeth me—'

'Mother, please,' said Luke, running back to her through the trees.

'Mother-please, indeed,' she said, holding up her injured hand like an accusation. 'Don't you go mother-pleasing me. Just look what you made me do.'

Luke reluctantly approached and made a pretence of attending to her wound, but his mind was elsewhere in the forest.

'Don't know what this nonsense is about any road,' she said, pulling her hand impatiently away. 'If you won't tell me what this trouble is that our Abel's got himself into, then it sounds like a fuss about nothing to me. I've had just about enough of this game. You can take me home.'

'Mother, please,' Luke implored her like a young child, 'Enoch's taken him in the forest.'

'Again, mother-please. If Abel's with his brothers, you can rest assured there'll be nothing to worry about. You're too old for this silliness, boy. Take me home. I won't say it again.'

As she turned and stumbled a few steps through the wild garlic on the riverbank, they heard a cry like an animal howling in the distance. The first call was echoed by another, though the second sounded further away, smothered by the mist.

'What's that, dogs?' Mother asked anxiously. 'Must be dogs, no?'

'No,' said Luke. He snapped a branch from a hazel bush and absently stripped away the leaves as though putting off what he wanted to say, what had to be said. 'Don't think it's dogs.'

'Sounds like dogs to me.' Mother shook her head and continued to tread carefully through the dense undergrowth. 'Suit yourself. I'll find my own way home.'

'Mother,' Luke called a little too sharply. He pointed his stick in the opposite direction along the riverbank, refused to look her in the eye. 'This way.'

'You sure?' she questioned him, though Luke had already turned his back and was walking slowly enough for her to follow. She thought that the stream had been on their left on their way out, that Luke must surely be mistaken and was leading her further into the forest, but the mist was deepening and her boys always seemed to know their way through the trees better than she ever would. Besides, those dogs were howling again. This time, they sounded closer.

'He restoreth my soul,' she said to reassure herself as she tried to keep up with Luke. 'He leadeth me in the paths of righteousness for his name's sake. Yea though I walk through—'

Luke left the shallow-running stream behind and approached a small clearing between several old trees where the afternoon sunlight broke through the forest canopy and illuminated a drifting thickness of mist. Silhouettes appeared in the white haze and passed out of sight – colossal leaves, a fishing net of woven branches, a giant bird whose head turned inquisitively, wing stretched out of all proportion: fragments of ideas channelled from the treetops above and projected onto the white fog below.

'I knew we were lost, I'm always right,' said Mother as she came to stand, breathless, beside him. 'Should trust my gut instinct, should know that by now.'

'We're not lost,' Luke replied, though he did not move. The mist thinned a little, dragging its tail wilfully and without a breeze between the shadowy trunks and leaving behind three majestic oak trees which stood guard around a patch of open ground, leaf mulch, mushrooms.

'Not lost, indeed,' she said bitterly. 'Well, home looks very different to how we left it this morning.'

She entered the clearing and glanced around, was about to turn and go back to the stream when she recognised the torn shreds of a black tarpaulin tent hanging from the oak trees.

'Like I said, we're not lost,' said Luke, crouching down beside a trunk. He stirred the damp, fallen leaves with his stick. The dogs howled again, one plaintive voice inciting the other and coming closer, though this time Mother chose not to hear.

'Luke Mann, you brought me here on purpose,' she shouted, turning on her son. 'Now you tell me why you've done this. You tell me this instant. This place, of all places—'

As she spread her arms to encompass the clearing, Mother caught sight of a black shape leaning against the base of one of the trees, a shape that she had initially assumed to be another strip of the ripped tarpaulin. Tentatively, she took a step through the thinning mist towards the material, which she could now see was not tarpaulin at all but a soft, woollen fabric like an old blanket, glistening with dampness and the silver pathways of meandering snails as though the thing—whatever it was—had been left to rot in the forest for weeks.

'Because I figured this is where they'd bring him,' Luke replied, his eyes fixed on the dank underside of leaves that he continued to unearth with his stick. 'Here, or hereabouts. I didn't think they'd do anything to him. Honest, I didn't. I mean, it's our Abel. He's one of us. It's not like he's one of them god-haters and unbelievers. They got what they deserved, didn't they? Those others all got what was coming. That's why I told them, Enoch and Mark, about what Abel had been up to. I thought they'd take that other one, that Lugh, out to the forest. I didn't think they'd take our Abel. They should have taken the other.'

'What have you gone and done now?' said Mother, barely listening to her son's hesitant, mumbled confession. Her attention was on that black shape at the foot of the tree. She approached it warily, becoming more convinced as she drew nearer that it must surely be a blanket that someone had draped over a low branch. Like all unexpected and indeterminate forms of a certain size, it gave Mother the impression of an almost human presence that she knew would dissipate once she had seen with her own eyes that there was nothing forbidding, nothing to fear beneath the old fabric, blanket, coat or whatever it was. And that smell too, she thought as she came closer, that rich, red, rancid smell of fertile earth, raw humus, that too would pass into nothing, it being nothing more than the essential stench of the forest, always there if she chose to notice it, only noticeable now because of her unease.

'I told them what I'd seen,' Luke continued, blushing as he concentrated on the hole he was digging with his stick. 'That's all I did. I told them I'd seen our Abel and that other boy together. Doing things. Alone in the big house. Don't know where the old man's gone but he's gone and they've got the whole place to themselves. They've been getting up to all sorts, Mother. All sorts. And it is a sin, I know it is. Worst sin of them all. So I told Enoch what I'd seen, thinking he'd deal with it, you know, in the right way, in the forest. I thought they'd take the other one, Lugh. Honest, I didn't think they'd take our Abel.'

Luke stopped talking and closed his eyes. The things that happened in the forest were unknown and unknowable, and best left that way. The Beast, when it came, was indiscriminate but that was beside the point, that was where the confusion lay. He pushed away those other thoughts. 'I didn't think they'd take our Abel.'

'And what did you see?' Mother asked vaguely, her attention evidently elsewhere.

Luke glanced up from the leaves, exasperated by his mother's indifference to the secret that had been so difficult for him to share. Maybe the idea of that sin was incomprehensible to her, or maybe he had simply not been explicit enough. While he had been confessing, he had pictured in his mind the vivid details of the acts he had witnessed in the drawing room, and Mother had always been so sharp at seeing precisely what went on in his mind. She cannot have been listening, he concluded. It was the gravest, most serious thing he had ever told her, and she had not listened. He watched her kneel down slowly on the other side of the clearing, her back towards him so her expression was hidden from his view. He watched as she reached out her hand to touch the tree, or something behind the tree. It was a gentle gesture, both affectionate and cautious, as though she were attempting to comfort a small wild animal or a frightened child, something that might run away or turn and bite her if touched wrongly. Before Luke could see what the hidden thing was, he heard something stumbling through the mist and the undergrowth behind him, heavy footsteps lurching towards the clearing and a deep-throated rasp like that of a bull or a horse struggling to breathe. Luke backed away from the noise, holding his stick defensively against the forest.

Mother did not turn around. Even if she was conscious of the disturbance behind her, she could not bring herself to look away now. She tugged the damp material between her finger and her thumb, and lifted the hood of the black duffel-coat open. If she had been here on her own, she knew that she would have reacted differently. If she were alone, she would have recoiled from the rotten, teeming sight, howled at it, closed her eyes and beat it with her nails until there was nothing left, not a trace of her daughter's expression, that gaping, laughing, accusing emptiness, for anyone else to see. But Luke was standing in the clearing: Mother could feel him coming closer. In a curious way, she was more aware of Luke's presence than she was of the other, that discoloured non-presence from which she could not lift her eyes. No, no one should see this, Mother decided, for their own good, for everyone's good. She let go of the hood and pushed the shoulder so that the body slumped harmlessly against the ground. Protruding from the coat sleeve, on which spores of fungus had already germinated in silver rings, Ruth's fingers still clutched the sharp fragment of Antarctica, though the snow had been dyed a deep, dark purple.

'Mother,' she heard her name being called behind her. She flinched at the sound and imagined that it was already too late, that Luke must have seen what none of her sons should ever see. Standing up to screen the body from his view, she turned her most anguished face on him.

'Quick,' Luke called to her again. 'Help me get him on his feet.'

Mother pressed her hands to her mouth and smothered a cry of relief that Luke had seen nothing of the coat, nothing of that grin within the hood, was not even looking in her direction at all. Instead, he was stooping over a bent figure on the other edge of the clearing.

'Can you walk?' Luke asked, peering into Enoch's face, his hands resting on his eldest brother's shoulders. Luke glanced up at Mother and shook his head. 'I don't think he can walk.'

'What's he gone and done to himself now?' she scolded, anxious to move her boys away from the clearing as quickly as possible. She knelt beside Enoch just as he leaned forward and heaved like an animal, retching a thin dribble of black liquid onto the leaves.

'Aye, I can walk,' said Enoch, wiping his mouth and struggling to stand. 'I'll be right as rain once you get me someplace warm.'

Between them, they helped Enoch climb to his feet and supported him towards the riverbank, where he stumbled to his knees and retched again, though this time producing nothing.

'Where's your stick, son?' said Mother, feeling the temperature of his forehead. 'We'd make it back quicker if you lent on your axe. Honestly, it's like trying to carry an ox.'

'Where are the others?' Luke added, glancing back at the way they had come, at the mist thickening through the trees. 'Mark and Abel aren't with you?'

Enoch spat and shrugged ambiguously, heaved himself upright.

MAYA HAD MADE THE LOFT spaces as homely as possible. Crawling through the small hole in the alcove beside the chimney stack, she had made a den of blankets and sofa cushions on the dusty floorboards in the neighbouring attic, set a ring of candles on an upturned box, and removed four or five roof-tiles to allow a current of fresh air to flow through the close, confined quarters. The loft hatch into this dormitory space she had weighted down with anything she could lay her hands on: planks of wood, the jerry cans of petrol and, heaviest of all, a wooden cask of water.

'I'd like to see someone move that now,' Maya said with a nod at the barricaded hatch. Satisfied with her work, she sat in one corner and combed her daughter's hair.

'They will, if there's enough of them. When they know we're up here, they'll find a way in,' said Ky. She was lying on the floor, eyes closed, her arms folded meditatively over a book on her chest. Beside her on the blanket Fran lay facing the wall, cradling her stomach.

'See them try,' Maya repeated confidently. 'You say, safe as houses, yes? Is safe as houses. Safe as Sofia, niña mia.'

Maya pressed her mouth against Sofia's bare shoulder and blew noisily, sending the little girl into a fit of delighted squealing.

'Is there a volume control on that child?' asked Ky. 'Can we turn her down a touch before she wakes the patient?'

'The patient is awake,' Fran murmured, although she did not move. 'Not been asleep.'

'You were, my love; you were talking in your dreams.' Ky sat up and leaned over Fran's shoulder to see her bruised and swollen face. 'Not exactly talking. You were barking, bow-wow, bow-wow. Sounded very trippy. How's the stomach?'

Fran twitched her shoulder a fraction, a gesture that could have meant anything.

'There, you see? The patient is much more lifelike,' said Maya, blowing her words into Sofia's ear. The little girl writhed within her mother's embrace and laughed loudly. 'And when the patient is on her feet again, Sofia, then we say adios, adios, and leave this shit-hole place.'

Ky turned to her sharply and said, 'Seriously, what's with all the noise? If they hear—'

'Okay, Comandanta,' Maya interrupted with a placating smile. 'I know, if those chicos hear us, then this safe house is not so safe no more. But those chicos are nowhere and Sofia takes her sleep medicine soon and then she'll be quiet as an angel, I promise it. But is important that Sofia goes to sleep feeling fine so she wants to wake up again. If she doesn't feel fine, then maybe she won't want to wake up, you know? Francesca, you know that feeling, no?'

Fran did not respond immediately. Taking her time, she laboured to roll onto her back and stare at the rafters overhead, the thick, white cobwebs stirring in the breeze.

'That woman over there,' Fran said after a while, 'the one that's talking, that's not Rhea.'

'No, my love,' Ky answered, brushing the hair away from Fran's damp forehead. 'That's Maya. Maya's our friend. She carried you across the road from the other house, you remember?'

'No, it's not Rhea,' Fran said decisively. 'I know it's not Rhea.'

'Rhea's not with us anymore.'

'Rhea's not with us anymore,' Fran echoed with a pained expression as though she were struggling to untangle the words. Finally her eyes fixed upon Ky's. 'So how come you're with us?'

'I found you in that bedroom, don't you remember? You told me about the toadstools. I made you very, very sick. Then we brought you here where it's safe.'

'I'm not an imbecile, Zachariadou, not yet.' Fran turned to the wall. 'I mean, how come you're with us now? You wanted to see how I got on without you, didn't you? Go that way, that's what you said. It'll be interesting to see how you get on, you said. Ta-da, here I am.' She tried to smile at Ky, genuinely amused though pained by the effort of stretching her lips. 'How do I look?'

'Same as always. Like a painting. Like a Rossetti, pre-Raphaelite.'

'A painting that Rossetti threw out the window, smashed on the pavement.' Fran coughed and closed her eyes. 'He's not with us now, is he?'

'Who, Rossetti?'

'Matthew.'

'No, Matthew's not with us now.'

'I knew he wasn't.' She allowed Ky to take her hand, squeeze her fingers. After a moment, she added, 'But Lugh is. I know he is. He sent me a present.'

'He's just over there.' Ky nodded towards the alcove where the bricks had been removed. Lugh was sitting in the neighbouring loft space, silently watching them through the hole in the wall though his face could barely be discerned in the shadows.

'He's keeping an eye on the other loft door, the one down to our house.' Ky considered mentioning the row of home-made munitions on the floor beside him: three glass bottles, each filled with petrol and stuffed with a rag that Lugh had put together according to Ky's recipe. She decided better of it. Such details, rather than providing reassurance, would only draw Fran's attention to the immediacy of danger, and Fran needed to rest.

'See,' Ky concluded, 'we've got everything covered. Safe and sound, just like Maya said.'

'Lugh sent me a present,' Fran repeated, 'a letter. Not puffball. He's full of surprises. You're full of surprises, O'Byrne. Always have been.'

Lugh did not reply. Instead, he gazed down at the box of matches in his hand.

'He's been watching out for you, my love,' Ky said to Fran, though she intended that Lugh should also hear the words. 'He's been doing his best.'

Through the gaps in the roof where tiles had been removed, the palettes of sky shifted hue: the deep, pacific blue kindling imperceptibly into flaming yellow, dusk-fire orange, an inferno of evening reds. Maya administered the fragment of a sleeping pill to Sofia, kissed her daughter's face in several places and covered her shoulders with a blanket.

'It's late, no? I think the young man wants to see what happens to his friend,' Maya said with a smile at Lugh. 'Off you go, guapo. I'll watch that door when you go.'

'It's still too light. If he goes now, they'll see him.' Ky threw a cautionary glance at Lugh. 'He can wait another hour at least.'

Lugh opened the box of matches. He knew that, if he was mindful and sensitive and paid close attention to his surroundings, he could go anywhere at any time of the day or night and not be seen. He knew how to take advantage of the long shadows at sunset, the moon-shadows at night and the protection provided by those secret pathways through the forest known only to him. Moreover, he came and went according to the dictates of his own say-so, no one else's.

He closed the matchbox and looked at Ky. Somehow, miraculously, she was now alive when only that morning she had not been. Throughout the long months of her absence, Lugh had not just believed that she was dead, he had known it as surely as he knew that Rhea was dead, that his mother was dead, and that his brother lay buried under hard clay at the old farmhouse. I want her to go, Lugh had said, and Ky had gone. It had been a simple curse, spiteful and ignoble, but one that had damned himself as deeply as it had her, cutting both ways. He had carried the shame of it every day, through each subsequent and associated loss. Now that Ky had returned, he knew that the curse was lifting. She had managed to accomplish in one afternoon what Lugh had failed to achieve in weeks. She had delivered Fran from Enoch.

Lugh put the box of matches on the floor and folded his hands. He was conscious that his fiddling could ignite the firebombs, burn the house down: it was a repulsive, fascinating temptation. He needed to get out, to take his secret path of shadows to Abel, find out what was happening down the lane. Something had drawn Enoch and his mother to the big house, and the street had been silent all evening. None of them had returned; none of them had come looking for Fran. Lugh determined that he must find Abel. He did not want to unsettle the fragile concord he had established with Ky, to risk reopening the curse by opposing her, so this time he considered his words carefully. It was Fran, however, who spoke first.

'We thought he was a tree,' she said cryptically. She did not turn around but lay motionless on her side, facing the wall, reminiscing aloud to the room. 'We took a boat to the mainland, arrived on the beach in that empty seaside town: you, me and Rhea. Rhea was always carrying her suitcase, that massive suitcase. I thought it must be full of lentils. We ate lentils for so long, nothing but lentils: her suitcase must have been stuffed with them. And then you said, do you trust me? And we said yes, Zachariadou, of course we do. And we followed you off the beach, out of that town, into the countryside. All those fields of wheat and rye. And there was O'Byrne, standing on the roadside, still as a tree. In fact, we almost didn't see him at all. He just blended in with the landscape, glaring at those mountains in the distance.'

Fran slowly turned over to look up at Ky and added, 'Trust is a two-way conversation, Zachariadou. I think we can trust O'Byrne to be fine.'

Ky looked at the alcove and saw Lugh watching her from the shadows.

'Go on then. Go and be a tree,' said Ky. After a moment's consideration, she appeared to throw a small object at him. 'Here, you'd better take this.'

'What is it?' he asked, looking at the nothing he had caught in his hand.

'The magical ring of invisibility. Let's see what you do with it.'

LUGH SENSED THAT THINGS WERE different at the big house before he had turned the corner in the lane. Others might have called it instinct, but Lugh was conscious of specific, empirical alterations in a miscellany of natural wavelengths. The blackbirds, nuthatches and song thrushes, which had grown accustomed to his comings and goings, held back from the house as though affronted by a change of regime within. He knew enough of the language of magpies to suspect that their unusual silence signified vigilance, attention, suspicion. Obsessed with novelty, the magpies were watching to see whether the new order would provide them with new opportunities. The crows were the only ones to gossip noisily, contentiously, at some safe distance in the twilit forest, their voices refracted by the mist rising from the trees.

Keeping to the shadows, a shadow himself, Lugh skirted the walls of the house and approached the drawing-room doors. Although the evening sky burned with sunset, the candles inside had already been lighted and the windowpanes reflected the quick dance of flames. Before he reached the French doors, he heard a man's voice within, a wordless moan like that of a suffering animal. Lugh crept closer, still clutching his scythe, and peered through the glass.

'Pray for me, Mother. Why won't you pray for me?'

It was Enoch who spoke, lying on the sofa and cradling a cushion against his stomach. His mother sat on an armchair near the fireplace and refused to look at her eldest son. She stared determinedly away, her eyes fixed on the hearth where Luke was attempting to kindle a fire from the splintered fragments of a chair and pages ripped from old books. A dozen candles flickered on cabinets and bureaus around the room, their yellow flames glittering on the surfaces of glass and silver ornaments. Crystal decanters twinkled on the polished lid of the harpsichord.

'You sat at my bedside last time, Mother,' Enoch said after another tormented groan. 'Night and day you sat with me. You did not leave till your prayers were answered. Prayer and faith, that's what you said. Prayer and faith. Will you not do the same for me now?'

Mother looked down at her lap and distractedly brushed the dried mud from her black skirt, picked at the thorns that pierced the cotton, inspected the cut in her hand.

Mark sat on the floor beside the fireplace, his muddy hands resting on his knees and his face hidden behind the alcove. He cleared his throat to break the acrimonious silence.

'I don't want to hear a sound out of you,' Mother said sharply before Mark could say a word. 'Neither you nor your brother. There's nothing either of you can say to make this right.'

'But, Mother,' Mark pleaded regardless, 'for all we know, our Abel will come through that door there any minute like nothing happened. For all we know, he ran off before the Beast got to him. We only took him out there to teach him a lesson, show him right from wrong. And he had gone wrong all right, Mother, no one can argue with that. He'd gone wrong and needed to be put right. Isn't that so, Enoch?'

'Aye, and then the mist came down and that Beast showed up and now no one knows what's become of your little brother,' she snapped, dismissing his explanation with a wave of her hand. 'Well, Mother knows. Mother always knows. When you two get together in them woods, something bad and bloody always happens. That Beast shows up and someone disappears, as it was with your father and your uncle and then Matthew. And now our Abel.'

She pressed a trembling hand over her mouth in an attempt to prevent further words escaping. Unable to contain herself, she stood up and moved to the window, keeping her face averted from her sons. Outside, Lugh retreated beneath the boughs of the apple tree, hidden from view but still close enough to hear what was said in the drawing room.

'I wish you'd think, Mother, before you opened that mouth of yours,' Enoch said after a considerable pause. His tone was cold, menacing.

'Oh, you do, do you?' she shouted, turning to confront her sons. Her expression was unrecognisable, twisted by emotions she hardly dared to own but were nonetheless played out for all to see. 'You know what I wish? I wish that all my children were with me still, all of them here like they should be, not rotting out there in the forest. You have no idea what it's like, as a mother, when you close your eyes and see that face, those hands—'

Her voice broke and, reaching blindly for the nearest armchair, she lowered herself down and continued, 'When I think of those god-given months I carried you, each and every one of you, nine months in my womb—you've no idea. And that's why it's mine, aye, it's mine, the right to give and take, not yours. Lying there on that sofa, stewing in self-pity and pride. You dare say I should think before I open my mouth? Dear God, you know what I wish? I wish that bloody Beast had taken you instead of our Abel, instead of them all. I do, I wish it had taken you and that was that.'

As soon as she had uttered the words, she covered her face and began to cry soundlessly into her hands. Luke exchanged a look with Mark and returned his attention to the hearth, stirring the burning wood with the poker. Around the silent room, the ornaments glistened in incandescent response to the rising fire.

'I didn't say that, I didn't say that at all,' Mother sighed, drying her face with her sleeve and regaining her composure. 'It's just the sadness speaking. Least said, soonest mended.'

'You know what I'd be thinking?' Enoch turned his face to study the ceiling, to the glass beads of the birdcage chandelier twinkling overhead, a tide of long shadows reaching and retreating. 'If I were you, Mother, I'd be thinking about what's out there in them woods, and what's in here in this room. And I'd ask myself which side of these walls I'd rather be on.'

'I meant nothing and I know nothing,' she replied, staring in mild surprise at the fingernail marks she had scratched on the back of her hands. 'Just as you know nothing and there's nothing you can say. Best we say nothing, all of us.'

Enoch leaned over the edge of the sofa and retched a black, foul-smelling liquid onto the rug. When he had finished, he pressed his mouth to the cushion, closed his eyes and whispered, 'Pray for me, Mother. Why won't you pray for me?'

'My prayers won't do no good, not if the Lord has turned his face away. I'll speak to Father Ambrose, that's what I'll do.'

'It's dark up them stairs. I'll come with you,' offered Luke. He stood up to accompany her, but she had taken a candlestick and was already halfway out of the drawing room.

'Father Ambrose doesn't want you traipsing up and down his stairs,' she replied. 'And he certainly doesn't want to be bothered by strangers when he's feeling so poorly. Besides, we have an understanding, the priest and me. He'll talk to me if we're alone. He's a man of God. If anyone has displeased the Lord, Father Ambrose will know how best to atone.'

From his place near the window, Lugh watched Mother leave the drawing room and disappear into the hallway, the light of her candle flickering into darkness as she ascended the staircase. He knelt for a moment under the apple tree, considered all that he had overheard, then turned to confront the forest. Under the cover of twilight, the mist had stalked beyond the shelter of trees. It stayed low, tentative in open ground, and drifted densely over the lawns so that the stone peak of the ornamental fountain seemed to float like a sail on the tide of cloud. Above that strange, disembodied object, the stars burned clearly overhead and a bone-white moon gazed over the forest. Abel lay somewhere out there in the darkness. Or perhaps Abel was not there at all. Perhaps he was no longer anywhere.

Lugh stared distractedly ahead as that old, familiar, intimate emptiness crept closer to him, kissed his face and punctured his skin. He knew the name of the Beast now. It was neither Enoch nor Mark, though both of them were implicated in the same nature. The Beast simply was and always would be.

Its appetite was infinite and it would take and take because it could, because it knew no other way, because it was not a thing of reason. It would keep going until there was nothing left to take, until it had devoured everything or was kept at bay.

The voices started up again behind the glass doors, but Lugh no longer cared what was said inside the house. Instead, he pushed himself up from the grass beneath the apple tree and walked silently, invisibly, towards the emptiness in search of what remained.

AFTER MAYA HAD PULLED THE stepladder up behind Lugh and taken his position in the alcove, they listened to his footsteps disappear down the stairs below and fade into the evening. Fran folded her arms over her stomach and curled into a foetal position. Ky stroked her shoulder, said she should try to sleep through the pain.

'I've been sleeping for weeks, months,' Fran replied. 'The pain's not so bad. I've had worse. Distract me. Tell me something. Tell me what happens after here.'

'After here?' Ky looked around the room. Sofia was sleeping peacefully beneath a blanket in the corner, the sky was darkening through the gaps in the roof and the circle of candles seemed to burn more brightly on the makeshift table. 'I suppose we wait a few more days until you're well enough to move, and then we move. Now, you tell me something. Tell me what you meant about Lugh and trust. What were you getting at?'

Fran did not reply immediately. She took a deep breath, either to manage the pain inside or because she was unable to form the right words. Eventually she said, 'You're a pushy cow, Zachariadou. But I wouldn't have you any other way. You do know that, don't you?'

'Stop flirting. Get to the point.'

'Before you went away, I said some awful things, unforgivable shit. I didn't mean it, not all of it. I said I didn't trust you, but that was a lie. I did and I do. The thing is—' Fran paused to contend with another spasm of pain. She breathed heavily until the wave passed and then continued. 'It is a two-way thing, trust. It's not a dictatorship. I wish you'd trusted me. I wish you'd talked to me. That was the other option, instead of running away.'

Ky said nothing, but stared at the candles, her glossy eyes reflecting the flames. Fran's body contracted again and this time she struggled to raise her head, to retch raw air into the bucket beside her. When she lay back down again, she said, 'Tell me something. Tell me anything.'

Still gazing at the candlelight, Ky considered the many things that she could say. Eventually, she settled on a verse from memory, 'My heart, burning like a volcano and deep as the void. Nothing will satiate that wailing monster, nor cool the thirst of the Eumenides.'

'It's Baudelaire.' Fran smiled at the recollection of their first meeting. 'Poems in the library on the day we met. You know, we shouldn't call the Eumenides by their name. It's not right; we might summon them. Safer to call them something else.'

'The Eumenides are ancient spirits of revenge,' said Ky, turning to Maya. 'Vicious things. Not nice at all. We're supposed to call them the Kindly Ones instead, so as not to attract their attention.'

'You've got a book here, haven't you?' asked Fran. 'Did I dream you were reading a book?'

'This one,' said Ky, picking up the hardback volume that lay with its torn pages open on the floor beside her. 'It was in Enoch's room. You told me to bring it with us. Laertius, *Lives of the Eminent Philosophers*. I don't imagine this was his usual reading material. Can he read?'

'Rhea left it for us. Did you see what she did at the back? She found her answer.'

'Her answer for what?' Ky flicked through the pages.

'To the question, of course.'

Turning to the final chapter, Ky found the annotations that Rhea had scribbled around certain passages. Sometimes the ink had bled through the paper, obscuring whole sentences with a smudged thumbprint, a finger that had pointed at some pleasing phrase.

'I think maybe this is a private question between you two,' said Maya from the darkness of the neighbouring loft space. She sounded bored, stifled a yawn. 'I think maybe I better not listen.'

Ky was straining to read the small text in the dim light of the candles, too occupied with the book to hear Maya speak.

'Nothing private,' said Fran drowsily. 'It's an old question, older than

Plato, older even than Rhea. It goes: is there any reason to be good, to be a just person, if there are no consequences? If there's no society, no law, no punishment, does justice still exist as an idea? That's all it was.'

'Justicia?' Maya asked incredulously. 'You asking if justicia exist?'

'Yes, and what is it.'

'I know injusticia, there's always injusticia. Since we were animals living in trees, injusticia.'

'And now, look at us. Back to living in trees.'

'I think I've found it,' Ky interrupted, holding the book as close as she dared to the candlelight. 'Natural justice is to prevent one man from harming or being harmed by another. Or one woman too, though it doesn't say as much. Is that it? Is that Rhea's answer?'

'Rhea's answer,' Fran repeated quietly to herself. She turned to the wall and closed her eyes. 'Yes, must be. Preventing harm. Otherwise there's only revenge, the Kindly Ones. We haven't done this in ages, have we? Talking like this. I missed it. I missed our nights.'

Ky closed the book and lay down on the blanket, gently resting one hand on Fran's shoulder. She listened to Fran's breathing gradually settle into the steady rhythm of sleep, broken occasionally when her stomach contracted with cramps.

'We say adios to this place when your friend is better,' Maya said quietly. Ky did not reply, so Maya continued, 'I know you, Comandanta. I know you're thinking something. You told me, you said we get out of here and we go somewhere safe. That's what you said. We don't go making war with those chicos. I don't want Sofia in danger. We say adios and we don't look back.'

'I'm not thinking about getting even,' Ky whispered so as not to wake Fran. 'I'm thinking about stopping them doing the same thing again, or doing something even worse.'

Before Maya could reply, they heard heavy footsteps in the lane outside, stones being kicked, a door opening and closing. Ky stood up and put her ear to a hole in the roof.

'He's not here,' said Maya, kneeling beside the loft hatch with the matches in her hand.

'No, he's over the road,' Ky replied. 'Won't be long before he comes over.'

Ky could hear noises in the houses over the lane: furniture being shoved aside, boots running up and down stairs, a front door opening and someone walking slowly across the lane towards their house. A man was making sounds, deep animal noises, under his breath.

'I think maybe we wake the sleepers now,' said Maya.

'Not yet. Let's see what he does.'

Ky crouched beside the barricaded loft hatch in the dormitory quarter and prepared to remove the heavy cask of water from what could be their only exit. If they made the slightest noise, if the floorboards creaked or the sleepers were startled awake, she knew that the man, Enoch probably, would be up there in no time. She looked at Sofia, looked at Fran, each of them sleeping in their corners, and felt a rising panic at the realisation that she had trapped them in the loft.

'I think maybe this was a shit plan,' Maya whispered from the neighbouring loft.

'I think maybe you're right.'

There was a loud bang downstairs as the back door of their house was kicked open and footsteps entered the kitchen. Chairs were thrown against the wall, cupboards opened, crockery smashed on the floor, and all the time they could hear the constant murmur of the man's voice. He advanced through the hallway and into the front room, breaking windows, pushing furniture aside and throwing things violently into corners. As he climbed the stairs, they heard the dull weight of his axehead thud on each of the steps. At the top of the stairs, he paused for a moment to listen to the sounds of the house. Directly above his head, behind the thin wooden board that covered the loft hatch, Maya tried to keep the matchbox from rattling in her hand.

'Mother-fucker, mother-fucker,' Mark said as he thumped the axe against the floorboards.

The echo of his voice faded into deathly silence. After a moment, he entered the bedrooms, exploring the darkness with his fists, overturning wardrobes and bedside tables. When he had ransacked the bedrooms, he descended the stairs, all the while growling incoherently under his breath. Ky and Maya listened as he searched through the houses next door, though it became apparent from the diminishing commotion that he had lost his enthusiasm for the hunt.

'He's gone,' said Ky as she listened to his footsteps disappear down the lane. She leaned against the wall and rolled herself a cigarette. 'Fucksake, this was a shit plan.'

'Is not so bad,' Maya smiled as she passed the box of matches to Ky. 'He come and he go.'

'He's not gone. He'll never go.' The voice was Fran's. Lying in the corner with her back to the room, she spoke the words dreamily and did not move. 'He'll never go.'

'I didn't think you were awake,' Ky said as she passed her cigarette to Maya. 'It wasn't Enoch. It sounded more like Mark, but he's gone now. He's gone and you shouldn't be awake.'

'He'll never go,' Fran repeated. Her eyes remained closed as she talked in her sleep.

CHAPTER FIFTEEN
APOCALYPSE

HE ARCHANGEL WATCHED OVER THE trees with her gorgeous wings outstretched, enfolding the forest in a white, feathery mist. Although she was many leagues above him, Abel could feel that she was drifting even further away. Sometimes she disappeared altogether when the mist clustered over his eyes and he could see nothing but the pale glow of her memory. When the air cleared again, she returned with a fierce smile of consolation, her tin-beaten face so attentive and immediate that she seemed to be looking at him for the very last time.

'What are you?' she asked in a gentle, teasing voice.

'Broken,' he replied. A spring-green chestnut leaf drifted down from the trees and touched the bloody wound on his forehead, stayed where it had fallen, was joined by another. He tried to brush the leaves away from his mouth but he was unable to raise his hand so, from behind the greenery, he whispered, 'What are you?'

'I?' she asked, mildly surprised. 'Why, I am also broken. I am the collector of broken things.'

'Have you come to collect me?' Abel asked as another leaf fell onto his face and covered one of his eyes. He blinked his eyelashes but the leaf would not move, so he gazed at the sky with his unobstructed eye and watched the mist drift overhead and shroud his view of the moon. He knew he was not able to communicate with her when she was hidden, so he waited for her to return. The mist carried an elfin music, the tinkling of crystal bells that played unevenly, sounded close and then scattered to a thousand distant corners of the forest.

'You want to play hide-and-seek?' said the moon when the mist cleared and her lucent, pockmarked face could be seen again.

'Will you find me if I hide?'

'You know the answer to that better than I.'

'Do I?' asked Abel. 'Why? Why do I know the answer?'

'Because it is your question.'

Abel did not understand what the moon meant but, before he could say anything, another leaf fell from the chestnut tree and buried his open eye.

'I will hide,' he said, though he could no longer see. 'I will hide and you can find me.'

The moon did not reply, so Abel started to count quietly, apprehensively, to the aching pulse of the wound in his head. The mist must have returned because the numbers were stifled in his mouth: barely spoken, much less heard. The tinkling glockenspiel, tin-bell orchestra now sounded more clearly around him than before although, this time, the music was accompanied by deep words strummed on rough, animal tongues: *come* or *run*, *where* or *dare*.

By the time Abel counted to a hundred or thereabouts, the leaves had fallen so heavily on his face that he could no longer move his lips. She will find me, he thought. One-hundred-and-one, I dare to be found.

The jangling bells drifted away in the mist, grew fainter and disappeared altogether at the sound of footsteps, leaves cracking under approaching boots, the regular pace of an axehead beating against the earth. Kicking his way through the undergrowth and keeping close to the edge of the forest, Mark passed by on his way back to the big house. He stumbled over a rotten branch and lurched a few steps forwards, cursing incoherently under his breath as he fell against a trunk. Sometimes the mist seemed to disperse and the moon shone so brilliantly that the glistening forest floor and the bark of trees were illuminated clearly. Now, however, the mist had regathered and he could see nothing through the dimly lit cloud. He listened to the sounds of the forest: a night bird or some other animal crying in the distance, branches stirring and breaking from trees, the rustling of fallen leaves as though something dragged itself after him. Mark thought of the Beast in the forest, of the thing that turned wild with the taste of blood, and he became afraid. He stumbled blindly forwards, broke into a run and lost his footing where the ground sloped down to the stream. The mist cleared and he found himself standing knee-deep in moonlit water. The axe, which had been in his hands just moments earlier, was nowhere to be seen.

THE REFLECTION OF THE CANDLE-FLAME danced over the lenses of Father Ambrose's spectacles, seeming to give life and expression to the dead man's face. Mother shifted to a more comfortable position on the stairs and absently scratched her thumbnail over a patch of dried mud on her skirt. She had tried to pull the priest up the stairs and into the attic room in the tower, but it had been enough of an effort to push the door open against his body that had set rigidly behind it. If she had managed to drag him upstairs to the moonlit attic, she would have finally met the Gentleman resting in his armchair, and so seen the wooden cross upon which the shrunken corpse gazed in perpetual concentration. For the time being, however, Mother decided to leave Father Ambrose where he lay at the foot of the stairs, his head resting against a step as though he were listening intently, compassionately, to her words. Besides, her sons downstairs were more likely to overhear her talking to the old man if they both remained close to the door. And that, to her, was vital.

'That's a fair thing to say,' she said, nodding in agreement to her own thoughts. 'I tried my best with my boys, with all my children. God knows, I set out to raise them same as my own parents raised me. Better, if possible. To love the Lord that brought us out of Egypt, to honour their mother and their father, to avoid the assembly of evildoers. I did my best and that's the most any mother, any decent parent, can do, isn't it? Aye, by His grace, I did try.'

White, moonlit motes of dust drifted down the stairs on the draught from the broken skylight, turning yellow as they approached the candle and settled on Mother's hair.

'If I had my time over again, there's not a thing I would do different,' she said, continuing the one-sided conversation after an attentive pause. 'Thank you, Father Ambrose. That's a kind word. It is, as you say, a sacrament.'

Mother bowed her head as though she were praying, or trying to catch the dead man's words, or staring attentively at his single black shoe that sat on the lowest step and wondering whether she should try to slip it back onto his foot. As she sat there in silence, she heard a door creak open in the drawing room below, the sound of Mark's voice as he returned to the house.

'Aye, Father,' she said more loudly, pressing the key into her palm. 'The wafers in the tabernacle, you say? Sure, I know where it is. If this is your wish, Father, I'll do just as you say.'

Before she left the attic staircase, she glanced again at the old man's shoe. Tomorrow, she thought as she locked the door behind her and slipped the key into her pocket. I'll put that thing back on him tomorrow.

Her boys stopped talking when they heard her footsteps descend the stairwell and saw the flickering light of her candle as she passed through the hallway on her way to the chapel. She had heard enough of their conversation to learn where Mark had been and that he had returned without that godless tramp. Small blessings, thought Mother as she opened the chapel door and entered the stale-smelling room for the first time since Holy Thursday. After genuflecting at the door, she looked up and saw that things had been moved since she had attended that last communion. The statue of the Virgin Mary still gazed forlornly from her station in the corner and the candle sat low and unlit in its holder before the tabernacle, but the silver crucifix and white cloth had been stripped from the altar. More than that, the wooden bench where Abel used to sit was now empty. She stood for a moment at the entrance and closed her eyes.

Father Ambrose must have said another communion after Holy Thursday because the door of the tabernacle was now closed and, inside the mahogany box, Mother found a white envelope of what she assumed were sacramental wafers. The rituals of the high church were still mostly a mystery to her, but she had received enough instruction to know that this was where the real stuff, the transubstantiated body of Christ, was supposedly kept. As she took the envelope and closed the tabernacle door, she caught again that tragic look on the face of the Blessed Virgin. The candlelight played with the statue's painted expression, raising her eyebrows, loosening the tightness of her lips.

'You lost just the one,' Mother said, straightening her spine as she confronted the Virgin. 'I lost more, much more than your stone heart could ever bear.'

She turned once more at the chapel door and bowed towards the empty altar, crossing herself with the same hand that held the small, white envelope of dried toadstools. Carrying her candle slowly down the hallway, she could hear Enoch complaining that Mark had been wearing his boots again, Mark answering in a low voice as though he did not want to be overheard. They all fell quiet as soon as she entered the drawing room.

'Don't stop on my account,' she said, laying her candlestick on the tea-table beside the set of china cups and saucers. 'If you've something to say, best say it aloud so everyone can hear, else hold your peace. I can't abide secrets, you should know that by now.'

'He lost the axe,' Luke said quickly with a nod at Mark. 'Dropped it out there in the forest.'

'That stranger that our Luke said he saw round the back of the houses,' Mark retorted, glaring at Luke, 'that foreign-looking woman with the baby, can't find her anywhere now. Luke didn't think to deal with her at the time, of course, and now there's no sign of her. No sign of Enoch's tramp either; looks like she's run off. Don't know how she managed it, but she smashed up the bedroom door and left the room in a right state. Wouldn't be surprised if Luke's foreign-looking woman had something to do with that. No sign of any of them now.'

'Small mercies,' Mother said under her breath.

'Bathsheba,' Enoch growled from the sofa. 'Her name's Bathsheba.'

'Don't blaspheme, son. The Lord may be slow to anger, but even He has his limits.' Mother sat in the armchair closest to the fireplace and laid the envelope from the tabernacle reverentially on her lap. She gazed down at it for a minute or more, enjoying her moment of suspense before telling Luke to open the Bible that lay on the mantelpiece. 'Find me that paragraph about the last supper. When you've found it, you can read it aloud. There's a good boy.'

'You've been talking with the old man?' Enoch asked her, though his eyes were closed. He clutched the cushion against his stomach as his body contracted in another wave of pain.

'Father Ambrose is a wise man,' she replied.

'You saw the Gentleman too?'

Mother thought for a moment before answering ambiguously, 'So long as we're no bother and respect his house, his rules, we can stay. Now, the priest and I have an understanding. He's a man of God and he sees what's in your heart. He knows your sins and your secrets. He's prayed and he's listened and, by the grace of God, he's spoken wisdom. If your body's sick, my son, it's because there's a sickness in your soul. That's what he said: that's the word of the Lord.'

Enoch relaxed on the sofa. He opened his eyes and watched long shadows ebb and flow over the ceiling, the birdcage chandelier twinkling overhead in candlelight.

'You're the firstborn, Enoch, and that's a mighty responsibility to bear on your shoulders, a weighty inheritance. If you're not fit to carry that responsibility, you'd best say so. Can't go hiding your sins from the Lord; that's where the real sickness lies. Now, you'd know if there'd be some shame in your soul, wouldn't you, son? You'd know if you'd done wrong, if there's something that needs saying to make it all right?'

The fire crackled in the fireplace. Luke looked up from his reading and exchanged a glance with Mark. Mother sat patiently with her hands on the envelope, waiting for Enoch to reply.

'Aye,' Enoch said at length. 'I am sorry, Mother.'

'I know you are. Mother knows. Is there anything else?'

Enoch shook his head. 'Pray for me, Mother.'

'I do. No more to be said.' Trying to conceal her smile of relief, she concentrated on opening the envelope and invited Luke to read the last supper.

'And as they did eat, he said, Verily I say unto you, that one of you shall betray me. And they were exceeding sorrowful—'

'Not that bit, son,' Mother said sharply. 'A little further on, the breaking of bread.'

Luke ran his finger down the page and continued, 'Jesus took the bread and blessed it, and brake it, and gave it to the disciples, and said, Take, eat; this is my body.'

As he read the words, Mother rose from her armchair and walked towards the alcove where Mark stood. He looked uneasy and backed away, but she smiled reassuringly and held the sacrament to his mouth. After serving Mark, she did the same with Luke and finally knelt down beside the sofa with Enoch.

'Don't think I can stomach a thing,' he said, looking sadly into his mother's eyes.

'Body of Christ, son,' she said, placing the slice of death-cap onto the tongue of her firstborn.

She sat back in her armchair and looked in wonder at each of her sons. They were good boys, faithful boys. The Lord has made his face to shine upon them and blessed them above all of her children. Made them strong, survivors. She put the last remaining sacrament into her own mouth and noticed at once that the texture was unlike any communion wafer she had eaten before. It was neither dry nor brittle, nor did it dissolve slowly on her tongue. Rather, it was sinewy, thick and fibrous, tough to chew and tasted vaguely like honey, like a sweet meat in her mouth. Take, eat: this is my body, said the Lord—and maybe, at last, it really was. Maybe this was the real miracle, she thought as she closed her eyes and allowed herself to smile. A real taste of the holy flesh, the first miracle of the new Heaven and Earth.

THE BLACKBIRDS WERE THE FIRST to wake, breaking into song before the moon had set or the eastern sky had begun to insinuate a lesser shade of night. Following the sound of lightly running water, Lugh returned once more to the stream and knelt down at the water's edge to drink. The mist had mostly dissipated, though ghostly strands still meandered through the forest, breaking against trees and fragmenting into finer threads. Lugh raised his head to listen to the blackbirds and was startled by a residual thickness of mist drifting purposefully along the opposite riverbank, seeming to take the path to the big house. It was not a sign, he told himself. All night long, he had followed signs that led nowhere. Sometimes it was the sound of branches breaking nearby as though someone were showing him the way to go, other times it was an owl crying with urgent information, and once a clear moonlit avenue had opened up majestically ahead of him in the fog. None of those things had brought him any closer to finding Abel. There were no signs, no leads, only dead ends. It was all too reminiscent of that endless, desperate, ultimately futile search for Rhea last summer. Drying his hands on the jumper that she had knitted him, he laid down to rest among the wild garlic leaves and gazed up at the patch of sky, a scattering of stars overhead.

Lugh did not remember closing his eyes but, when he opened them, all the stars had gone, burned themselves out, and the sky was an empty, early morning blue. He sat up and looked around for the source of the noise that had disturbed him. The sound was crisp in his memory, had been vivid in his dream: a clear voice close at hand, so close as to have been whispered into his ear. It had left a trace of warm breath on his cheek, although there was no one to be seen.

He drank handfuls of cold water from the stream and then stood up to stretch and take in the sights of the clear, sunlit forest. It would be easier to search for Abel in the daylight, but it would also be easier for him to be seen by the brothers. Not Enoch, of course: Enoch was evidently suffering from a dose of the death-cap. The others, Luke and Mark, however, might be up already, hunting for Fran or for himself in the forest.

As Lugh reached down to pick up his scythe, he heard that sound from his dream again, a coarse, cracked, rugged word lowed like a warning or a wary greeting. He took a step towards the trees where the voice seemed to come from and almost tripped over something buried beneath the leaves, kicking it clear of its hiding place. It was a stick of smooth, polished wood like the handle of a broom or a rake from the tool-shed. It was surprisingly heavy too and, as he pulled the blade free from the undergrowth, it took him some seconds to recognise the thing as Enoch's axe.

The voice spoke again from behind the trees. Taking the axe with him, Lugh walked towards the sound. He did not see the creature at once, so camouflaged was it among the textured spectrums of sunlight, shadow and green foliage. As Lugh crept forwards, he stepped on a blanket of fallen chestnut leaves that rustled beneath his feet and attracted the attention of the face in the undergrowth. The creature turned to gaze intently at him, opened its whiskered mouth and revealed a set of large yellow teeth as it bleated the same meaningless utterance. Lugh and the goat stared at each other, neither of them moving until, after a minute or more, they each heard the sound of a man singing in the distance, coming closer.

'Walking in a garden at the break of day,' the man sang. His deep voice rose and fell as he wandered among the trees. Verses were cut and sentences lost altogether as the man turned his head this way and that, forgot his words, picked up the tune at a later line, 'But he turned towards her, smiled at her and said: Mary, spring is here to stay, only death is dead.'

Lugh crouched down to hide behind a thicket of brambles and watched as the scrawny, shirtless man with wild hair and a wilder beard, a crown of leaves on his head and a branch shaped like a shepherd's crook resting on his shoulder, came strolling casually through the trees. When he caught sight of the goat, the man stopped walking.

'Seen you, he has,' he said, taking the staff from shoulder and pointing the hooked end at the goat. 'Been waiting for you, he has.'

The goat bleated once more and nodded its head. The tin bell that hung from a rope around its neck jangled lightly as, with a farewell glance at Lugh, it turned and tamely followed its shepherd away. Lugh remained hidden behind the brambles, watching and waiting until the tinkle of the goat-bell was lost in birdsong and the pair had disappeared, one leading the other, among the dark depths of the trees.

When he was certain that they had gone, Lugh stood up and listened to the forest bristling around him. A crow cried plaintively from the canopies overhead. Branches stretched in the altered ambience of early-morning air, dew-water dripped from the ducts of unfolding, spiralling ferns; small things crept over the detritus of larger bodies, breaking down, dividing and redistributing the common particles of life. The carpet of chestnut leaves crunched beneath Lugh's trainers as, axe in hand, he walked towards the place where the goat had been standing just a short time before. One more step and the ground flinched from his tread. Another, and a body of leaves rolled over to reveal a leg of denim, a shoulder in chequered fabric and a thick mass of black hair. Startled by the sudden movement below, the crows in the upper branches broke into a commotion of wings, a riot of screeching.

Lugh knelt down and cleared the leaves away from Abel's face, saw at once the gash on his forehead and the blood that had dried where it had flowed down his pale cheek. Abel moaned without regaining consciousness as Lugh exhumed his body from the forest floor and carefully inspected his arms and legs for more injuries. There were no signs of other wounds, but Lugh's gaze returned to that grotesque, dirty cut on the forehead. Although it was no longer bleeding, the skin gaped open and Lugh knew that it had to be cleaned. It was too far for him to carry Abel to the Mews, and he would not leave Abel alone, not again, not in this forest. After a moment of blind panic, Lugh remembered the nearby stream. He sprinted down to the riverbank, slipping off his jumper and t-shirt as he went. It was only after he had ripped his shirt into strips and was soaking them in the cold water that he noticed how much his hands were trembling. When he returned, he lifted Abel's head onto his lap and dabbed the damp rags to the wound as gently as he could. Abel flinched at the contact and feebly raised a hand to push the cloth away.

'I'm sorry, I am sorry,' Lugh apologised, wincing each time he touched the fabric to Abel's tender skin. 'Just trying to get you cleaned up a bit.'

Abel muttered something incoherent and tried to pull away.

'There, all done,' Lugh said, as he pulled the longest strip over the gash and tied it in place around Abel's head. 'Guess we should think about getting you into a bed.'

Abel's eyes remained closed, but he muttered, 'My trousers aren't clean.'

'Doesn't matter,' said Lugh, absently reaching down to brush the dirt and leaves from Abel's jeans. 'We just need to get you inside.'

Abel smiled faintly. 'You won't let me in if my trousers aren't clean.'

'Maybe I'll make you wear my pyjamas again. Do you think you can stand?'

'Doubt it.'

'Can we try?'

'I'm thirsty.'

Lugh frowned distractedly at the riverbank just a few metres away. Now that the crows had fallen silent overhead, he could hear the water running softly along its course. After a moment, he said, 'Look at that. I dare you to look.'

'What is it?' Abel raised his head and opened an eye.

'If we get to that stream, you can have a drink. Can we try, please? Just to that stream?'

'Looks very far away.' Abel dropped his head back onto Lugh's lap and closed his eye. 'Further than the moon. Further than that red planet.'

'Mars. It's not as far as Mars. You're just looking through the telescope the wrong way.'

'What telescope?'

Lugh glanced around. He saw the handle of the axe, lifted it into the air and said, 'This one.'

'That one?' Clumsily and with painful effort, Abel raised himself into a sitting position and flinched at the sight of the blade. 'That's Enoch's axe. Why did you say it was a telescope?'

'I don't know. To see if your head still works, I suppose. It seems to. That's something.'

'Aye, though it does feel funny. Feels like I don't weigh a thing, like I'm going to float away. Hold on to me, will you?'

'Look, if you put one arm over my shoulder and lean on this,' Lugh waved the wooden handle, 'then perhaps we can get as far as the stream. And then you can have a drink.'

'Bollocks, I am thirsty.'

Taking Abel by his elbows, Lugh tried several times to hoist him from the ground. Abel slumped first to one side and then to his knees, but eventually Lugh managed to heave him unsteadily to his feet. Even using the axe as a walking stick, Abel foundered with each step so that he had to be practically carried towards the bank. They stumbled onto their hands and knees at the water's edge and Abel put his mouth to the stream.

That was not so easy, thought Lugh. The way back to the houses on the Mews lay much further along the meandering stream, further than he could imagine he could carry Abel. This way, however, just across the stream and hidden behind those old grey trees, lay the ivy cottage. If they took it carefully and rested when necessary, Lugh guessed that they could reach the cottage in less than half an hour. The sooner they reached shelter, the better. The brothers were much less likely to be hunting out that way and, besides, the overgrown building had already proved itself a decent sanctuary to them both.

THE BROTHERS DID NOT GO hunting in the woods that day. Lugh could see that they had already been down the lane, that they had coursed through the Mews the night before, leaving a scene of desolation in their wake. The garden was littered with traces of their violation: sheets that had been dragged from beds and clothes from wardrobes, temporary substitutes for real bodies, real violence, strewn over the stones and hanging from windows. They had ransacked the kitchen, broken chairs and overturned tables, emptied the contents of drawers and cupboards over the floor. Lugh was met by the same miserable sight in each of the rooms. It was more than mere pillage, the disorder caused by searching: it was a deliberate, knowing debasement.

Treading carefully over fragments of glass in the hallway, Lugh bent down to pick up a book that lay face down at the foot of the stairs. It was Fran's bible of herbs. Its pages were torn and its spine had been twisted. Lugh closed the cover, carefully flattening the remaining pages—rosemary for remembrance, thyme for courage—and carried it with him up the stairs. There were more clothes, more splintered wood and broken glass on the floor of the landing. The loft hatch, however, was still closed overhead and appeared to have been undisturbed. Lugh rested the axe against the bedroom door and knocked on the wall three times, paused and repeated the signal.

'Maya, it's just me,' he called, knowing they would have been listening to his movements.

It was Ky who removed the wooden board and looked warily out of the hatch, gauging the scene of disarray on the landing below, making certain that Lugh was alone. She said nothing but reached across to lower the stepladder for him to climb.

'No, I'm not coming up,' he said. 'I need you to come down.'

Ky inclined her head, a sharp, interrogative gesture of distrust, and said nothing. In a few words, Lugh explained that Abel had been injured and was resting in the ivy cottage. He needed her to come at once with her medical kit. Ky did not move.

'Why leave him there?' she asked quietly, suspiciously. 'Why not bring him here?'

'Because he could barely walk, and we were so close to—' Lugh's explanation dried on his tongue. He recognised that guarded look on her face, had seen it before, understood her entirely. 'You think it's not serious?'

'No, not necessarily,' Ky shrugged off the accusation. 'Maybe Abel does need help but, if I do come, who's keeping an eye on things here? What if Mark or Enoch return and there's trouble while I'm gone? It's too risky.'

'Maya can stay with her. Maya can keep—'

'Maya has a daughter to look after. She can't manage alone if those fuckers return.'

'But Abel's head, it's open. It's actually cut open,' Lugh gestured the wound with his hands, gazed helplessly up at her. 'Ky, you have to come. Don't you trust me?'

'Oh, enough of that already,' she said, losing patience. 'Of course I do, but I have to think. Don't look at me like that, Lugh.'

'No one's going to that town.' Lugh spoke the words in a different voice, a dead voice that silenced Ky and disturbed himself. He sighed, sat down on the top step and pressed the book of herbs between his palms. Resting his head against the bannister, he continued more placidly. 'That's what you said. You said, no one's going to that town to get medical supplies. And no one did go, and Michael died.'

'I've always been sorry about your brother, Lugh,' she said, taking care with each word. 'We did try to save him, honestly we did. I need you to know that we tried.'

'I know,' he said, looking directly up at Ky. 'I know you tried. And I know that, if you'd had the medicines then, Michael might have lived or he still might have died. Fran told me. She said you felt guilty, though you shouldn't have. But Michael wasn't your brother. He was mine.'

Lugh lay the book on the floor and, after a moment, he continued, 'Michael had terrible taste in music; he was seriously uncool. He didn't have many friends, but he looked after me. When mum was out all night, we'd stay up together and watch films. Sometimes he'd give me a taste of his beer. Sometimes he let me use his aftershave. You didn't know him but, if you had, if he had been someone you were close to, like Fran, would you have said the same thing? Would you have said no one's going to that town? Or would you have gone yourself?'

'That's—that's academic.' Ky closed her eyes, ran her fingers through her short hair.

'Abel's hurt. He's really hurt, like Michael was. You've got the medicines this time, and you know what to do. If you don't try to help, if you do nothing, then—well, you'd be no different than the thing that did it to Abel, to Michael, to all of them. You'd be no different to that Beast.'

Ky could feel that he had finished talking, that he had said all he could and all that he needed to say. She glanced up and saw Maya watching her through the hole in the alcove, her eyebrows raised in a look of immanent judgement. Fran and Sofia lay peacefully on the floor behind Maya, the edge of their bodies traced by a line of soft sunlight.

'Tranquila, Sofia,' said Maya, pretending to address her sleeping daughter, though she smiled directly at Ky. 'The Comandanta is acting like she don't know what to do. But she's going to help the young man, you see. Any time now, she'll be asking for her kit. You watch, Sofia—'

'Of course I'm going,' said Ky as she reached for the stepladder and lowered it down to the landing. 'Hand me my kit. I'll be back as soon as I can. And, Maya, don't take any chances.'

'If it makes you feel better, we can leave this with her.' Lugh lifted the handle of the axe through the hatch. He waited for Ky to take it, but she stared mistrustfully at it.

'It was in the forest where Abel was hurt. I think it's what they used on him.'

'Nothing will make me feel better till I'm back here,' she replied, pulling the axe into the loft.

'And then what?' he asked. 'What happens when you're back here?'

'What do you mean?' she said as she climbed down the ladder.

'You plan to hide in the attic forever?'

'I don't know. Until it's safe to leave. I don't have a plan.'

'And then where will you go?'

'You have a better suggestion?' Ky reached up to collect her black rucksack from Maya and turned to face Lugh. 'What do you propose?'

'The petrol can,' he said, coolly returned her gaze, 'and one or two of those bottles.'

Ky slipped her arms through the straps of her rucksack and tightened the belt buckle. They stood on the landing and looked at each other, each considering the unspoken.

'WE SHOULD ALL BE TOGETHER,' Ky said quietly, more to herself than to anyone else. She dropped the needle, tweezers and remaining thread into a bowl of sterilising solution and gently pressed the clean lint over the stitches she had sewn in Abel's forehead. With her free hand, she gestured towards her rucksack. 'Bandage. We shouldn't be in two different places: you and Abel here, the rest of us in the house. It doesn't make any sense. It's fucking ridiculous. And the surgical tape.'

Lugh rooted through her bag and placed the items she had requested in her hand. He watched as she wrapped the bandage around Abel's head and fastened it tightly with the tape.

'You said I shouldn't have moved him,' he said when Ky had finished with the dressing, removed her plastic gloves and was washing her hands in the bowl. 'Can we move him now?'

'You shouldn't have. But I also see how you couldn't have left him in the forest.'

'I couldn't.'

'Well then.' She stood up from Abel's bed of blankets on the floor and fumbled in the pocket of her boiler-suit for tobacco. Walking to the front door of the ivy cottage, she rolled a cigarette and lit the end with a match in one quick, seamless movement. 'But we can't move him again, not yet, not while he's sleeping.'

'So, what do we do?'

'It's getting late. I should head back to the loft. Maya will be wondering what's become of me.' Ky leaned against the door frame and breathed a funnel of smoke at the dusky sky, listened to the sounds of forest birds settling down for the evening. After another draw on her roll-up, she asked in a hoarse voice, 'Why do you think they did it to Abel? He's one of them, isn't he? A flesh-and-blood Mann? What made them turn on one of their own?'

'I thought it was because of the old man,' Lugh replied after a thoughtful pause. 'Because of what we did to him—had to do to him—locking him up in the attic and all that. Apparently, it wasn't that at all. Abel told me what happened. It was because they'd seen us together.'

'Together?' Ky asked. She looked curiously at Lugh as though seeing him for the first time. Kneeling on the floor beside the bed, Lugh held Abel's hand and returned her gaze. Having understood, Ky nodded and returned her attention to her cigarette, to the darkening sky. 'I see. They'll come for you next, I suppose.'

'They'll come for all of us. That's the nature of the Beast.'

'On the balance of probabilities.'

'We can end it all tonight,' Lugh suggested so softly that Ky barely caught the words.

'Maya says she doesn't want to start a war.'

'We're already at war.'

'Yes,' said Ky, dropping her cigarette and extinguishing it beneath her boot. 'I had noticed.'

—

THE FOREST HAD ALREADY FALLEN quiet as they followed the riverbank behind the gardens of the Mews, keeping their bodies to the shadows and their thoughts to themselves. Where the stream turned around the boundary of the big house, Lugh held the jerry can against his chest and slipped through the gap in the garden wall. Ky walked closely behind, a bottle in each hand.

'There's a light in that downstairs room,' she said as she came to stand beside him. 'They won't be asleep for some time yet.'

'That's just the light of the fireplace. And they're quiet. You usually hear them before you see them, haven't you noticed? Not tonight though. Tonight there's nothing.' Lugh closed his eyes for a moment and listened to the stillness of the house, a slight breeze combing spirals over the long grass, rustling the trees, then silence. 'It's okay to go.'

They approached the French doors along the path, treading so carefully as to not make a sound, and peered around the edge of the window. Inside the drawing room, as Lugh had anticipated, the dying fire in the hearth provided the only illumination. It was difficult to make out much in the low light, but eventually Lugh's eyes grew accustomed to the dimness and he gauged that the room was empty. He reached for the handle and opened the door without a sound.

The last flames flickered along the edge of some piece of broken furniture in the hearth. Lugh gathered handfuls of twigs from the log basket beside the fireplace and scattered them over the flames, rekindling the fire. Ky struck a match and lighted a candle on the mantelpiece. They looked at each other uncertainly, exposed in the sudden light.

'They're not here,' Ky whispered. 'I should be with Fran and Maya.'

'No, they are. I know they are.'

Ky gestured with her hands: *Where?*

'The smell,' said Lugh, as though it were the most obvious thing in the world and, for the first time since entering the room, Ky became conscious of the sweet, sickeningly overripe odour of faecal matter that hung in the air. Lugh pointed at the dark stains on the sofa, the rugs, the wooden floorboards leading into the darkness of the hallway. With the beginnings of a smile, he said, 'It was Fran. She got them. She must have got them all.'

'She told me that she only gave the toadstools to Enoch. But this,' Ky gestured at the stinking mess around the room, 'it's like a massacre.'

'There may have been another batch,' said Lugh vaguely, remembering the death-caps that he himself had placed in the chapel. In the bedroom overhead, they heard a long, low, agonising moan, an answering lament from some other room up the stairs, and then the dull weight of a body sliding or being dragged over the floorboards. Without hesitation, Lugh retrieved the jerry can from the patio and began to splash petrol over the sofa, the chaises longues, the harpsichord and the curtains.

'Lugh, no,' Ky called in a louder voice as she tried to keep her candle at a safe distance. 'If they are sick, then we don't need to do this, not now.'

'Why not?' He turned at the entrance to the hallway. He looked fierce, angrier than she had ever seen him before, a dangerous excitement in his eyes.

'Because,' she faltered, looking around the room at the paintings, the mirrors, the silver ornaments, crystal vases and glass decanters glittering in the light of her candle. 'Because, if you're right, if they are all poisoned, then it's no longer necessary. They're not a threat anymore. We don't need to go this far.'

'It has to end, you said so yourself,' Lugh replied, quietly determined. 'We have to burn it down, all of it. The attic, the chapel, the old man, Enoch: all of them. We have to bring it all down.'

'Not this way, not if they're already harmless. Abel won't forget it. Neither will you.'

He appeared to consider this, then turned and disappeared into the hallway.

In the dim light, he could barely see anything except the first few steps of the stairwell, yet he knew for certain that the brothers were somewhere in the house, and he knew what lay up those stairs and beyond the first floor, behind that door into the attic. Ignoring the urgency in Ky's voice as she shouted his name from the drawing room, he poured the last of the petrol over the wooden stairs and then threw the jerry can aside. It was only as he slipped the matchbox out of his pocket that he became conscious of another sound closer at hand: the raw, fevered breathing of someone watching him from the darkness. After the sound, he became aware of the smell. Lugh hesitated for a second before he struck a match against the side of the box.

In the sudden phosphorous glare of the flame, he saw her at once. Wrapped in a blanket at the first turn in the staircase, her back resting against the wall and her legs stretched across the step so that no one might pass, Mother regarded Lugh through half-closed eyes. She seemed to have aged immeasurably, to have become a reduced and desiccated version of her former self. Her skin was pinched tightly around her cheekbones, the whites of her eyes had turned a lurid yellow, and her mouth hung open as though it was no longer of use. The flare of Lugh's match lasted only seconds, but it was long enough for him to see that the woman was already half dead. In the renewed darkness, all he could hear was Mother struggling to breathe, to utter a word.

'I can't,' Lugh whispered, almost inaudibly. 'I can't.'

He turned away from the sick woman as Ky entered the hallway and the light of her candle fell over the stairs. Ky stared intently at Mother's face, assessed her condition, said nothing. She reached out her hand, but Mother recoiled and crossed her arms to ward off the touch.

'I shall not want,' Mother rasped, strenuously pushing her body away from the wall in an effort to prevent anyone from climbing the staircase. 'He maketh me lie down in green pastures. He leadeth me beside still waters –'

'She's hallucinating,' Ky said gently. 'What can she see, I wonder?'

'She's guarding them,' said Lugh. He glanced up the winding staircase towards the darkness of the first-floor gallery, the hushed bedrooms overhead. 'She's put them to rest up there.'

Ky laid her candlestick on the lowest step, crouched down and attempted to hold Mother's gaze as she asked, 'Are they up there? Did you put them all to bed? Enoch and Mark and Luke—'

'Yea, though I walk through the valley of the shadow of death,' Mother whispered as she tried to brush the sight of Ky away with a limp hand, 'I will fear no evil.'

'—and Ruth too?'

At this mention of her daughter's name, Mother's expression changed. Her eyes narrowed, she glared ferociously at Ky and then, without warning, she lashed out at Ky's face.

'Unnatural. Wicked,' she cried, swiping the air. As she flapped her hands, the gold wedding ring, which had become too loose, slipped off her bony finger and tinkled down the dark hallway into silence.

Retreating from the woman's nails in time to avoid being scratched, Ky fell backwards and skidded on the petrol-drenched floorboards. Satisfied, Mother slouched against the wall and continued to pray quietly, breathlessly, to herself.

'Can't we do anything for her?' Lugh asked as he pulled Ky to her feet.

'You wanted to burn them all a minute ago.' Ky made a face as she sniffed the petrol on her fingers. 'It has to end, you said. What's changed?'

'Look at her,' he said, staring at Mother, who had gone silent, cowering from the pain inside.

'That's the thing, Lugh. Now we can see her. It's not so easy, is it?' He did not reply, so Ky picked up her candlestick and lifted it away from the petrol on the floor. 'The colour of her eyes, her skin, that's the late stages of liver failure. Kidneys too, most probably. There's no treatment for the toxin, not now. If she's protecting the others, their condition is likely to be the same or worse. And they will suffer before it ends. Two or three days, then it will be over for them all.'

'We can't do anything for her?' Lugh repeated, his eyes still fixed on Mother's face.

'There is one last thing.'

Lugh looked directly at Ky. She tightened her lips into a sad, strained smile and shrugged slightly as though to say, there is a choice and there is no choice. The light of the candle in her hand cast long shadows across the floor, bars from the bannisters over the walls, monsters taking flight on the ceiling.

THERE WAS A WINDOW IN her room. Fran knew it was open because she could feel the breeze playing freely over her face, a hint of that intimate hour before dawn, an aftertaste of smoke. She opened her eyes and did not recognise the room. There was no dusty brown lampshade hanging like a dead sun overhead, no chair poised at her bedside nor piss-bucket beside a mean fireplace. She still lay with her arms crossed over her chest, but the fabric of this blanket felt different against her skin. Her skin felt different. She was no longer naked. She breathed differently.

The noise that had accompanied her dreams all night long was still playing in the distance, that peculiar background crackling like an un-tuned radio in a neighbour's house, residual static from the big bang. On some level, Fran must have been aware that the sound had gradually decreased as the night had advanced, as though the owner of the radio had a growing awareness of the irritation it caused for the neighbours and had reduced the volume accordingly. Now, the noise was negligible, only perceptible when she chose to concentrate on it.

Through the open window, the window without glass, she heard a cockerel crowing in the forest. Another male bird answered its call, a challenger usurping the claims of the first. Their premature announcement of the dawn exposed them both as losers. Fran smiled at the thought, cautiously lifted her head from her pillow and looked around. As her eyes became accustomed to the dim light, she could see that it was a large room. The walls, the ceiling, even the doors and window frames, seemed to be carved from wood or made of tree roots. In the proud open fireplace at one end of the room, a late fire burned, unwatched and unguarded. That would not have been permitted before. Her bed was a nest of blankets on the floor, not a hard mattress on a metal frame. The most extraordinary thing of all was that she had it all to herself. She stretched her legs under the blankets and was astonished by the expanse, the experience of no boundaries.

'You awake?' a voice whispered from another corner of the room. Fran knew it at once.

'O'Byrne,' she replied warmly. 'I think so. Although it feels a little like a dream.'

'How is your poor belly?'

'My belly?' Fran frowned, slipped her hands beneath her t-shirt and carefully explored her stomach with her fingers, probing for areas of sensitivity. It did feel tender inside, but more from hunger than any lingering soreness. 'I'd completely forgotten about that. Isn't it funny. When you're in pain, that's all you can think about. You just want the hurting to end. But, afterwards, you don't notice the absence of it, not for long, anyhow. I mean the physical pain. Where are we?'

'The ivy cottage. Don't you recognise it?'

'I've never seen it look so homely before. Must be because the fire's alight. I thought it was an enchanted tree-house: a house made of magic trees.'

'It is, almost.' Lugh reached out and stroked the wall of ivy. 'You've been Sleeping Beauty.'

'How long have I been out of it?'

'All day and all night. We had to carry you here on a sheet like a stretcher.'

'Typical princess,' Fran smiled. She pushed herself up into a sitting position, rested her head against the wall and turned to Lugh. He was sitting cross-legged beside another bed on the floor, keeping watch over a sleeping body. 'Who's that?'

'Abel. Another Sleeping Beauty.'

At the sound of his name, Abel stirred beneath his blankets and drowsily complained, 'I'm not a Sleeping Beauty. You're a Sleeping Beauty.'

Abel tried to touch the bandage on his head, but Lugh took the hand away and clasped it in both of his own. 'We've had this discussion. You're supposed to be asleep.'

'I was. I was dreaming.' Abel opened his eyes slightly and looked up at Lugh.

'What were you dreaming?'

'That you were there, right where you are.'

'I am here, see?'

'And it was raining on the roof. I was listening to the rain.'

'Then it's a good dream. You should go back to it.'

Abel smiled and closed his eyes again. When his breathing had returned to the settled rhythm of sleep, Lugh glanced up at Fran and explained, 'He's also been through the wars. He's had a run-in with the Beast.'

'The Beast?' Fran repeated, growing agitated as the memory of danger returned. She pushed herself up from the blankets and steadied herself against the window frame. 'What are we doing here, Lugh? Whose idea was it to come here? Look at these windows—and there's no front door, nothing to stop him. What were you thinking?'

'He's gone.' Lugh came to stand beside her at the window and gestured for her to keep her voice low so that Abel would not hear. 'Enoch's gone. They're all gone.'

'You don't get it,' said Fran, enunciating each word slowly and precisely so that Lugh would hear and understand. 'He will never go.'

Lugh leaned out of the window and pointed around the side of the house to the overcast sky above the trees.

At first, Fran thought that he was merely indicating the dawn over the forest, a deep-red blushing of clouds before the sunrise. As she gazed outside, however, she noticed the presence of flakes drifting in the air, a blizzard of dust that fell from the crimson sky and covered all things – the trees, brambles, path and stone table in the front garden—with a ghostly layer of grey. She could also hear that crackling sound more clearly at the window. The static of the big bang was coming from the forest, from beneath the red clouds, from the place that Lugh was pointing at.

'The big house is burning,' he whispered. 'Enoch was in there. And the mother. All of them.'

'Burning.' Fran echoed the word as though hearing it for the first time. 'How do you know he was in there? You can't know that.'

'I do. I started the fire. Enoch was in there. They all were.'

'Oh,' she said simply, her mouth slightly ajar, catching butterflies. They stood together without speaking for a while, gazing at the red clouds reflecting the fire. Eventually, Fran asked, 'And Ruth and Luke too? Surely not Ruth. Not her as well?'

Lugh shrugged and said evasively, 'We didn't see her.'

'We haven't seen her for months. Poor Ruth, I hope she got away. I'd like to think she's far away.' A flurry of ash drifted through the window and settled on Fran's face, on the fabric of her long white t-shirt and pyjama trousers. Brushing herself down, she said, 'It's like Pompeii, like the end of the world all over again. The end of another. Do you think the chickens will be all right?'

'We set them free in the forest, just in case. Ky didn't think the fire would reach as far as the chicken coop, but the greenhouse went up straight away: the glass shattered everywhere. Ky got worried that it might spread to the houses on the Mews. With all the smoke, it was impossible to breathe down there anyway. That's partly why we came here. That and the helicopters.'

'That's right, we were in the loft,' said Fran remembering. 'Helicopters? What helicopters?'

'Ky says the fire might attract the attention of some militia or other. Says it's happened before. She's with Maya and Sofia right now, keeping watch in the attic,' Lugh nodded towards the ceiling overhead. 'In what's left of the attic. The ivy has taken most of the roof. They're looking for lights in the sky. If the house is still burning by morning, she says there's a danger the smoke will be noticed. If the helicopters come, we're to run into the forest.'

'This house is so camouflaged, I doubt anyone would see it. It's more ivy than cottage.' Fran turned away from the red sky and sat on the window ledge. Looking over the firelit room, she added. 'I never did like that big house. It always gave me the creeps. Oh, and the old man too?'

'And the old man too.'

'Poor old Rumpelstiltskin.'

'One day, I'll tell you all about poor old Rumpelstiltskin,' Lugh said as he returned to sit on the floor beside the bed. He retrieved Abel's hand from the blankets and tenderly ran his thumb around the dry scab in the centre of Abel's palm. 'We did manage to salvage a few things from the big house. That's probably why it looks so homely in here.'

'Things like the books?' Fran had already noticed the collection of old hardback books that had been placed in a row on the mantelpiece. Another stack of volumes stood in a pile at the end of her bed.

'Yes, the books,' Lugh said. 'We used the wheelbarrow to drop them down the lane, a fair distance from the fire, then went back for more. Ky's going to make a library for you. Bollocks, that was meant to be a surprise.'

'It's fine, I can act surprised. And this...' Fran knelt down reverently beside the wooden case of the antique gramophone. 'Rhea would have loved this.'

'That's why it's here.'

'You think we still have those classical records of hers? All those old composers preserving the soul of humanity?' Fran opened the lid of the gramophone and peered at the dusty turntable and brass horn inside. 'She really would have loved it. Damn and fuck it.'

'I only salvaged it because of her,' Lugh reflected. 'Wouldn't have thought of it otherwise.'

'So Rhea saved the music,' said Fran contemplatively to herself. She closed the gramophone lid and returned to the window, listened to the sound of the crackling static diminishing in the distance. 'That's what she always wanted. She would have been pleased with that accomplishment.'

Lugh frowned, uncertain what to say, and decided to say nothing. Instead, he concentrated on Abel's hand which lay open on his lap, drawing gentle shapes across the palm, harvesting dust and ash from the skin. Not for the first time that night, Lugh took an object from his pocket, the small gold wedding ring that Mother had let slip onto the hallway floor, and rolled it smoothly up and down Abel's forearm. He thought that Abel would be pleased with the keepsake when he woke up again. He thought that Abel would never forgive him. Placing Abel's hands back under the blanket, Lugh decided not to disturb him any further, to let him sleep a little while longer.

Outside the window, the window without glass, the ash of the burning house continued to drift over the forest, following vague currents of air that died just as they had been born, by chance, divining whims and determining that this and then this should be the way to go. The breeze dropped and the ash settled casually, incidentally, on leaves, on the uppermost branches of old trees, on Fran's eyelashes, on her outstretched hand. The clouds in the eastern sky turned leaden grey: an overcast dawn without a Morning Star, without colour or grace, but a dawn nonetheless.

The birds of the forest did not announce the sunrise. For once, even the magpies had nothing to say. Fran was considering the substance of this unnatural silence when she heard a voice overhead: Ky shouting from the broken rooftop of the cottage. She knew that Ky must have seen something, that something must have happened. It was a cry of warning that the lights of helicopters had appeared in the sky perhaps, or else one of relief that rain was falling through the empty expectancy of air, extinguishing the fire.

ACKNOWLEDGMENTS

HERE IS A SECRET: all writers are thieves, whether knowingly or not. Their books are the body parts of countless lives, fragments of humanity, stitched together and rudely reanimated, and then put to some strange and unlikely purpose. *The Kindly Ones* can be no exception. And so, to anyone from whom I have unwittingly stolen a kiss or an eye or a colour of hair, a love of music or a game of dares, I have to say – as should all honest thieves – that I am extremely grateful.

To those who have knowingly contributed to the life of this book, my primary thanks go to the great Steve Berman, for his kind appreciation of my earlier stories and for warmly welcoming both myself and *The Kindly Ones* into the Lethe Press family: we could not be happier. I am also grateful to the talented Staven Andersen for designing the perfect artwork for the cover of this book.

For the untold hours that were sacrificed to reading and editing my works, for the honest truths and the hard-hitting advice, and for a lifetime rich with friendship, adventure and magic – both ritual and spontaneous, I always have been and ever shall be thankful to Caroline Howlett and David Booth.

I am particularly grateful to the Reverend Ros Hunt for providing a house full of books during my more homeless moments; to the gorgeous Torsten Højer for still opening windows after all these years; to Melanie Rhind, Matt Hall, Castiel and Rael for hosting waifs and strays, book launches and unforgettable parties; to Karen Taylor for sharing a past and creating a future; to the poet Andrew F Giles for friendship and refuge in the pagan mountains; to Judith Stone and Sarah Farrell for the wisdom and wit that keeps utopia a possibility; to my fellow writer-in-exile Heléna Stakounis for putting a better world into words; to Janet Farrell, Baz Inquai, Jo Hickman and Jamie Beagent for postage stamps and the printing of manuscripts; to Julieann O'Malley and Sam Irvine for artistic and cinematic sorcery; to Anne Irvine, Holly Hero, Andy Dixon and Zac for providing a safe haven for lost books; to Colin Wolfe for the inspiration of unfinished stories; and to Ed Bixter, prince among thieves, for keeping the words flowing.

Most of all, I am grateful to Alvaro Gallegos, my compañero, for accompanying me on this particular path and from whom I have probably stolen the most.

321

Lightning Source UK Ltd.
Milton Keynes UK
UKHW010710020822
406728UK00001B/29

9 781590 216903